I0544703

All's Fair in Love and War

Written by T.L. Cordes
https://tlcordes.com
tlcordes@yahoo.com

Created 10/3/2018
Copyright 2-119-374
ISBN 978-0-578-45020-9
Published 14 Feb 2019

Published by
FooDog Publishing
foodogpub@aol.com

Suggested Music Playlist

✓**Adele -** Set Fire to the Rain
✓**Alice in Chains** - Grind / Man in the Box / Rooster
✓**Creed- Bullets** - My Sacrifice / One Last Breath
      Stand Here with Me / Weathered / Hide
✓**Daughtry -** Crashed / There and Back Again / Battleships
✓**3 Doors Down** - Changes / Dangerous Game
      Going Down in Flames / It's Not My Time
      It's the Only One You've got / Kryptonite
      Let Me Be Myself / The Road I'm On / When I'm Gone
✓**Enigma -** Endless Quest
✓**Evanescence** - Bring Me to Life / Going Under
      Taking Over Me / My Last Breath
✓**Godsmack** - Changes / Dead and Broken / I Am
      Releasing the Demons
✓**Kenny Loggins.-** Danger Zone
✓**Lover Boy.-** Turn me loose
✓**Machine Head.-** Darkness Within
✓**Moreza.-** Crimson Moon
✓**Nickelback.-** Believe It or Not / If Everyone Cared
      I'd Come for You / Savin' Me / Never Gonna Be Alone
✓**Rush -** A Passage to Bangkok
✓**Shinedown** - All I Ever Wanted / Better Version / Second Chance
      In Memory
✓**Sia** - Never Give Up
✓**Lindsey Stirling** - Crystallize / Elements / The Phoenix

Dedicated to those who serve

My cousin wanted to pilot the 'Millennium Falcon' but since space travel did not happen before he turned eighteen he chose to join the Air Force instead. However his plans changed when he could not pass the flight eye exam without his glasses so the Army took him in and made a Ranger out of him, where he seemed to excel.

When Desert Storm began he was not sent over seas but remained in the U.S. training troops going over seas, one of those training exercises included gas mask training in case of poisonous nerve gas. My cousin was exposed over and over again to the gas used training his brothers in arms to survive.

Three years after Desert Storm my cousin was diagnosed by a military doctor with 'Military induced Cancer'. He was given the prognoses of one week to live but refused to die for another six months, once he was certain as best as he could be, his wife and daughter would be taken care of. It was only then did he stop fighting and allowed himself to die, he literally starved to death from intestinal cancer.

My cousin was proud to be an Army Ranger and was a casualty of a war which was already over as many of our military veterans often are.

Chapter 1
Somewhere in Saudi Arabia.....

Five players from two different flights of U.S. Air Force pilots began a volleyball game, each team with two fresh players waiting on the shaded sidelines, but the participants are dropping like flies. Hot sand shifts beneath military issued combat boots while the remaining participants wearing military ABUs consisting of cargo pants and long sleeve button down shirts in desert camouflage of heavy durable fabric and matching caps stand in the blazing Arabian sun.

On one side of the net is Captain Hank Andrews whose resemblance to the actor Tom Hanks and the fact his first name is Hank has earned him the call sign of Tom Tom and only two men of his flight remain standing next to him as he prepares to serve the ball. Across the net his opponents are down to Captain Carolyn Callahan call sign C.C., and First Lieutenant Jack Roecheck call sign Check who stand ready to return the ball only one of Tom Tom's remaining teammates staggers for no apparent reason going down on one knee before catching his balance and rising again but this is enough to cause a delay as two men from the shaded side lines, spectators up to this point, run out to retrieve the man who is insisting he is fine. Tom Tom is forced to order him from the game.

Now the teams are even once again as airman, mechanics, and other base personnel including off duty medical personnel give a rather desultory cheer from the sidelines but their entertainment options are limited and their off duty time seemingly endless. Playing basketball has proven not only unsatisfactory but nearly impossible dribbling a ball on hard packed sand sand so the basketball hoop mounted outside the mess hall has been deemed only suitable for games such as Pig because Horse takes too long to play to its natural conclusion.

Heat stroke and dehydration are factors not to be taken lightly in the desert, or in the Air Force, which is why a short time later Tom Tom takes the damp towel from around his neck when his own knees become shaky and tosses it to the sand effectively surrendering the game.

"Ah, Tom." His remaining Airman moans regretfully. He walks slowly beside Tom Tom to be sure he makes it into the shade but glancing over to the other side of the net he sees C.C. almost jogging off the makeshift volleyball court toward the recreation area in the main command building. "Honestly C.C. must have ice water running through her veins. "She's not even suppose to be here." His airman mutters under his breath.

"Let's not go there." Tom Tom warns and it is a well known fact as a female C.C. should not have been given combat status in a war. "You make a deal with the Major and I'll make sure you're sent back home with her."

I'm not talking about doing anything like that, but it's the money you understand." The Airman quickly defends his position and he would never give the Major even the time of day unless ordered to. None of the U.S. Air Force personnel nor even the Allied personnel on the base are willing to give the Major what he wants which is to send C.C. home. "But the woman isn't human I'm telling you. Pool, cards, and volleyball she's like a machine."

"There has to be something she isn't good at." Tom responds and maybe if they look hard enough they will find it.

Just off the recreational area is a lounge where personnel sit at tables drinking though normally these bottles would include alcoholic beverages only per some agreement between countries no alcohol can be served so what would have normally been called the Dive Bar, Bombay Bar or some other creative name this area has been unaffectionately the Juice Bar. The lounge area is full of personnel formerly players or spectators of the recent Volleyball game sucking down bottles of juice or water like they just crossed the desert without liquid.

At a table on one side of the room is a little victory celebration which includes Airman First Class Jamal Royal call sign Prince as in a royal prince and he resents any references to the singer called Prince. Prince is presently wolfing down a snack rather then refreshments since he was the first player to drop out of the game claiming black skin was never meant to be out in the desert sun.

Also present is Airman First Class Paul Putty call sign Silly which most assume was given to him because of the children's play dough, but that is not the reason. Seated next to him is

Senior Airman Mark Doberman call sign Pincher only not because of the dog breed but because of an incident involving waitress whom is responsible for the small scar over Pincher's left eye.

"No." C.C. answers in her gruff four packs of cigarettes a day voice though she has never smoked a day in her life to Check's unasked question. She saw him making the rounds and she knows he is up to something. The fact she does not smoke or drink or have any vices she is rather proud of but her flight seems to have developed a serious gambling habit.

"It's only a game of darts." Check insists leaving out the added incentive of money since C.C. cannot be swayed by money but she can be motivated by fair play. His captain looks like a little girl wearing grown up clothing though she does not sound like a child and she could be part elf with a pointed chin but she lacks the height even if her bright green eyes and pointed chin says other wise. "This gives them the opportunity to win their money back."

"If you thought they could win you wouldn't have made the bet." C.C. responds bluntly and they both know this is fact. "Have Egor play them."

"The medics are hanging on to him." Check informs her regretfully because Egor, Airman First Class Ed Gorman, is their second best dart player. "He might have over done it a little on the volleyball court."

"He's milking it." C.C. responds confidently while frowning at Check who looks like a farm boy from Indiana, which he is, and back home he probably sings in the choir every Sunday morning in church. His fresh faced boy next door good looks and sunny personality hides a barracuda when it comes to money. "There's a nurse in the infirmary he wants to know better than just saying hello to when passing in the hallways."

"The brunette with the mongo bongos?" Prince wants to know instantly.

"Brunette he said with extraordinary knockers." C.C. answers with a shrug not knowing the difference and her flights descriptions of women only involve hair color and some body part in man code.

"It's her." Prince rages pounding a fist onto the table top rattling the juice bottles sitting there but with all the laughter and talking of the other personnel no one even glances over. "She just transferred in last week. That lousy fuck is making time with my girl."

"If she's yours he won't get very far then will he."   C.C. reasons not concerned by his out burst.

"She doesn't know it yet." Prince confides indignantly.

"Delusional much." C.C. responds and it is times like these she is reminded she may be willing to take a bullet for one of her flight but they are after all just men. They treat her like one of the guys and speak freely around her about the opposite sex continually reconfirming what she already knew, men are pigs and she does not want one or need one in her personal life again.

"C.C. come on. It'll be a fun way to cool off." Check wheedles knowing she will eventually give in because C.C. is a good sport and she knows they are not just lining their pockets. He plans to buy property adjacent to his family's farm, Sin, Senior Airman Alex Sinclair, has a pregnant wife back home, and Egor is financially supporting his elderly parents so the extra cash from a few friendly wagers is for good causes.

"Fine." C.C. responds caving because it will take her longer to argue than it will to play the game but afterwards she plans on taking a shower like she intended and she knows she has sand in places she really does not want to think about. "Set it up."

Also somewhere in Saudi Arabia.....

Army Private Millhouse J. waits impatiently for his passenger to arrive so he can proceed with his mission, well, it is not exactly a mission, but more of an errand to his mind. He is on foreign soil in the middle of a war but he is expected to play taxi driver to some Army Colonel and if this Colonel is in such an all fired hurry to get to an A.A.F. base he should have flown there. While he continues his silent litany of why he should be doing more important things than driving a Humvee a pale tan canvas back truck pulls into the sandy cross road on this clear, yet again hot sunny day, and Millhouse steps forward to the passenger door finding only the driver who motions him with a thumb toward the rear of the truck.

Walking to the rear he finds the back gate down and a Military Police officer standing on the ground cradling a rifle in his folded arms. Glancing into the back of the truck over the mans shoulder he sees another M.P. in the shadowy interior unchaining a large man from a chair bolted to the floor in the center of the truck bed, but having a difficult time of it. The man in the chair is not just cuffed but wrapped in chain, shoulders, chest, and legs while even seated the prisoner looks massive as the M.P. works diligently unlocking what Millhouse estimates to be at least fifty pounds of chain. This is not his problem though as they unwrapped their nasty Christmas gift because he is here to drive some fancy stiff necked Colonel on a sight seeing tour no doubt so he turns his attention to the M.P. on the ground.

"Do you have orders for me since Colonel Red Eagle is a no show, or is he arriving in another truck?" Millhouse asks and the M.P. motions over his shoulder back into the truck so Millhouse looks again but there is just the other M.P. and their prisoner.

"Colonel, sir, your ride is here." The M.P. on the ground calls over his shoulder while smiling at the private who is looking justifiably confused.

Millhouse checks again but does not see anyone resembling a superior officer as the large prisoner rises from the chair leaning sideways to walk to the end of the truck and Millhouse quickly backs away hoping the M.P.s can handle their prisoner. The prisoner jumps down from the truck dressed in desert fatigues a couple sizes too small he judges from the way the tee shirt is stretched to the seams by massive arms and shoulders and the cargo pants normally loose might actually burst at this guys thighs and calves.

The prisoner is red skinned like an American native and his black hair is not short but he appears incredibly fit capable of breaking a man in two with his bare hands. Millhouse takes another cautious step back watching this prisoner now standing in the bright sunlight. He is taller and twice as wide as Millhouse first thought and he can now clearly see scars marring bronze skin on his arms and face but glancing towards the M.P.s who have rifles only neither of them are pointing them at their prisoner as the massive man raises tree trunk like arms up over his head stretching as the tee shirt seams make little noises of distress.

"Good." The prisoner comments in a deep harsh voice as he lowers his arms with his face still tilted upward toward the sun unaware he looks like a bronze carved statue. "Wouldn't want to miss the war."

"Colonel, sir." Millhouse addresses the prisoner coming belatedly to attention and saluting while ignoring the M.P.s who are no doubt amused but in the absence of common logic he must go with the illogical which is this is the Colonel he came to collect.

Colonel Johann Red Eagle slowly lowers his chin to his

chest as the sunlight and heat begins to seep into the cold dark places of his soul then he turns his head slightly to glance at the Private now standing at attention and saluting him. He can feel the low hum from the two M.P.'s of repressed amusement at the Privates expense but how is this poor grunt suppose to know he is still a prisoner and a Dog on a very short leash.

"At ease." Dog offers after returning the salute then lifts his head looking out over the barren desert surrounding them closing his eyes just breathing in the scent of freedom, sweet freedom.

"Sir?" One of the M.P.s cautions shifting nervously now as they continue to stand in the open.

"Let's get this Dog and pony show on the road." Dog suggests knowing full well what is making the M.P. nervous because he is not truly free yet. "Since I'm the only Dog present that makes you three the ponies."

"Sir, the Humvee is right over here." Millhouse responds motioning toward the front of the truck finding himself backing away for some inexplicable reason but he does not feel comfortable turning his back on this man so instead he moves toward the Humvee in a sideways crab walk with the three men. He thinks his unease is caused by the Colonel's eyes rather than his sheer massive size making him feel ill at ease. It may be his imagination but for a moment when the sunlight hit the Colonel's seemingly brown eyes there was an sudden red glow in them much as he thinks a hell hound's eyes would look looking straight out of hell.

Millhouse chastises his over active imagination as he moves to the drivers side door with one M.P. following him but when he opens the drivers door he can see the other M.P. on the other side has opened the front passenger door but he and the Colonel seem to be staring at one another while standing motionless. Millhouse glances at the M.P. beside him through the window of the now open rear driver's side door waiting to see what this M.P. will do since there seems to be a silent disagreement about the seating arrangements going on and he decides he is safer not getting into the drivers seat before the disagreement is settled.

"Sir?" The M.P. across from Millhouse warns respectfully as the Colonel towers almost a foot over him and his shoulders are nearly three times as wide.

"I need to get the lay of the land." Dog explains responds knowing what their orders are but he is not going any where until this is over. "I can't do that from the back of the bus."

"Yes, sir." The M.P. agrees after a moments consideration then glances at his fellow M.P. who now climbs into the back seat of the Humvee first positioning his rifle across his lap so it points at the back of the front passenger seat before the other M.P. moves to the back door on the other side.

"For some reason I get the feeling these guys don't trust me." Dog comments as he leans down in the open doorway looking directly across the front two seats to the frozen Private.

"Yes sir, I mean, no, sir." Millhouse responds practically stuttering but this has to be the strangest situation he has ever found himself in. His orders were to drive a Colonel to one of their allied air bases yet the Colonel came chained to a chair as if a prisoner.

"You were right the first time." Dog informs the Private as he folds his large frame into the doorway.

Millhouse quickly takes the drivers seat thinking the sooner he delivers this Colonel the better but discovers once all the doors are closed he feels claustrophobic, which has never been an issue for him before. The Colonel's large form seems to crowd him yet he is no where near crossing the small space between them or maybe it is a lack of oxygen in the front half of the Humvee as if the Colonel's large form is sucking up all the air. He resists looking back at the M.P.s to see if they are having the same problem he is getting enough air as he concentrates on putting the Humvee into gear but one thing he is certain of, this will be the longest ten click drive he has ever made in his life.

C.C. showers in the only male restricted building on this slapped together base and often the military does not accommodate women in the military with their own bathing facilities enacting instead a coed showering system designating showering hours for each gender. Given the fact ground grew, command staff, and medical personnel are mostly women the genders are nearly equal so two large block buildings were erected.

Each building is divided in two creating a bench area for drying off, dressing, and storage while the other half is all shower with shower heads sticking out of the wall every three feet and no stalls since personal privacy is not something the military is concerned with. The shower half is big enough it is estimated to shower four camels at once or twenty people but one slight miscalculation was made when they only put in one floor drain in the center which is perpetually clogging with hair and sand.

Nearly every woman on base contributes to a running supply of skin lotions kept in the supply lockers with the towels and she contributes to this skin lotion supply with the contents of her care packages from her brother Carter back home in the States who has yet to master the art of gift giving to women. Lotions are Carter's only notion of a female gift and if she horded her lotion supply it might last her a month leaving her waiting another two months until Carter found a holiday or reason suitable enough to send her a gift again. Skin lotion is referred to as the Nectar of the God's when dry skin chaffing can land them painfully in the infirmary or have them standing in the mess hall to eat unable to sit.

The echoing sound of female laughter bounces off the cinder block walls along with the spray of water greets C.C.'s entry into the large outer room and one of the long wooden benches contains three piles of clothing so at least three women must be present in the shower area beyond. She undresses while hearing the hollow distorted voices talking followed by more laughter but something about the laughter is not comedic in nature so she is not overly shocked when she enters the shower area to find two naked women have made a man sandwich with one standing in front and the other standing behind a naked man as they rub soap on him front and back. This would not be so bad if she did not know the meat in their sandwich by name.

"Egor." C.C. moans with resignation and unconcerned with her own nakedness not having mongo bongos or their other term is a bodacious booty which her flight tends to gravitate in that direction. She can also add she is not tall, not curvy, and not well endowed so not interesting but at least she has been told she is not ugly.

"Oh, hey, C.C." Egor, greets his Captain from his position under a shower head. "These nurses thought I needed complete re-hydration."

"Of course." C.C. responds and why not would have been Egor's first thought at the suggestion without even a small consideration for the violation he is committing by being in a male restricted area. She realizes now if she had skipped the dart game she could have showered and missed this party entirely but instead she has been placed in a very sticky situation as she considers her options which there are none as she walks up to a shower head a good distance from the trio. "You know I have no choice but to report you?"

"What?" Egor asks momentarily blank but then there are two beautifully naked women with their hands on him.

"I have to report you" C.C. repeats grimly as she pushes the button below the shower head and leans on it while water cascades over her short spiky blond hair before lifting her hand from the button effectively stopping the water then raking her longer top hair back from her face she continues with a short synopsis of the situation. "Major on base, he wants to send me home, and any infraction of regulations will serve his purpose. Does this ring any bells?

"Oh shit C.C." Egor moans as he disentangles himself from the women to lope across the wet floor to where she is standing. "I didn't even think of that."

"Obviously." C.C. responds as she wipes more dripping water from her face wondering what she did to piss God off today because if it is discovered she did not report him for this infraction, a small one on her part though not on Egor's, she will be sent home.

"Don't report us Captain, we can have a foursome." One of the nurses offers with a bright smile as the two women are now soaping each other.

"Yeah, that would be great." Egor interjects with a fake grin. "Right up to the part where C.C. cuts off my balls and feds them to me that is." Egor turns his reluctant attention back to C.C. as he scrambles for a solution to this problem until he hits upon the very one. "I'll just make sure no one sees me leave, I swear."

"You can't guarantee that." C.C. informs him and he does not seem to realize the two nurses are the only witnesses the Major needs. "You know what's at stake here for me, yet you pull something like this, and right in front of me no less."

"I wasn't thinking." Egor admits and glancing at the two women who seem to having a good time without him and no court in the world would convict him if they saw what he is looking at right now but C.C. will not have a trial. "No one will see me."

"You're killing me." C.C. responds because he was not even paying attention to anyone coming upon them while they were previously engage. The odds of his leaving without being seen are between zero and no way but as she considers her gaze drifts downward then quickly back up. "Stop pointing that thing at me."

"Sorry." Egor responds with a grin turning sideways but he knows she is reconsidering and no one in the flight wants to loose her because she is an ace pilot which somehow she makes them all look top notch. "I swear if someone even looks side ways at me when I leave I will let you know so you can file a report first, you know it."

"Just get out." C.C. replies because neither of them will know if anyone saw him leave until the Major Agitator arrives at her door with M.P.s to escort her to a plane back to the States.

Chapter 2
Somewhere in Saudi Arabia....

As Egor and the nurses leave C.C. leans against the wall with her palm on the button sending water cascading over her washing away the sand from her body but unfortunately not the thoughts from her mind. She can feel sand running with the water under her feet and has accepted this as just a fact of life but the Major Agitator, also known as Major Alexander, is not something, or someone, she is willing to accept.

From their very first meeting she felt a strong dislike for the man which has only grown with association over the past three months. The U.S. government may have decided females should not engage the enemy in this war but the Air Force made it clear in stationing her here she is qualified but the Major Agitator has made it clear with veiled insinuations he does not believe she is qualified, and not just because she is female.

The Major has recently given up asking her to reassign her position voluntarily and now carry's misconduct discharge papers just waiting to implement them if she sets so much as a toe wrong. He no longer just wants her gone from this base but out of the military all together and Egor may have just given the Major the misstep he has been looking for, dereliction of duty, but she cannot bring herself to toss one of her flight into disciplinary action to save herself from what is only a return trip to the states.

Once she has shampooed and rinsed her hair twice she returns to the outer room and dries off where no evidence of Egor and his two nurses remain. She did not even hear the outer door open and close over the spray of the shower so how did they hope to hear anyone coming upon them let alone where would he hide. Sitting on a bench she engages in the best part of showering, the body lotion, and for a short space in time she feels clean and her skin is not dry or irritated which only lasts for these few precious moments before she leaves the shower building and is instantly hit by floating sand once again, the stuff just does not stay on the ground.

On her way back to her quarters she stops at the

commissary in another part of the main command building which sells just about everything from abrasive cleaners to zip ties but it also acts as post office passing out mail. She finds a letter from her brother and normally this would be a cheerful event only recently his letters have become more focused on a woman he has met then details about himself. The words wonderful, beautiful, and brilliant appear regularly but she cannot bring herself to be happy for him when she herself has been married four times to date.

She is certain she knows every pitfall involved regarding relationships from firsthand experience and she would rather risk walking through a mine field than ever fall in love again, or have her happiness tied to someone else. Happy ever after is a fairy tale and she can only hope her brother does not find out the hard way it is not all wine, dancing, and roses.

Entering her cinder block building housing enlisted officers she finds the prerequisite pile of sand blown just inside the doorway then walks along the narrow hallway passing closed doors while contemplating her brother's hand writing on the letter she carries when she turns a corner with more closed doors and two uniformed M.P.s standing on either side of her closed door and she sighs.

She knew this was going to happen but there is nothing she can do about it now so she steps up to her door finding these are not the regular base M.P.s but Army and they are holding rifles. They regard her with curiosity but with no particular interest so now she wonders if the Major Agitator is waiting inside for her and the M.P.s are unaware of her changed status, or they are to keep her here until he has her transport to the States arranged.

"Am I restricted to quarters?" C.C. inquires just to be certain.

"Not that we're aware of." The taller curly brown haired M.P. offers.

She realizes she can just walk away right now and they will not stop her but this will only delay the inevitable and filing a report on Egor at this late date will do no good. She can still requisition a jeep and leave the base but go where and this could be construed as AWOL getting her kicked out of the military any way so why bother. She briefly considers taking this opportunity to kick Egor but she is the superior officer here so blaming him for not attending her duty will do little good even if it might make her feel better.

She reaches instead for the door handle opening the door but seeing no one waiting inside she turns to close the door and the M.P.s are simply looking at her over their shoulders until the door closes completely cutting them from view. She stands for a moment staring at the closed door finding this strange and maybe the Major Agitator was only bluffing about having misconduct discharge papers ready, or he requires more time to make it official.

Turning she glaces about but it is a small open room with no places to hide with two door frames leading into two smaller rooms just big enough for a cot and to walk around it. She has a spare cot serving as a couch and to reach the small wall air conditioning unit taking up the only window she has to slide side ways along the wall to avoid the cot to reach the controls.

There is a small counter to her right made of a piece of plywood nailed to an open wood frame only big enough to hold a single hot plate or a coffee maker if wants continuous jolts of caffeine which she does not require.

Tossing the letter from her brother onto the little counter effectively taking up half the available space she has no idea how long before the Major Agitator arrives so she may as well proceed with her day as usual and the first thing she normally does is remove her outer clothing while standing just inside the door shaking out each article before moving on to the next. This little tip she learned from a nurse in an effort to keep most of the sand in one spot to be swept up two or three times a day.

Now standing wearing only her military issued boxer shorts and same issued sports bra she carries her clothing to the couch spreading them out before the air conditioner. Another trick from another nurse so when she puts her clothing back on she can get part way across base before her clothing feels like it is being branded to her, okay maybe two steps, but those are two glorious steps.

"Now there is a sight I haven't seen in a very, very long time." Comes a deep grating voice from beside her.

C.C. straightens from arranging her clothing on her make shift couch knowing to her right is a door frame to an empty room. Turning she finds a huge man standing in front of the door frame blocking it from view with wide shoulders but beyond his impossibly narrow waist she can see the door frame.

Her first impression is he is incredibly fit, her knowledge tells her an entirely different story. His broad bronze scarred face has sunken hallows around his eyes over very prominent cheek bones, the cartilage in his throat looks as if carved from redwood in grave detail, and his collarbone stands out like a shelf out lined perfectly by a tee shirt plastered to him like a second skin. The tee shirt also reveals what appears to be an excessive number of abs but when a person is so shriveled from lack of food other organs can be seen as lumps under the skin. Despite the ropes of muscles of his large muscular arms there is not an ounce of body fat on this man so even his wrist bones stick out like softballs. Meeting his reddish brown eyes that remind her of a hawk's she knows she is looking at a man who has not seen many solid meals in days.

"Jesus, doesn't anybody feed you?" C.C. blurts out without thinking but she is certain this man's body is virtually surviving by feeding off his muscle and once the muscle is gone so is the man. The shear bulk of him means this could take a while but the result will be the same.

"Occasionally someone throws me a bone." Dog confides finding it interesting this short nicely shaped woman in a matter of seconds deduced what no one has yet realized, or guessed, and technically he is as close to being dead as he has ever been in a very long time without excessive blood loss but if she is the last sight he sees he is not complaining.

Short, nicely built with a muscular compact body, and short spiky blond hair with large wide green eyes she stares him directly in the eyes. There is no fear, caution, or sign of intimidation in them and some might describe her as cute but all he sees is dangerous so he is not falling for the over all look.

"It seems our travel agent double booked." C.C. concludes grimly knowing this is clearly a mistake because no male, officer or not, can be assigned to these quarters while she is here.

"Not surprising." Dog muses and they are both in the military where terms like 'snafu' were invented. "I suspect in this instance it has more to do with necessity. I don't think they really have a place to put me."

"I'll speak with the housing Sergeant." C.C. responds because he cannot stay here and she lived through the horror of nursing a man starving to death once so she is not about to go through it again. If this man is terminally ill then they can keep him in the infirmary.

"I think you know neither of us has any real say in the matter of living arrangements." Dog comments realistically and there is possibly an explanation neither of them know at this time. "Although I must say the addition of women to the military does have it's merits."

"If one of those supposed merits includes touching me then plan on having your hands and privates cut off then fed to you." C.C. warns just to be certain he understands there are very clear boundaries and regulations regarding fraternization if they are not clear enough for him.

"Not that hungry, yet." Dog confides having no doubt she will do exactly as she warns even though she is no taller than his armpit but he is not taking her warning personally. Many men have no doubt been fooled by her soft and cute facade but he can see this woman is hiding a serious load of pent up hostility behind those wide green eyes, not just directed at him. She appears calm, cool, and controlled, her hands and teeth are not clenched, obvious signs of anger, and even her voice does not hold even a hint of the rage he can feel radiating from her. "You're one cool little cat aren't you? But all I want is to sleep on that cot right there."

"You're not sleeping here at all and there is a cot in the room behind you." C.C. informs him and he should know since he was just in there but apparently he plans to hog the air conditioning.

"I'm not sleeping in there." Dog responds flatly which is absolute fact since he only lasted eight minutes in there before she arrived and he would loose what little sanity he may have left if he tried to sleep in that little room.

"Fine." C.C. concedes because he will not be sleeping here at all once she files a complaint, which is best done sooner rather than later as she begins putting her clothing back on. "It's all yours. I'll speak to the housing sergeant before going to the mess hall to eat. Do you need directions?"

"I'll just follow my nose but my friends outside the door will probably be escorting me there." Dog assumes feeling a twinge around his middle at just the mention of food but he is a prisoner still.

"So you're their prisoner?" C.C. guesses finding she should have realized this sooner and now she has to wonder if she is in a small room with a psycho killer.

"Yes, and no." Dog replies as honestly as he can earning

himself a frown. "Things aren't always what they seem."

"I get that a lot." C.C. responds grimly. "Right up until they're far worse then they seem."

Dog follows her toward the door keeping a safe distance and when she throws it open it is the first outward sign of the rage burning within. The M.P.s turn startled by the suddenness of her exit then continue to watch her as she marches past them looking neither left nor right while Dog watches as both M.P.s do the neck craning thing men sometimes do checking out a woman's back side and he wonders absently just what these men expect to see when she is wearing Air Force regulation ABUs. He leans against the door frame after she has gone around the hallway corner out of sight as both M.P.s grin at their prisoner.

"Looks to me Colonel like your living accommodations just got much better, sir." The shorter M.P. on the right comments while the one on the left nods in agreement.

"She could take you both out." Dog informs them and he does not doubt it for a minute just from what he has seen so far.

"No need to be insulting." The taller M.P. on the left objects because neither of them are about to be taken down by the short woman they just saw. "We're just following orders."

"No insult intended." Dog assures them looking from one M.P. to the other finding they are clueless but then they were looking at her back side and not into her eyes, or anywhere else apparently. "Have you looked around you at all? This is an NCO (Non Commissioned Officer) building so there for the Cool Cat you just saw is an enlisted officer. Woman, or not, promotion is based on intelligence, skill, and leader ship ability so not only is she air combat trained but while you were ogling her unseen ass did either of you notice how she walks?"

"Yeah, really nice." The shorter one responds and the taller snickers.

"I seriously hope the two of you do not end up in a combat situation." Dog responds sighing at their lack of attention and finding it rather alarming given where they are presently, in the middle of a war, but he decides to educate them. "She walks on the balls of her feet which suggests she may have more than a brushing acquaintance with boxing or another form of hand to hand combat. I'm going to even go so far as to guess she has had some martial arts training. Never judge a man or woman by height or hair color because soft and cute in this case can hide cold, and calculating. She's proven she can size up a man with a single glance and she pegged me accurately within thirty seconds, which is also a command requirement you either have or you don't, and she's got it."

"Colonel?" The shorter M.P. divulges having his doubts about the woman in question. "I know you've probably been out of circulation for a while now but in my experience most women are cold and calculating."

"But most aren't deadly, that one is." Dog maintains which could prove problematic for him. "I'll be sleeping with one eye open if she decides she really doesn't want me staying here."

"Personally, I would keep them both open so I can see what I'm touching." The taller MP advises and his partner laughs with him.

"Are the two of you going to be guarding the door the entire time I'm here?" He asks now having positive proof he is dealing with a pair of not too bright soldiers and they will find out what the Cat is made of if they cross her.

"Just until your gear arrives." The shorter M.P. sobers enough to answer. "But we will be around base to keep tabs on you."

"Not worried I'll sneak out after dark?" Dog asks though he has no intention of doing do so but they are suppose to be guarding him from escape, which is laughable given their apparent blindness to what is around them.

"This is a fortified base on foreign soil during war so nothing moves around here without someone knowing." The taller M.P. imparts but this situation is very unusual and they are not completely unaware of what could have happened. "You've had every opportunity to escape regardless of how careful we were but you haven't taken any of the advantages you have to ditch us so we assume you want to be here."

"It's not really a matter of want but a matter of having given my word." Dog confides grimly and all he really has left to call his own. "I made a deal and I'll keep my end. It's as simple as that."

"What do you get out of It?" The taller M.P. inquires while his partner is looking at him as if he has lost his mind for asking.

"Probably dead." Dog responds honestly as he closes the door separating him from his keepers once again.

C.C. wastes a good deal of time looking for the housing

sergeant in the command offices with no success then proceeds to the crowded mess hall realizing a single officer will be like finding a needle in a haystack inside. She carries her tray along the line in the mess hall as the servers behind the serving stations slap food into the divided sections but she has given up identifying the food by sight because spaghetti and meat balls can look similar to goulash, which can easily be confused with what passes for ravioli here. It is all just some kind of pasta with tomato sauce and it tastes the same regardless of what name it is given.

Meat loaf, roast beef, and Salisbury steak are interchangeable tasting the same and even suspiciously shaped in similar sponge like squares regardless of what it is purported to be. Most just try to identify the food by taste as a game while others say pretending it is what the daily board on the counter claims then it actually taste as it should.

With her full tray in hand she finds her flight seated together at one end of a long table but no sign of the housing Sergeant as of yet and she sits in the empty space next to Check placing her next to Sin on her left. Across the table from her is Egor and on either side of him are Pincher and Prince. Silly is on Check's other side creating strange shapes coming up out of his tray using his fork and spoon as styluses.

She is no sooner settled when Egor is tapping his finger on the table between them to get her attention then gives her the thumbs up signal. It takes her a moment to remember what he is trying to tell her because the shower incident seems like it happened years ago now and it remains to be seen if anyone saw Egor leave the women's showers or not but she has a bigger problem, a much bigger problem, as she contemplates silently what she knows about her current problem.

The guy either was, or still is, a military prisoner, not Air Force because they have yet to build a cockpit big enough to hold his bulk, and they might be transferring him else where for medical treatment of some kind though it must have been unexpected whatever the reason hence his remark about necessity rather than planning was involved when they assigned him to her quarters though this still does not explain why he is not in the infirmary. This whole situation smacks of something the Major Agitator would think up only she is not certain he has the clout and it seems ironic he would use a violation of regulations to some how catch her violating regulations.

"C.C., hey, wake up." Check beckons softly finding C.C. staring at her tray while he is laying out their next course of action for separating another flight from their pay packets.

C.C. glances at him frowning knowing she really does not want to hear what he has cooked up this time so ignores him while glancing around at the tables near them hoping to spot the housing sergeant when a commotion near the mess hall door snares her attention. People still waiting in line to reach the serving stations are moving aside for someone, someone tall with long black hair in a pony tail. It seems her problem has arrived but why he is being stepped aside for by those first in line she has no clue until there is a break in the line and she sees his uniform. Brown not the lighter colors of desert fatigues but a dress uniform with gold eagles riding the collar.

"Shit." C.C. mutters under her breath because this one word says it all as far as she is concerned and it says it so well she repeats it. "Shit."

"C.C?" Check asks looking from the Army Colonel who apparently lost on his way to the commissioned officers dinning room and wondering if anyone will be brave enough to tell him he is in the wrong place but his attention is firmly caught by this one word uttered not once but twice from the woman seated next to him whom he has come to know, he believes, fairly well. C.C. does not cuss or swear and for her to do so requires something really bad to have happened, or it is about to happen.

"He's my new barracks mate." C.C. grits out striving for her normal calm but right now she is not feeling calm. "They put him out of uniform in an enlisted officers quarters with this captain and I didn't salute him."

"They put him in with you." Sin asks to be certain he heard correctly. "But they can't do that. That's against regulations."

"Whatever gets the job done." C.C. responds realistically and the Major Agitator has to have something to do with this but as far as moves go if they were playing chess this is checkmate for her. "He got me, he wasn't in uniform, and I assumed he would be of equal rank just by his being in my quarters. I'm as good as gone."

"Maybe he won't report you." Silly whispers softly leaning forward to see her around Check in the sudden quietness of the mess hall as all eyes are presently following the Colonel without actually looking at him as if he is a large bird of prey and they are not quite certain where he will perch.

"Of course he'll report her." Pincher snarls keeping his voice down. "What other possible explanation can there be for why they put him in with her against regulations? They don't expect her to be staying long so he'll have the place to himself."

Which is exactly what she is now thinking and she was so worried about Egor dumping her in the suds she did it to herself. She has been so cautious and careful but if in doubt she should have saluted him only she did not. This is all on her but glancing from the corner of her eye she sees he is coming toward their table then he stops just behind where she sits.

Chapter 3
Somewhere in Saudi Arabia.....

"Attention." C.C. calls out standing as does everyone the entire length of the table.

"As you were." Dog responds leaning forward between his new, but not very happy roommate, and a First Lieutenant pushing the Lt's tray over one space further down the table to place his tray in the cleared space. "Make room Airman."

Check grits his teeth having no choice but to move down the table one space as Silly does the same beside him and so on down to the end of the table bumping a man off the end who collects his tray moving to another table allowing this Colonel room to sit down. Once he is seated they are allowed to be seated again but the whispering of the over all mess hall is unusual and the silence in the vicinity of the Colonel is absolute which this Colonel seems oblivious to as he scoops up a fork full of mashed potatoes and shovels them into his mouth.

"Sir. Enjoying your meal, Sir?" C.C. asks grimly because meekly being run out of the Air Force is just not her thing.

"Yes, actually I am." Dog admits treating himself to another fork full of mashed potatoes and he honestly cannot remember anything tasting so good but the people seated in his vicinity are not eating. "I said as you were."

"Sir, for some reason I have lost my appetite, Sir." C.C. responds being certain to use the perquisite sirs though why she is bothering at this late date since one infraction, or ten, will not matter one way or the other now. "Sir, so sorry, Sir."

"If you're trying to 'sir' me to death, or just trying to irritate me, it's not going to work." Dog warns and hostility is practically radiating from her even though outwardly she looks as if they are discussing the weather. "You're more cunning and diabolical then this pathetic effort suggests. If you're planning on going toe to toe with me you're going to have to hit with something much harder."

"Sir, a strong wind could take you out right now, Sir." C.C. points out because she saw the evidence with her own eyes even though the formal uniform hides his emaciated form better but maybe she will have the opportunity between now and being discharged to shove him out into a sand storm.

"Possibly." Dog allows as he already feels his shriveled stomach beginning to stretch as he eats and soon he will be too uncomfortable to continue eating. "But your sharp tongue won't do the deed so you need to rethink your strategy here."

"Colonel, Sir." The shorter of the two M.P.s interrupts from behind him and when the Colonel looks up he continues. "The base C.O. requests your presence in the Command office, Sir."

"The Major General is here then." Dog surmises as he looks down at his plate knowing he could have gotten at least six more bites in but now he has to get this meeting over with and there must be some way he can stash food for later. Most would find it surprising three solid meals a day will not cure his current condition but he considers his alternatives and options. He turns his head to the Cool Cat addressing her for she saw what was wrong with him so she must know something useful. "What time does the commissary close?"

"Sir, eighteen hundred hours, Sir." C.C. answers and for some reason he directed this question to her like his favorite class pet.

"Does it work on cash or credit?" Dog asks thinking quickly since he must get to this meeting.

"Both, Sir." C.C. confirms while watching as he rises and of course they all stand as well but then he does something she finds odd. He holds a hand out to one of the rifle carrying M.P.s who looks at him for half a second then reaches into his pocket as does the other M.P. and they both hand him money.

"Here." Dog offers setting the money on the table next to her tray. "You know what I need."

"Sir, is this an order, Sir?" C.C. inquires just to be clear and wondering if he sees her as some kind of personal errand girl but surprisingly he leans toward her giving her an up close look at the white scars on his other wise dark face. Some of these marks are large like the hook everyone can clearly see but there are a multitude of small ones along the sharp edges of his cheek bones.

"If I were to order you to do things for me, I don't think it will work out well for either one of us." Dog imparts candidly because for some reason she already hates him and the added resentment of being ordered about by him will probably get him knifed in his sleep. "Let's try asking nicely and go from there."

C.C. nods her agreement and she could argue she was not asked nicely to run this errand for him but he seems satisfied with her mode of consent as he gives her a steady incomprehensible look before turning to follow his M.P. escort leaving her to return to her seat to count the money he left next to her tray. Putting the money in a pocket she considers what just occurred between them and it is obvious he is not expecting her to go anywhere so she needs to rethink her position as he suggested earlier.

"Colonel or not that guy has some nerve asking you to do him favors." Egor carps grimly unable to hold his piece any longer. "He's here to get rid of you."

"Yes, partly I think he is." C.C. agrees with this much as she picks up her fork while thinking out loud. "He just doesn't know it yet and there is something else going on here with him."

"So what, you're going to get him his late night munches?" Pincher asks in disbelief and he knows C.C. is not a push over so he cannot believe she is just going to go along with this.

"Kind of hard to say no to a starving man." C.C. confesses knowing exactly what he needs but not exactly munchies. He needs carbohydrates, protein, and yeah, fat but sugary starch is not going to cut it as she runs through a list in her head of what can be found in the commissary.

"Right, I wish I looked that built, maybe I should try starving." Sin snickers in disbelief as the others chuckle along with him, all except for C.C. and Check.

"He use to be much bigger." Check interjects looking at C.C. and knowing what she is saying is probably true, no matter how impossible it seems. "His uniform is loose. His shoulders use to be wider and his chest fuller. The jacket is sagging where it didn't once before. His pant legs are brushing the floor so I'm guessing his waist was bigger and even his belt is too big to help keep them up."

"Some times it worries me when you notice things like how a guys pants fit." Pincher jokes while looking at Check with comedic concern.

"Why? Because it means he'll be looking at his next promotion before you will? He paid attention to details." C.C. criticizes as she continues in the same lecturing tone. "You all need to be keeping your eyes open and start noticing what is going on around you. If I'm not here much longer you won't have me and Check watching out for you and he can't be expected to do it alone. Something is going on right now, on this base, and you're all clueless."

"Sorry." Pincher apologizes sincerely feeling justly chastised.

"Yeah, we'll start paying attention." Egor agrees because C.C. has a point. It is easy to sit back playing around and only getting serious when in the air but what happens in the air often starts on the ground.

"So what kind of Colonel walks around with two armed M.P.s as body guards?" Sin asks looking at his flight to see if anyone else may have noticed anything to explain this.

"The kind who isn't being protected but being kept from escaping." C.C. reports knowing this much from what the Colonel inferred but then he claimed nothing is as it seems. "The kind who doesn't get fed regularly, but what I find extremely interesting, and I'm fairly certain of this, the M.P.s just handed him their own money to buy him food."

"They respect him. They like him." Silly offers with a grin because he gets that.

"Exactly." C.C. concurs thoughtfully because dipping into your own pocket has nothing to do with rank and neither M.P. even put up a token resistance when he held out his hand to them. They only hesitated for an instant and never made comments such as 'you owe us' or any other derogatory quips used by really good friends.

"Don't guards and prisoners form bonds over time?" Sin speculates as it seems to him this is something a friend would do for a friend without question.

"But he's not exactly a prisoner any more." Prince points out the obvious after listening to the conversation for a few minutes. "They didn't escort him in and sit here with him. They've released him, here, on this base."

Now the question that seems to linger in the air over the table is just what have the M.P. s unleashed on their air base and no one seems to have the answer or even a good guess.

Dog is motioned into the base commanders office by a young man seated behind the outer desk wearing a uniform and finds three men, not two, as he suspected to find. He recognizes Major General Aimhurst, a distinguished elder man with steel gray hair and matching eyes, and obviously the shinny domed black man seated behind the desk has to be the base C.O. General Ridgeland as the plaque clearly reads on the desk before him but the man with dark beady eyes and close cropped hair is more difficult to identify. He can tell from the dark uniform with no insignia and the way he is standing the man was once probably a Marine but Pentagon grunts sometimes shed what they now view as their inferior enlisted affiliations donning the dark uniform of a station they feel is apart and above the common military. Dog finds it hard to respect a man who changes allegiances to such extremes as to put off his uniform and insignia which made him the man he is, but then maybe the Marines are relieved to have no known association with him.

"Colonel, have a seat." The C.O. offers as this is his office therefore his party and he waits as the Colonel takes the seat before his desk beside Major General Aimhurst to continue. "I have been instructed to ask the two of you to allow Major Alexander from the Pentagon a few moments of your time before turning my office over to you for your meeting."

"Then by all means proceed Major." Aimhurst agrees not certain what the man has to say but it must be of some importance given the C.O. is probably taking his orders from higher up.

"First, I must say Colonel, it is an honor to meet a man with your record of exemplary heroism." Major Alexander begins finding in his past dealings compliments help loosen up men he wants something from regardless if he is sincere or not.

"I assume you're referring to my record previous to being charged with desertion." Dog responds wondering just how much of his military record the Major managed to see given most of what he did was classified and buried so deep it would require scuba gear and a shovel to locate. Any one who manages to see his entire file would find themselves buried six foot under where they found it because classified takes on a whole new meaning when it comes to his military record.

"I believe a grave error was made in your circumstance, either in communication or clerical, but now apparently the Army intends to rectify this error." Alexander replies only knowing the bare minimum of the actual facts but this explanation stands to reason as to why the Colonel is here. He suspects this Colonel with his long list of medals and commendations walked over the dead soldiers under his command to obtain them which is exactly the type of man he needs now. "Clerical errors have been known to happen in all branches of the military and with grave consequences. Such an error has presently occurred here within the Air Force which you may be able to help me rectify."

"I'm listening." Dog assures him but at this point he is not promising anything until the Major gets to the point but from the grim look on the C.O.'s face this should be interesting.

"There is a person assigned to this base by clerical error who should not be here." Alexander presents firmly. "It is a woman and you may know the type, or have seen them, so when I tell you she is rich and has been pampered all her life you will understand my concern with her being placed within arms reach of a war."

"Then change her orders and send her home." Dog suggests but he has been watching the C.O. and thinks there is far more to this story but if anyone would be concerned about this woman then it would be the C.O. who has her under his command only he is sensing a good deal of anger radiating off the man who has yet to say a word.

"Given her financial situation she could generate a good deal of bad publicity for the military if she does not agree to leave voluntarily, which she has refused to do. Since women have been admitted into the military there have been some rather sticky areas regarding discrimination but for a simple clerical error she has been placed in harms way." Alexander explains but surely the Colonel is aware of these issues as the President is taking considerable heat from several women's rights groups over his decision. "What the enemy would do to a woman held hostage in a military uniform is something I personally do not want to even consider nor does the President of the United States."

"I passed at least ten women just to get here so I don't see what the issue is or what this has to do with me?" Dog admits honestly wondering what it is this Major will not come right out and say.

"Those women do not have combat status, they will not be ordered to engage the enemy behind enemy lines, but regardless of her gender due to a clerical error, as I stated, Carolyn Callahan is a combat pilot in a war." Alexander responds with a smile as he focuses his attention on this Colonel. "I personally saw to your accommodations while you're on this base."

"Ah." Dog comments because he understands very much what this has to do with him now.

"Your superiors have already been informed of your gross violation of military regulations." C.O. inserts and he has been attempting but failed to remain neutral during this discussion but Major Alexander has over stepped his authority. "And when you speak of one of my officers you will do so with their appropriate rank."

"Captain Carolyn Callahan does not belong in a cockpit flying over enemy territory and I have been granted the authority to have her removed from this base by whatever means I deem necessary." Alexander reminds the C.O. sternly who has been of no help in achieving his directive.

"Captain Callahan is six times more qualified then you are to be here and three times more qualified then half the pilots on this base." The C.O. mutters attempting to regain control of his temper and the Major always makes it sound as if the Captain's qualifications are in question when it is only her gender. "Both the Navy and the Marines have been trying to lure her away from the Air Force so personally I'm proud to have a pilot of the Captain's caliber here."

"And as you just heard Colonel, Captain Callahan has other options which will place her in a much safer position." Alexander manages to say holding his temper but he intends to derail this C.O.'s career in any way possible only at the moment he must concentrate on what he thinks might sway the Colonel to help him with his objective. "It is unbearable to think of what our enemy would do to a woman shot down behind enemy lines which should be avoided at all costs."

"True." The C.O. mutters and it is a concern but this goes for any pilot shot down in enemy territory not just this captain. "I would bet money on Captain Callahan making them really sorry they came within a foot of her."

"She's hand to hand combat trained, isn't she?" Dog asks because he was certain.

"She has cross trained with other branches of the military. Navy fight school and SEAL training missions." The C.O. explains with a slight smile. "She was suppose to be a hostage the a SEAL team intended to extract from a group of Marines. The Captain is not the type to sit around and wait to be rescued. All the SEALs had to do was walk in the front door by the time they arrived and that's when the Marines began trying to recruit her. She reportedly each one of them at various times during her escapes and the only escaped them five times and they are still scratching their heads trying to figure out how she did it. She also managed to take down reason she was captured again is because she let them since she was suppose to be the hostage but she was not making it easy for them."

"This is not a training exercise, this is a war." Alexander reminds them and she obviously caught them unawares given she volunteered to be the hostage. "All I want from you Colonel is to report any infractions you may see, or may experience, from Captain Callahan."

"You may as well have painted a target on me." Dog comments as the Major has the audacity to smile at him as if he has no clue what he has done. Anyone in the Cool Cat's quarters would be suspect so he understands the rage she concealed but now she knows he out ranks her and she might just burst into flames frying him in the process. Bunking with a superior officer normally would require saluting and siring morning, noon, and night and the Major is looking for infractions of regulations so she will be doing just that unless he can convince her he is not her enemy. He glances toward the Major General who shrugs so the Army apparently has no interest in this internal problem so neither does he. "I'm not going to be your stool pigeon but I'm going to be paying for your little stunt. I'm fairly certain Captain Callahan is at this time planning my early demise and once she gets past the obstacle of disposing of my body where no on will ever find it I'm toast."

"I'm so glad you find this predicament amusing." Alexander replies not appreciating his humor given situation.

"I'm being completely serious." Dog responds and also dead if he is not careful. "I've met the woman who is a small keg of dynamite and I'm hoping she doesn't blow up on me or blow me up."

"No demolition training." The CO offers freely with the hint of a smile.

"That you know of." Dog corrects and the C.O. nods looking thoughtful. "The worse part is if she ever does get training then somebody better slap a warning sign on her ass because apparently that is the only place men like the Major here are going to look."

"And where were you looking Colonel?" Alexander inquires

grimly because the woman has obviously gotten under his skin and he can see his error now not taking into consideration a man who has been in prison would side with a woman hoping for compensation in some form.

"I was looking her straight in the eyes and what I saw there told me all I need to know." Dog responds and the Major had best be doing the same. "Captain Callahan is ice cold and they don't call killers stone cold for no reason. I've seen that look in the eyes of men before and I am not ashamed to admit I take a step back because crazy or stupid they are not. You push a man or woman like that up to a point and they are going to mess you up bad. I'm not going to push and will be trying to stay on her good side so I don't get messed up."

"Obviously we're not taking about the same woman." Alexander responds with a frown because a single look and the Colonel would understand why this woman should not be here.

"Small, blond hair, and cat green eyes." Dog replies and the Major frowns nodding. "She looks people straight in the eyes, walks like a caged tiger, and growls softly every time she speaks. You probably think she's cute and helpless, which makes you not very observant."

"Even so she does not belong here." Alexander responds and maybe he will have to do more looking into her previous records.

"People like her and I don't really belong anywhere." Dog admits grimly but the Army decided a cage was best for him and the Cat apparently chose the Air Force as her cage. "If here is where she wants to be then here is where she will stay. I'm not going to help you."

"I must say I expected more cooperation from you Colonel." Alexander comments as he moves directly to the door seeing his business is concluded but not as satisfactory as he would have liked.

"I'm fairly certain I can't alter your accommodations, thanks to the Major, but I will pass along your refusal to cooperate." The C.O. offers as he rises from his chair heading for the door himself.

"I don't think it will help but thank you." Dog replies because he doubts the Cool Cat believes anything anyone tells her about anyone she feels is a threat.

"Yes, thank you General." Aimhurst adds before the door closes behind the C.O. leaving him and the Colonel alone at last but he has to wonder. "Are your accommodations a problem?"

"Not if I can convince the Cat I'm not a threat to her self imposed asylum. She is better suited for the Army." Dog comments and he wonders why she is in the Air Force of all places. "I might be able to gain her cooperation if needed but that's a big empty hole of unknown given I was intentionally positioned as a threat to her which she knows."

"I pushed for an extension but as it is you have three weeks to prepare for this mission." Aimhurst admits and so far his progress on this issue has been like rolling an elephant up hill. "I'll keep trying."

"So much for getting back to my fighting weight." Dog mutters and three weeks of eating regular meals will only take the sharp edges off but not build a nice healthy layer of body fat needed to keep his muscles happy.

"The Intel I have indicates nothing regarding this mission has changed." Aimhurst informs him which is rather telling in its self.

"And we both know that's a load of bullshit." Dog responds bluntly because he was approached with this offer of a second chance two weeks ago. The information was probably a week old by then and things change all the time in a war so he will not only be physically unprepared but going in blind. The powers that be higher up probably including this Major General do not want him coming back so why wait for him to be ready or give him the Intel he needs.

Chapter 4
Somewhere in Saudi Arabia....

Just as C.C. suspected when she opens the letter from her brother enjoying what will likely be her last few moments of privacy since the housing Sergeant was less than cooperative and where the Colonel is presently she could care less as long as he is not in her space. Reading Carter's letter about some woman he seems fixated on while seated on her cot with her back to the wall does little to cheer her.

From her prospective Carter just met this woman but realistically a month or two have passed between his letters so he has actually known the woman possibly four months and her responses are brief notes. She cannot tell him where she is and mail is read to be certain no one divulges military information so what is there really for her to say except she vaguely remembers feeling over the moon and starry eyed once only sometimes it seems like it happened to someone else.

Bobby was her everything so when he asked her to marry him she did not hesitate saying yes but she was only seventeen to his nineteen. The age difference was the least of her problems as it turned out because her parents did not know she was dating nor were they pleased Bobby did not attend church regularly. The blow up over her marriage announcement was loud and vicious but what she remembers most about it is the fact it was Carter standing by her side and not Bobby who seemed to feel he had done his part by asking for her hand.

Married by a justice of the peace they moved to a new city where Bobby was an intern at a prestigious business and attending college. She received her GED through the mail and landed her first job doing what she could to help support the two of them. It felt like they were playing house and all they had to do was pass GO but then the phone calls came and the hung ups when she answered. Bobby became secretive until one sobbing woman who did not hang up on the wife confessed to having an affair with Bobby, she did not know he was married. She confronted Bobby and her first marriage ended when he stopped coming home. She signed the divorce papers one year and two moths after their marriage began but the worst part is she no longer cared.

Hearing the outer door open and close she puts aside her memories refolding Carter's letter placing it in the military issued trunk beside her cot acting as storage, night table, and dresser held securely closed with a combination lock. The cot, a tall narrow locker, along with the trunk are the only furniture in the room. Moving to the door frame where no door exists she finds the Colonel picking up one of the items she purchased at the commissary earlier from the couch.

He seems to be making himself right at home wearing only his briefs as he studies a package with a frown and emaciated is the only way to describe him yet he has far more muscle then she thought possible given the other obvious signs of his near starved condition. His hip bones are the only thing holding up his boxer shorts and the elastic is not even touching his skin between but he is bronze all over which is not a question she needed answered.

"How long?" C.C. asks as he is currently unwrapping a breakfast bar and it seems she has the right to know just how long he will be here before he shrivels to nothing.

"I'll be gone in three weeks." Dog informs her figuring would be her first concern and he does not take it personally but her straight forward question is surprising given her precarious position in this war. "What no salute, no sirs?"

"Damage is done." C.C. mutters grimly so why bother at this late date when the Major Agitator has all he needs to send her packing but he did not really answer her question, so is he going to be dead in three weeks or transferred for medical help?

"I told the Major no deal." Dog continues wondering if she will believe him and knowing probably not. "The Major pissed off your C.O. and you're right, I'm not suppose to be in here, but I am. I'll not be here long."

"As long as I'm not expected to nurse you through some wasting disease until you're 'gone' I can deal with it."   C.C. responds bluntly feeling it best to lay it right out there.

"No problem." Dog assures her on this point as he bends picking up something else he does not recognize and finds it to be good. "I knew you would know just what to get. Sorry, you apparently learned the hard way."

"No problem, my marriages tend not to last long any way."

C.C. replies not wanting to get into the details about number three.

"Ouch." Dog responds with sympathy seeing no tears only a hint of sadness but she hides it well. "Show me the gym tomorrow?"

"Cals O'five hundred." C.C. agrees as everything runs on military time and no consideration is made for airmen who do not get back to their bunks until after O'three hundred after flying night runs.

O'five hundred and C.C. is at the gym which is a large building with a sand floor and given the size of the openings in the sides it was most likely built to be another mechanics hanger but the crates at one end suggests it is also being used for storage. The building is in no way air conditioned given the doors were never hung but at this hour the temperature is sixty degrees Fahrenheit. As far as gyms go she has found it to be more complete and compact then her home base gym state side where the obstacle course and running track can be reached by going to different parts of the base but here it is all under one very big roof.

She is with her flight part way through their five mile jog but very much aware the Colonel is also here pumping weights with his two M.P.s acting as his spotters and she does not need her flight's comments every time they pass the area to remind her.

"Jesus God." Pincher mutters as they jog past as the Colonel bench presses a bar loaded with weights so heavy the bar bends in the middle as he pushes upward.

"Mommy, can I touch the gorilla." Silly whines in a little kids voice.

"Someone should put him in a cage." Prince remarks because he does not like this guy being in the same quarters with C.C. One of them would be no problem because they respect her but this guy does not look like the type to give a lady her space.

"I'm almost certain they just let him out of a cage." C.C. responds although she still is not certain whose cage or where, when, or why.

"He didn't say any thing last night about why he's here?" Check asks because surely she knows more now than before.

"He just said he will be leaving in three weeks so I only have to put up with him for that long." C.C. repeats but she is still not certain what he meant by 'gone'.

"He has to be a spy for Major Alexander." Check responds confidently because what other reason would they overlook regulations and let him stay in her quarters.

"Well, if he is, he's not a very good one." C.C. comments knowing the Major Agitator does not need much to send her home and in this case it would be her word against that of a Colonel so they would take his word. "I'm still here."

"We're going to find out what is up with this guy." Sin promises because they need to know what they are up against and this is not just about her, C.C. is one of them.

"Captain Callahan, report to the C.O.'s office."

This message is being verbally relayed across the gym from one of the large open doorways where a staff orderly is standing after passing his request to the first person walking by going into the gym. C.C. acknowledges the message has reached her to the staff orderly who leaves having completed his assignment as she continues to jog since this will take her past the same doorway.

"Ah shit." Egor blurts as C.C. peals off going out the door thinking this is probably not a good thing and might have something to do with his extracurricular activities.

When C.C. arrives she is admitted directly into the C.O.'s office where she stands sweating in tee shirt, fatigues and combat boots while standing at attention knowing the Major Agitator is also present from her first glance but now she has to stand staring straight ahead while sand is clinging to damp places on her clothing making itches she does not dare scratch. The Major Agitator usually accosts her on the parade grounds and likes having her stand at attention in the hot sun never allowing her to relax as he regales her with all she is missing by not being state side. The only thing he accomplishes is reinforcing her decision joining the Air Force was the right thing for her and the only place she has ever really belonged.

"I knew it was only a matter of time Captain before you gave me what I needed to send you home." Alexander greets her with a confident smile and gives her time to explain herself as he studies this woman who stands maybe five foot with a manly looking crew cut longer on top combed to stand up like a razors edge but dangerous the Colonel implied, definitely not. "I'm giving you this one opportunity to explain yourself Captain before I proceed."

"Sir, nothing to explain, Sir." C.C. informs him and she knows a fishing expedition when she hears one but the need for it escapes her when the Colonel could give the Major Agitator a list.

"I imagine you were surprised to find a man assigned to your quarters. Must have been an unpleasant surprise and understandably you may have forgotten your position in this military." Alexander comments certain she will tell him what happened even if the Colonel refuses to cooperate. He is certain she did not address the Colonel correctly because he made sure his kit was delivered here and not before he was released.

"Sir, the M.P.s stationed outside my door were more of a surprise Sir." C.C. responds truthfully and a rather nasty surprise considering the timing.

"M.P.s? What M.P.s?" Alexander asks because no one told him about any M.P.s. "I didn't approve M.P.s coming to this base."

"I believe they are bunking with the enlisted men." The CO offers as if this helps matters while being amused by the major's discomposure regarding this information.

"I was not aware men came with him." Alexander mutters angrily and the woman was clearly forewarned which is not what he planned at all and her being caught unaware is part of the reason he offered the Army this base to use as a launching point.

"I was not aware you intended to bring a military prisoner to my base." The C.O. replies dryly without sympathy. "The fact he came with armed prison guards should not be a surprise to you."

"My arrangement with the Army was strictly on a need to know basis and you did not need to know." Alexander dictates still staring at the woman who has become a thorn just under his skin. Just looking at her irritates him and he moves up into her face knowing he is going to break her to his will soon. "You and I are not finished Captain."

C.C. remains silent as he stares at her then he backs up shaking his head before going out the office door closing it with a bang and if she did not know better she would think the Major is seriously rattled about something other than his plans going awry but with his terminally irritated attitude it is difficult to tell. The office is now quiet as the C.O. sighs reminding her she is not the only one who has had to suffer the Major Agitator.

"At ease Captain, have a seat." The C.O. instructs and waits as she complies before continuing. "This is a hell of a situation and I have issued complains which I am certain fell on deaf ears given the Colonel needs a launching point for a very important mission. If it helps at all the Colonel was very definite in his refusal to assist the Major in his objective but as to his sincerity

I have no idea."

"Sir, understood Sir." C.C. replies and he is basically telling her to make up her own mind whether or not she should trust the Colonel.

"Well I'm glad one of us does." The C.O. mutters and as base commander he should have been notified but something about this situation reeks of classified top secret. "I cornered the Army Major General who flew in here to meet with the Colonel hoping for an explanation which was unhelpful then did a little digging on my own but all I have is more questions. I feel you have a right to be aware of the situation, or as much as I could find given your enforced proximity to the man. Colonel Johann Red Eagle is, or was, a Ranger assigned to Black Ops during and after Vietnam. He apparently went AWOL, was charged with desertion, and was sentenced to life in prison."

"Sir?" C.C. asks because the sentence seems a little extreme so there must be more only he is looking at her as if this some how explains something she may have missed.

"Now you have the same questions I do." The C.O. comments and he goes on because it becomes even stranger. "There is no record of a hearing or tribunal just his sentence, he was not stripped of his rank, and the Major insinuated there was some kind of error made and went on to suggest the military intends to rectify this error at this time. From what little of the Colonel's military record I could obtain he is a highly decorated soldier but given the dates not much of his record is accessible and doing the math the man is, or at least should be, in his early fifties."

"Sir, he doesn't look it, sir." C.C. responds but the Colonel's words come back to her, 'nothing is as it seems', but how much is the question she has.

"The Major General did go so far as to assure me the Colonel will in no way harm anyone on this base which tells me at some point he may have on another." The C.O. warns her and he did not find the information comforting.

"Sir, I am not concerned about that, Sir." C.C. replies honestly because one thing she has not felt while in his presence is fear for her life, only her status in the military.

"Then I will be concerned enough for the both of us." The C.O. informs her because putting a man who has been incarcerated for years in close quarters with a woman is not what he would call a good idea. "I have a daughter about your age and my father instinct is kicking in so deal with my concern."

"Sir, yes sir." C.C. replies maintaining a straight face while granting him this one concession to her gender since the C.O. made it clear the decision to stay or leave was entirely up to her when the Major Agitator first arrived and has treated her no different than any other officer under his command.

"It is my understanding as of this morning this middle aged Colonel with a mile long list of Purple Hearts is bench pressing what I am told must be well over five hundred pounds." The CO comments just so she is aware his concern for her is valid.

"Sir, by my estimation nine hundred pounds, sir." C.C. informs him because she knows the weight each size of those disks represents and he was pressing them twenty reps slow and steady so working out, not showing off.

"Great. Maybe I should be more concerned with him lifting the Humvee's in the motor pool." The C.O. responds finding this not comforting at all. "But they don't send a man to prison for AWOL and desertion usually results in the same punishment, a dishonorable discharge is usually the result, which means he did something far worse."

"Sir, I will keep that in mind, sir." C.C. responds because the punishment is suppose to fit the crime so whatever the crime it was very bad.

"If he attempts anything regardless of you being capable of handling it or not you report to me. Is that understood?" The C.O. orders looking stern.

"Sir, yes sir." C.C. confirms but she finds this silently amusing she is expected to report any infractions the Colonel should make when he is suppose to do the same with her. Irony abounds.

"So this is what you hotshot pilots do when not flying." Dog comments standing in the door frame where a door should be but is not so either the military made some budget cuts or they simply ran out of time. It seems he found the Cat laying stretched out on her cot as if intending to take a nap.

"Squadron run to night." C.C. explains simply and she does not have to explain herself or her actions to him but she does open her eyes to glare at him.

"Night bombing runs." Dog mutters wondering what the world has come to in his absence but what he has learned still does not explain how this war is being fought. "No troops on the ground, just bombing runs."

"Your point?" C.C. inquires wondering if he is getting to one.

"Just not the way I'm use to things being done." Dog admits where the fighting was heavy on the ground and they called in for air support.

"Well, a lot has changed in say, ten years." C.C. responds hoping he will either correct her or explain but no such luck as he simply stares at her so she tries to goad him. "If we had this technology during the Vietnam war we would have won, oh sorry, you lost that one didn't you."

"I was there and it's hard to win a war when there is no clear objective." Dog replies finding himself grinning for the Cat is curious but then he never doubted her intelligence as the Major seems to be doing because there is only so much which can be hidden by a pretty face.

"You were there." C.C. repeats not pleased by his answer because it tells her nothing so she decides to lay out what she has found and put together herself. "Fine, correct me where I'm wrong. You've been in prison for ten years charged with AWOL or desertion, which are not entirely the same, and sentenced to life with no hearing or tribunal then you were starved nearly to death by the U.S. military which completely does not wash nor is possible."

"My sentence was death curious Cat." Dog confides bluntly even though he probably should not but tenacity should be rewarded. "I was taking too long to die."

"So they dump you in the middle of a war." C.C. responds dubiously for she is not sure she believes this but what better way to get rid of him. "One way mission?"

He grins while touching his index finger to the tip of his nose then pointing at her as if they are playing some sort of game before he leaves and she is left staring at the vacant space he left behind still knowing little more than she did before. She is now under the impression he is just playing a game with her and maybe after all this time this is all life and death situations are to him any more. Death sentence or not the U.S. does not starve prisoners and he is lucky because at one time they did shoot deserters but not in a very long time. She pounds her pillow with the back of her head and refuses to think about any of this any longer closing her eyes again and willing herself to sleep.

"So, O'nine hundred at the shooting range." Check finishes quickly for C.C.'s benefit as he sees the Colonel with his tray heading their direction so he instantly moves down leaving space between himself and C.C. without being asked before standing at attention.

"Attention." C.C. calls out as she and her flight, along with the entire table, stand at attention while the Colonel sets down his tray.

"At ease before you get indigestion and it is not necessary to stand and salute me in a mess hall, except for the Cool Cat here." Dog advises as everyone sits back down then he looks over the mess hall seeing Major Alexander standing by the door with a grim look on his face. "He even looks like a vulture."

"Sir, he was waiting outside the showers for me this afternoon, sir."
C.C. comments not glancing in the Major Agitator's direction but it is getting to the point she can feel his eyes on her and there is a creep factor to this.

"Check for a peep hole." Dog suggests with distaste. "The man doesn't respect you or your rank. Former Marine is my guess and might be looking for a little pay back."

"Sir?" C.C. questions wondering why he would think a Marine would have it in for her for any reason.

"My military record might be buried in the deepest dung pile but yours is not." Dog confesses and he can tell by her frown she does not like his knowing anything about her. "Hey, you were as much a surprise to the Army as I was to the Air Force and they want to be sure you don't kill me off before I reach my objective."

"Sir, such concern for a condemned man, sir?" C.C. asks finding this totally contradictory to what he expects her to believe and the payback comment does not fly either as those Marines learned never underestimate short and cute again.

"No, just determined I do what they want done before I die." Dog informs her keeping his voice low for only her to hear which has him leaning toward her and getting a heady whiff of Cat which is not perfume or sweat but something rather intoxicating in between. "Not many can do what I can do."

"Sir, like bench press a Humvee, Sir?" C.C. asks not seeing what else he might be good at given he stands out like a sore thumb.

"Among other things." Dog replies saying no more on the

subject as he straightens and concentrates on his meal.

"Check?" C.C. calls to get his attention frowning as she has to lean forward to speak to Check because of the mountain seated between them and she is still frustrated by this man's unwillingness to give her a straight answer. "Did they put my bird back together again?"

"Yes Ma'am." Check affirms leaning forward to see her. "Ran final checks this morning but if it so much as spits you should take up the trainer again."

"Mac Levies people are good, I'm not worried about it." C.C. replies confidently because they do have the best aircraft mechanics around on this base. If it gets off the ground then it will stay up until she decides to bring it down herself.

"She caught a broad side meant for a bomber last time out." Pincher informs the Colonel who is looking curiously from Check to C.C. seated on either side of him "She limped home."

"An exaggeration." C.C. corrects because the damage was not nearly as bad as it looked. "Just a few holes."

"Right through the fuselage into the heads, your bird was choking on it's own fuel." Silly reveals to no one in particular. "She had to cut the engine and glide in or when she reduced speed to land it would have flamed, but C.C. knows all the tricks."

"If she says ditch a bird, we ditch." Prince comments because they trust her word and she has far more intensive training then they have. "They pulled her into the Navy pilot training program when she was still in Air Force flight training. She's a top gun and they offered her a position as a Navy trainer."

"That's so not happening." C.C. mutters and shudders at just the thought as those chosen for the program have egos too big to fit through doorways. It was not a pleasant experience being the only woman pilot but what she learned was worth the aggravation but she would never put herself in a position where she would have to deal with those egos day in and day out or she might commit murder.

"Something went wrong with my bird during a training flight. She told me to ditch and just after I pulled the ejection handle and was going up the bird went boom right out from under me. I was thinking I could make it back to base." Sin recounts because he will never forget.

Chapter 5
Somewhere in Saudi Arabia...

"Hydraulic hose burst in the landing gear." C.C. comments as she tries to figure out what kind of meat wishing they would just shut up. "You probably felt go but chalked it up to air turbulence, just another bump in the road. Landing was already out of the question but the fluid ran into the electronics which is what was smoking and playing hell with control. There was nothing else any one could do."

"Just a malfunction." Egor responds. "No big deal."

"It was to me." Sin objects frowning at Egor.

"Guys" C.C. warns not wanting them to get into an argument over something that happened over a year ago. "If in question protocol is ditch the bird."

"But you didn't." Dog comments with interest.

"Sir, there are different degrees of damage, and electronic malfunctions which I have been trained to asses because a bird coming in hot on a Navy carrier will make a hell of a mess." C.C. informs him. "Aerial combat is not all they teach and the only two choices a Navy pilot has is landing on a carrier or in the ocean so the decision to land or ditch becomes a little more precise, sir."

"But." Silly interjects grinning knowingly. "Given lots of options for landing and C.C. can land a plane on nearly anything no matter what condition the bird is in."

"Every leave from base state side she finds a vintage plane to fly." Sin explains and really some of them do not look like they should be air born. "Bi planes, crop dusters, and she's on a list of pilots with the military who fly vintage fighters to museums all over the States."

"If it has wings, rotors, or a propeller," Check adds because he feels it needs to be said. "C.C. can fly it."

"She has more flight time than most, if not all the pilots here." Prince brags with a grin.

"Simulations don't count." C.C. warns them knowing there are several pilots here with more flight time than she has.

"Don't need too." Egor mocks with a laugh. "Your feet are off the ground more than they are on it. Civilian life for you will be hell on Earth unless you fly an air bus but even that would be too tame for you."

"Flying is hell off Earth." Dog interjects his opinion and they all just stare at him. "I hate flying."

"Sir, if you're an Army Ranger, you have to fly Sir." C.C. comments dryly because if what the C.O. gleaned from his record is correct he would most likely have to be inserted into where they need him by plane or helicopter.

"I am, and I breath a sigh of relief when I jump out, or it lands." Dog confides seriously.

"Sir, is that why they stuck you here, sir?" C.C. asks because if the Army knows of his fear of flying then they would know he will not jump in a plane to get off this base.

"Probably has more to do with convenience." Dog responds truthfully. "I can't be driven to my destination so have to be dropped."

"Sir, the military usually weeds out people with phobias or assigns them to other positions, sir." C.C. comments not certain she believes him or if it is as bad as he would like them to believe.

"It's a well documented military fact." Dog replies grimly. "Given my skill set and training they choose to over look my white knuckles and trepidation."

"You don't like to fly." Pincher mutters unable to wrap his mind around this.

"Sir, you're trained to pilot aircraft aren't you, sir?" C.C. asks.

"If I must." Dog responds which is worse then being a nervous passenger but he is surrounded by pilots who are now looking at him as if he has lost his mind.

The pre-flight briefing is short, their orders have not changed since this began months ago which simply states S.E.A.D., Suppress Enemy Air Defenses, and roll them back. Flying patrol routes they pick off radar posts and anti aircraft missiles with air to ground missiles from their F-15 Eagles while Night Hawk bombers undetectable by radar fly their own missions with targets predetermined as key military targets.

Dressed in flight gear C.C. climbs into her jet sweating buckets while waiting on board seated in the second seat behind her is the WSO assigned to her this night. Weapons Systems Officer's control the air to ground weapons and track missile signatures along with enemy radar leaving her free to fly so Wilko is with her this night, real name Roger.

The air temperature is a nice sultry eighty two and will drop down to near fifty on the ground only the jets are not air conditioned only once in the air they cool off nicely, though at the moment they are large ovens on wheels. Pre-flight checks, control tower clearance and she along with Wilko are roaring down the runway then streaking off into the night leaving fan tails of swirling sand to blow across the base on the slight breeze.

Dog is making use of his time moving about the base unseen studying the base defenses finding they are adequate but just as he thought set to keep enemy forces out not personnel in. He could leave at any time, but not just yet since he has more to learn here first though when he passes the woman's showers he cannot resist taking a closer look. No peep holes he can find and he cannot explain why the very thought of the Major spying on Cool Cat possibly naked sets his inner dog howling with rage.

It is not like him to be jealous, not in his genetic make up before or after the DNA patch, and he would not know what a relationship is if it walked up to bite him but for one instant there, in the mess hall, just the thought of the Major spying on Cat while she was naked made his blood boil.

He has played slap and tickle more than a few times but once the sheets untangle both he and the woman part ways, no need for names, they will never see each other again, and he has never wanted, or expected more. Such is his acquaintance with Cat if she crooked her finger leading him to her cot he would be looking for land mines the entire way but follow he would. He would not be able to resist if she gave him the green light but the odds of this happening are somewhere between none and never. A man can dream and his dreams use to involve food but now they center around a woman, so maybe he is normal after all.

Laying on his cot in the living area Cool Cat returns at O'three hundred and by O'five hundred she is up again at the gym. O'nine hundred she is at the outdoor shooting range with her flight and another flight in what appears to be a competition. He is joined by his two M.P. guards who seem to be doing nothing more strenuous than wondering around the base this morning.

"Have the two of you placed any bets yet?" Dog inquires motioning to the two flights.

"No, but if we do they would be on Captain Callahan." The shorter one replies confidently.

"Word is she can't be beat, except possibly with a really big stick while she's asleep." The taller M.P. confides with a laugh. "Pool, Darts, Volleyball, and anything else they can come up with she and her flight are raking in the dough. They also say she doesn't sweat except in the gym and only to make everyone else feel better."

"You two seem to have heard quite a lot." Dog responds wondering why this strange feeling is circling his innards again.

"Boredom." The taller M.P. admits. "And Captain C.C. is about the only interesting thing on this base. Even people who don't like her respect her which says a lot about a person. Those who don't like her it becomes pretty obvious it's envy and not a specific incident."

"I'm surprised the envious have not found a way to help the Major get her off base." Dog comments with interest.

"That's because they hate him, not dislike, but actual hate." The shorter M.P. explains as they watch the two flights gathered around the two participants. "The Major has a real hard on for the Captain, and not in a good way."

"Has he tried to convince the two of you to play stool pigeon for him?" Dog inquires out of curiosity.

"Oh yeah." The shorter M.P. admits with a frown. "Wanted to know what she did, or did not do, when she saw you. Wanted to know if she saluted you or if she was disrespectful in any way. We told him we didn't see anything so we don't know then he promised us promotions if we testified to any infraction, seen or not was implied, but I got the feeling I would be selling my soul to the devil cutting a deal with him."

"Yeah, don't do that." Dog responds seriously. "Look, in a couple of days I'm going to disappear for a while."

"Ah shit Colonel," The tall M.P. mutters and why would he tell them his escape plan. "You shouldn't be telling us things like that. We're suppose to keep you here."

"I promised to complete this mission but there are some things I need and things I need to do first." Dog responds leveling with them as they are looking anything but pleased. "I'll be back and the Cool Cat is going to help me but I need the two of you to help her cover my absence in case someone comes looking for me, like the Major."

"The Major is exactly why the Captain is not going to help you." The shorter M.P. informs him seriously.

"She will, she just doesn't know it yet." Dog responds confidently and he does not miss the doubtful looks they exchange but he keeps silent.

"Okay, I think I can spit farther than you." Senior Airman Debronski call sign Deb offers his hand gun back into his holster.

"You can." C.C. replies as money changes hands around them. "No need to prove it."

"Are you sure?" Deb remarks laughing but he sobers quickly when Check holds his hand out to him and he has to fork over the money before Check moves on. "Your pal Check is one greedy bastard if you don't mind my saying so Ma'am."

"No, you've got it right." C.C. agrees finding Check is getting worse in his money making endeavors. Friendly competition is one thing but this continuous need to feather his nest is getting out of hand. "I'm thinking he needs a lesson."

"Oh goody, can I watch?" Deb asks seriously.

"Possibly." C.C. admits seeing the Colonel and his M.P.s approaching and Check is smiling up at him. "I don't think I'll have to do anything."

"You think that Colonel can beat you?" Deb asks looking at the Colonel as Check seems to be talking, a lot.

"Army Ranger." C.C. replies and to her this says it all.

"Hot damn." Deb proclaims hustling over to where Check and the Colonel are in conversation as they move toward the shooting range then money is changing hands.

"C.C., we have another bet." Check announces smiling big approaching her in advance of the others.

"A word First Lieutenant." C.C. instructs moving away from the others as he follows and he should know she is upset about something since she just used his rank.

Dog stands at the shooting line as he watches what looks like an disagreement between the Cool Cat and the First Lieutenant. Her previous opponent is standing before his flight as they grumble over their loss but he is motioning them to silence and looking over catching Dog's eye while smiling confidently so something is up but what is unclear. The Cool Cat is not stupid nor does she take anything at face value so she is no doubt trying to talk her airman out of this match and does not succeed by the grim look on her face as she moves back to the shooting line.

"I haven't fired a gun in ten years." Dog confides if she is concerned she might loose.

"Sir, I'm sure they gave you free run of the prison gym, sir." C.C. counters because he certainly had no trouble handling weights.

"No." Dog admits not having access to anything.

"Yeah." C.C. mutters already knowing there is something about this Colonel which is not normal so why should his shooting be the exception. "Sir, do you have a gun, sir?"

"Uh, no." Dog admits looking back at the two M.P.s close by motioning toward a side arm and they hesitate for a second then one is taking off his side piece handing it to him then he backs off looking concerned while his partner has the rifle off his back and in hand. "There is just no trust in the world any more." Dog mocks as he familiarizes himself with the gun in his hand.

"Sir, yes, sir." C.C. agrees glancing at Check who is still smiling big. "Sir, a few practice shots, sir?"

"No." Dog declines the offer.

"Sir, I figured that too, sir." C.C. comments dryly as she pushes the button running her target out. "Sir, where should we start, sir?"

"Right about there should do." Dog decides as he sends his target out matching her distance.

They both take five shots before the targets are brought back and the score is totaled by one of the watching men. Both score evenly hitting only in the round marked area of the heart. The targets are moved farther out by ten feet and they fire again but when they are brought back one of the Colonel's shots has hit outside the mark.

"Thanks for the heads up it pulls to the right." Dog calls back over his shoulder to the M.P. as he puts in a fresh clip.

"Sorry Sir, didn't know it either." The taller M.P. admits. "I've never attempted to shoot that far before."

"Well, now, you know." Dog informs him as they run the targets out again and the Cool Cat is leading in score.

"Heat warning flag has gone up, yellow." One of the men behind them calls out meaning they do not have much time to finish this competition because red means everyone has to be under cover and this happens quickly in the desert.

"Let's send the targets out farther and make this the last five shots." Check announces and a discussion ensues as to whether this is fair to both participants since the Colonel is one shot behind.

"If you turn and shoot him the Major will have good reason to send you home." Dog cautions the Cool Cat hearing her low growl at her airman's suggestion and now even more money is changing hands.

"Sir, do not tempt me, sir." C.C. responds and it is now obvious the Colonel is not use to distance shooting with a hand gun when he is probably use to rifles at this range which Check has no doubt guessed at this point.

Dog remains silent since it seems Cat has had enough of being used but right now the Cool Cat cannot afford animosity. It is a wonder half the base does not hate her already given her flights penchant for taking other peoples money but then they could just say no too.

"Run the targets out another ten feet." Checks confirms finally after a good deal of debate.

"Ever shot this far out before?" Dog asks as they hold down the buttons sending the targets out farther.

"Sir, not my problem , sir. C.C. responds and whether she can or cannot is really no longer the issue.

"Might drift like a rifle which is usually to the right." Dog confides in good sportsmanship. "I have no clue why."

"Sir, if I truly cared I would try that, sir." C.C. informs him just as honestly.

"And here I was hoping for a little friendly competition." Dog responds grimacing as he aims.

"Sir, you came to the wrong base, sir." C.C. replies as she aims. "Sir, there is nothing friendly about this any more, sir."

"Understood." Dog agrees and he is beginning to see it too but not his problem as he takes his five shots and when targets come back he is the clear winner.

As the men from the other flights cheer he can only stare at her target because the Cool Cat shot a line right next to the heart circle, a straight line with no deviation at all. No one else seems to have noticed as money exchanges hands nor understand how incredibly difficult it is to do but he knows and would have said it was impossible given the kick of the gun along with the distance.

"Sir, you're correct, a bullet at this distance does drift to the right but the reason is we're both right handed so the torque of the stronger hand on the gun butt effects the velocity. If we were left handed at long distances it would drift to the left, sir." C.C. informs him so now he knows but she doubts this is information he will ever need since rifles are more commonly used by soldiers in all branches of the military and with those distances wind speed and direction are more of an issue.

"Did the Navy teach you that?" Dog asks looking at his target finding they are all towards the right side of the heart circle and two are to the left because he over compensated but the Cool Cat could have placed those bullets even at this distance any where she wanted.

"Sir, second husband, sir." C.C. admits but says no more as she notices the two M.P.s approaching cautiously. "Sir, "I think your guard wants his gun back, sir."

"Just no trust anymore." Dog mutters turning the gun and handing it back to the guard butt first and the M.P. takes it with a sigh of relief but then he is looking past the two of them. He knows exactly what the man is looking at by the way his eyes widen and his mouth drops open. "Let's just keep this to ourselves, they're Airheads, they don't know any better."

"No offense Colonel but if we need back up, we'll be calling the Captain." The M.P. informs him.

"No offense taken and that would be a very wise decision." Dog agrees and maybe now the two men are beginning to see the Cat for what she is as they walk away glancing back as if to make sure their eyes were not deceiving them.

"I'm sorry C.C., I should have checked the distance with you first." Check laments as he walks up to her and the Colonel only she turns walking away without a word. "I guess she's not use to loosing."

"If this were scored like poker she won. Her royal flush beats my full house hands down." Dog comments turning to walk away.

"If she had hit the circle all five times would have been a royal flush." Check comments but she did not even hit the circle once.

Dog pauses knowing he should just walk away but the fact this First Lieutenant cannot see what is right in front of his face burns so he turns back while chastising himself for getting involved.

It is one thing the Major doubts the Cat, and can be used to her advantage, but someone as close to her as this man is, this is not a good thing, and the man is blind to what just happened here.

"Do you see that line?" Dog asks pointing to the Cat's target. "That is perfect aim."

"She missed the heart." Check replies because that is what she was suppose to be aiming for.

"And you would probably say if that line went straight through the heart she won but that would have been easier than what she just did." Dog responds wondering why he is wasting his time with this.

"You're saying she did that on purpose?" Check asks frowning as he considers while looking at the line then realizes there is no way she could have done it unless she intended to even by accident. "She threw the match."

"Partly my fault." Dog admits and he should have kept his mouth shut. "I told her guns at long distances pull to the right like I assumed she would not know. She just showed me she knows then proved it five times."

"But that wasn't the bet." Check mutters woodenly and she intentionally threw the match which is now obvious to him.

"I wasn't aware either of us made a bet." Dog remarks looking at the target and if he had a wall he would have it framed. "I believe you made a bet and you lost but in our competition she won. Maybe you should have listened to her because what happened here had nothing to do with you and you're the only one having a problem with loosing."

Dog walks away this time because it is time to get moving on his own plans and maybe it is best this happened now because he is going to need Cat's undivided attention soon. If she is not speaking to her flight then it could work to his advantage.

Sitting on her cot C.C. rereads her brother's letter but still has no idea who this woman is Carter has met only she knows where his words are leading and she does not want him to make the same mistakes she made In the marriage lottery. She apparently did not learn her lesson the first time and her second marriage was far worse then her first but she did learn how to shoot with a hand gun really well if nothing else.

She met her second husband when he gave her a speeding ticket having caught her at a very low point in her life. She was crying so hard she honestly had no idea how fast she was going.

Surprisingly he asked her to dinner and it was not until after they were married he liked making her cry which fed some sick macho aspect of his character. When she stopped showing any emotion at all he became increasingly violent and began to control every aspect of her life. A victim of domestic violence with no job or means of support she walked away from her marriage anyway. She just packed up what little she owned into her car and drove away on what little money she took from his wallet. She lived in her car working odd jobs to make money, so she could drive farther, but her car broke down in between towns which is when she met husband number three.

Refolding Carter's letter placing it back in her trunk she intends to nap before her squadron flight only memories of Melvin The Great causes her smile sadly because she would have gladly spent the rest of her life with him. After picking up a hitchhiker from the side of the road he agreed to drop her off in the next town but during a forty minute drive she learned a good deal about Melvin The Great.

Divorced himself he offered her the job of being his magic assistant but it was his old fashioned charm which won her over. Living like a gypsy traveling the country in an RV with a man not her husband she wore a sequined and feathered costume in hospitals and nursing homes assisting Melvin the Great who preformed magic tricks bringing smiles and laughter where ever they went.

He built up her confidence, made her feel like a real person, and she began to trust him enough to tell him some of her past. He paid for her divorce from number two then asked her to marry him not needing a wife so much as wanting to protect her. He meant and she accepted his proposal because she could no longer imagine life without him.

Two months after they married he began having stomach pains and the diagnoses was intestinal cancer then a month later he was gone. Two days later lawyers and his children from previous marriages descended upon her. Melvin The Great was Melvin apparently incredibly rich and if she wanted any part of what was rightfully hers she would have had to fight for it. Instead she took the RV and the money in their joint checking account moving on once again because without Melvin the money meant nothing.

Chapter 6
Somewhere in Saudi Arabia...

Having had little to no sleep C.C. enters the mess hall but the Colonel is suspiciously absent given his need to eat continuously and her flight is suspiciously silent for a change then she sits through pre-flight briefing trying not to yawn before going out on patrol where her lack of rest seems to vanish.

Returning to her quarters she finds the Colonel apparently sleeping peacefully on her makeshift couch since he does not stir as she passes to her room. She bares clenched teeth in his direction which he cannot possibly see in the dark even if he were awake and not more than an hour later she is up participating in calisthenics. Her only goals for this day are taking a shower then a nap but crossing the parade grounds returning to her quarters after the shower Check begins walking beside her. She is not in the mood to hear whatever plan he has cooked up this time to rook men from their money and their silence the night before makes her inclined to believe she will not like it. Right at the moment her only thoughts are of stretching out on her cot to sleep but they are nearly to her quarters and he has yet to say anything so she stops waiting for him to spit out whatever is on his pee brain.

"What?" She demands as she turns to him just wanting to get it over with before she answers no.

"I'm trying to figure out how to tell you I'm sorry which does not sound like the hundred other times I have told you I'm sorry so you might actually believe I am actually sorry this time." Check contemplates out loud but so far he is coming up empty.

"Well, that is different." C.C. responds blinking at this strange and convoluted apology.

"Still not quite what I was going for but if you believe I'm sincere then good." Check concludes and he may have stepped way too far out on a limb this time. She has gone along with his plans with only token resistance only this time she had been adamantly against his betting. "It has occurred to me if I applied myself a little I could earn my next promotion and a pay upgrade."

"Don't go over board." C.C suggests wryly as this is a point she has been trying to make for a long time now.

"I know, you've mentioned it a few times." Check hedges but it was far more than a few times only he was having more fun this way. "I've been letting you do all the work."

"On the ground." C.C. replies generously because he is a good pilot only he never goes that extra step like being in the Air Force is just lark. "You've got what it takes but you're not using it to its full potential."

"Are you saying I'm lazy?" Check asks just to be certain.

"Yeah." C.C. agrees with no difficulty at all.

"Then why didn't you just say something sooner." Check responds throwing up his hands. "Gees, women, they think we're all mind readers or something."

"Get out of my face." C.C. warns because at the moment she is tired and incautious enough she might just lay him out teasing or not.

Dog takes his customary place in the mess hall between the First Lt and Cat after spending a good deal of time reconnoitering the base and he is not certain taking his customary place is safest after the shooting range incident the other day and an internal flight war could be very dangerous to innocent bystanders, or not so innocent like himself.

"Sir, do I need to draw you a map to the commissioned officers dinning room Sir?" C.C. asks because the day before it was nice not having his large form in the way even if no one said a word and his disrupting their meals is getting old fast.

"I know were it is." Dog replies, he knows were everything is now. "I just choose not to eat there."

"Sir, we feel so privileged, sir." C.C. mutters wishing he would just disappear.

"As you should." Dog goads but before he can say anything more everyone in the mess hall rises to their feet.

"As you were everyone." Comes Major General Aimhurst's voice as he moves through the mess hall to stand behind the Colonel. "Colonel, I have been called back to Washington."

"I'll sorely miss you Sir." Dog replies without guile.

"Be that as it may." The Major General manages continuing with a smile. "I've given your situation considerable thought and spoken with the base C.O. He agrees, as long as it does not interfere with regular duties, and if Captain Callahan is agreeable, her flight may participate in a flag game. On the stipulation you do not, and I repeat Colonel, do not maim or disable any airmen."

"Kill joy." Dog grumbles under his breath. "And you left out the Captain who would very much like to maim me for life."

"True, so I'll add the stipulation she does not maim or disable you." The Major General responds making this clear looking at the Captain seated next to him without amusement or a hint of teasing.

"Sir, agreed Sir." C.C. responds just as seriously though she will have to find out what this flag game entails before she agrees to anything else.

"I need you in fighting form Colonel." The Major General admits leaning down with a hand on the Colonel's shoulder and saying more quietly into his ear. "I need the man who can walk on water."

"Yeah, well it didn't work out so well for the other guy." Dog responds just as softly glancing up into the Major General's face. "Sir."

"I believe the flag game will help you." The Major General replies straightening and it is all he can think of which might at this point be of use. "If the Captain agrees her flight can participate."

"I'll spell it out for them." Dog agrees knowing he will probably enjoy this more than Cat's flight which is something to look forward too.

"Good." The Major General replies then adds before turning and walking away. "I want you coming back."

Dog glances over his shoulder at the Major General's departing back uncertain he heard correctly then finds Cat giving him a questioning look so maybe she heard but the content makes no sense to him. The whole intention and purpose of this mission is he will not be coming back but then maybe the Major General is not on board with the plan or thinks the success of this mission is contingent upon his return since the mission seems to be all the man really cares about.

"Sir, what is this flag game, sir." C.C. prompts seeing the Colonel really does not believe he is coming back and if walking on water is required then he probably is not.

"Fine." Dog mutters pulling his mind from the Major General's parting words. "You hide an article of clothing or what we decide to use as a flag. A wallet maybe?"

"Sir, no, sir." C.C. informs him flatly.

"It must be hidden on a person and can be passed off at any time. I have to find the flag and get it back without being seen." Dog explains looking to see if they all get it.

"How are you going to get it off of us and not be seen?" Sin responds laughing because this is not possible.

"Well if it were easy, they wouldn't need me." Dog replies.

"But this method is used in training, so other people are doing it." Pincher reasons out loud.

"They practice capture the flag and the flag is either an actual flag or a person. Same principle, whoever takes it has to do it without being seen, looks kill." He explains once again since they seem to think it cannot be done.

"When you get the flag, what happens next, sir?" Egor wants to know figuring there has to be more.

"I give it back and you hide it on someone else." Dog responds shrugging because this is all he can do given the situation.

"But what would normally happen if you were not warned off by the Major General, Sir?" Prince persists wanting to know why he was warned off to begin with if looks kill.

"Whoever looses the flag has to get it back in hand to hand combat." Dog replies which is why this is so not going to happen. "If he is not able too then game over and another hunter is selected and so on."

"But you're the only hunter here so it's going to be you hunting every time." Check reasons seeing why the C.O. would not agree to a real flag game being played on base. "So you have to keep giving it back Sir."

"Yep." Dog confirms as he realizes once again being the last man standing is not all it is cracked up to be.

"Sir, you are literally the last one left, aren't you, Sir?" C.C. comments looking at him because he did this flag game with men trained like him.

"I am." Dog replies with a grim laugh glancing down at the front of his dress uniform then to her. "I would show you my unit insignia but they seem to have removed it from my uniform."

"We need something small which will fit in a pocket, easily concealed, and passed without drawing attention." C.C. dictates suddenly because she does not want to dwell on how cold blooded it is for the military to have taken his unit insignia from his uniform, not only to the men gone, but to the one left who now has no visible connection to the men he served with. It is like they have erased him, no past, and apparently no future.

Everyone is going through their pockets pulling out change, looking through wallets, and then Silly tosses a small furry pink thing into the center of the table with a small silver ring around one end. Egor gingerly reaches out to touch it, one can never be too certain what Silly might keep in his pockets, then he grins.

"It's a rabbits foot." He informs them.

"My sister gave it to me for luck." Silly explains grimly. "She hopes I never come back and as long as I have it, and she doesn't, she might get hit by a car."

"You may need some family counseling." Check responds.

"I have six sisters, no one is going to miss one." Silly assures him just as seriously.

"I like the way he thinks." Dog mutters with a smile but looking at the pink thing on the table his smile fades as he looks to Cat. "Are you really going to make me spend part of a war looking for a pink rabbits foot?"

"Sir, it's the perfect size, sir." C.C. informs him because, yes, it does look like he is going to be looking for it. "And Silly doesn't seem to care if it gets lost."

"Just as long as my sister doesn't get it back." Silly adds with a smile.

"Fine then." Dog acknowledges resigning himself to the fact he will be searching this base for a pink rabbits foot and this is so not what he envisioned his last days on this earth being like.

"C.C. hold up a minute." Check calls out before she can turn to her jet for this nights squadron flight. "I want you to let me take this."

"The squadron sure." She replies not having a problem with this.

"No, well, yes. What I mean is with the Colonel and the flag." Check corrects her assumption but he does need the command experience as well.

"This flag thing is not something any of us have trained for." C.C. responds logically so who hides the flag really does not matter.

"I know, and you're probably more qualified to handle something like this." Check admits because she palled around with Navy S.E.A.L.s and probably picked up a few things from them but he thought of something she may not have yet. "You live with him and I sleep with twenty men."

"Good point." C.C. agrees because she will have to close her eyes some time but Check and the guys sleep in the barracks with a total of twenty other airmen.

"Do I still get the squadron?" He asks hopefully.

"Of course." She replies because he needs the experience. "I got your six."

"Thanks Captain." Check responds grinning as he moves on to his jet.

"You're welcome First Lieutenant." C.C. replies softly feeling like a mother whose child has just done something very adult like and Check will do her proud or she will mop the runway with him when they get back.

"You know, this makes it harder." Dog comments in the darkness when Cat returns at O'three hundred after what she calls a squadron run but why they do not just call it a mission, or a patrol, he has no idea.

"Excuse me." C.C. responds because she could not have possibly heard him correctly nor does she want to know his personal business.

"These night patrols cut into ideal searching time." Dog explains and he does not have to wonder what she thought he meant which is interesting.

"I can't do anything about that." C.C. responds and her mind obviously derailed when she thought he meant something else entirely.

"What about the other?" Dog inquires with interest just to see what she will say.

"What other?" C.C. asks wondering why he seems to be talking in riddles all of a sudden.

"What you thought was harder when you began undressing by door?" He asks simply.

"That's your problem and I don't want to know anything about it." C.C. responds gritting her teeth as she moves by memory to her room in the darkness.

"You started it." Dog accuses grimly.

"I didn't start anything." She responds going to her cot laying down hoping he shuts up and goes to sleep.

"I wasn't even thinking about it until you said something." Dog admits and now thanks to her he cannot think of anything else.

"I didn't say anything." C.C. retorts as she stares up at her dark ceiling but he said harder and her mind made a near fatal leap.

"You were thinking it." He grumbles back.

"Great, you can read minds as well as bench press Humvee's, and walk on water." C.C. mutters and the only reason he does not fly is because he fears flying. "So what is your supper hero name?"

"Dog, just Dog." He replies but there were others like him once. "Axle, Brick, Creek, Dog, Elk, and Falcon is what they called us."

"And not a single shred of imagination among you." C.C. responds realizing he must be talking about his unit.

"We thought it was better than subject A,B,C,D,E, and F." Dog responds but thinking back they thought they were clever coming up with their names only she is right they could have done better, or maybe not.

"What happened to them?" C.C. asks wondering if she should and if he will tell her but by the lengthening silence he may not want to answer or went to sleep.

"Brick lost it first followed by Elk then Axle and Creek, Falcon and I were the only ones left until he lost it." Dog replies as he stares up into the darkness able to picture their faces still. "I killed the only family I ever had and my best friend."

"Mission went wrong?" C.C. inquires figuring it is something like that and he feels survivors guilty.

"If only it were that simple." He replies grimly and he could have accepted fate rather than murder. "Killed in action they would have been, buried with honors instead of disposed of like so much unwanted trash, and now I'm the last bag of garbage they need to take out."

"The Major General sounded as if he expects you to come back." C.C. remarks and there is somethings off with what he said or maybe just the way he said it.

"Orders are sometimes interpreted differently." Dog responds with a sigh and the Major General may not understand or have been told the true purpose of this mission. "Sweet dreams Cool Cat."

"Back at you." She replies but for some reason she doubts

he has pleasant dreams and the evidence of this is written all over him in scars.

Dog spends his morning watching the cool Cat's flight without them being aware he is even nearby though he knows they are keeping an eye out for him and the one carrying the flag is super twitchy but he will leave retrieving it for later. He needs to speak with the cool Cat so he shadows her from the gym back to the housing block sliding in behind her into their quarters before the door closes completely from her backwards heel tap and while he is silently congratulating himself for a perfect execution of his old skills he clears his throat to get her attention.

Suddenly he is flying ass over end through the air landing ingloriously with a splintering crash on his cot where he lays sprawled looking up at her from the floor. Her eyes are wide and she has a hand over her mouth as if he is not the only one surprised.

"What was that?" Dog demands as he picks himself up off of his ruined bed and rolls the impact out of his shoulders.

"Sorry." C.C. offers removing her hand from her mouth stunned by her own actions enough to admit. "Flash back, second marriage."

"Really." Dog replies with interest and now understanding why people compare their marriages to battle fields so it must have been bad enough to have flash backs.

"He use to sneak up behind me and." C.C. begins but realizes he does not need to know about her personal life. "Just forget about it."

"I would like to hear what comes after the 'and'." Dog admits truthfully. "And you obviously haven't forgotten."

"Just don't sneak up on me." She suggests but she seriously over reacted which rattles her and has never happened before.

"So noted." He responds since she apparently does not want to fill in the blank only he has a good idea of what happened but this is not what they should be discussing. "I need you to do something for me."

"What?" C.C. asks not feeling all that sorry or generous despite being the one at fault.

"I need you to get me off base." He requests point blank and to her credit she does not even blink.

"No." She replies with a smile finding that answer simple enough.

"There are things I need the military is not going to supply me with." He explains and the truth about his mission is one of them. "I promise to be back in two days."

"Oh, you promise." C.C. responds sarcastically knowing he is not suppose to leave this base or he could requisition a vehicle and go without her help.

"No one will even notice I'm gone." Dog responds and it is not as if he has to be any where or do anything at any given time so who would notice his absence except her. "The M.P.s know I'm leaving and if the Major or Major General comes snooping around they'll help you cover my absence."

"No." C.C. responds again but after a moments thought. "Why don't you have the M.P.s take you off base?"

"They're as much a prisoner here as I am." Dog replies because they are suppose to be watching him on base. "They can't leave base and I was going to come up with a legitimate reason for you to go to town but I think you just did it for me."

"So I requisition another." She responds looking down at the broken cot he is pointing at.

"But you can save yourself the paper work and waiting for the paper work to be processed. Just take this one into town to be repaired." Dog explains reasonably.

"You're going to have to do much better then that. Tell me why you need to leave base?" She asks as she folds her arms not budging on this.

"I told you, I need information no one here wants to give me." He responds honestly but then the military is not big on collecting gossip or in this case passing it along to him.

"No, you say a lot but you don't actually tell me anything." C.C. accuses and much of what she does know she has gleaned on her own from bits and pieces which makes absolutely no sense.

"You're bright enough I don't have to spell it out for you." He replies and she has figured out a good deal but she just does not want to, nor will, believe it.

"You're going to have to throw me a bone Dog." She warns him and she is not about to take a blind leap of faith on a man she knows nothing about when she thought she knew four other men in her life only to find she was wrong.

"So what do you want?" Dog asks her but he knows she is

not going to be happy with anything he can tell her.

"Tell me about the mission when your unit was killed?" C.C. inquires point blank and the quickest way to learn about someone is by looking at their mistakes. He obviously carries the guilt for his units deaths and this says a lot about him no mater if it was actually his fault or not.

"There was no mission." Dog informs her again and if only it had been that simple and that quick. "I killed them."

"Why?" C.C. asks because there must have been a reason and he was not imprisoned for murder which would have made far more sense. "I killed them tells me nothing."

"Does it really matter?" He asks given what he did was horrific enough without details. "I killed them, it's that simple."

"No, it's not." C.C. maintains knowing enough about him to know nothing about him is that simple. "You didn't wake up one morning and just decide to kill them all without a very good reason."

"The reason is classified." Dog responds and he is brushing as close to the truth as he dares not wanting to have to kill any more people he loves or cares for again. "I can't tell you."

"Classified." C.C. repeats finding this convenient but she was told most of his file is Black Ops so this is believable if not helpful. "I know you didn't just kill them and my guess is you were following orders for some reason but you saw no alternative except to follow them. The fictitious charges were to keep you silent about those orders and probably a good deal of other things. You're right, eventually I will figure out just what is up with you."

"Which is exactly why I have to be very careful what I say around you." Dog responds seriously. "I don't want anyone coming to take you out like so much garbage and I've only told you things which can be found if you look hard enough. The government can only cover up so much garbage before something begins to stink and draws attention. This is when they step back and say let it stink because no one will connect all the stink to one thing."

"But you can." C.C. replies confidently and this definitely explains why they put him in prison for AWOL.

"Yeah." Dog verifies but it is not even the icing on the cake. "I'm the only one left who can follow all the sink right back to the source which makes me a problem."

Chapter 7
Somewhere in Saudi Arabia...

"Then tell me why you joined the Army?" C.C. inquires realizing she is not going to get him to tell her more so she will go to the beginning hoping to find out more about his motives which should not be classified.

"Ironically, to keep from starving to death." Dog informs her and he never really thought about his reasons nor can he remember anyone asking. "My father was an alcoholic, and my mother ran off. He could hold a job and the money we had he drank. I hunted rabbits, snakes and lizards for dinner when I was young. Found work when I got older and the pay was next to nothing. When I looked old enough to enlisted I ended up eating frogs and snakes in Vietnam most of the time I was there."

"You have serious food issues." C.C. responds and she quickly does the math in her head. "So you're roughly forty two."

"I honestly don't know." Dog confides because this is one piece of information he could give her if he only knew. "Does my age really matter?"

"No, I was hoping it would give me another bone but if you don't know then it really isn't useful." C.C. explains grimly and so much for gaining some insight into this man.

"Not bad." He compliments and she is correct in this giving her something to base a personal insight on. "I can only tell you I have not set foot in the United States in something like thirty six years and I really would like to go home but preferably not in a box."

"Ten years In prison." C.C. reminds him so he must have been in the States though it may seem to him like he never went home.

"There are military installations all over the world." Dog mutters and governments sometimes hand over prisoners to other countries if they want them buried deep enough.

"Okay." She remarks not having thought of this but it also

raises another question which might explain why he wants off his base. "So if you leave here you still can't go home and after all this time is it really home to you any more?"

"You know if there is a price to be paid for admission into the United States and the currency was blood and sweat, don't you think I've paid it three times over?" Dog asks and simply holds out his arms toward her hands palms down then slowly turning them over for her to see all his scars which are obvious for all to see. "I've done everything my country has asked of me, I have given everything I have mind, body, and soul for my country, and I would like to be allowed to see after thirty six years just what I've been protecting without question. Am I really asking for too much?"

"I'll sign out a jeep." C.C. manages to say past the lump that has formed in her throat but it is not the evidence of the scars which changed her mind but the look in his eyes. Lost is the only word she can find to describe what she sees there and she knows that feeling. He has done everything he was suppose to do yet nothing was as it seemed or went as it was suppose to and she has done the same thing four times only for her there is nothing left but he is clinging to one dream, going home. How can she say no in the face of that when he is not willing to give up like she has so if she is only waiting to die does where she waits really matter. "Be ready in fifteen minutes."

Turning on her heel she goes out the door not looking back to see if he now has a self satisfied smirk on his face at her capitulation after having shredded her with only a look. She does not want to know how badly she has been taken in this time as she tries not to even think about what she is about to do as she crosses the parade ground to the motor pool. She knows better then to trust men but there is something not right about the Dog in her quarters and maybe the sooner she is rid of him the better.

When she pulls up in the jeep by her building Dog is waiting along with the two M.P.s as they keep watch for anyone passing close by as the cot is loaded in back then Dog is concealed beneath it and as one of the M.P.s closes the tailgate the shorter one gives her a brief nod. She rounds the jeep climbing into the drivers seat wondering if they will toss her in the brig for this instead of on the first plane State side as she pulls the jeep up to the entry gate where two base M.P.s look into the jeep then wave her on through.

Who knew violating regulations and possibly committing

treason could be so easy? She puts several miles between her and the base until it is completely out of sight behind her before stopping the jeep and climbing out to open the tailgate and the Dog climbs out.

"They're more worried about what comes in and not so much what is going out." Dog informs her after a glance finding the anger she keeps locked behind ice is beginning to boil.

"Just tell me where I'm taking you and when I should pick you up." C.C. replies grimly but he is taking his clothing off. "What are you doing?"

"I'm going from here on foot and you don't have to pick me up." He responds as he places his clothing under the cot leaving on only his undershorts.

"So you're going to run around in the desert naked? And how do you plan to get back on base when you just said security is set to keep people out? C.C. asks but it seems obvious to her now he is not planning on coming back and it is one hundred ten in the shade yet he is standing bare foot in sand only wearing his boxers. It did not occur to her before but it is clear now he is insane.

"My body has to get acclimated to the desert again." He responds not going into detail as he shuts the back tailgate and it is all rather complicated and clinical which he does not understand the half of nor important to anyone but him. "If I can't get back on base without being detected I'm probably a dead man as far as the mission goes."

"An infiltration unit." C.C. comments as another piece of the puzzle just hangs out of reach. "Or you're mental."

"I hear that a lot." Dog replies honestly. "But out of my mind or not they keep using me to suit their own ends then I'm suddenly everybody's best friend. Just go into town and have the cot repaired but when you go back don't forget to take my clothing out of the back when you unload the cot."

"I can't go to town." C.C. admits with a sigh and she really was not thinking clearly, nor thought this plan clear through. "I forgot to bring a face cloth."

"A what?" Dog asks then he realizes what he should have thought of too. "Arabia, yeah, the face cover for women. Been a while since I've been here."

"It's against regulations for female personnel to go into town without one." She replies though what is one more broken regulation after all, except this one could get her possibly arrested and/or stoned to death in the street, which ever came first. "I'll wait a while then head back to base and tell them I forgot to bring it. By then it will be too late to go back."

"Right." Dog responds since she has this complication covered. "Of course, that means I'll be sleeping on the floor when I get back."

"My heart bleeds." C.C. mutters dryly but she is fairly certain she is not going to be seeing him again.

Dog gives her a smile before jogging off over the hot sand wishing she would trust him just a little but this would be asking far too much. He keeps to a slow steady jog as the heat of the sun sinks into his skin then under it while also being drawn up his legs from his feet. His skin becomes burning hot so he kicks up his pace to a long loping stride and his skin cools but soon his skin is burning again so this time he hits a full out run as another feeling steels over him, something he has not felt in a very long time, freedom.

It is a rush better than any drug as he breaths the hot open air as his bare feet fly over the hot sand and his hair like a living thing wants its freedom as well so escapes the band holding it in a tail until it flows along behind him like a black banner. He settles into a smooth thirty mile an hour, heart pumping, blood rushing clip, and at this moment he truly feels alive again.

C.C. sits in the hot jeep sipping water thinking she had at least one working brain cell when she grabbed a bottle of water before signing out the jeep and she probably should have offered it to the idiot running around in the desert in his underwear. He is going to wish he had on more clothing when the sun goes down when his skin will be so burnt by the time the temperature drops into the sixties it will feel like the thirties, if he has not already died of heat stroke, dehydration, and/or snake bite.

She should never have agreed to this in the first place and this is yet another perfect example of why she belongs in the military where there are clear set of rules of conduct but Check is a perfect example that nothing is fool proof. She should have said no to him a long time ago but she fell for his dream of rolling fields of corn and she let him talk her into every hair brain money making scheme he came up with because it was not against regulations.

She decides there is obviously something genetically wrong with her which her parents must have seen upon her birth and why at the first opportunity they washed their hands of her. Their strict rules and set expectations for her should have been simple to follow whether she liked or agreed with those restrictions but no matter what she did she was always in trouble. Maybe if they had updated their beliefs to include the modern world she might have stood a chance but manners, marriage and having children was the sum total of their expectations for her future.

Again this did not seem to work as it should have and how billions of people succeed is beyond her while one or both participants have careers as well. Her parents were very explicit after her first marriage failed that they did not want her back and she has not spoken to them in years. Carter is still in their good graces but rarely mentions them. She knows her father had a stroke a couple of years ago but other than knowing he recovered Carter wrote little else about it and she did not ask for any further information.

Their parents stringent religious beliefs ruled out any possibility of any relationship since a divorced woman in their world means whore and she is now one three times over but some of her childhood lessons have stuck so she does not cuss, break the law, though she may have just done so by sneaking Dog off base but she would also never commit suicide. But if she should become a casualty of war then what better place for it to happen than in the middle of a war and she starts the jeep heading back to base hoping she did not just ruin her last and final future plan.

The first thing to seriously annoy C.C. after Dog's departure is her flights repeatedly asking where he is as if she is some how Dog's keeper. She tried calmly explaining infiltration and possibly espionage are the reason they are engaged in this flag game and why not being seen is the whole point so he will not be seen if he is playing the game. This does not seem enough explanation for them, and it is hard to believe since Dog has stood out among them for so long, but the game requires stealth so he is not going to report his itinerary to her in advance.

This approach does not seem to be working and the M.P.s are not helping because when asked they say they just saw him coming or going to some place on base so they keep expecting to see him. She supposes the M.P.s think they are helping but this approach is not going to work for long when out of sight should include from everyone but the noose she feels around her neck really begins to tighten when the Major General returns to base the same evening Dog left base.

She is beginning to feel like a tight rope walker standing on only one foot but when the Major Agitator mentions he has not seen the Colonel around base also inferring she should know where he is like she is some how the Dog's secretary she feels her foot on the rope begin to slip until she is only holding on to her career with one toe.

Two days later after returning to her quarters at O'three hundred then rising at O'five hundred she has to face the fact the Dog is not coming back nor ever intended to. She is waiting for her flight to arrive for calisthenics but at O'five hundred zero five she goes looking for them after receiving a very disapproving frown from the sergeant in charge this day. She has not had to wade through the male barracks in a while as Check has been making sure they are in attendance on time so now entering the male dominated area of the base she passes closed doors but as she draws closer to the door where her flight should be she hears shouting and laughter.

Entering she finds most of the double stacked bunks are empty and a group of men are gathered around three sets on the far side of the room. At first she suspects a fight has broken out but as men begin to notice her they stand aside or suddenly find somewhere else to be leaving her with a clear view of her fight tied up in their bed sheets while those who should have been freeing them were taunting them instead.

"I warned you one of these day someone would try to get even." C.C. mutters under her breath as she attempts to untie Check but it must have been more than one person who did this so they have a group of disgruntle losers to deal with. "Who where they?"

"I have know idea." Check replies angrily more embarrassed than he can ever remember being in his life. "I was asleep and so were they." Once he can extricate his arms from the sheets over him he instantly reaches under his pillow as he has done every morning only to find what he is looking for is not there and he is astonished. "It had to be the Colonel."

"No way." Pincher objects needing to use the latrine and wishing C.C. would hurry up. "It had to be a group or flight. They had to have done us all at once or someone would have seen them."

"Unwrap the others." C.C. orders once she frees Check because there is only one way to find out.

"Where are you going?" Check asks as she simply walks away while he needs to use the latrine and he cannot do both.

"To see a Dog about a rabbit's foot." C.C. informs him simply over her shoulder as she keeps walking. "We can't hide it if we don't have it."

As she crosses the parade ground she feels a fleeting moment of relief but if Dog is back he is already causing her problems and his need to show off rather than just taking the rabbit's foot will be all over base. This was not part of the game and needs to stop before retaliation leads to stupidity.

Dog hears Cat enter as he lays on the floor where his cot use to be and he briefly considered taking the cot from the other room but just walking in there makes his head swim. Besides, this is apparently where Cat wants him to be or she would have pulled the other cot out herself and he has slept on a hard floor before. He catches her ankle just before she can kick him in the ribs and it was not going to be a gentle tap either by the way she drew back her foot.

"Oh sorry, I didn't see you there." C.C. offers with a grim smile as she looks down at him. "I almost tripped over you."

"That would be bullshit." Dog replies point blank because she had to go out of her way from the path she normally takes to her room to get to him.

"The rabbit's foot." C.C. demands holding her hand down to him after he releases her ankle.

"Your Lt is lucky I didn't play tooth fairy and put something in return back under his pillow." Dog comments but she simply clicks her fingers at him and he pulls the rabbit's foot from under the blanket he is laying on but holds it just out of her reach. He considered daring her to search him for it but Cat does not appear to be in a friendly mood this morning, or any morning, afternoon, or night. "I'm a little disappointed."

"I hear that a lot." C.C. responds snapping her fingers again as she notices he does not seem to have so much as a sun burn on his face or arms to show for his desert romp. "I excel at disappointing people."

"I find that difficult to believe." Dog replies surprised by her response and confused. "From what I've seen and heard you excel at everything, except hiding a rabbit's foot."

"Give it back." C.C. instructs him calmly finding this discussion tedious. "And curb your over enthusiasm. The deal was this game wouldn't interfere with our required duties. My flight is going to be late for Cals just as I'm late having to come back here to retrieve the foot."

"If we were really playing this game you would have to take it from me." Dog offers wondering if she will take the bait.

"We're not playing by those rules, remember." C.C. reminds him but she would very much enjoy kicking the stuffings out of him.

"I remember." Dog responds wondering just how much longer before she takes a swing at him. "We're playing by our own rules which is going to make this so much more interesting."

She has the impression he is not referring to the same rules she is when he suddenly rolls into her legs over balancing her forward and she cannot regain her balance before pitching forward right on top of him. She rolls quickly off of him only he rolls on top of her before she can roll to her side and regain her feet.

Anger comes to her hot and quick at being so easily out maneuvered but her attempts to dislodge him are met with no success as he has effectively pinned her arms and legs. This is when a sick hollow feeling of helplessness hits her and it is a feeling she has sworn never to feel again as her heart begins to pound to fast and she swallows hard the metallic taste of all consuming fear in her mouth.

"Cat?" Dog mutters as his triumph turns to shock by what he is interpreting from her and this is not a woman who should know what fear is. "I would never hurt you Cat."

"Get off me." C.C. manages to growl as she tries to set this feeling aside knowing it is irrational and just a gut reaction left over from her second husband.

"I will." Dog assures her but that momentary look of fear concerns him and physically twists his guts. "I miss calculated and didn't consider the fact fear is partly what drives you. Why else would you be hiding in the Air Force?"

"I'm not hiding." C.C. responds having run through every technique she knows to free herself and he has effectively nullified all her options simply by using his shear weight. She briefly considers head butting him, which is something she tends to shy away from, but she is certain hitting him would be like slamming her head into a cement block.

"Oh you're hiding, or maybe you don't know what you're

capable of." Dog replies though he is not certain how this would be possible but he intends to reassure her his intentions are not sexual. "I'm just an old Army dog trained and conditioned to come when ever my country calls even knowing I'll most likely get kicked in the teeth but I always come with my tail wagging hoping maybe, just maybe, this time will be different. My hopes and dreams have dwindled to just wanting a warm place to lay my aching bones, a nice blazing fire on a cold night, and maybe someone around who wouldn't mind scratching my belly every once in a while. That's the sum total of my expectations so you've nothing to fear from me."

"Fine." C.C. responds and this is really more information than she wanted to know. "If you get off of me now I won't kick you."

"Oh, you're going to kick me and probably try to kill me but for some reason you've built a cage around yourself which is probably why you like flying it's the only time you're free of the cage. We make a hell of a pair but instead of facing our own personal demons, let's play a game." Dog suggests as he places the rabbits foot in her turned up palm before rolling quickly away from her snapping up to his feet without using his hands but he is not surprised when he finds Cat jackknifing her body and doing the same as they face each other across his make shift bed.

"I believe it's common knowledge Dogs and Cats don't usually play well together." C.C. informs him as she tightens her fist around the rabbit's foot and backs determinedly toward the door not willing as of yet to turn her back on him but mostly uncertain what he means by playing a game other than the flag game.

"But we're playing a game, just not by anyone's rules, not even those of nature." Dog reminds her with a grin. "We can do whatever the hell we want."

"Except murder." C.C. mutters because she is certain the Major General took this out of the game.

"Oh, you're going to want to kill me and you might even try." Dog responds with certainty while still grinning because he is looking forward to it. "You won't be able to help yourself, it's part of who you are and what you fear."

"So you think I'm some kind of vicious killer?" C.C. asks just to be certain she understands him correctly as he seems to have a strange idea of who she is and could not be farther from the truth.

"Vicious to the bone." He agrees and if pushed she will kill he has no doubts about it. "Blood thirsty while on the hunt."

"Right." C.C. replies wondering what he was smoking while he was out wandering near naked in the desert or this might be a sign of heat stroke because he sounds like he is hallucinating only she walks out the door thinking this is his problem not hers.

"We got this." Check assures C.C. when she hands him back the rabbit's foot but of course being C.C. she has some idea of what he should do only he cuts her off first. "Don't worry about it, he's not getting it again."

And just that simply the game is out of her hands but she is not really playing this game anyway nor is she certain she wants too. She was not permitted to play games as a child so why should she begin now but two days later two of her flight are found tied up with their own clothing in a latrine and the whole base is laughing which is when the game takes a turn. She offers to retrieve the rabbit's foot for them but they insist on doing so themselves.

Part of her feels Dog is going to far and intentionally humiliating her flight for no reason other than he can but another part of her thinks he is trying to instill just how important this game is to his mission which her flight is not really taking this game as seriously as they should. The flag game is a training exercise not a real game as it suggests but meant to teach survival skills and so far no one is really learning anything except what humiliation feels like.

Chapter 8
Somewhere in Saudi Arabia...

"You're flight seems to be having issues with their uniforms lately." Major Reese, call sign Grease, comments when C.C. rounds the interior corner of the officers housing and he is hoping for an explanation because for the life of him he cannot think of anything to explain what he is now seeing or has heard about base.

"A training exercise with the Army Colonel on base." C.C. explains simply resigned at finding her flight seated in the hallway in their briefs tied up with their own clothing and she just knew this was not going to turn out well.

"You're letting Army do this to our guys?" Captain Delmar, call sigh Mars, remarks not pleased by this as this is no prank or rivalry with another flight so this makes them all look bad.

"They're doing this to themselves." C.C. comments ignoring the pleading glances from her flight who cannot seem to grasp the concept of what they are involved in and since they are presently gagged with their socks tied about their heads can say nothing in their defense. "We're engaged in a flag game with the Army Colonel and he must retrieve a rabbit's foot from them without being seen."

"Well, that sheds a whole new light on this. We can't have Army doing this to Air Force." Mars responds with disapproval.

"Not good for morale if everyone finds out." Grease agrees and they knew nothing about this before. "It's funny now but later on it won't be."

"Which is exactly what has happened." C.C. confirms agreeing with his opinion and part of her understands why Dog is doing this but she knew her flight would not get the message. "This is a training exercise meant to assist the Colonel to prepare for an important and extremely dangerous mission, not a real game or a lark. Looks kill which means if anyone sees the Colonel he's as good as dead but my flight seems to think all they have to is guard whoever has the flag when the Colonel has proven twice now moving it from man to man is the only way to hide it yet they came in force just retrieve it."

"So you're not part of this then." Grease comments from what she says so gathers she is not participating.

"Since the Colonel is in my quarters I have apparently been disqualified and they think I can some how spy on the Colonel for them." C.C. replies grimly and wonders if they see the error in this thinking.

"That's not how this type of flag game operates." Grease responds looking at the men on the floor wondering if they thought they were playing keep away. "Obviously this Colonel infiltrates enemy installations so he's not going to walk up and take the flag, he has to find it without being seen. Walking through security is probably a cake walk to a guy like this but it's finding what he is looking for while inside unnoticed that requires the kind of stealth this training exercise should give him."

"But is spying on only six men really much of a challenge for this Colonel. From what I've heard, now that I know the reason, this Colonel has found the flag twice in two days." Mars remarks as he considers all the angles. "It has to be moved around from man to man all over the base and no one should be guarding whoever is carrying it or he knows who has it."

"Exactly." C.C. replies pleased she is not the only one who understands how this game is suppose to work.

"If you have more men we could really make this more of a challenge for this Colonel." Grease adds but someone will still have to over see and plan the hand offs as he stares at C.C. "Could you orchestrate this?"

"I learned a few tricks from some S.E.A.L.s but Major General Aimhurst set this up with the C.O.'s approval for this flight to participate. It would be up to the C.O. if more flights can be involved." C.C. informs him honestly. "And given what has happened already he might not be willing to allow this exercise to continue."

"But if you were in charge of it and you kept the flag moving this wouldn't be happening." Grease comments because she clearly understands the concept of the exercise better then her flight.

"I can't guarantee that. If someone gives themselves away the Colonel is going to make an example of them such as we have here." She replies indicating her flight as perfect examples. "If whoever looses the flag takes it personally rather than as a lesson they might do something stupid and go after the Colonel who can probably bench press a Humvee as well as do very inventive things with clothing."

"We'll talk it over with some of the other captains and speak with the CO." Mars responds intrigued by the entire concept. "But I think if you're on point this shouldn't happen again and we'll make it clear something like this could happen only I don't want it said we didn't do our part to help a fellow soldier train for a mission."

"He's right. It's our duty to do what we can." Grease agrees and he likes the idea of having one person responsible for where the flag goes or the Colonel will find it. "You'll be the only one who knows where it is other than the carrier. He's going to have a hard time finding it just by looking for some schedule which probably is also a piece of cake for him."

"No, nothing should be written down or pre-planned." C.C. agrees and she is certain Dog has been into every record kept on this base by now so with a nod both captains leave her to untie her flight.

"Some day I'll learn to listen." Check comments as she is untying shirts after taking off the gags.

"Part of being a leader is knowing when to seek other counsel and when to back off if you don't know what you are doing." C.C. informs him as she tries to get Silly untied only he seems to be enjoying the whole thing and fighting against her rather than helping. "When to charge and when to retreat. Pride can't be part of the equation because it just gets in the way of good judgment."

"Yes, and I realized something else." Check agrees with her somberly. "He could've just as easily killed us."

"He promised not to." C.C. reminds him with a smile or she would have been cleaning up another type of mess.

"No." Check counters as he gathers how to express what he wants to relate, or even just the feeling he had. "The Major General ordered him not to harm us, yes, but I took that as just a joke like, 'don't hurt the little guys', you know. But C.C. he handled us like we were little kids and we couldn't do anything to stop him. It was six of us to one but this gave us no advantage what so ever, he didn't have to even throw a punch, and we were down."

"What's your point Check?" C.C. asks because he is not telling her anything she did not already know.

"He could, and no doubt has, killed men with only one

hand." Check responds simply because it hit him like a ton of bricks when they were all down and despite the scars, the brown/red soulless eyes, he never really saw the Colonel as dangerous until that moment.

"Check." C.C. replies looking him straight in the eyes. "We have killed men we've never even seen. We are at war and there are people on the ground manning those antiaircraft guns and missiles."

"I know that realistically, though it's not something I choose to think about, and like you say we never see them, or know, but the Colonel does. He faces those men, looks into their eyes, and he has killed them." Check explains and he knows he is not explaining this very well but he never really considered this aspect before which was a very unsettling experience. "It just hit home, so to speak, what a man like the Colonel has done and is capable of."

"And like us he is here making sure this war never hits our home." C.C. reminds him and she does not like Check inferring Dog is some kind of killing machine. "The Colonel has fought in one war and engaged in countless battles people will never know anything of to protect his country which he hasn't set foot in for something like thirty years he told me. He's part of the reason we were born in a country where we were able to chose our government, our path in life, and who leads us but now he needs our help.   That's what we're suppose to be doing so he can complete his mission and go home to enjoy all the things we've taken for granted because he fought to protect those things for us. So do you think you can pull your head out of your ass long enough to remember this is not some sort of game and help him reach his objective?"

"Yes Captain." Check agrees and maybe for the first time he realizes he is part of something much bigger than he is. This is not about what he can get out of it before going back home or just passing the time until he can go home. Even the possibility of being shot down here is just a game of chance to him but now he is beginning to see the big picture, and C.C. is cussing so she is seriously pissed.

"Is your head on straight now?" C.C. demands as she finishes untying Silly as the other men have remained eerily silent as they had been dressing themselves as they are freed. "Because the urge to take you over to the gym and beat the living shit out of you is almost more than I can control."

"I'm good." Check replies then risks a grin. "You probably should've done that a long time ago."

"Yeah, I'm beginning to see that now." C.C. informs him earnestly and maybe she does need to get vicious to get through to the bone heads she has to deal with on a daily basis. "Wait here and I'll get the foot back then you're going to do exactly what I tell you."

"Yes Captain." Check answers instantly not daring to do any thing else.

C.C. enters her bailiwick which must have been a war zone a short time earlier only it appears just the same as she last left it and Dog is stretched out on the floor again probably faking sleep. She passes him going into her room to her trunk retrieving something she stole from her second husband. Something she keeps as a reminder or maybe a warning, to never be so stupid over a man again. She needs this reminder now she is certain since none of the men around her are listening to anything she says and causing her more trouble then they are worth so with the small gun in hand she reenters the living area and points it at the Dog.

Dog from his prone position has had his eyes closed but he knows she is staring at him so he opens them to gauge what kind of mood she is in only to find she is holding a small caliber hand gun on him and she does not look as if she is in a very good mood. Being sensible he lifts his hands palms up knowing she would not be pleased with what he did to her flight but he was almost certain she would not attempt to kill him just yet. He knows she means business but he has difficulty containing a smile because the fire always just behind those green eyes is no longer banked but burning bright and likely to burst into full flame all over him. No one would say she is cute right now but she is incredibly beautiful if deadly.

"Give me the rabbit's foot." C.C. orders not falling literally for any more of his tricks this time.

"I think this might be against the rules." Dog informs her just to hear what she has to say because once this woman discovers she can and should be making her own rules she will be a force to be reckoned with as he slowly takes the rabbit's foot from his pocket holding it up in his hand.

"I seriously doubt you know, or have ever played by the

rules." She responds because she is now certain he makes them up as he goes along. "Toss it to me and if you don't toss it too me so I can catch it you're going to have a small hole in you. It won't kill you but it will hurt."

"They attacked me you know." Dog responds just wanting to be clear.

"I know." She replies simply and that is not the reason she is holding a gun on him. "Toss it to me."

He could probably take her before, or after, she shoots him but why bother when he has to give the rabbit's foot to her any way so he tosses it to her. She catches it while never taking her eyes off of him then as he watches from his prone position she moves to the door opening it slightly and calling to the First Lieutenant holding the rabbit's foot out the door.

"C.C., I...." Check begins.

"Later." C.C. responds cutting him off and shutting the door in his face as she lowers the gun. "From now on we'll be doing this my way."

Dog watches as she disappears into her room then jackknifes silently to his feet entering the room to find her bending over a trunk. Grabbing her around the waist with one arm he grabs her hand holding the gun with the other before she can return it to the trunk where she must have taken it from. She lands an elbow into his side as he keeps her bent forward or his shins will take a beating and she is actually growling which causes him to smile.

"Let me go." She snarls and this is exactly what she hoped to avoid, being close to him, but her elbow gained her nothing and once again she is at his mercy.

"Ouch. Your bony little elbows should be listed as lethal weapons." Dog comments as he pulls her captured wrist closer so he can see the gun because something about it is not right but he has to avoid a back kick aimed for a very sensitive place. "Stop it. I just want to see what this is because it's not a gun."

"Fooled you though." C.C. reminds him because now he has turned slightly so she cannot kick him in the privates so she presses the trigger of the gun and blue flame comes out the end. "Satisfied?"

"That's not regulation and you don't smoke." Dog replies even more curious now as to why she went to the trouble, and the paperwork, to bring something like this on base with her.

"It's a reminder." She responds then realizes she may have said too much as she lets go of the trigger and the flame goes out. "A keep sake, that's all."

"A keep sake for what?" Dog asks finding this even stranger. "No it's a reminder like you said at first but of something bad. You were really mad when you walked in and grabbed this to hold on me so a bad memory and this had to be part of it."

"Have you ever heard of the term 'personal business'?" C.C. asks and she has no intention of telling him anything.

"It just means you don't want to tell me." He replies simply but the problem is he really wants to know and curiosity is not something he indulges in often given his line of work. Once someone starts asking questions they tend not to know when to stop then draw attention to themselves which can be deadly but he really wants to know and part of him feels it is important that he knows. "Just tell me, you know I won't be around long enough to tell anyone so what does it matter."

"You're like a Dog with a bone." C.C. mutters not at all pleased by this turn of events when she wanted distance so she used the gun.

"Precisely." Dog agrees proving his chosen nickname was also fortuitous and not just lack of imagination. "I've been told I'm rather single minded sometimes. Deacon or Deck wouldn't have suited me as well."

"I'm leaning toward Dickhead myself." She remarks finding this an odd time and position to be having a conversation since he has yet to release her but one thing for certain is he talks too much.

"I'll be eternally grateful you weren't there at the time." He responds seriously as she tries to pull away but he is not willing to give up this slight advantage. "Just tell me about the lighter and I'll let you go."

"It's no big deal." C.C. responds but she is really not in a position she wants to wait him out as her back is pressed to his front and it is becoming more difficult to ignore the bulge now poking her in the back so she rattles off quickly. "My second husband kept this lighter and a small caliber hand gun on the bedside table to play his version of Russian roulette when we were in bed together when he wasn't using this one to light his cigarettes. Happy now, let go of me."

"Not until you tell me what you did to him in payback?" Dog replies visualizing what a woman like this would, and could, do to a man after a stunt like that. "I'm going to need details."

"I never did anything to him." C.C. hisses angrily because how can number two's actions be blamed on her.

"No, I mean after." Dog begins thinking she misunderstood the question but she said never which cannot be right. Before she can reply he knocks the lighter from her hand then spins her around backing her quickly into the wall while avoiding a knee meant to make him sing soprano for life. He expected her to make some kind of attempt as this is not a woman to be manhandled without serious repercussions but she allowed a former husband to mentally abuse her which makes no sense what so ever. "Why didn't you stop him?"

"I didn't exactly know what he planned to do." C.C. replies honestly then she sort of hoped number two in his condition would grab the real gun by mistake ending her nightmare of a marriage permanently.

"You could've feed him the lighter or better yet popped him in the balls with the gun." Dog responds seriously and he knows she is capable of it. "Why didn't you?"

"Because I loved him." C.C. replies not certain what else to offer as a reason for not committing murder.

"Bullshit." Dog growls angrily and what she is telling him is she allowed her husband to abuse her but he knows not for some sappy reason like love. "I'm not buying it and no court would've convicted you for what would have been self defense no matter if he held the real gun on you or the fake. Try again."

"I don't know." C.C. responds unable to answer.

"You know." He counters angrily as he stares down at her in disbelief. "What could you have possibly done to think you deserve what amounts to torture?"

"I don't know." C.C. repeats and this subject is not open for discussion but she is starring at his collarbone rather than return his intense gaze noticing he has gained some weight.

"Why?" Dog mutters again only she will not meet his gaze and he rests his forehead on top of her head but even this proximity does not clear up this gray area he cannot comprehend. "There is nothing you could've possibly done which would require enduring torture as some kind of self punishment. You should've handed him his ass like I know you're capable of and I fully expect you to hand me mine if I ever go so far as to hurt you. I expect, and know, you'll make me pay in triplicate."

"You don't know anything and I'm fairly certain you're insane." C.C. informs him pulling her head back and he quickly raises his head out of range as if he is expecting some form of retaliation but again she is certain head butting him would be like hitting a brick wall.

"Sort of a prerequisite for the job." Dog admits but there is insane and completely nuts which is where his problems with the military begins and ends. "I'm also in something else but if I told what you would probably slaughter me in my sleep. I have a mission to prepare for so we will have to fight about this later."

"What later? I thought this was a one way mission." C.C. counters and she is wondering yet again just how much is fact and how much is fiction but one thing is certain she has no intention of fighting with a dead man.

"I have to find my own way in but if there is more than one way then I might be able to find a way out as well." Dog informs her so this makes anything possible but he had been thinking along the lines of this being his last mission only he has found the motivation he needs to buck the status quo.

He just wishes he did not have this feeling he is missing something really important here, something he should be seeing when he looks into her eyes only it is just out of reach but if possible he will have plenty of time later to figure it out. He promised to release her but retaliation will be at the top of her list so he spins away from her going out the door only when he stops he hears nothing nor does she follow. He now knows without a doubt there is something seriously wrong here because this Cat is far from tamed and he is still standing.

"I'm afraid my mission was not successful, Colonel." Major General Aimhurst begins earnestly while seated across from the Colonel in what the enlisted men here refer to as the Juice bar.

"Not your fault." Dog replies simply, because it is not, and the Major General is not calling the shots here.

"This mission is important." Aimhurst responds which is partly why he pushed to get the Colonel for this mission and hoped to buy him more time. "We need this done and it could very well end this war before we have more American's fighting on the ground."

"I'll accomplish the mission." Dog assures him which is all he can be certain of at this point.

"Yes, I have no doubt you will, but you would be more effective in top shape." Aimhurst responds grimly.

"Then there would be more of a chance of my coming back." Dog replies with a grin because they both know the other side of this coin.

"You are coming back." Aimhurst responds emphatically. "I have three units moving into place as we speak who are only there to bring you out."

"How did that get approved?" Dog inquires surprised since he figured he would have to fight his way out then walk or swim from there.

"Surveillance." Aimhurst replies simply.

"You're not getting behind the real spirit of this mission." Dog informs him finding this rather amusing and not very smart in terms of long term career moves on his part. "You know the score."

"I hate waste." Aimhurst remarks deciding this maybe the time to lay out his cards. "Tossing a soldier into a hornet's nest after spending millions of dollars creating said soldier is a gross misuse of a proven tool which should be used more carefully and retrieved to use again as needed. I also have a personal gripe with how the Steel Man project was handled not only on an ethical level but on principal as well."

"And what would you know of my unit?" Dog asks and they are entering dangerous waters here.

"I suspect I know more than you. Soldiers died before, during and after being attached to that project who deserve recognition for their actions of bravery and personal sacrifice but instead they were all swept under the rug." Aimhurst mutters quietly as he glances about them but no one in the crowded bar is paying them any attention.

"You might want to pretend you never heard of Steel Man." Dog suggests because right now he is the only loose end needing snipped.

"Did you know they only chose men with no family on record? But the military made an error as Major Alexander was quick to point out and one of those men had a brother." Aimhurst informs him and he did not go into this assignment blind.

Chapter 9
Somewhere in Saudi Arabia...

"Falcon." Dog responds simply because there is very little in a fighting unit as close as the six men of the Steel Man were that they did not know about each other. The two brothers were orphaned at a young age but Falcon full of youthful rage and resentment directed at everyone was sent to a disciplinary home while his brother was adopted.

"My brother and all of Steel Man, as I said, deserve recognition for the sacrifices they made on behalf of our country." Aimhurst repeats and yes this is very personal to him. "You deserve better than being treated like a criminal."

"I don't think you know how Falcon died." Dog responds which might change his opinion and murder is still a crime.

"The project he volunteered for killed him, not you." Aimhurst insists because he also knows the moment his brother was assigned to project Steel Man he was a walking dead man. "You're the lone survivor of a project forged in hell and a violation of every law dealing with genetic manipulation we had then and still have today. Then you were imprisoned by what can only be called a travesty of due process even by military standards and they couldn't even come up with a descent excuse for your incarceration, and to make matters worse, I just recently discovered you have been treated worse than the Geneva convention allows us to treat enemy prisoners. Honestly Colonel, there is nothing about this damned situation that does not piss me off."

"Okay." Dog replies fighting the urge to say to the man, now tell me how you really feel, but there is something else the Major General should know. "They're not going to honor their end of this bargain you know. If I come back, I'll probably be sent back to my little cell to count the little dimple things on the concrete block walls for the rest of my life, however long this will be, given their past record of feeding me bread and water."

"Not if I can help it." Aimhurst responds and he thinks he has figured out a way to end this travesty once and for all. "In pulled you out for this mission because it's important but it also gives me an opportunity to prove you'll not go out like the rest of your unit but in order to do this you'll have to play their game for a little while longer and when you return having proven once again you're an asset rather than a liability I'll have another mission ready. A mission they'll be so set on needing you for they'll have to grant you an honorable discharge or look like fools. My intention is to get you home because you've earned that right."

"While I appreciate your efforts, and don't take this personally, but I don't think you can do it. I'm living proof of every violation you just mentioned and they don't want me walking around." Dog reminds him simply.

"Just by allowing you on this base they've proven they know you won't talk." Aimhurst responds.

"I don't think my talking is their main concern." Dog assures him because there are things which are just not normal about him. "They don't want me to be looked at by a regular doctor and they most definitely don't want me going out like the rest of my unit did, especially on American soil."

"I have a doctor on stand by and I'll have proof their fears are unfounded." Aimhurst replies because he saw the files and he knows what to look for. "Fact is Colonel you've proven what they believe is false just by still being alive but if they need reassurance then I'll provide it for them."

"You can't prove anything." Dog responds and neither can he.

"I know what to look for." Aimhurst replies but most of what he needs hinges on this mission. "All I need is for you to trust me on this and come back preferably in one piece."

"I'll take it under advisement." Dog responds but the man is going to dig up years of lies and in his experience this will not make anyone happy no matter what the Major General thinks he found.

"I just need a little more time." Aimhurst admits and there are a few gray areas yet to be worked out but he is positive this will work. "I've had a long time to think about this and what I could've done, and should've done for my brother but I wasn't given the chance. I couldn't save him but I can save his brother in arms who showed him compassion and gave him peace at last."

She is procrastinating C.C. knows this and cannot put off going to the mess hall any longer because like everything else in the military there is a time to eat, miss it and do not eat, or the alternative is buying a bag of something from the commissary. She is seated on her cot not wanting to face Dog after divulging some very personal information which was humiliating enough the first time let alone talking about it now and she does not want to face him, sit next to him, or talk to him.

Dog is smart enough to fill in the details and apparently curious enough to ask for more but he is not her counselor or even a close friend. She does not need some one telling her how she should or should not feel and husband number two caught her for speeding right after she proceeded with a course of action she was already regretting.

After her first marriage failed and her parents told her they no longer wanted anything to do with her she decided she would probably fail at motherhood as well so she opted out which is perfectly legal only she was completely unprepared for the ramifications. She was still feeling like a failure then she went on to prove she is deficient of any moral or ethical considerations which made her feel less than human because what kind of woman would kill her own child.

It is a question she has asked herself repeatedly ever since so in an effort to prove she is a normal human she married number two intending to correct her deficiencies and be a wife then eventually a mother. She failed again on both counts and now the option of children is completely off the table because she ruined her one and only chance which was probably for the best but that one decision is like a splinter festering just under her skin. It is a regret she has been trying to live with only she cannot figure out how.

Joining the military has done much to restore her confidence, if she ever had any, and proven she is capable of being something other than a wife but unfortunately the military is not a magic eraser so she is still a widow, a three time divorcee, and most likely a coward as life just keeps running over her but standing up and fighting back seems to be beyond her. Now the military even wants her out but the military has been the one place she has been able to stand up and fight back so she rises from her cot determined not to let Dog drive her into hiding. This is her base after all and he is the interloper here so going to the door she finds someone has slipped a note under it then while reading it she smiles.

When she reaches the mess hall since Dog is already seated and eating with her flight she is forced to stand at attention until he invites her to sit down which he does with a omnipotent wave of his hand. This irritates her but it is her own fault for procrastinating and luckily he seems lost in thought so says nothing then he is asked by one of the M.P.s to have a private word leaving the table.

She eyes the remaining food on his tray for a moment and knows what she is thinking is childish, and petty, but she cannot seem to resist and he practically told her pay him back so taking the salt shaker she applies it liberally to everything left on his tray while her flight at first wide eyed with shock wisely turn their heads looking else where making no comment. Suddenly she feels much better as if a weight has been lifted from her chest and she can breath easier as Dog returns then begins to eat only he pauses after the first fork full looking resigned as he swallows.

"That's mean even for you." Dog informs her but she is looking at him as if she has no idea what he is talking about and she might fool everyone else only he knows this calm cool woman seated next to him has the heart of a tiger with the claws to match whenever she decides to stop playing kitten to use them. "You can shoot me, stab me, or beat me with a baseball bat while I sleep, or even awake, but don't mess with my food."

"Sir, in the Commissioned officers dinning room they have waiters Sir." C.C. replies simply and maybe now he will go there.

Dog watches as she continues to eat and considers stealing her tray but then decides to fight fire with fire so he turns to the First lieutenant and orders him to get him a new tray. When he looks back at Cat she is looking at him through narrowed green yes but he smiles.

"I know you'll make me pay for that too." Dog comments without concern. "But you better be quick about it because I leave in three days."

"Sir, good to know, sir." C.C. replies but she will not be waving him off and she does have glad tidings from the note she found under her door. "Sir, I have news as well, there will now be six flights involved in the flag game instead of one, sir."

"Which flights?" He asks instantly.

"Sir, that would be cheating, sir." C.C. responds with a smile and let him go through them all looking for the rabbit's foot because there are only about a thousand men and women on this base and over half are in flights. "Sir, you only have three days to find it, sir."

Dog watches as she manages to eat with a smug smile on her face as he looks to her men who are suddenly very interested in what is on their trays while knowing he did provoke her knowing all the while she would find a way to make him pay so he is not going to complain. Of course if he were the complaining type there is no one here to complain to as they would side with the Cat regardless but he is relieved to see she is no longer sulking in her room, and apparently he is going to have a very busy three days while trying to decide if he can trust Major General Aimhurst.

"C.C. is there a problem between you and the Colonel we should know about?" Check asks at they walk out on to the airfield.

"No problem." C.C. replies confidently. "He and I just had a meeting of the minds over something. No problem at all."

"So who has the rabbits foot?" Check asks curiously.

"That's for me to know and the Colonel to figure out." She responds. "You'll know when it's your turn, don't worry.

"Okay." Check agrees but something is off here and he is not certain exactly what it is because C.C. does not normally resort to what she calls childish pranks and if one of them had salted the Colonel's tray she would have voiced her displeasure. She has verbally put him in his place twice now, and rightly so, but normally she does this in a more delicate way, for lack of a better word, and now it is like she has taken off the gloves and anyone who crosses her is going to get bare knuckles. She is normally so cool and controlled but he is beginning to see some signs of recklessness and he is not certain if this is a good thing or bad.

During calisthenics the following day Captain Veronese, or call sign Ron, asks to have a word with her in private so she steps aside for her flight to continue without her as the other Captain proceeds to inform her in no uncertain terms he does not feel she is qualified to handle the flag training game with the Colonel demanding she give him the flag so he can handle it. Normally she would insist they take this matter to the CO for him to decide and this is not the first time her qualifications have come into question by a long shot only the words refuse to form and her throat seems to close.

Something comes over her and her hands close into fists at her sides as her entire body seems to have frozen solid in objection. She is not even listening as he rattles on as she seems to be focused on his sharp chin knowing with one solid punch she could shut him up as she attempts to breath and regain control. She blames the fact Dog is never sleeping on the floor when she returns from her squadron runs so she can kick him black and blue and thus being repeatedly denied this pleasure she would like to take a shot at anyone but just as she feels herself regain control and intends to inform Ron they should take this matter to the C.O. his rattling nonsense sinks in.

His over inflated ego, macho assumptions, and basic bull sets her off again so she flatly tells Ron in a calm controlled voice exactly where he can go with his suggestion, which is not the CO's office, and shocks those who unintentionally over hear just passing by who stop so suddenly they run in to each other. Ron responds by inferring if she were not a woman they could settle this in the boxing ring which C.C. responds without a second thought asking at what time.

With a derogatory parting comment pertaining the her finger nails the time is set and she watches him swagger away while wondering just what the hell is wrong with her and the only answer she can come up with is Dog. She has been immune to the slights from the men around her and even some of the women but this time she could not simply take it and to her this is a weakness having given into this urge to pound Ron but the dye is cast so she is not going to back out now. Truth be told she is looking forward to it and she knows there is something fundamentally wrong with that.

An airbase is like a small town so not everyone knows everyone but they have acquaintances or they have made friends who have acquaintances and so on. Word has spread fairly quickly and she did not tell her flight but of course they heard about it and intercept her before she is half way across the base back to the gym where the boxing ring is located.

"You don't box." Check informs her looking concerned as he strides next to her with the others falling in behind.

"Neither does Ron." C.C. counters because technically what he does is not boxing but a combination of martial arts, boxing, and wrestling.

"She's right full contact fighting is not actually considered real boxing." Egor agrees as they keep stride with her.

"So I don't need to know how to box." C.C. remarks wondering if this will reassure Check who is looking even more concerned. "I can kick him all over the ring."

"Since when?" Check asks because she never steps foot in the boxing ring to do so much as spar with them or anyone else to his knowledge.

"Since I was nine." C.C. replies truthfully but it was a secret kept between her and her brother Carter for a very long time.

"You and I are going to have a talk if you're still conscious afterwards." Check demands firmly as they enter the ring area of the gym finding it packed with Airmen and other base personnel.

The roar of talking echos about the large building making a low private conversation impossible but Check intends to pursue this conversation later. He thought he knew almost everything about her but apparently not and as he watches her move through the crowd parting before her he realizes she has only told him the basics. Four failed marriages, overly zealous religious family, and a twin brother but none of the details so what does he really know about her after all?

C.C. pauses slightly when she reaches the ring seeing Chief Master Sergeant 'Mic' McAllister standing in the ring with Ron who is wearing government issued sweat pants, the soft boots used in boxing, head gear, and with boxing gloves on. Ron has the look of a man who could one day be a professional boxer, pudgy faced despite his lean body and five nine in height while his smile exudes confidence along with pride but she knows instantly when Mic sees her standing at the edge of the ring and there maybe a problem she failed to remember at the time when she let her anger carry her along.

Mic is in charge of the gym acting as referee for bouts between airmen in the ring so he almost literally owns the boxing ring and everyone has to go through him to use it. He is also the reason she does not spar with anyone because he will not allow her in his ring, not on his watch, as he put it to her when she once considered sparing after she first came to the base.

She climbs through the ropes into the ring hearing no objections as she begins taking off her combat boots leaving her sweat pants and tee shirt on but she does not wear boxing shoes preferring bare feet. One of the Chief Master Sergeant's men assists her in putting on the boxing gloves because it is difficult if not impossible to do by herself and the noise level from all the people crowded around to watch has become a dull roar as excitement and expectation seems to bounce off the block walls but Mic motions to ring the bell to get everyone to quiet down.

"Listen up." Mic announces loudly getting everyone's attention looking toward the grinning confident Captain Ron who has yet to be beaten in the ring and then to Captain C.C. who is standing demurely to one side like sugar would not melt in her mouth and he shakes his buzzed cut head because this is the problem with this woman, she looks so sweet no one suspects she is capable of driving a piece of straw clean through a man. "I'm telling you both right now I'm dead set against this match but the C.O. insists everyone here needs a diversion but I consider this sheer stupidity."

"Come on Mic, she agreed to meet me in the ring." Captain Ron replies smiling congenially as there is whooping from the watchers as Ron raises his gloved hands getting cheers.

"Did she also mention she is a sixth degree black belt and she might inadvertently kill you?" Mic inquires grimly once the noise settles again as he looks at Captain Ron whose smile falters as the crowd mummers. "Which is exactly the reason I don't allow her in my ring."

"No, she didn't mention that." Ron admits grimly looking at C.C. skeptically wondering how this information did not come to light sooner.

"Would you have believed me if I had told you?" C.C. asks grimly and she should have considered she would not get this past Mic and only the C.O.'s approval has gotten her as far as into the ring with Ron. This is not much better than going to the C.O. in the first place for dispensation because this settles nothing and she did not get to hit anyone.

"Maybe." Captain Ron admits grudgingly but if the Chief Master Sergeant says she is then it is so but the question he is asking himself now is does he fight her and make a fool of himself not to mention risk life and limb over a dispute rather than in the defense of his country or should he bow out now. "Do you want me to forfeit?"

"Call it a draw." C.C. replies and her intention was not to humiliate him but for some reason she really wants to beat on someone so his arrogant male attitude at the time made him the perfect candidate. "I'll go back to the punching bag."

"How about using me instead?" Dog asks over the airmen and base personnel voicing their disappointment around him.

"What degree of black belt?" Mic asks looking skeptical as the crowd quiets at this turn of events to listen and he knows most military men do not bother with belts and degrees. They get hand to hand in basic training then pick up the rest as they go along unless they have hobbies like Captain Ron who finds full contact boxing to be an outlet for his excess energy.

"Tenth." Dog informs the big Chief Master Sergeant while watching Cat's face and her eyes narrow into a near scowl but he glances back at the Chief who seems to be calling the shots here and looks like the kind of man who once boxed himself.

"Of course, he's a freaking Ninja." C.C. mutters realizing she should have guessed by how easily he managed to subdue her. He was countering every close up move she made before she had the chance to make them.

"C.C?" Mic looks to C.C. questioningly. "Normally I don't allow more than one belt difference in my ring and I'm only going to allow the two of you to spar. No submission and if I call a halt you two break it off or I'm calling in the M.P.s to haul you to the brig. I'm not messing around with either of you."

"Fine." C.C. agrees as Mic looks to Dog who nods but at least she is going to be allowed to thump on someone and it being Dog only makes this more appealing.

"No problem." Dog agrees as everyone around the ring cheers and they may not be getting what they were hoping to see but will settle for this as he takes off his boots stepping into the ring barefoot in combat pants and tee shirt.

Men at ring side put gloves on him then the Chief Master Sergeant is patting them both down for anything which might cause injury.

"I'm calling a halt to this after twenty minutes." Mic informs them as they stand face to face in the center of the ring. "Just a nice easy work out, nice easy taps."

"No worry Mic." C.C. replies as she looks up at Dog who towers over her.

"I see this guy working out in here." Mic replies pointing to the Colonel. "You miss a block at his full out and you're going to be broken."

"I know." She replies only she is not worried he will land anything but if he should miss a block she is going to make sure he feels it for a good long time.

"Engage." Mic commands backing off with a chop of his hand down between them as they circle one another.

C.C. does a round kick which he easily blocks then she throws some punches which he blocks as they circle each other. She tries a quick combination and he blocks but all without so much as trying to touch her which is aggravating and insulting.

"Only my grandmother is afraid to hit me." C.C. informs him and he smiles as he does a kick of his own which she blocks easily but at least she no longer feels like she is shadow boxing with herself.

They trade kicks and punches as both manage to block so she turns up the heat moving faster and he complies by doing the same. When C.C. drops down to the mat trying for a leg sweep to her surprise he avoids it by leaping up and doing a back flip. C.C. jackknifes back to her feet and they both stand posed facing each other in the classic Jujitsu stance as Mic calls a halt as the men and women watching begin to boo and hiss the interruption.

"Are the two of you fucking serious?" Mic snarls. "Is that Jujitsu I'm seeing in my ring?"

"Looks like it from here." C.C. replies with a grin.

"Yeah looks that way from here too." Dog adds with a straight face.

"Oh you two are a riot." Mic snaps not amused. "Just keep it careful. Engage."

Punching, kicking, and leaping they work their way all over the mat. When the bell rings at Mic's signal there are cheers from the watchers along with disappointed groans. Mic stands between them raising both their gloved hands calling the bout over.

"I almost hated putting a stop to that." Mic admits with a smile which quickly disappears. "I don't ever want either of you in my ring again. Is that clear?"

"You're such a kill joy." C.C. informs him feeling more relaxed than she has in a long time.

"Kill is what I'm hoping to avoid." Mic reminds her grimly. "You two are far too dangerous to be playing with anyone, even each other, as far as I'm concerned."

Chapter 10
Somewhere in Saudi Arabia...

"C.C. that was great." Check declares as C.C. steps down out of the ring but then looking over her head he sees the Colonel standing on the ring apron looming over them. "Sir, we're headed to the Juice bar. Care to join us, sir?"

"Can't." Dog replies looking at Cat grimly. "I have a rabbit's foot to find."

"Yeah, good luck with that." C.C. offers feeling generous because he is going to have a few bruises by morning since blocking still requires contact of flesh and some times it can feel like bone. She is going to have a few too because no matter how careful Mic insisted they be there is no way to avoid it

"Enjoy the show?" Dog asks when he sees Major General Aimhurst by the door as Air force personnel slowly leave the building and his two M.P. guards are standing off to one side mouths still gaping.

"Actually I was just picturing what that fight would have been like if Major Alexander had the guts to step into the ring with her." He admits because the Captain is a very impressive woman. "They would be scooping up what was left of him off the mats with a shovel."

"Not a member of the Major's fan club." Dog mutters keeping his voice down as a large group passes them going out.

"No." Aimhurst replies sincerely. "Hard to respect a man like him. He's under orders but there are ways of carrying out those orders without attempting to belittle the woman's record or inferring she is far less than what she is."

"And that would be?" Dog asks out of curiosity wondering what the Major General sees.

"A highly qualified combat pilot who is unfortunately female." Aimhurst responds easily. "It's a shame too. I would give the Navy a fight for her except when the Major is finished she won't be able to remain in the military and why would she if every war despite her qualifications she knows she'll be sidelined. She's a fighter, needs to be in the thick of it, not trainer material or she would've taken the job the Navy offered. You could see by her smile she enjoyed kicking you around."

"Oh yeah." Dog agrees because he noticed the smile too. "The problem is she doesn't see herself that way. She doesn't see or accept what you and I see."

"Interesting." Aimhurst admits thoughtfully trusting the Colonel living with her to know more about her. "If that's the case then what the hell is she doing here?"

"Just a little glitch, but I'm working on it." Dog informs him as he moves on toward the door leading out of the building but the question of why Cat is really here has been gnawing at him for a while now. Ever since the lighter incident he has been turning this over in his mind and the only thing to come out of it so far is the whereabouts of the rabbits foot only he wants to check a few things first but he is fairly confident he knows who has it.

"So why didn't you tell us?" Check asks C.C. once they are all settled around a table in the Juice bar before mess as they do not have a squadron run this night so no one is in a hurry to be any where.

"Why?" C.C. repeats seeing no reason and every time someone brought up sparing or practicing hand to hand in the gym she just told them no. No reason to tell them Mic already warned her off or why. "It's not like you needed me to beat anyone up for you."

"Well." Check hedges then smiles.

"Not like you could make money off of it." C.C. adds knowingly.

"We could have." Check replies then groans. "Which is exactly why you didn't say anything."

"Bingo." C.C. responds because she does not need a match promoter in her flight any more than she needs a gambler.

The Dog does not appear in the mess hall nor does C.C. see him in their bailiwick this evening and she wonders if he let himself off base this time. His deadline for departure is some time the day after tomorrow but where he is, is not so much her concern, as long as he is not sneaking up on her since she has the rabbit's foot. If he approaches her any where on base she will know it and he cannot approach her in her quarters or she will see him for there is no place to hide or at least not any where he is willing to go. She has gone over her decision to keep the foot a hundred times and there is no way he can get it if he sticks to the rules.

It is while she is bending over her trunk to retrieve a book Check wants to borrow it suddenly occurs to her, she and Dog are not playing by any rules when she is suddenly grabbed from behind, lifted off her feet then dropped, and pinned face down on her cot. She tries to twist free pushing up against him only he is covering her from hip to shoulders and not letting go. After an embarrassingly short struggle she stops realizing just how useless this is and she turns her head to the side so she can see the side of his face.

"You're dead you know." C.C. grits out because she can see him and looks kill.

"Figuratively or literally?" Dog asks unconcerned as he shakes off the jitters from standing in that little cell like room across from her room waiting for her. Funny how being in this room which is no bigger than the one across the living area does not bother him but then she is always in here with him. He did not bother riffling through her room once he finally figured out she has the piece of pink fur he has been scouring the base personnel for. It finally dawned on him after their sparing match the safest place to keep it is on her.

"I can see you." C.C. informs him. "This is suppose to be a game of stealth, not assault."

"If I pussy foot around with you I'll be long gone before I get the flag." Dog reasons as he sends one hand under her searching the pockets of her uniform.

"You're about to be gone all right." C.C. warns as his hand goes to the pockets on her shirt starting at the ones over her chest.

"I'm not copping a feel here." He informs her then sighs. "Okay, I am. If you put it there everyone would see it but in my line of work it's best to be thorough."

"Why didn't I remember you said the rules don't apply to us?" C.C. grits out banging her forehead into the cot beneath her for being so stupid only her head bounces back up. This is totally not what she wanted to happen. "Turn me loose and I'll give it to you."

"Like I'm to take your word just like you take mine." He replies in disbelief. "I let you go and I'm going to end up with a mouthful of loose teeth."

"I promise to be good." C.C. responds because he has one large hand roaming all over her chest and the errant thought of wishing she were not wearing clothing just hits her out of the blue so this has to stop, now.

"Right, like the government promises to set me free and the Major General promises to help me get out of this." Dog grumbles as anger suddenly surges forward most and he stops moving as he fights for control. "It's to the point I don't have anyone to trust any more. I had six guys I could trust with my life and I ended up having to kill them. Now the brother of one of them says trust me and I'll help you get free of the Government then issues orders to the M.P.s to shoot me on sight if I come back here without his chosen escort. There's trust for you."

"What the hell are you talking about?" C.C. demands in the sudden silence after his outburst as he lays across her back not moving. He is breathing much too harshly for a man who is using his weight and not his muscle to hold her down. "Whose brother?"

"We were chosen for project Steel Man because of our intelligence, abilities, and our dedication to protecting the United States at all cost." Dog mutters taking a deep breath and knowing he should not be telling her any of this, but the reality is, he is not coming back. Not because he does not want too but because there will be nothing left of him to bring back and one of his many sorties here on base was to gather as much information as he could on the situation and his mission. He found out what he needed to know here, and in the nearby town, and as far as one way missions go this one qualifies in spades.

"Steel Man." Cat repeats softly while hoping he continues.

"We also didn't have family. No one to ask about us and there were no pesky care packages floating around looking for us but they missed something. Major General Aimhurst is Falcon's biological brother even if not on paper." He continues more quietly and hell the cat's so far out of the bag what is the point trying to stuff it back in. He should be shot for involving her in the first place but she has a brain so he might as well use it.

"One of the men you killed." She breaths now more interested in what he is saying than trying to get free. "He blames you."

"He says he doesn't, he says he blames project Steel Man." Dog replies laughing gruffly because fact is fact, he killed the mans brother. "Wants me to rendezvous with one of his pick up teams after the mission to be brought back here. He thinks he can get the government to agree to maybe one more mission in which he'll magically get my discharge papers and I can go home."

"You don't believe him." C.C. guesses and really she would not believe the man either. If Dog fights free after this mission he could very well be walking right into an ambush.

"Would you?" Dog asks her with interest. "I put his brother down like a rabid dog."

"No." She disagrees and she does not believe this for an instant because there was a reason and he would not have done it that way.

"See." Dog replies knowing she would agree with him. "Sad fact is, without help I'm not going to get out but worse than being gunned down by enemy forces is being gunned down by my own. I really don't think I deserve that."

"So what are you going to do?" C.C. asks even though she doubts he will tell her and why should he when she can tell someone else and mess up his escape plan.

"The only thing I can do." Dog informs her because he has given it a lot of thought lately and there is only one alternative. "Complete the mission and if that doesn't kill me, hug a land mine."

"A bit dramatic don't you think." She responds dryly because she does not for an instant believe him. The man is a mass of scars and determination so intentionally killing himself is not his style, or in his make up.

"Are you jealous I might accomplish my own demise before you can achieve yours?" Dog asks point blank. "I would trade places but I'm afraid they would notice the exchange before the transport even took off."

"What are you talking about now?" C.C. replies quietly because she must have misunderstood him.

"I finally figured it out." Dog responds simply. "What do you have to gain by staying here?"

"I belong here." C.C. informs him angrily. Gees what is it with everyone and her qualifications.

"Yes, but once it was made clear they wanted you to stand down you should have and easily could've taken a position as a trainer but there is no chance of catching a stray bullet or getting blown up by a SCUD missile in the States." Dog explains what he finally realized. "No way of ending your life without having to do it yourself."

"You're insane." She informs him trying to put some heat behind her words as her heart leaps into her throat because he cannot possibly know what he is saying is fact.

"I think both of us are." Dog admits sadly. "We don't belong anywhere, do we. I want to go home but where is home? I'm not going back to the reservation I grew up on and except for a few Army bases State side where I was stationed I've never been anywhere in the U.S. I've spent my whole life fighting for a country I've only seen three cities in three states. I could've settled anywhere in the world but the States are home to me. I know the streets aren't paved with gold and at some point I'll have to pay taxes, if I can actually get a job. Jesus, who would hire a guy who looks like me? But the need to go home has kept me alive all this time. It's not logical, or even practical, but it's home."

"I get that." C.C. admits and honestly she does while hoping to change the subject. "But you might be close to getting home."

"Might is even slimmer than maybe." Dog informs her.

"You still have twenty four hours to reconsider." She reminds him because it seems a shame to have gone through all he seems to have and just give up on his objective.

"Nothing is going to change in twenty four hours." Dog responds flatly. "Falcon will still be dead, his brother will still be an enigma, and my own government is set on seeing me dead."

"Then you just have to prove you're of more use to them alive." C.C. replies suddenly because it makes perfect sense to her. "They need you now, so they may need you again."

"Funny, that's basically what Major General Aimhurst said." Dog replies frowning down at her but all he can see is the side of her face. He would like to have this conversation facing her but she is not going to simply hand him the blasted pink piece of fur and he has not accomplished this objective yet. "I'll tell you what I told him, it can't be done. The government fears what I'm capable of doing and what I might do at some point when I set foot State side."

"Which is?" C.C. asks wondering what could be so horrible and if they are worried he will talk about what ever this project is he could be silenced in more ways if he was close at hand.

"Picture, if you will, me drooling and raving with a weapon in hand and several close by shooting everyone in sight while a civilian police force tries to subdue me." Dog explains painting the picture for her. "They'll not succeed so more lives will be lost and by the time they call in the big guns I'll have left a bloody swath through some town or city. Then the questions will begin and the tap dancing around answering them."

"I take it you've seen Rambo." She responds dryly or he has an over active imagination.

"No." Dog replies but he has heard of the movie and wondered who is plastering his worse night mare all over the big screen. "I saw what Axle did to a small area in Saigon, I just followed the trail of bodies. Women, children, old and young all butchered in a place which was one of ours in the war. People we were suppose to be helping and he gunned down something like twenty of our own soldiers before I caught up to him and killed him. Brick went a little less dramatically when he lost it, all though not any less gruesome. Someone noticed animals were missing in the towns we were stationed near and a Brigadier General brought his dog to camp then it disappeared. It was while searching for it we discovered Brick was killing animals all over the place and when we tried to confront him he lost it completely. Luckily only one soldier was injured and not badly but God only knows what he would've done State side or next. Elk killed three women in a whore house and a couple of local police as well and one of our soldiers before I got to him. Creek lost it on one of our last missions before we were to pull out of Vietnam. We had taken out an enemy command post and when the call came to cease fire he didn't cease fire. The were all unarmed and surrendering to us then he wounds a couple of ours who try to stop him until I did. It was just me and Falcon left by the end of our involvement in Vietnam."

"So what happened to Falcon?" C.C. asks even though she is not certain she wants to know but it really is strange a whole unit went seemingly mad and too such an extreme.

"We were posted to another base on foreign soil then sent on covert ops. He wanted me to bet him I would be the one to loose it next for whatever was in my gear when he killed me but I didn't take the bet because I was sure he was right so he would get all my stuff anyway." Dog admits honestly. "Of the two of us it looked like I would be the first to go over the edge. Falcon had a wife, pretty little Asian girl named Songhai who stood not much taller than my belly button. What she lacked in height she made up for in temper. Cross that woman and she would lace your food with whatever was handy, but wouldn't kill you, just make you wish you were dead. I came back from an op and I had a standing invitation from Songhai if I came back hungry I better stop in to eat. I took her up on it often, I didn't want to face the wrath of Songhai which is exactly what Falcon warned me would happen. Falcon expected me to keep an eye on her when he was out but this time he was home." Dog pauses because he can still see what he walked into that night. "Falcon was sitting in a chair when I walked in and laying on the floor is Songhai cut open and Falcon was covered in blood. I actually looked for the body of her killer because there is no way Falcon could've done that to her but there was no one else there. He didn't say anything, just sat staring at her body, so I had to ask him why because I couldn't imagine him harming her for any reason and he told me Songhai was pregnant but she refused to show him the baby."

"Oh God." C.C. manages to mutter and for some reason Falcon must have lost touch with reality.

"He had lost it long enough to kill his own wife and he was just sitting there trying to figure what happened. He knew what he had done but he couldn't understand why he became so angry when there was no way she could show him a child not even born yet." Dog concludes and both he and Falcon knew what it meant. "He was waiting for me to end his life just like I had the others and he didn't even attempt to run or fight. He just sat there as I snapped his neck."

She presses her face into the cot and she does not need to see his face because she could hear the sadness in his voice. There is a lump in her throat but not for his friend but for the man who witnessed it all and had to do the unthinkable killing men whom he knew which were his only family. It takes two attempts to clear the lump in her throat before she can even speak but men just do not go insane this way without a reason.

"What made them go crazy?" She asks having to clear her throat yet again as the man who is holding her captive has gone still.

"No one knows for certain." Dog replies honestly but something with the project went wrong that was for certain. "No one really cared enough to find out so they wrote us off. We were suppose to be the men of steel twice as strong, three times as fast, and intelligent enough to know if we were looking at nuclear plans or common power plant designs. Photographic memories, stealth, and not stopped by a single bullet or two. I've found over the course of time my limit seems to be five or six so you might want to keep this in mind but it did take twelve to bring Axle down when he lost it."

"They think you'll go nuts too." C.C. gasps as it dawns on her the enormity of over coming the military's fear of him and now it is beginning to make sense but she already suspected there was something just not normal about him. "They couldn't starve you to death in ten years time because you are a Steel Man."

"I can go weeks without water." Dog admits and he has. "Months on very little food which is not pleasant but doable."

"This project did something to you." C.C. mutters wondering just what they did to Steel Man but they did make five men totally loose their minds. "They're just fooling themselves if they think this mission will kill you unless you give up. They would've been better off to have put a gun to your head."

"Might bounce off and kill the one who fired the gun." Dog responds amused and there was speculation about that at one time.

"You're human, so no, that wouldn't happen." She replies seriously. "You bleed just like every one else."

"Are you sure?" Dog asks wondering what makes her think so.

"Let me up and I'll show you." She offers hopefully.

"Ah, and now we're right back where we started." He mutters sighing because he is a Steel Man and there is a reputation he is the only one left to defend. "I've never not completed a mission so I have to find the pink fur."

"Have you ever heard the saying there is a first time for everything." C.C. suggests as his hand is moving under her again.

"Doesn't apply in this case." He replies confidently as he continues searching her clothing which is rather awkward since she is laying on most of the pockets. Then he finds what he is looking for in one of the smallest pockets and he has difficulty retrieving it while she growls. "Oh you knew I was going to find it."

"No, I planned on you never finding it." C.C. responds angrily as she presses all her body weight down on the pocket to make his job more difficult.

"Just give it up." Dog advises still struggling only he is certain it is not the size of the pocket at fault as much as the smaller size of the ABUs to fit her.

"You first." She invites because it sounds like he has given up.

"You were first when you decided to keep your combat status." Dog reminds her and just by her lack of reaction he knows he is correct but the change of subject was a dead give away.

"You don't know anything." She responds confidently and she is qualified to be here.

"Oh you made it easy." He informs her. "The scum bag you were married to kept botching the job and was suppose to kill you but he was obviously inept. Definitely not cold blooded enough for you."

"He was a cop." She responds so murder was out of the question which had nothing to do with marrying him though it would have been a nice side benefit in hindsight.

"Then he would know just how to dispose of your body wouldn't he." Dog replies easily not seeing what his occupation has to do with anything. "If there is a two then there was a one so he must have something to do with why you didn't care any longer if you lived or died. So was he the love of your life, died in a tragic accident, and you discovered you couldn't live with out him."

"I caught him after about his sixth affair with women he worked with." C.C. replies grimly. "By then I seriously considered killing him myself."

"So what did you do to him?" Dog asks with interest. "I want details so don't leave anything out."

"I divorced him." She responds blandly wondering what kind of details he expects to hear or if he is fishing for a good divorce lawyer.

"That's it. That's all." He comments surprised and some what stunned. "You didn't do anything to him. You nearly busted my spleen in a friendly sparing match yet this guy cheated on you and you just divorce him."

"It's rather obvious you've been living in foreign countries in some not so nice places when you ask questions like that." She informs him with a sigh and there was nothing else she could have done. "There are laws and rules you better familiarize yourself with before going back to the States."

Chapter 11
Somewhere in Saudi Arabia...

"Yeah, I'm familiar with what laws are and I'm not saying you should've killed him." Dog growls and why she does not assert herself is beyond him. "Busting his balls is not murder, assault possibly, but you could've pulled it off. Might get you a stiff fine but I doubt any jail time."

"Registered black belt." She reminds him which could get her possible prison time.

"Then you don't touch him." He modifies but that leaves a whole range of opportunities she does not seem to have even considered. "You should've torched his car, thrown out his favorite toy, or what ever he holds dear."

"Cheated a lot have you?" C.C. guesses and women have done these things to him.

"No." He replies but he has never had a woman he has not paid to be with him. "But you're not the type to tamely let someone get away with treating you like that."

"You keep saying that." She snaps at him wondering why he expects her to throw temper tantrums. "Obviously I am or it wouldn't have happened."

"Exactly my point." He confirms triumphantly. "Neither husband one nor two saw you as anything other than an object because you never stood up to either one of them and showed them who you really are. If you had stepped up into their faces and told them you'll cut off his balls, or if one of them laid a hand on you in anger you would, destroy his stamp collection."

"Stamp collection, really." C.C. replies finding this is getting more bizarre by the minute.

"You know what I mean. Hell you told me right where I stood the moment I met you." He reminds her.

"Yeah and look how well that has worked out." She mutters.

"Oh you've no idea of how badly I want to flip you over." He informs her wondering if hell has prostitutes and if he will have anything to buy one with. "But I know I'll be choking on my own spleen before morning comes and I knew that before I knew anything else about you. So we're participating in a flag game while I take any advantage I can get knowing you're going to make me pay for it but not doing anything completely stupid or you will kill me. I'm hoping at some point you might come to like me."

"Not happening." C.C. replies flatly but then she has an idea. "If you leave me the rabbit's foot I'll like you."

"Tease." He accuses as he finally works the foot free of her pocket but his ah of triumph is cut off by a wicked elbow to the center of his chest from an arm she has slowly been freeing from his control but rather than subdue her again he rolls quickly off one side of the cot while she has rolled off the other and they are now facing each other over it but he has completed his objective having the rabbit's foot in his fist as she glares at him. "Don't be a sore looser."

"I haven't lost anything." She informs him except possibly some dignity as she reaches down the top of her tee shirt pulling out the pink rabbits foot and holding it up for him to see. "You would be surprised what a woman can hide in a sports bra."

"What the..." He begins staring at her because he is positive he has the scarp of fur in his hand but when he opens his hand he finds a white rabbits foot. He shakes his head at the absurdity of these things. "Who in their right mind carries these things?"

"It's a war, rabbit's feet are good luck." C.C. explains not really caring one way or the other as she waves the pink foot in front of her. "Now you see it, now you don't."

"Now there's a talent." Dog replies honestly as with a flourish of her hands she made the pink rabbit's foot disappear while he stood watching with no idea how she did it.

"Third husband was a magician." She admits with a slight smile. "I thought I might need a decoy and there seems to be a few of these floating around but I have the only pink one."

"What happened with number three?" Dog asks which he finds more interesting than how many idiots carry rabbit's feet into a war.

"He died." C.C. replies with a sigh. "Intestinal cancer."

"He starved to death." Dog responds now understanding the underlying sadness he caught once before when they met but this begs the question. "Just how many times have you been married?"

"Four." C.C. replies which tells a story all by itself about her aptitude for relationships and predilection for failure. "I sold myself to a rich man the last time but he turned out to be a crook. Once I was cleared and the divorce was finalized I walked into an Air Force recruiting center and the rest, as they say, is history."

"But you're not." He informs her grimly. "Or not yet any way. I see it but I still don't understand why."

"This from a man who is talking about hugging a land mine." She responds with disbelief.

"I'm tired of fighting a loosing battle because no matter what I do I can't change their preconceived notion about what I might do regardless if I accomplish this mission or not." He replies bluntly which is a problem he sees no solution. "You on the other hand have just barely begun to fight whatever preconceived notion you have of what you should be doing with your life. You've made your own prison by following along in someone's wake or trying to live up to someones expectations not your own.

"Is that why you sat on your ass in prison for ten years rather than escape?" C.C. asks being equally blunt because she knows now he could have escaped but something else occurs to her. "A lot has changed in ten years."

"Not enough to make and difference." He replies grimly and he certainly did not stay in prison by choice.

"Just a minute. Do you know what makes this war different from any other war?" She asks him.

"It all seems to be fought from the air." He grumbles instantly because this is the first thing he noticed.

"The media." She replies and he has no clue it seems so she goes on to educate him about what he has missed not only by being in prison all this time but having no access to the states. "I know what Major General Aimhurst is going to do and it may cost him his rank but if handled correctly he could focus public opinion toward you."

"What the hell are you talking about?" Dog asks because from what he knows of public opinion after Vietnam veterans returned home they were spit on or called baby killers which is not going to help.

"There hasn't been a coalition action like this since World War I and those men returned heroes." C.C. explains to him and the more she thinks about it the more certain she is. "The public is always looking for a hero and this war is almost over. Everyone knows it, can feel it. We're going to win and the media will be looking for uniformed men to hold up to the public."

"I'm not liking the sound of this." Dog informs her honestly because having his name and face plastered all over the news is not something the government will want and neither does he.

"But if done correctly, and the Major General is careful, the public will only know of an Army Ranger pulling off key missions. They don't need your name or likeness but the public will take interest in Army Rangers." C.C. continues as the options click over in her head. "If the Major General keeps you just below the surface yet within public knowledge there are going to be indirect questions about where you are and what you're doing after the war is over. Once you have public scrutiny it'll be harder for them to just make you disappear or keep you in any military installation."

"More reason to want me dead you mean." He replies seeing this as their response.

"It's been over twenty years since whatever project you were part of operated so only a very few probably even know about it so you'll be proving yourself to a whole new generation of military higher ups. The reasons you were swept under the rug are gone and forgotten except for a few who are not going to want to explain why you have to be neutralized." She responds grinning because she is certain she has figured out what the Major General intends to do.

"Just say dead." Dog mutters grimly but even if she is correct, and he still is not certain she is, there is still one major loop hole. "You're basing all this on the contingency I can trust Major General Aimhurst and I'm not thinking I can do that."

"Well either way you're dead so why not take the chance he's trustworthy and come back?" She asks him because it is possible but a good deal does hinge on the Major General.

"Oh, just a five by five reason and lack of food." He informs her with a sigh because he now fears being tossed back in a cell more than death.

"This room and that room are eight by five and the door is wide open." She corrects him.

"Doesn't matter. Even the five by five feels like two by two after ten years." He grumbles and this is fact.

"Big baby." She accuses in disbelief. "You're going to let your fear of small rooms get you killed."

"That's rich coming from a woman who is afraid of living her life by her own rules so she is looking to get killed." He snaps back and once again he is reminded of what a pair they make.

"I have lived four lives." She informs him. "Six if you count my childhood and the military."

"And every one of those you apparently lived by everybody's rules but your own." Dog mutters in frustration because he cannot believe she does not see it. "You're so use to doing things the way other people want you to it's no wonder you fit in so well in the military. If they were smart they would've ordered you home already and you would've gone without a fuss which is what they fear you'll cause but you won't do it. You follow orders."

"It's the military, of course I follow orders." She responds finding he is being an idiot.

"But you won't act outside those orders to do anything for yourself. They fear the stink you'll cause, not because you told them you would, but because they expect it." He explains sighing again. "You're a square peg trying to pound yourself in to everybody's round hole and guess what, it isn't working. You're afraid to be yourself because everyone wants you to be something else. Boo hoo for you. Just stand the fuck up and tell them all to screw off. What could happen that would be any worse than the shit you've already had done to you? Think about it. What can anyone do to you that hasn't already been done?"

"Same goes." She replies angrily. "What can they do to you, you already know, you can live through. You come back first and I'll believe you're not full of shit."

"Deal." He agrees with a smile because the battle lines have just been drawn, or redrawn as the case maybe, as he leaves her room.

What the hell just happened?

She throws herself down on her cot wondering for the thousandth time what the hell is wrong with her and why does she even care if he hugs a land mine? Why talk him out of it when most of the time she wants to kill him herself? Now she has let him goad her into making a rash statement to do who knows what? He expects her to believe there is nothing wrong with her and it is everyone else who has a problem? Stand up for herself like that will solve everything or change anything. He can get away with telling people to screw off, look at the size of him, but that is not going to work so well for her, might get a laugh out of some.

She is not even sure why she is even still thinking about this because it is nonproductive. She knows what she needs to do because she may have just talked a man back into a five by five cell so he can starve to death. She is already dragging around enough emotional baggage and she does not want his return to a cell to be another.

After giving Check the blasted book she is now waiting out side the commissioned officers dining room when Major General Aimhurst exits but she follows him at a distance trying to decide just what kind of man this is as other base personnel move about this time of evening when it is cooler so she is just one of many. He is a distinguished looking man which most top officers are simply by adhering to regulations involving personal grooming but some do not keep up the physical regiment and go to fat but not Aimhurst.

He has kept fit moving like a man who knows he is in charge of most everyone he sees returning salutes with not exactly a smile of friendliness but not a grim stare of do not bother me or waste my time, which is a custom of the Major Agitator's and his aloofness transcends to everyone on base he is just doing his job and does not really care about anyone under him or around him. The Major set himself apart the moment he stepped onto base which is why no one really trusts him and one of the reasons both American and allied pilots will not help him get rid of her. The first thing learned in basic training is how to assess an officer in seconds to know if you will get kicked or a hand shake.

"Sir, Major General, sir." C.C. calls out before he enters the building housing the commissioned officers and when he turns seeing her there is an instant look of concern on his face.

"Is there a problem Captain?" Aimhurst asks immediately.

"Sir, no, sir." She admits knowing exactly what kind of problem he might fear now. "Sir, I would just like to have a word with you in private, sir."

"Very well then." He responds some what surprised but willing to hear what she has to say. "The Juice bar works fairly well for privacy without drawing undo attention."

"Sir, that will be fine, sir." C.C. agrees as she stands aside for him to proceed her to the Juice bar and a senior male officer speaking privately with a female officer without having to throw the C.O. out of his office so they can speak without tongues wagging about fraternizing is best.

"How is the flag game going?" Aimhurst asks after sitting at a table to one side of the room away from the more vocal point in the Juice Bar thinking this might be what she wishes to discuss.

"Sir, fine, sir." C.C. replies seeing her flight has left the bar as she pulls the rabbit foot from her pocket showing him before waving her hand and making it disappear again.

"Impressive." Aimhurst comments.

"Sir, the Colonel wasn't very impressed when his most recent attempt to retrieve it failed, sir." She responds with a slight smile.

"I'm certain he wanted to be." Aimhurst responds but still wondering what the problem is and there must be one or why would this Captain wish to speak to him. "Are the two of you getting along then?"

"Sir, not really. But even a cat and dog thrown into the same cage must make concessions if they hope to survive and this truce will only last until someone opens the cage door, sir." She explains earnestly.

"I imagine so." Aimhurst responds so it seems the Colonel and the Captain may not become life long friends after this.

"Sir, there is a problem which you attributed to in a way you may not realize, sir." C.C. replies or at least she hopes his intention was not to drive Dog to his death.

"Is the flag game causing you a problem then?" Aimhurst asks wondering if this is what she is referring too.

"Sir, the easiest way to explain is to tell you what little I know or have guessed, sir." C.C. informs him as she leans closer over the table. "Sir, project Steel Man is still the problem and did you know they were starving him, Sir?"

"No, not until his release was authorized." Aimhurst admits but then keeps silent because he probably should not be admitting even this much and she already knows far more than she should.

"Sir, I was hoping not, sir." She confesses but his answer is not confirmation of his intentions and even hardened killers will not kill a dog but maim and slaughter people. "Sir, my condolences on the loss of your brother but you have dangled the key to the Colonel returning to the States in his face, and he feels very responsible for your brother's death, sir."

"He told you." Aimhurst responds wondering if he has made a mistake if the Colonel is divulging information.

"Sir, dead men tell no tales and he is convinced he is a walking dead man, sir." She informs him earnestly. "Sir, the only men he trusted explicitly are dead and the one man he is suppose to trust should want him dead for killing his brother. You tell him you want him to come back yet you told the M.P. s to shoot him on sight. So you see Major General he's a man with few options and dwindling confidence in ever seeing home again. If this is what you intended then we are done here, sir."

"No, Captain, that was not my intention at all." Aimhurst admits understanding now he may have miscalculated. "I have spent four years cutting through red tape, making myself not so popular in certain circles, and all done with the objective of seeing the Colonel released and allowed to return home. Before that I would occasionally receive letters from my brother so you see it's as if I've known the Colonel for a good number of years when I forget he just met me not more than a month ago. For some reason I expected him to trust me and now I realize he doesn't even know me."

"Sir, understandable, and I've managed to dare him to return without meaning too. I also wanted to be certain I didn't just direct him to walk into an ambush from your pick up team, sir." C.C. responds and if anyone kills Dog she would like to be the one to do it which is an absurd notion she cannot seem to shake.

"I should've realized the M.P.s would relay my orders." Aimhurst mutters because he does know a good deal about the Colonel. "Even those within the project monitoring Steel Man categorized him as a nucleus meaning he draws others to him. People trust him, like him, and gravitate towards him whether they realize it or not. I was following my orders."

"Sir, I thought it might be something like that. I don't know how long the M.P.s have been guarding him but only a glance at his paperwork probably convinced them he pissed off the wrong Brigadier General somewhere and his sentence was revenge, sir." C.C. responds but this nucleus thing she is not so sure about. "Sir, combined with what the M.P.s told him and his feeling you should be angry with him for killing Falcon adds to him not seeing a way back, sir."

"He did what he had to do." Aimhurst replies and he knows his brother was no longer sane.

"Sir, you don't believe he is just a machine programmed to kill as your superiors obviously do, sir?" She asks flatly but she knows Dog is not a soulless machine because he still feels it all and it weighs on him.

"That is what Steel Man was all about but what they did was take brave intelligent soldiers and turn them into raving animals in the end." Aimhurst admits and it is what started his hunt for the Colonel after he found all the secrets he never knew about his brother. "Once a Steel Man began loosing touch with reality it was a downward spiral into madness and killing. What the Colonel did was a mercy because my brother wouldn't have wanted to hurt innocents or civilians which is what would've happened and did."

"Sir, you don't think Dog will 'loose touch with reality', sir?" She asks and to her it seems if it has not happened by now it never will.

"No, he will not." Aimhurst replies confidently because he has been doing some research of his own. "Once he comes back I intend to prove it."

"Sir, proof may not be enough, sir." She responds knowing proof to the contrary or not people still believe in the boogeyman. "Sir, you're planning on using publicity, sir?"

"Very astute Captain." He comments feeling like a glass window and she seems to be looking through him but then publicity is the very thing which has her in a tail spin with the Air Force at the moment.

"Sir, word of warning there, sir." She cautions him. "Sir, you can't splash his picture or name all over the front page, sir."

"It's the only way this will work to his advantage." Aimhurst replies why else bother and the Colonel has to be the focus of media attention.

"Sir, the media will dig if they have his name and face. They'll want to know far more than any one should which is what those involved with the project don't want, sir." She explains having given this considerable thought since her conversation with Dog. "Sir, you're proving the Colonel is still a viable asset to the military but too much focus on him will also make him a liability if ever needed again. Better to focus attention toward Army Rangers as a whole and the media will dig in the general area but not close enough to make any of the older generation of officers too nervous, and sir, this would also be a good time to bring the Colonel to the attention of the newer generation of officers who might see a future need for the Colonel's particular talents. His record can stand alone without all the top secret information along with what he is going to do here and now, sir."

"Have you ever considered a career in the Army, Captain?"

Aimhurst asks point blank because in the mater of only two weeks she has found a way to clear some of the major hurdles of his plan which he had yet to find away around.

"Sir, the Army has yet to incorporate jets and tend to use helos more as taxis so no sir I have not, sir." She admits truthfully.

"A pity." Aimhurst replies because he was thinking more along the line of tactics but even he cannot picture her seated sedately in an office directing the action and not participating.

C.C. is about to leave the Juice Bar following the Major General when a large frame settles into his vacant seat as Dog stares at her while she stares back and she should have considered he would be following her since she still has the rabbit's foot. Unless he failed lip reading one-o-one he knows everything which she and the Major General just discussed but just in case he did not have a good view she asks.

"Sir, everything clear now, sir?"

"Yes." Dog admits but there is still a matter which is unclear. "If not the Army then why not accept a position with the Navy?"

"Sir, same issues apply and I'm really not fond of large bodies of water, sir." She replies and she was not offered a pilot position with the Navy but that of an instructor which is so not for her.

"Can't swim?" He asks finding her answer oddly phrased.

"Sir, I love to swim, sir." She informs him. "Sir, give me a nice big pool and I'm good to go. Smelly fish water with creatures swimming and living in it, not so much, sir."

"I find I sometimes forget you're a woman until you undress or say something like that." He responds though that is not entirely true because he is very much aware she is a woman at all times.

"Sir, disliking large bodies of water is not a female issue, sir." C.C. replies with a frown though it is the closest he has come to making a sexist remark when some men trying to side step the fact she is a woman have said much worse to her unintentionally.

"Smelly fish water and creatures is most definitely a womanly way of saying what a man would say is crappy water and sharks." He informs her.

"Then it's a good thing I'm not a man." She comments wondering what his point is and deciding she does not want to know as she stands and walks out.

Chapter 12
Somewhere in Saudi Arabia...

Standing under a shower head C.C. has happened upon the rare anomaly of having the whole building to herself but this is short lived when she hears the outer door open after a few minutes only no one enters the shower area. She assumes whom ever opened the outdoor must not have changed their mind as she slices excess water from her body with her hands before stepping out into the outer room to retrieve her towel and encounters the Major Agitator standing by the benches between her and her towel but more unnerving is the fact he is holding a stun gun aimed at her.

"I have better things to do than to babysit you." He growls angrily and it is time to end this farce. "I am not going to spend the entire war stuck here watching you make a mockery of the uniform you wear because it's obvious you don't belong here and never have."

"Sir, this area is male restricted, sir." C.C. reminds him and surely he knows this but there is something wrong with his eyes, they look unnaturally glassy.

"You may have fooled everyone but I know exactly what you are and I knew before I arrived." He responds and how dare she attempt to tell him where he should or should not be when he out ranks her. "I know you latched on to an up and rising young executive in an attempt to pull free of your blue collar roots but he found solace in the arms of others escaping your cold money grubbing fingers. Then you married a police officer up for a promotion but he was smarter than you thought and must have caught on to your social climbing ways. He attempted to teach you your place only you ran off and some how landed yourself a millionaire. A man twice your age and it's obvious to anyone who looks your greed has no shame but he out smarted you leaving his money to his adult children but you still didn't learned your lesson and place managing to land a billionaire. How you managed to slip free of all criminal charges is beyond me."

"Sir, Major, sir."   C.C. attempts to interject again but he raises the stun gun higher towards her face and snarls from behind it.

"You are nothing more than social climbing lower class trash."   He bellows raising his other hand holding a packet of papers. "You're going to sign these discharge papers and willingly go back to the States or I'm going to make you wish you had. And if you're waiting for someone to come to your rescue, don't bother, I put the out of order sign on the door. Shall we begin."

"Sir, a coerced signature will not hold up in court when I contest this and you'll go to the brig, sir." She warns wondering how he thinks he can get away with this and he should know he cannot.

"But you won't say anything." He mocks with a knowing grin. "You never stood your ground with any of your former husbands or risk everyone finding out you were using them and manipulating them. Your personal history is nothing more than a greedy little girl who runs away when she's about to be caught in the wrong. And I'm certain an investigation into how you reached your present rank would prove very interesting but I don't have time for a lengthy legal investigation so we'll do this my way."

Until this moment she never considered how her previous actions, or lack there of, may appear to others laid out and reviewed as the Major Agitator seems to have done. By simply walking away not wanting or caring enough to fight back the Major Agitator has construed her actions as an admission of blame for some kind of criminal behavior. She is certain if Dog were standing next to her now he would be saying, 'I told you so.'

Her first thought even now is to simply sign the papers and fight about being coerced later but would she actually go to the legal hassle knowing she will be sidelined if the U.S. comes under attack again. Why fight to stay in the military when women are not considered assets in combat? The Major Agitator will have won and what will a voluntary early discharge say about her to any one who looks into her back ground again. Will they automatically assume she could not handle the training or the discipline so willingly bailed. Does she really care what other people think of her? Not for a very long time now because it only brought pain and endless frustration her life, but maybe she should be asking herself what does she think of herself when she has done nothing but take the easy way out most of her life.

"Sign the papers." The Major demands waving them before her again after giving her a moment to realize she is firmly trapped this time and cannot wiggle out as she has done countless times before.

"Sir, no, sir." C.C. manages and of all times for her to pick to fight back she knows she chose very poorly.

She is presently standing in a puddle of water where she has been dripping on a concrete floor known for being slick despite the finish to make it non slip. She is stark naked facing a stun gun with no where to hide but sign she will not.

"Sign the papers now." He yells at her and it echos around the sparse empty block room.

"Sir, no, sir." C.C. responds again as she scrunches her toes hoping to judge just how slick the floor is beneath her feet as she never takes her eyes off him.

"Stupid bitch." He mutter with a leering grin. "I'm going to enjoy this."

Just as he pulls the trigger C.C. lunges through the doorway back into the showers as she hears the electrodes hit the wall behind her bouncing off falling to the floor but she does not go far because there is no place for her to go, the room is wide open. She stands with her back to the wall just to one side of the opening waiting to see what he will do next only so far all he is doing is cursing.

The Major is apparently unfamiliar with stun guns and is having difficulty reloading the electrodes as she considers her limited options of which there really is only one if he enters the showering area gun first. She can only hope he does not look right or left when he enters assuming she is cowering against the far wall. She only has one shot at this and if she cannot disable him the first time she doubts she will have a second chance.

The gun appears through the opening aimed straight ahead and she shoves the gun up as she rounds the cement wall delivering a chop with the edge of her hand across the Major's wind pipe. He falls back gagging as one hand goes to his throat. Unfortunately he does not drop the stun gun but while he is gasping for air as she runs past him he is too occupied to aim. Running the distance to the outer door she hits it at full speed catching a glimpse of men passing by at the far end and two she recognizes as Dog's M.P.s.

"Help." C.C. calls out but for some reason her legs no

longer work as she pitches head first over the railing carried by her momentum.

She wakes wondering why she is laying in sand and the bright sun is blinding then a shadow moves over her. She is looking up into the face of a stranger as she wonders what has happened and why there is a neck brace on her but it becomes clear she is laying outside the shower door.

"Don't try to move." The man instructs as he looks into her eyes. "You have a nasty bump on your head. You hit the cement approach to the door when you flipped over the railing. Do you remember anything?"

"I think so." She replies as she pieces together what she was doing before then realizes the Major must have hit her with the stun gun and she is not feeling much of anything at the moment. "Could you at least tell me I'm decently covered?"

"You're covered Captain but you're laying on sand. Is it too hot?" He inquires with concern.

"I really can't feel much of anything but apparently I'll need another shower." C.C. responds grimly but his smile does not convey sympathy as he seems to be addressing two base M.P.s who are now standing in her sight. "I don't want her moved until I'm certain she doesn't have a neck injury I can't check her responses until the stun wears off."

"Understood." One of the M.P.s responds before the medic rises from her side and an M.P. now squats where he was blocking the sun from her eyes. "Can you tell me what happened?"

"I was showering, heard the outer door open, and didn't think anything strange about it. I came out of the shower into the outer room to dry off and Major Alexander was waiting by the benches for me with a stun gun in one hand and my voluntary discharge papers in the other, or so he said they were. He told me I wasn't leaving until I signed and he had put the out of order sign on the door." C.C. recounts and it would have worked too because when the out of order sign goes up it usually means a water pipe has busted or the drain is clogged which makes the showers totally useless for anything else as this is its only purpose. "I refused and he missed me the first time he fired when I darted around the corner back into the showers. He reloaded and came in after me. When the gun cleared the door way I gave him a chop to the throat then ran for the outside door."

"Why didn't you attempt to take the stun gun?" The M.P. asks looking curious.

"Wet floor sometimes slippery so grappling for a gun or kicking it out of his hand was risky and I had no place to run from there." C.C. explains simply.

"Good move." The M.P. compliments agreeing with the Captain's assessment of the situation.

"Critic me later okay. Preferably when I'm not laying flat on my back and I can demonstrate." C.C. replies dryly causing him to smile.

"Which is why I asked now because if you took offense it's safer for us." The M.P. responds with a smile because he saw with his own eyes what she is capable of. "The Major is lucky to be alive."

"Which is another reason I didn't go for the gun or I might've been tempted to kill him." C.C. replies honestly. "I made it to the door but he hit me from behind after I called out for help."

"Anything else we should know?" The M.P. asks looking at her seriously.

"His eyes were glassy like he's been drinking." C.C. admits knowing how stupid this sounds but it is the only explanation she can think of.

"Now there's a trick we should look into." The M.P. responds looking toward his counterpart standing to one side who moves off before he returns his attention back to her. "I was going for dumb ass stupid as the cause of this incident."

"Well there's that too. Systems are beginning to reboot." C.C. admits finally managing to raise her hand just as the Dog approaches into her line of sight and she growls. "Bed side manners."

"You're laying in the sand like a beached whale with a bump on your head turning purple. I'm not seeing a bed here." Dog informs her grimly as he looks into the open door way at the Major being treated and questioned in the shower building.

"They ran straight to you didn't they." C.C. reasons knowing the two M.P.s are loyal to only one person on this base and it is not the Major General.

"Of course." Dog replies because what else would they do.

"Remind me to explain the chain of command as it applies to everyone else." C.C. grumbles as the medic comes back so she raises her hand to show him. "One hand and I think the other."

"Good, what about feet or just toes would make my day." The medic instructs as he watches her feet sticking out from beneath the sheet they draped over her and they wiggle so he removes the neck brace. "You're good to go Captain but you've earned your self twenty four hour med leave before you fly again."

"Great. He accosts me and I'm the one being punished." C.C. mutters because she is grounded until they clear her to fly.

"Head injuries, you know the drill." The medic replies without sympathy then turning to the M.P. "I want her on a liter and taken back to her quarters unless you're keeping her."

"No we're not but by regulations she is restricted to quarters for twenty four while we look into this so it works out just fine." The M.P. informs the medic.

"How convenient." C.C. grits out not finding neither restriction to her liking.

"Actually it's usually forty eight but I don't see any possible way he can explain being in a male restricted building which will be plausible." The M.P. explains grimly.

"He says she lured him in." The other M.P. fills in when he returns.

"I said plausible." The other M.P. counters. "All officers have rendezvous's in male restricted areas while carrying stun guns?"

"Says he feared for his life." The M.P. replies with a grin.

"Now that I can believe." The other M.P. responds with a laugh. "If he was so scared he shouldn't have entered a male restricted area and if he knew it was her he should've brought something bigger than a stun gun."

"Medics think she's right, he's on something. Not conclusive yet." The M.P. adds.

"All right get her on a liter and back to her quarters." The M.P. orders as they both walk away.

"So where were you?" C.C. asks frowning up at Dog.

"Where was I suppose to be?" Dog asks as he crouches down next to her taking the M.P.s place blocking the sun from her eyes.

"Not charging to the rescue obviously." C.C. replies grimly. "You've been dogging my every step, now when you could've been useful you suddenly disappear."

"Then you should've kept this with you." Dog informs her pulling out the pink rabbit's foot from his shirt pocket and holding it up for her to see. "I was busy woman."

"Apparently." C.C. responds with a grimace while wondering what he did to the airman carrying it and decides to worry about that later.

After being carried back to her quarters on a stretcher she is deposited on her cot but as soon as they clear the outer door she is up on her feet putting on underclothes and once finished she turns to find Dog standing in her doorway with a slight smile on his face.

"He got you butt good." He comments having seen far more of her than he expected but he is not complaining.

"Yes, I noticed." C.C. responds frowning because she found the two little holes in her rear end, one on either cheek, and this day has turned into the day of ultimate humiliation.

"You don't strike me as the overly modest type." Dog replies and they have had most of their conversations while she is in her underwear and he is in his so why does this seem to bother her.

"There is a difference to being nearly clothed and being naked for all the world to see." C.C. explains and this is a big difference to her but back to business as she holds out her hand to him demanding without speaking.

"Can't I just enjoy the moment?" Dog protests but she is not looking cooperative so he reaches into his pocket and hands her the rabbit's foot. "Happy now?"

"Not really, what did you do to the guy carrying it?" C.C. asks hoping it does not incite more stupidity.

"I doubt he knows it's gone yet." Dog responds smiling since she gave him what he needed to pull this off. "He'll check it at some point then wonder why it's not pink any more."

She forgot he has the other white foot and now the guy carrying the rabbit's foot still thinks he has it on him. This is just wonderful and she cannot go tell him he lost the game because she is restricted to quarters so officially the game is over but she does have the rabbit's foot again and not Dog so this is a plus. As far as this day is concerned it is a total loss as she is restricted to quarters, unable to fly until cleared, and she might be looking at time in the brig, again.

"I can practically hear the devious wheels turning in your mind from here Cat." Dog mocks amused by her predicament since she is restricted to quarters and can do nothing to fix the situation.

"When do you leave?" C.C. asks suddenly because all she knows is tomorrow.

"Ouch." Dog comments but not surprised she is anxious to be rid of him. "O'five hundred."

"Did they get you everything you need?" C.C. inquires looking about her room absently because she really is probably concussed if what she is thinking seems like a good idea.

"The Major General informed me my gear and kit are on the plane coming to pick me up. I'm not to be trusted with anything sharp, pointy, or blunt until then, which means they'll probably toss me out of the plane and then toss my stuff out after me just to be on the safe side." Dog explains with a grin but she is not smiling back or even looking at him. "Problem?"

"I'm just thinking." C.C. replies, or not thinking, as the case may be. "Let's do something wild and crazy."

"Strip poker?" Dog suggests instantly because they cannot do much as she is stuck in quarters and she only put on her underwear while he is fully clothed, advantage his.

"Close." C.C. admits as she moves to stand before him as he instantly straightens in the doorway and when she reaches to rest a hand on his shoulder he jerks away. "Jumpy much?"

"Self defense mode." Dog replies seriously as he watches her. "It kicks in when women with multiple black belts say they want to do something wild and crazy."

"Well, at ease." C.C. instructs him as she reaches up placing her other hand on his other shoulder but she can feel the muscles in his shoulders jumping around. "Are you shaking?"

"There's some name for it but basically it's my muscles building." Dog explains looking down into her cat green eyes as she looks at him skeptically. "Fine, I'm shaking."

"No, I believe you." C.C. replies honestly as she slides her hands up the sides of his neck but she has to stand on tip toes to do this. "This would be a little easier if you bent toward me."

"Okay." Dog agrees not certain what she is about to do but whatever it is he is certain it is going to hurt as he bends his head down toward her and then she does the most incredible thing by putting her lips to his giving him a kiss which nearly causes his eyes to roll up into his head. When she breaks off the kiss by dropping down from her tip toes he can only stare at her as she is frowning and looking at her hands still on his shoulders. "Yeah, now I'm shaking. I just did the math and I haven't been this up close and personal with a woman in fourteen years."

"Seriously." C.C. replies astonished but then he was in a military installation for ten of those years so what options did he have. "You've been here nearly two weeks."

"Is there a question in there somewhere?" Dog asks because he is not certain if she is asking if he found someone here in that time or is she inferring he is slow at picking up women. "I've not asked and I've not accepted any offers."

"I'm sure there were many offers so why not?" C.C. asks him while taking off her sports bra because for some reason she already knew his answer.

"Why not what?" He repeats staring at her breasts finding them perfect.

"I think I just actually saw your brain cells fly out the window." C.C. comments while frowning at him as he is staring intently at her bare chest.

"There is no window in here." Dog informs her flatly. "Believe me I would've noticed."

"Would you like to go out into the living area?" C.C. suggests having gathered he is not comfortable in small rooms.

"Only if you and those are coming with me." Dog replies honestly as he looks to her face to see if she is joking. "If this is the case then I really, really, like the way you think even though you're going to hate me in the morning."

"Why? Aren't you leaving?" C.C. responds grinning as she puts her hands on his chest and pushes him backwards out into the living area where she begins unbuttoning his shirt.

"You know it." Dog replies undoing the upper buttons since she started at the bottom. "But I'm coming back."

"Don't spoil this." C.C. warns him grimly.

"And that is when you're going to hate me." Dog informs her as he shakes his arms out of his shirt then pulls his tee shirt over his head quickly but now she is staring at his scars then tracing her fingers over them causing him to shiver. "I have a lot."

"Shh, I'm counting." C.C. orders him but really she is trying to catch her breath and he gives a whole new meaning to the term ripped. She saw and knew what to expect under his tee shirt but now not so starved and the shear size of him in the flesh is truly drool worthy. "Four bullet holes."

"In the front." Dog mutters and she slips under his arm to get behind him.

"Okay." C.C. agrees looking at the mass of scars on his

back including what look like whip marks. "Three more holes." C.C. continues moving back to stand in front of him.

"Four." Dog corrects her.

"One went clear through." C.C. replies wondering if he thinks she is too stupid to figure this out.

"Did not?" Dog objects.

"Yes, it did." C.C. counters and too bad for his bullet riddled ego if he wants to claim he has been shot eight times but facts are facts and scars do not lie.

"Where you there?" Dog inquires grimly. "No, I think I would've noticed."

C.C. rolls her eyes as she leans forward placing her lips to his chest in one of the few unscathed areas and she feels his muscles jump under his skin. She finds this interesting as she begins testing other places on his bare upper torso finding his muscles jump like this all over, it is as if he is vibrating under his skin.

"Uhm, Cat, if you're just messing with me this would be the time to back up and laugh." Dog warns her because he is getting light headed and he might not be able to appreciate the joke soon.

"Not messing around." C.C. informs him as she begins to undue his belt then reaches down into his pants but she is willingly and knowingly breaking the rules because just for once she is going to do what she wants and to hell with what she should or should not do.

"Please be kind Cat." Dog mutters as he locks his knees to keep from dropping to the floor at her feet.

"I think it goes, please be gentle with me." C.C. corrects as she lets her hand roam.

"No, because that would be totally against your nature." Dog breaths or at least tries too. "I wouldn't ask you to do anything against who you are."

Chapter 13
Somewhere in Saudi Arabia...

"Has anyone ever told you, you talk too much?" C.C. replies to his blather about her true nature but he was some what correct about her lack of action or reaction in the case of her previous husbands.

"Not in the last ten years." Dog admits but no one ever complained before he was put in prison.

"I thought you said fourteen." C.C. responds thinking she just caught him in a lie and giving his privates a none to gentle squeeze because what kind of fool does he take her for.

"For being with a woman." Dog clarifies quickly before she ruptures him. "Speaking to another human being ten years."

"You were not in solitary for ten years." C.C. replies. "The proof are the two Army M.P.s walking around on this base now."

"I only met them three days before we arrived here. They were to make sure I didn't take any detours." Dog explains wondering why she would think he has known them longer. "I haven't talked or seen anyone until I was transferred here or what would be the point of locking me up to insure I don't tell anyone military secrets if I was allowed to speak to the guards who rotate in and out?"

Her mind recoils at what he is saying but she pushes this new information aside even while wondering if the Major General knew and the answer she is certain is no. She sets her mind to giving the man in her hands fourteen years worth of pleasure in one night and before long he is the one who is quiet and she is the one making all the noise.

C.C. turns in her sleep and something is poking her in the side of her face so she puts a hand under her cheek pulling out whatever it is then focuses on what she is holding finding a pink rabbit's foot. Jack knifing to a sitting position on the blanket covered floor she finds Dog is gone but he obviously found the rabbit's foot before he left, not that she hid it having only tossed it onto her bed, but he placed it on the pillow to goad her no doubt which for some reason makes her smile.

It amazes her she can smile given she may have to chalk up sleeping with him as just one more dumb decision she has made in a long line of dumb decisions, more so than she even realized given the Major Agitators character assassination based on her past failings.

Not knowing what this day will bring she dresses then straightens the living area putting everything back where it should be including pulling the spare cot from the other bed room for a couch. Looking about her it is as if Dog was never here only he was and it angers her that she will not soon forget him. When the walls feel like they are closing in on her after just a few hours she knows what he meant, her stomach growls having missed breakfast in the mess hall while he lived for years on bread and water, and she paces from the door to the couch wondering if he spoke to himself just to hear a voice as she is now tempted to do. Barely twelve hours into the twenty four of her restriction she is ready to throw open the door and run down the hallway when a knock comes to her door.

"The Colonel should reach his drop zone within the hour." Major General Aimhurst informs her grimly so now what happens next is completely up to the Colonel. "I wanted to let you know I'm going back to the Pentagon and start the ball rolling in his favor but if you need to get in touch with me just inform the M.P.s who will remain on base as they will be able to contact me without drawing undue attention."

"He can't go back to prison." C.C. responds flatly and she has no idea how he remained sane.

"I'll do everything in my power to see he doesn't." Aimhurst agrees and they established this before they share the same goal.

"No, I'm saying no matter what happens he can never go back." C.C. replies adamantly. "Your superiors left something else out of his paper work so not only was he existing on bread and water but he was in solitary confinement for ten years speaking to no one."

"Well, that would explain why he was reportedly a model prisoner." Aimhurst mutters and it is as if they wanted to make the man insane to prove what they feared would happen.

"How is this even possible?" C.C. asks angrily because what prison would follow the dictates of superiors which over rules human rights but this is beside the point now. "No matter what he can't be treated the way he has been again. Cleared or not by the military he is better off staying over seas then returning to the U.S."

"Agreed, and I'll work on a contingency plan if I should fail in getting his discharge papers." He replies grimly but he is not willing to give up yet. "I'll make sure, one way or another, he is free."

"Thank you." C.C. responds not certain what else to say or why she feels so strongly about this but he only nods before turning away walking off stiffly and obviously angry but before she closes the door she sees two base M.P.s approaching and one is carrying a tray so she opens the door wider to let them in. "Can I request mystery meat number three and substance two for lunch?"

"You know where the mess hall is so you can get it yourself." One M.P. suggests with a smile. "Major Alexander was drunk and is facing a number of charges so he's not going to see the light of day without bars for a while. Is something wrong?"

"No nothing." C.C. replies only it just hit home what else Dog might not have seen in ten years.

"He gave up trying to convince us you some how forced him into the woman's showers after we showed him the tape of his arriving and entering under his own power." The other M.P. adds so there can be no doubt what really happened.

"You have surveillance cameras on the woman's showers?" C.C. asks and apparently someone did see Egor leaving the showers despite what he believes.

"No one views them regularly and only base security has access but in matters such as this they are viewed." He explains and they are not interested in minor infractions but in a serious situation such as this they can see who comes and goes. "You are willing to press charges we assume."

"Only if it doesn't require I have to go State side to testify against him." C.C. replies or the Major Agitator will have gotten his way.

"Wouldn't that be rich." The M.P. comments knowing her leaving this base was the whole goal of the assault but it is much simpler then that as he pulls the paperwork from his inside pocket. "Your written statement will stand for you. We took the liberty of writing in what you told us so read it over and sign it then you're done with the whole deal. The medical restriction still stands until they clear you for flight but you're no longer restricted to quarters."

"Well that's something at least." C.C. mutters as she

accepts the papers and begins reading then signs but when the M.P.s leave satisfied she leaves the tray following them out. Suddenly she is not so hungry any more because if she is feeling itchy just by being made to stay in one place she cannot even begin to imagine the torment Dog felt. She heads for the Juice Bar intent on making her own contingency plan but just what that might be she has no idea.

"You look recovered." The shorter Army M.P. offers when the Captain stops at their table.

"Nice goose egg." The tall M.P. compliments admiring the bruise on her forehead. "The header you took really freaked us out."

"I honestly don't remember hitting anything." She responds so being stunned at the time seems to have had one benefit. "Thanks for the rescue."

"Part of the job Captain." The short one replies honestly and it was nice to be useful once again. "Not that we really have one here."

"So since you've seen me naked I feel I should at least know your names?" She asks as she takes a seat at their table.

"I'm Pete Harvey." The taller dark haired one introduces himself before motioning to his partner the shorter blond haired one. "Greg Mossgrow."

"Harv and Moss, or would you prefer Grove or Grover?" She replies instantly.

"Moss." He responds laughing. "You pilots and your nicknames."

"Radio conversations have to be short and in code so it's easier to use call signs and safer in some respects." C.C. explains as they nod seeming to get this. "You only met the Colonel when you brought him here, am I correct?"

"Per orders, pick up a prisoner and turn him loose here but make sure he doesn't jump ship in between." Harv agrees which was strange only it turned out to be stranger then they expected. "Seemed simple enough."

"When did begin to get complicated?" C.C. asks with interest.

"It could've been really difficult since he still had his full rank." Harv replies with a laugh and if that was not a kicker. "Most prisoners are striped of rank but not him so there we were with a full blown Colonel who could order us to remove his chains at any time and if we didn't obey a direct order we could've been facing charges for insubordination."

"Did he order you to remove them?" She asks wondering what happened on the ride here.

"No, he never did." Moss admits and was seriously relieved. "He could've had us hopping around like idiots."

"Did you notice anything else strange when you picked him up?" C.C. asks wondering if they will tell her if they did.

"Well, he squinted a lot at first." Moss comments looking to Harv for confirmation and gets a nod so goes on. "Really chatty and asking questions about basically the world in general. Things like who is the president of the U.S. now, what movies are showing, and things people know so we wondered if he was just trying to make conversation to kill time."

"Did you stop to eat along the way?" She asks knowing Dog would not have known those things with no contact with the outside world.

"No, our orders were not to stop until we met our driver to this base. We were supplied with two drivers on the longest leg who took turns driving. There where even cans of fuel in the truck and we were supplied with MREs. The Colonel's meals were packed separately." Moss explains which reminds him of another odd thing. "We assumed he would be eating much better then us but it was just bread and water so we thought he was on some kind of restricted diet because his paper work said he use to weigh three fifty something but he is a really big guy so maybe he went to fat sitting around. We offered him one of our meals but he refused."

"Probably because he knew what your orders were." C.C. replies simply as she considers what they have told her. "Which is also why he didn't ask you to remove his chains."

"He could've made our trip hell if he started throwing his rank around." Harv responds knowing they were very lucky the Colonel is a mellow type of officer.

"Did his paper work mention why he was imprisoned in the first place?" She asks to see if they were even curious.

"Not really, which is again strange and we had no idea what type of man we were dealing with." Moss replies with a frown. "They had him chained to a chair bolted to the back of a truck bed when we got there. We had know way of knowing if we were escorting a mass murder or what but we sort of got to know him on the trip here. I figure he stepped on a superiors toes or something equally minor but the payment was a little over the top if you ask me."

"What if I told you his crime was AWOL, he was imprisoned for life, but had only served ten years of it in solitary confinement existing on only bread and water for those ten years?" C.C. asks seeing their disbelief instantly and their indecision as to whether to laugh but she is not laughing so they are now curious how she intends to explain this when it should be impossible, not that they believe her. "The two of you stumbled into a classified military secret and a gross violation of human rights all at the same time."

"So you're saying he wasn't just making conversation." Harv responds as his mind goes back to what they spoke of and he cannot just laugh off what the Captain is telling them given the questions the Colonel asked them.

"That's not possible." Moss interjects but if it were possible this would explain some of the strange things they noticed.

"Now listen closely and don't repeat what I'm about to tell you but I think the two of you like the Colonel. You've both helped him in ways a little beyond what would be considered your duty to a prisoner." C.C. reminds them and for some reason she knows they are trust worthy so she is just going with it as she leans in closer to them. "Dog was imprisoned for AWOL some time after our withdrawal from Vietnam which is public record and common knowledge but not made public was his participation in a project called Steel Man, which from what I gather was a very classified black ops outfit. Of the six men in the unit five are dead leaving only the Colonel who is one of the few people left to know what Steel Man is and why five men went insane requiring elimination. Certain ranking members of the U. S. Military have been trying to kill him accidentally on purpose after capturing him and failed in starving him to death. They attempted to make his incarceration look legitimate but unimportant using a very minor infraction and using solitary confinement to keep any one from finding out what they were doing to him."

"It's just not possible." Moss comments again shaking his head and the Colonel would be dead. "He would've starved if what you're suggesting is true."

"Nope, not possible." Harv agrees and highly unlikely.

"How much weight was he bench pressing in the gym?" C.C. asks not disappointed by their skepticism because at face value they are correct as they look at each other and do not seem to know the answer. "Any normal man can't continually bench press nine hundred pounds yet he was doing it and the two of you were having trouble helping him lift the bar back to the cradle. Imagine what his maximum must be if that is what he was just working out with."

"You mentioned the bar was bending but did you see how much was on it?" Moss asks Harv who is looking equally stunned.

"One of the big ones had one hundred on it, four the same size were on each side, and I know the small one on my end was fifty." Harv replies but he did not actually read them all. "I think some of them were on the rack next to the bar but he went over to two other racks to get the others."

"Because each rack at each bench only has two one hundred pound weights." She informs them and they can check this themselves. "He had to get them to have enough and that size weight is only one hundred pounds. They were all the same size but for the ones on the ends and you saw those were fifty."

"The two of us would have never gotten the bar off of him without his help." Harv remarks and that is what a spotter is suppose to do.

"We thought it was heavy even with his help." Moss comments as he considers what he saw but did not make this connection. "It had to be nine hundred pounds and he was lifting it in sets of twenty for almost an hour."

"Intelligence, speed, and strength beyond what any normal man should have and the military called them Steel Man." C.C. informs them and just so they don't forget what else they should know. "He was trained to slide in and out of military installations, or enemy camps, like he owns them and he slipped right back onto this base with no problem. Now they intended to send him on a one way mission with very little chance of his surviving but he plans to come back."

"He could've just left here at any time." Moss comments looking at Harv. "He didn't have to go through with the mission."

"He said he gave his word." Harv reminds him and despite how he was treated the Colonel seems to be keeping it even if it could be the death of him.

"Loyalty is one of the other things they looked for in a Steel Man." C.C. adds grimly. "He has fought for his country in two wars, as of now, and in countless other arenas all over the Middle East and foreign countries but he hasn't been home in something like thirty years. They won't let him go home but that is exactly what I intend he is going to do."

"But how?" Harv asks confused because what could she possibly do.

"The Major General chose Dog for a reason that has nothing to do with this mission." C.C. admits. "His brother was a Steel Man unbeknownst to the U.S. Military and I'm guessing the only way to get Dog out of prison was by insisting he be sent on this mission which was probably deemed too dangerous and low in probability of success to make it feasible to send anyone."

"His deal with the devil." Moss mutters as he listens.

"As far as I can see the military's mistake is they continually under estimate what a Steel Man is capable of. If there is any possibility of completing this mission and returning Dog will find it." C.C. replies.

"And if he does come back we're ordered to shoot him." Harv replies grimly because now this order is beginning to make a sick sort of sense.

"What exactly did the Major General say when he gave you that order?" C.C. asks certain this is not exactly the order they were given and now she is really glad she decided to speak to them. "Was there something about his returning alone, or un-escorted, in that order?"

"Yes, but how else would he return?" Moss counters her question with his own. "They dropped him in alone if what you say is true so who would be coming back with him."

"The pick up teams the Major General has on stand by." C.C. explains and she really hopes they remember that part of their order if Dog does return, which he is going to.

"Now that makes more sense." Harv comments but there must be some reason she is telling them all of this. "What do you want from us?"

"Just eyes and ears." She replies simply because they are Army and may hear things not channeled through the Air Force. "The Major General is attempting to arrange a second mission, which Dog and his particular skill set will be needed for, so he won't be sent directly back to some military instillation when he returns. He is also working on a little public awareness not to mention getting Dog known among some of the newer leaders in

Washington and the Pentagon."

"If they need him now then they might need him again so he has to be alive." Moss comments understanding only there might be a problem. "What if they don't go for it?"

"That's when plan B takes effect which I haven't worked out all the details yet but he can't go back to where he was before or anything similar." C.C. responds seriously.

"Look, we're willing to help as much as we can." Harv replies understanding the gist of this conversation now but really there is not much they can do. "We're not career military and only entered the Army for the educational benefits. Computers are the future and we were rocking right along with our computer science and language classes until we were pulled in for this."

"It's part of the deal when we signed on and we don't want bite the hand feeding us computer courses." Moss explains to make their position clear. "We've already missed a chunk of computer advancements because we were too young to get in on the ground floor but we don't want to be too old sitting in prison or cut off from the funds to continue."

"I understand." C.C. replies and unlike her they seem to have a future planned they do not want to disrupt which is understandable. "Just let me know if you hear anything."

"We can do that." Harv agrees easily because traveling three days with a man in the back of a truck and he feels they know the Colonel fairly well. The man never once complained and even kept them amused with his wry humor about military life all the while chained to a chair and they began to admire him then. Now finding out how he has been treated yet keeping his word speaks volumes about the kind of man he is. They will help the Colonel as much as they can without disobeying a direct order.

"Well you're all so much fun." Egor comments to his flight seated at a table in the Juice Bar because now they do not have the flag game to keep them occupied and Check is reading a military manual rather than finding them something better to do.

"And our whole point of being here is to have fun." C.C. responds before rising and leaving the table.

"Was it something I said?" Egor asks those still at the table.

"The Colonel left this morning and she's still grounded." Silly replies and even he can figure out what is wrong with C.C.

"You think something was going on between the two of

them?" Egor asks now but this seems highly unlikely as Check glares at him from over his book. "What?"

What the hell is wrong with her C.C. is asking herself two days later and there has been no word from the Major General about Dog one way or the other. She was examined after her mandatory down time and cleared to fly only she still finds herself pacing her quarters or walking aimlessly around the base when not attending to her duties. She does not understand why she feels so restless and unsettled when everything should be back to the way it was before Dog arrived and less stressful with the Major Agitator gone but nothing feels normal now. She completes her night squadron runs feeling itchy under her skin and rather than tired she is still awake looking for something else to do so has taken to using the punching bag late at night.

She is in the showers four days later finding every female on base seems to have had the same idea so the outer room is crowded with women all talking in high pitched voices of excitement or some type of drama. She showers finding she is not alone in her self erected bubble of silence as Marge one of the jet mechanics and the closest woman she has ever considered a friend gives her a commiserating grimace when their eyes meet. They never seek each other out but if they should happen to meet they occasionally talk about jets, military life, and the weather as they both seem to be disinclined to socializing which instantly gave them something in common.

She has never had a woman friend as her parents disapproved of anyone she chose to call friend male or female so she does not understand why these women seem drawn to each other or insist upon talking so continually. The outer room echos with their laughter, shrieks, and as she dresses after her shower she finds a woman being consoled by others who is crying but when the outer door opens all sound trickles to a stop.

Chapter 14
Somewhere in Saudi Arabia...

The most powerful person on base is standing in the doorway and every woman comes to attention but it is not a man. Major Webster A. is the base Chief Medical officer and has the final word on all medical matters pertaining to base personnel and in some respects she out ranks even the base C.O. Pilots keep a respectful, almost fearful, distance from her as she can ground them with a single word and half the women in the shower building at this time are under her command along with all the medics and Doctors. The fact she has come personally to the shower building does not bode well for someone as no one seems to even be breathing and the woman crying her heart out moments before stands as if made of stone without daring to shed a tear or sniff.

"Captain Callahan." Major Webster calls out into the quiet except for the sound of dripping water.

"Sir, here, sir." C.C. replies stepping forward to be seen and she wonders absently which of her flight she will have to kill if the Chief Medical officer came looking for her personally.

"Are you aware the Army Colonel is back on base?" She demands to know.

"Sir, no, sir." C.C. answers honestly and now she knows whom she needs to kill and leave it to Dog to be causing her trouble once again.

"Medical personnel aboard the carrier reported him as critically injured yet he was not taken to the base hospital but directly to your quarters." The Major accuses eyeing the Captain whom she has been watching with absent interest given her status on this base as a woman combat pilot but all her possible sympathy and allegiance for this woman just went out the window. "Do I need to explain to you the difference between critical and seriously injured? Are you a qualified doctor Captain Callahan?"

"Sir, no, sir. C.C. responds feeling firmly caught and even the two questions make it clear the Major is looking for a reason to pounce on her. "Sir, I was not aware nor do I agree with his being placed in my quarters, sir."

"I hoped not." The Major responds satisfied with the Captain's response. "This serious disregard for protocol has been brought to the attention of the base C.O. and regardless of the Colonel's branch of service he is on my base and therefor under the care of my personnel not a civilian doctor."

"Sir, yes, sir." She agrees again but she has no idea what civilian doctor she is talking about.

"I expect to hear of your complaint filed with the C.O. immediately." The Major informs her and noncompliance is not an option.

"Sir, yes, sir." C.C. responds the only way she can or her feet may never leave the ground again.

"Good answer Captain." The Major replies before storming back out the door.

"Did she just infer there is a dead man in your quarters?" Marge asks to be certain as talking begins to build around them.

"If he's not then he will soon wish he were." C.C. replies as she quickly gathers her things.

"I figure you know the score." Marge comments with a frown.

"Score?" C.C. asks not certain what she is referring too.

"Men are nothing but trouble." Marge explains and she was certain the Captain knows this.

"Yeah, and the bigger they are the more trouble they are." C.C. agrees as she rushes out the door only to have her flight meeting her halfway there but she is not stopping. "What ever it is not right now."

"Reports are beginning to come in of a munitions bunker taken out by ground troops. They are claiming it was Army Rangers." Check informs her as he falls in beside her as the rest of the flight follows since she seems to be in a big hurry to go somewhere.

"Good." C.C. responds not knowing why they are telling her this as she keeps walking.

"Intel reported it was a school so they needed someone on the ground for a closer look." Check adds and it seems obvious whom that someone was but C.C. does not seem to be following along his train of thought as she says nothing. "It had to be the Colonel."

"Most likely." C.C. agrees but this is not her immediate

concern at this moment. "Apparently they brought him back badly wounded."

"Then we should head over to the hospital and see how he is." Sin suggests wondering why C.C. is heading in the opposite direction as they come to the door of her building. "We can wait for you."

"Where in lies the problem." She informs then turning to look at them as she opens the door. "They took him to my quarters and the Chief Medical officer is not happy about it."

"Why would they bring him here?" Check asks confused by this.

"He must not be badly wounded then." Pincher adds because other wise he would be in the hospital.

"That's what I intend to find out." C.C. responds to both questions as she enters her building and thankfully they do not follow. She rounds the corner finding Harv and Moss are once again positioned outside her door as she walks down the hallway.

"He doesn't look real good Captain." Moss offers upon seeing her then warns. "Major General on deck."

Forewarned C.C. steps inside her quarters closing the door then stands at attention taking in what she can see of her living area while staring straight ahead . A man wearing a white coat is bent over the cot that was her couch which Dog is now laying upon but she can smell blood even if all she can see of him around the Major General with his back to her is Dog's legs and head.

"Sir." C.C. voices so he will know she is present.

"At ease Captain. Do what you can for him doctor." Aimhurst instructs the doctor before turning to her.

As the Major General approaches he moves to stand at her side leaving her a clear view of Dog and his chest is a bloody mess causing her to swallow with difficulty because it seems the Chief is correct about the extent of his injuries. Personally she has never seen anything so horrific outside of a horror movie, or splattered on some highway, and to make matters worse the doctor is humming as his gloved hands pull what looks like the bloody remnants of Dogs clothing from his chest or it could be gauze for all she knows as she turns to face the Major General.

"Sir, I was told he was critically injured, sir." C.C. comments and presently she is not certain if he is dead or alive.

"Contrary to the rumors probably circulating the base he is not dead nor dying." Aimhurst replies grimly knowing how quickly word spreads. "I gave specific orders to the pick up teams not to attempt any form of medical treatment if he should be injured. Unfortunately my orders were disobeyed and they attempted to resuscitate him then radioed ahead a visual of his condition along with his lack of discernible pulse."

"Sir, they thought he was dead, sir."   C.C. responds understanding now where the Chief received her information. "Was he?"

"Steel Man were trained and conditioned to withstand just about anything." Aimhurst responds only she has no idea of the full extent of the project the Colonel was part of. "Increased metabolic rates, enhanced physical strength, and mental capabilities.   His blood vessels were already sealing themselves along with tissue knitting together before he even arrived here but I imagine he looked much worse when they picked him up. He has been trained to drop his heart rate to lessen blood loss and maintained a comatose state while all his physical energy is directed to healing his body. His pulse would be nearly undetectable and they used this state in certain situations so the enemy would think they were dead."

"Sir, no pulse and they reported this to the base Chief Medic whom is very emphatic I file a complaint, sir." C.C. informs him and it seems this Dog can play dead very convincingly.

"Which is exactly the type of attention I was trying to avoid." Aimhurst replies ruefully though seeing the Colonel himself he cannot blame the pickup team for reacting as they did but now he has to undo the mess they have created. "I have to find some way of down grading his condition and smoothing the waters."

"Sir, part of martial arts is meditation. Every one, or most every one, on base is aware he is a tenth degree black belt, sir" C.C. suggests but he is looking doubtful. "Sir, it's a plausible explanation and outside the medical norm so you really don't have to explain it to make it fly. When he is up and around in only a few weeks they will have to acknowledge you were correct, sir."

"Try days."   Aimhurst informs her as he considers her suggestion and he may be able to pull it off saving him from divulging classified information which he has been directly ordered not to do.

"Seriously?"   C.C. asks and in her surprise she forgets to address him proper protocol and rank.

"Doctor Hellsker here is a genetic scientist working in a

similar field and predicts the Colonel will be up and nearly healed in a matter of days. Three is his guesstimate though the doctor works more in the civilian usage of such research where this type of wound is not often found but he is the top in this field so I have to believe him." Aimhurst explains though he is having difficulty believing it himself only this brings about another problem. "The Colonel is required for a second mission and certain higher officials have taken an interest in his abilities."

"Sir, that's good news, sir." C.C. replies relieved as her back up plan was beginning to look as if she would have to fly him out herself to some foreign destination but the Major General is not looking as if his success is good news.

"He has to ship out in five days." Aimhurst responds and he is not seeing this as likely despite what the Doctor says. "This mission will be watched and vetted by more than just the military. If successful this will give him the opportunity to pick and choose basically any position he wants even beyond the military orbit. He can't be denied an honorable discharge or from returning to the states."

"Sir, what about the project issues, sir?" She asks seeing why he is concerned but there is still the problem of some fear.

"The doctor has all the samples he needs to prove not all aspects of the DNA patch used in the Steel Man project worked on the Colonel." Aimhurst responds candidly given the Captain already knows a good deal more than she should but her concern for the Colonel he feels is genuine so he continues. "By now you've guessed they were attempting to create super soldiers and one of the prerequisites included telepathic ability as they hoped to build a unit which could act as one soldier. The others all tested highly in this area but in the end I believe it destroyed their minds. The Colonel tested so low in this area they wanted to pass him over for the project but they didn't given the fact he could basically predict the others actions so closely it was almost as if he were mentally connected to them."

"Sir, you've based your entire career on an assumption, sir." C.C. comments and talk about the ultimate gamble.

"I know it may sound extreme to you but it's the only difference I could find so it must be the reason he didn't go insane years ago." Aimhurst responds with a slight smile because she is correct and his career is riding on this. "But I will go so far as to tell you there were twenty men slated for the project and only six made it into the Steel Man unit, the rest died."

"Sir, I don't even want to know how they explained that, sir" C.C. responds but dead men tell no tales comes to mind and no family to ask questions no doubt helped.. "Sir, we still have the Chief Medical officer to contend with and I must issue a formal complaint with the C.O. And to be perfectly honest, sir, I was never cut out to be a nurse, sir."

"I understand Captain and after the M.P.s help the Doctor clean him up they will be responsible for his care though really there is nothing they or you can do for him." Aimhurst assures her and he really cannot picture her as a nurse either. "I'll use your suggestion and down grade his injury as best as I can and assure the C.O. your duties won't be interrupted."

"Sir, I'll have to disagree and appear reluctant to have him back in my quarters, sir." C.C. warns or the C.O. will know something is off and his not disrupting her life again she does not want to even get into.

"I'll have to talk you into it." Aimhurst replies understanding what her position in this will have to be and this woman has a very quick and agile mind which begs the question. "What exactly did you do before joining the Air Force Captain?"

"Sir, I got married, I got divorced, and I was widowed by a magician, sir." C.C. replies giving a short synopsis. "Sir, it is what I learned from my late husband which I have found most useful as misdirection has a wide variety of uses. I seem unintentionally to be very good at it. My intention wasn't to misdirect the military as to my gender but some how I managed to do just that, sir."

"Computer generated orders and you're a combat pilot assigned to a war." Aimhurst muses and now he can see just how this misdirection happened. "An error several of your commanding officers saw yet no one bothered to correct probably because in peace time it really was of no matter until now."

"Sir, yes, sir." C.C. agrees and it seemed something of a standing joke but no one seems to laughing any longer. "Sir, should we go in to the C.O. together or separately, sir?"

"I think we should argue about it on the way over for appearance sake." Aimhurst suggests then looks towards the Doctor. "Doctor, I'll send in some help to clean and bandage him."

"There's really no need Major General." The Doctor replies with a wave of his blood smeared gloved hand. "Not to mention a waste of bandages."

"Be that as it may, Doctor, it would be better for everyone concerned if he was more presentable." Aimhurst responds with a grimace because the man is entirely too cheerful about a man being wounded then he finds seemly.

"Very well." The Doctor agrees. "It's a shame I can't stay to watch the process. Very remarkable really."

"Yes, I'm sure it is." Aimhurst replies motioning the Captain toward the door then as he steps out orders the M.P.s to assist the Doctor.

"Sir, Genetic Scientists don't seem to have much in the way of bedside manner, sir." C.C. comments as they walk down the hallway.

"Given most of his patients are lab rats I suppose it's not necessary." Aimhurst responds with a frown. "Don't worry, Captain, I've forbidden him to dissect the Colonel. As soon as this meeting is over I'll have him on the first plane out of here."

"Sir, let us hope he listens, sir." C.C. mutters not really liking leaving the man alone with Dog but the M.P.s will be there watching over him at least.

Once they reach the C.O.'s office the arguing begins in earnest and continues becoming more involved when the Chief Medical officer is also present. The C.O. appears to be listening intently to all three varying points of view involving the Colonel without comment or question until C.C. pretends to relent pertaining to the Colonel's presence in her quarters then the C.O. silences them with his decision declaring the Colonel remains where he is but he grants the Chief Medical Officer one concession by allowing her to have the Colonel visually examined by one of her doctors. Clearly not happy with the C.O.'s decision but unable to object further with no proof of the Colonel's condition until the examination is complete the Chief Medical Officer storms out.

"Captain, stand fast." The C.O. orders as the Major General follows the Chief Medical officer out of his office. He takes a moment to study his Captain who has maintained a relatively low profile while on his base with the exception of showing extraordinary skill at darts, fire arms, and a dogged inexhaustible approach to volleyball when all he has expected of her is her aerial combat skills, which she is exceptional, but since the Colonel's arrival he has noticed a change in his captain. "For an officer who recently challenged one of our top full contact fighters in the ring then faced a superior officer holding a stun gun basically ending his career in the military you gave up a little too easily when it came to the Colonel's present location. I have to wonder why."

"Sir, I've become privilege to some classified information which must remain confidential, sir. C.C. explains hoping he understands because she cannot tell him all she has learned.

"Then by all means don't enlighten me." The C.O. responds but he is concerned. "I only want to caution you to be very certain you know what you're doing."

"Sir, I'm hoping so, sir." C.C. admits because she may have made a grave tactical error and angered the Chief Medical officer by capitulating to having the Colonel in her quarters.

"All in all, if I were a betting man, my money would be riding on you." The C.O. concedes which brings them to another topic. "I am not a betting man however and the military frowns upon such endeavors which is why I suggested the flag game with your flight. It seems to have kept them thoroughly occupied but I trust your flight will find something better to do with their time if the Colonel is unable to participate."

"Sir, yes, sir." C.C. responds to the veiled warning knowing it will be the only one they receive before action is taken.

"Very well, dismissed." The C.O. replies satisfied she understands the thin ice she and her flight are skating on.

She finds her flight in the Juice Bar but before she reaches their table she is asked by several people the Colonel's condition which she chalks up to morbid curiosity at first given what has probably spread about base only their concern seems genuine as are the offers of assistance. It is apparent they are not just asking to satisfy their curiosity and by the comments made they genuinely like Dog and are concerned for his welfare. A nucleus the Major General had said and she is beginning to understand what this means by the 'good guy' and a couple of 'he's so sweet' comments made.

"So how bad is he?" Check asks when C.C. finally arrives at their table but she seems to have become popular with everyone suddenly by the many times she was stopped before reaching them.

"He'll be fine in a couple of days." C.C. responds as she takes a chair at the table.

"Well that's good news." Pincher comments relieved.

"He humiliated you twice." She reminds him and he sounds

very sincere when by all rights he should still be slightly out of joint.

"We're over it." Pincher replies shrugging it off. "When the other flights were included he told us why he did what he did."

"Really." She responds looking at them wondering when this happened and what could he possibly say to explain what he did that would make them okay with it. "So his obvious dislike for pilots was simply explained away."

"He likes us." Silly objects frowning at her. "But the game works both ways."

"Yeah, we were failing at subterfuge which is what the flag carrier is suppose to learn." Sin explains and wondering why C.C. does not get this aspect of the game. "You were the one telling us we were doing it wrong."

"We're getting better at it though." Egor adds.

"The flag game is over." C.C. responds plus they do not have the flag any more so how can they get better.

"We're still playing." Silly responds looking about the table. "I mean if the game were real we all would have been dead not tied up for everyone to see."

"One of us has our flag but we're sitting here acting normal and none of us knows who has it." Egor explains then adds "Sorry we didn't include you but the Colonel warned us if you played we would loose."

"He said you're a master at subterfuge." Sin comments and he believes it. "All this time and we didn't know you were a black belt."

"It's not quite the same thing." C.C. responds and it is not a subject that ever came up.

"I'm sure there is a lot we don't know about you or each other." Silly remarks confidently. "But that's not the point of the game."

"No, it's self awareness, conscious effort, and calm reasoning in all situations." Pincher responds listing them off as the others nod agreeing.

"You have it, we need to learn it." Egor adds.

"Well I'm so glad you all seem to have found something else to do." C.C. responds feeling like she has stepped into some alternate universe and warning them not to return to their betting habit seems unnecessary at this point. "Carry on."

Rising from the table she leaves them smiling at each but too brightly so they are only fooling themselves if they think a table full of men smiling for no apparent reason is normal.

Walking out of the Juice bar while silently disagreeing once again with the Colonel's assessment of her abilities since she has never felt self confident in her entire life and the only conscious effort she exerts is what is required just to get through a day. She will give Dog credit however because he has managed to focus her flight on something just as pointless as betting but less likely to get them into trouble with their superiors. She has tried to lead by example but her example was used to line their pockets not their minds.

When she arrives at her quarters she is for some reason carry containers of soup for a man she is not taking care of from the commissary where she stopped finding yet another letter from her brother which is unusual. Entering her quarters she finds all appears normal except Harv and Moss are seated on either side of her air conditioner unit looking a little green around the gills. She is now stuck with the two M.P.s until Dog is up and around considering them a necessary evil but not willing to let this stop her from going about her daily routine.

"I can see you're here." C.C. comments when one clears his throat as she begins undressing by the door. "And you've seen me in far less. I'll be here for a while so grab something to eat or whatever."

"Thank you Captain." Moss responds instantly as they rise but food is the last thing on their minds after what they just did and saw.

"And Harv quit staring at my ass." C.C. comments as she moves away from the door as they pass.

"I wasn't exactly." Harv admits honestly as Moss pauses to look at him as if he has lost his mind. "No disrespect intended Captain but I noticed a small birth mark or tattoo on the back of your leg which looks remarkably like the state of Florida or a gun."

"Birthmark." C.C. mutters but it strikes her as odd as they file out the door that complete strangers comment on the dark birthmark on the back of her upper thigh only none of the men she married seemed to notice at all. Dog noticed and she wonders why this occurs to her now as she approaches the cot where Dog lays while holding the letter from her brother.

Chapter 15
Somewhere in Saudi Arabia...

Staring down at Dog he looks much better than he did and only looks as if he is sleeping other than being a little pale with a white bandage wrapped around his chest. She catches herself reaching out to touch and pulls her hand back not certain what has come over her as she moves quickly to her room then seated on her cot she opens the letter to see what catastrophe has struck back home which is the only explanation she can find to explain this letter second letter so soon.

Unfolding the printed page a five by seven engraved and embossed card falls out laying face up on the cot before her. Disaster has struck as she looks at Carter's wedding invitation with entwined hearts and a myriad of flowers while the letter is full of happiness and hopeful wishes for her to attend his wedding.

Stuffing the card and letter back into the envelope C.C. feels like someone is trying to strangle her as her throat closes with tears she cannot seem to ever shed. She rises pacing her small room, three steps one way three steps back, and it is not happiness clogging her throat but anger.

The miles between her and her brother have never bothered her until now and she will not be granted leave to attend a wedding though it would be her intention to stop the wedding not wish them happy. There is no such thing as happy ever after and she does not want Carter to learn this lesson the hard way she did.

Finding her room too confining she strides out into her living area forgetting for a moment Dog is even there and if there is proof there is no justice in life he is the perfect example. The M.P.s are not back yet so storming over to the gym is not possible so she drops down next to his cot folding her legs leaning back against it as she tries to remember what her brother wrote about the woman he is soon to wed. This woman obviously has her hooks so deep into Carter he cannot even form or write a coherent sentence but she does remember something about her kids. Previously married so probably looking for a man with a steady income and who better than a lawyer but does this woman care about Carter or is he just a convenience.

She feels something brushing the back of her neck and reaches up to brush it away thinking dried sand but encounters Dog's fingers instead as his hand is resting on the cot behind her. Glancing toward his head she finds he is looking at her with dull eyes and she has the odd impression he is asking her a question as his fingers move once again. Still staring into those eyes like black bottomless holes it suddenly occurs to her he wants to know what is wrong and without second thought she tells him not holding back the pent up anger and fear she has on her brother's behalf.

"My twin brother is getting married in a couple of months." She offers hating this feeling of helplessness because there is nothing she can do about it. "A divorcee with kids from what I gather but he can't seem to focus on any details other than how wonderful she is. If love is blind then Carter is deaf, dumb, and stupid with it. She bagged herself a successful lawyer but what is he getting out of the deal other than being saddled with kids."

Dog can feel the rage rolling within her along with the fear which he concentrates on rather than his own pain. His Cat is in pain only of a different kind but as always it is leashed, contained, and poisoning her. He does not understand what barrier she created, or someone else created, that she will not cross but if she does not over come it she will continue to batter herself endlessly until she dies which is what she wants and why she is here. He can only keep pushing her as he moves his hand again knowing he is only irritating her as she moves away from his hand but if he pushes hard enough she might break through that barrier, or so he hopes.

"Stop it." C.C. orders wondering if he is even listening or cares and the answer is probably not. "He left out any pertinent information such as her age and career, if she has one, or she's a stay at home mother which will please the parents to no end but the fact she's divorced should have stopped this marriage right from the start. She must be widowed."

"We have a deal." Dog manages to say with difficulty since she is now pacing from the door to his cot.

"What deal?" She snaps and he obviously has not been listening but looking at him she realizes she can stew about her brother's wedding later. "I knew this would happen."

She grabs a bottle of water and a straw while wondering

where Harv and Moss are who are suppose to be attending him but honestly she is not so certain they can even take care of themselves. Drawing water up the straw she stops one end with her finger then inverts the straw dribbling water into his mouth by lifting her finger. She does this several times until he seems satisfied before capping the bottle of water but then he smiles.

"You're not welcome." C.C. comments as she goes to her room and when she hears Harv and Moss return she dresses quickly and heads over to the gym to punch something.

"We have a deal."

C.C. hears his soft whisper in the darkness aware Harv and Moss are sleeping on the floor by his cot when she returns from her squadron run later at night. What he means by this she has no idea because she dared him to return alive that was all but what he seems to expect in return she has no idea nor does she want to know.

"You're obviously delirious." She hisses back as she undresses by the door.

"I'm not coming back again." Dog responds and he knows this so he has to make sure she is squared away before they ship him out again.

"Don't talk like that." She whispers harshly back not wanting to hear it. "You're halfway home already."

"We had a deal." He repeats too tired to have this conversation now but they will be having it soon.

"Oh for Pete's sake." She mutters on her way to her room wondering what he thinks she promised him when she promised him nothing.

"We're not finished." Dog warns her softly as he stares up at the ceiling with a slight smile knowing she did not hear him but she will be listening soon.

"Was he blown up?" Egor asks C.C. when she joins them in the mess hall where the Colonel is still absent.

"Not to my knowledge." C.C. responds wondering why he asks and she has not asked nor heard but wounded is wounded so what does it matter.

"Shot or stabbed?" Sin asks with interest. "And if so how many times?"

"Check?" C.C. growls because she now has an idea of why

they are suddenly so interested in Dog.

"I have nothing to do with it." Check replies and the fact she thought he did really hurts. "This is all on them."

"What?" Prince responds as C.C. turns a dark look on himself, Egor, and Sin. "It's not like we're betting on if he dies or anything."

"Oh well that makes it so much better." C.C. mutters sarcastically as she looks past Check to Silly but he does not usually instigate money making deals.

"I said no." Silly informs her feeling her stare and looking back at her. "Man is down, don't matter how, and I ain't paying to find out."

"Good answer." C.C. responds with approval and some times it is surprising just how smart Silly is when his every action on the ground says other wise. "The man is down and deserves more respect then his wounds being used to line your pockets."

"Sorry C.C." Sin replies contritely though it seemed a sure deal with C.C. having the inside track.

"Did you have any takers?" She asks bluntly.

"Actually, no." Egor admits hesitantly and most everyone on base turned away from the bet.

"Which should've been your first clue." C.C. comments dryly but yet another indicator she should have done more than simply put her foot down earlier about this gambling addiction as it seems contagious. "What happened to the flag game you were all so keen on playing among yourselves?"

"Sin lost the flag." Check responds grimly.

"I didn't loose it, I miss placed it." Sin responds grimly. "I was pretending I didn't have it and forgot where I put it."

"It's suppose to be kept on you at all times." She reminds him so how could he loose it.

"I change clothes you know." Sin replies innocently but he was putting the flag someplace safer and someone found it just not any one in his flight.

Sin has clearly been cheating even if none of the others have caught on to this fact yet but she has a bigger problem and once again it is Dog. She still has no idea what deal he is talking about but she simply avoids being alone with him which Harv and Moss are unwittingly helping her do until she returns from the mess hall one evening finding Dog standing next to the cot rather than laying on it. The two M.P.s are no where in sight and other than the bandage around his chest Dog looks back to normal which only took three days as the Genetic Scientist predicted.

"What are you after?" She asks bluntly just to get this over with.

"Teaching you how to live." Dog responds just as bluntly.

"Some how I don't think you're qualified to give life lessons." C.C. responds honestly. "So far your life choices haven't worked out so well."

"As far as choices go, I have few regrets." Dog replies being completely honest because serving his country was his intention. "As far as orders go, I have issues, but I would do the same again. Without Steel Man I might not have been able to accomplish what I have or save the people I saved. Being different doesn't bother me as much as it seems to bother you. You're exceptional but you seem to be trying to hide it."

"Which would be my business not yours" C.C. responds bluntly.

"Fine." He agrees grimly seeing she is not willing to listen but she is going to hear it just the same. "I want you to go back to the states and make sure your brother is not making the biggest mistake of his life by marrying a money hungry harpy."

"Well, we don't always get what we want." C.C. informs him earnestly and he should know this if nothing else.

"Why stay here when you can't achieve your goal because of your deal with me." Dog responds attempting to reason with her. "This war is almost over so one month or two months you're going home whether you like or not and other than trying to figure out your brothers situation you don't have a clue what to do State side, do you?"

"I'll think of something." C.C. assures him but it is her worst nightmare coming true.

"May I make a suggestion?" Dog asks having let her mull this over for a moment knowing she is hitting block walls which are only partly due to her gender.

"Sure, why not." C.C. invites knowing this will be interesting if not helpful.

"Hear me out." Dog warns her but he has to sit down before he falls down so he moves back to the cot. He stifles a groan as he sits then has to catch his breath but she is still glaring at him from the doorway. "It seems to me you need ammunition people will respect without question."

"What ammunition?"   She asks surprised and does he expect her to start some kind of war.   "Ammunition for what exactly?"

"To wage the real war you've been avoiding."   Dog answers and this woman has always viewed life as a battle field only she has never fought back.   "You're a beautiful weapon but without the proper ammunition you're only being admired not respected."

"And you have this so called ammunition."   She comments still not understanding what he is referring to.

"Lots of it."   Dog admits with a slight smile.   "I did go AWOL as I stand accused.   It became obvious before my last official mission I was being set up to fail so consequently the men under me were dying.   They wanted me dead, which is fine, but I couldn't risk any more men dying because they were simply following orders and me into an ambush.   I became a mercenary then built a business using dummy corporations and even the CIA contracted me for work through a middle man.   Basically I was doing the same work I did for the military without having to worry about the men with me walking into a death trap because of me."

"So what went wrong?"   C.C. asks because something did or they never would have caught him.

"Greed is a horrible task master."   Dog mutters almost absently and a sad fact as he continues.   "I underestimated how badly the military wanted me dead but I should have known by the number of men they were willing to sacrifice in their previous attempts.   They put an international bounty out for me and it was more than my go between could resist."

"Scumbag pig."   C.C. mutters because this is exactly when his ten years of hell began.

"I've had ten years to come up with much more creative names than that."   Dog manages to grin at her.   "The point is I have money which is the ammunition you need to gain some of the respect your physical presence does not."

"Money doesn't buy respect."   C.C. counters because she has seen this for herself.

"But it does make people pause and consider."   Dog replies which is all she needs so they take a second look and realize they should be stepping more carefully.   "I met a soldier in Vietnam by the name of Malinowski who claimed once he went back home he was joining his families banking and financing empire without one more complaint about how boring it is. He volunteered for the Army to escape what he considered to be a fate worse than death and found out other wise. I signed the paper work and turned over most of my pay packets to him before I was shipped else where. When I went AWOL I contacted him because I was cut off from my regular pay."

"And he didn't have it?" She guesses because who trusts a man they just met in war then hands him all of his money.

"Of course he did." Dog replies stunned she would think other wise. "He not only had my money but he invested it and made more. He gave me the information to tap into one of my accounts in Switzerland and I sent him every thing else I made on those mercenary jobs through foreign banks. He is one of three brothers and he wanted to go into the banking and investment business on his own so he did, with my money. He tripled what I gave him and not only do I have accounts in the states under dummy corporations but accounts in banks all over the world."

"Have you contacted him since you've been here?" C.C. asks because Dog might not have any money if the guy assumed he was dead for the last ten years.

"That's one of the reasons I had to leave base." He admits as he grins at her because she is sharp if suspicious of just about everyone. "And no he didn't take it. He's made his own money from my money but if something does happen to me the money will likely be taken by what ever banks it is in because he won't touch it. He checks on it making sure the accounts are considered active and shuffles it around to keep it this way. He apologized for a bank employee in the states managing to get most of one of my accounts and several other peoples money before being discovered. I have no clue how much it was nor do I really care but he had gone through all the legal paperwork to get it back as if it were my last dollar. He takes money in his charge very seriously."

"Apparently." C.C. mutters wondering what this has to do with anything as she waits for him to continue.

"Just follow the money Cat." He instructs her with a smile. "Do whatever you want with it but it's the ammunition you need and it could be used to pay off gold digging harpies. Buy a plane or a whole airfield of planes, and basically live your life by your own rules because you won't be considered different just eccentric with the kind of money I'm talking about. You could even buy a magical statue for husband three or an angel for his grave."

"Magic dragon." C.C. corrects because this shows how little he knows but this is only a fairy tale after all. "So you're just going to sign all your money over to me is that it? Some kind of bandage to fix everything wrong with my life."

"Three days Cat." Dog reminds her simply and why not but it is what it will do for her he is most interested in. "I'm not going to be ready and I would rather give it to you because I know you'll do something with it. But I can't just sign it over to you without serious legal maneuvering so the easiest way for you to gain access is to marry me."

"No." C.C. replies flat out, not again, and she does not even need to think about it.

"Okay, Ouch." Dog comments watching her expecting her response but he did not expect it to hurt quite so much. "Think about it."

"Nothing to think about." C.C. responds because this is so not going to happen. "You're going to live then I'll be stuck married to you."

"Would that be so bad?" Dog asks wanting to know how bad she thinks it would be.

"I'm not cut out to be a wife." C.C. replies simply as she moves toward her room because she has a trail of failed marriages to prove it. "With your money you can almost marry anyone you want."

"What I want and need is a good pilot because if I come back I have a business to run." He informs her frankly and he knew this would catch her interest as she pauses. "I lost my last negotiator slash go between when he cashed in on selling me out and he also helped me handle a lot details and acted as my second in command."

"Okay." C.C. replies intrigued as she turns back toward him because this is the possibility of a job which would allow her to make use of her training. "Hire me."

"No." Dog responds adamantly. "I'm not sleeping with women I pay any more. There is no way I can work with you and not sleep with you."

"Great, just great." C.C. mutters throwing up her hands knowing she would end up regretting sleeping with him. "Sex just gets in the way of everything. If I hadn't jumped in bed with you we could have worked together."

"We still can. I don't see what one has to do with the other."

Dog replies grimly. "I wasn't looking for a wife but marriage is the easiest legal way for you to access my money which you're going to need because you know all the little details of what we are going to need if I come back."

"When you come back." C.C. corrects him dryly.

"Fine, when." Dog grumbles wondering if it would have made a difference if he got down on one knee but he instantly envisions her laying him out on the floor with one kick to the head and he cannot help but grin.

"What?" She asks because she knows he just thought of something he finds amusing.

"You can always kill me later." Dog reminds her.

"With what, a bazooka?" C.C. asks because if three armies, and who knows who else, cannot do the job then what chance is there she can do it.

"We could use some rocket launchers." Dog admits. "Need rifles and ammo for my guys, if they're still alive. Might want to start buying this stuff up."

"Sure, I'll just go to the local supper market and stock up." C.C. hisses at him and he knows she cannot just buy stuff like that. "Then I'll put it all in the kitchen cabinets of our little house in the suburbs. Talk about la la land."

"Well, probably not on U.S soil, find us an island or something." Dog suggests then realizes she is just being snarky. "I know, a wife's work is never done."

"This wouldn't be a marriage, it would be a mercenary's retreat." C.C. informs him just picturing what kind of house they would have with loaded weapons hidden all over the place and an armory in the basement. No, the shooting range should be in the basement, the armory should go on the first floor then she grabs her head with both hands. "Gees now you've got me doing it."

"You can see it can't you. Make sure the island is big enough for a runway." Dog reminds her with a smile. "Our marriage will be whatever we want it to be and I want us to be partners, lovers, and friends, if somewhat reluctantly on your side. I trust you with my life Cat and maybe some day you'll trust me with yours. Until then you're financially set to walk away from me any time you want."

"After all this I would think you would want to live in the States." C.C. informs him which is the whole point of going home but she has no idea where to find an island in the U.S. big enough for what he wants and why is she even thinking about it.

"We can live there or anywhere else in the world we want but we need a base of operations and it can be any where." Dog explains but he can see she is giving this some thought which is enough for him. Mission accomplished he feels as he slowly and carefully lays down on the cot aware she is still staring at him but he is tired.

And just like that the man falls instantly asleep as if he did not just mentally hand her a grenade without a pin. Throwing herself onto her cot she tries to ignore all the memories just the word 'marriage' invokes but the job aspect does intrigue her so she concentrates on that instead.

Money has never impressed her though she knows it impresses some people and husband number four taught her that some assholes with money just become bigger assholes but there is one aspect of having money she did like. Large sums do tend to keep people at a distance and acts as an insulator.

Objectively she worked well with husband number three which was no hardship and she was just window dressing to his act. She could very well end up nothing more than a shuttle pilot with Dog but where she believes they will be flying in and out of will give her ample opportunity to use her skills. Only what she has learned from her previous marriages is what was good before marriage suddenly becomes bad for Carter she is willing to take the chance.

Chapter 16
Somewhere in the U.S. of A...

"Yes, I'll marry you." C.C. informs Dog as she passes to the door to dress knowing he is awake and it seems he has dismissed his nurses since the M.P.s have not returned.

"Are you sure?" Dog asks having given what he said some thought as he rises slowly from the cot and approaches her.

"What?" She replies looking up at him in disbelief. "Now you want me to reconsider?"

"I backed you into corner." Dog informs her which was not his intention. "It's not either me and the money or nothing so I'll find out what I need to write up to transfer the money to you."

"Marriage will be easier." C.C. admits and he was correct. She finishes buttoning her shirt then looking up finds him frowning at her which is probably a look she better get use to seeing the rest of her life, or his. Moving on impulse she reaches up framing his face with her hands and he leans slightly back causing her to smile. "This way if you change your mind you can't just take the money back and if you annoy me too much, I can kill you leaving me a rich widow."

"I always keep my word." Dog informs her.

"I know, and that's part of the reason I said yes." C.C. admits and it's the only thing she can count on at this point. "Bend down just a little."

"You'll need to clear permission with your C.O." Dog begins after she kisses him and maybe his brain cells did just fly out the window as she stares at him. "Which you already know."

"Count to ten before you speak." C.C. suggests helpfully as she turns going out the door.

"Keep kissing me like that I won't remember how to count." Dog mutters to himself as he moves back to the cot knowing he needs to tread more carefully. It is definitely too soon to tell her he loves her.

If she is going to do this, and she cannot believe she is

getting married again, she decides it is better to just get it over with much like pulling off a bandage. She enters the command office and is directed into the C.O.'s office wondering just how much explaining she will have to do when she presents her request.

"At ease Captain." The C.O. grants motioning her to a chair. "I was planning to call you in so you've saved me the time. Night Hawks are going on standby only as of o three hundred tomorrow, Eagles will follow two days after, and the whole base will be on stand by for an indefinite time."

"Sir, we knew this was coming, sir." C.C. replies and it means the war is nearly over.

"I've been directly ordered to send one flight back state side next week." He continues grimly knowing he probably does not have to spell it out for her.

"Sir, my flight is being reassigned, sir." She guesses and the air force is finally ordering her home with no concern now of her claiming discrimination because more than her flight will be leaving.

"That's the gist of it, Captain." He agrees not happy about it because a decorated Captain deserves better than being tossed off before the final solution.

"Sir, I've done my duty here sir so there's little left for me to do but sit around and wait, sir." She responds and the writing was more than on the wall. "Sir, the place really doesn't matter now, sir."

"I realize your enlistment will be up in a matter of months." He comments grimly and he fears she will not reenlist. "I'm hoping what has happened here hasn't clouded your judgment of the Air Force."

"Sir, no, sir." C.C. replies honestly but it is clear no matter what branch she is in she might be waiting for years to be taken truly as an equal. "Sir, I've been offered another position, sir."

"The Navy." He remarks grimly and he is not overly surprised.

"Sir, no, sir." She admits but understands why he may think so. "Sir, nothing would really change if I went with Navy so I'm not reenlisting. I'll be working for a business in the private sector which I'm hoping will allow me to use what I've learned from the Air Force and Navy to its full potential, sir."

"Well it's our loss but I wish you the best of luck Captain." The C.O. responds honestly hoping she will not be disappointed and even in the private sector she may find difficulties. "I assume you came to see me for another reason."

"Sir, I have a rather strange request, sir." C.C. admits and when he folds his hands on his desk she knows he is listening. "Sir, the army Colonel and I are not in the same branch of the military so I need to know if a joint venture between us would violate any regulations?"

"A joint venture?" The C.O. begins then realizes what she is asking. "Marriage?" When she nods he gathers for the first time ever he is seeing this captain embarrassed so he continues by answering her question. "There's nothing against it. All that's required is permission from both commanding officers but as with marriage in the states, marriage in the military is legal and binding in any court."

"Sir, I am aware, sir." She responds and she knows just what it means all too well but Dog is correct, it is the simplest way to achieve what needs to be done.

"Very well." He replies since her mind seems to be made up as he considers what needs to be done which really is not much of anything. "I'll grant my permission. Once his commanding officer does I can preform the ceremony or the clergy can. I believe he's Methodist this month."

"Sir, I was hoping we could just sign the paperwork. I'm not sentimental, sir." C.C. responds as the word ceremony gives her a bad feeling about this.

"There is a process to these things Captain. There must be witnesses and words spoken." He informs her and sentimental or not this will be done correctly or not at all. "Only two witnesses are required but it should be a cause for celebration."

"Sir, yes, sir." She agrees and so much for just signing her name on the bottom line

"You know, upon further consideration Captain this would present an excellent opportunity for a base celebration." The C.O. comments as he has a sudden inspiration. "This war isn't officially over yet so a victory celebration would be rather presumptuous and as of next week your flight along with more will be returning state side. This presents the perfect opportunity for a celebration while everyone is still on base."

"Sir?" C.C. asks afraid she heard him correctly and their wedding has suddenly progressed from two witnesses and a clergyman to the whole base in a matter of seconds. "Sir, the Colonel leaves in three days, sir."

"I think I can get cake by then." He counters this obstacle as his idea is continuing to form. "Mess hall two days from now and if you wouldn't mind I'd like to give the bride away. Perfect practice for when my own daughters do the march."

"Sir, that would be fine, sir." C.C. responds helplessly.

"You'll have to come up with a bridesmaid and a best man." The C.O. instructs as he sits back liking this idea more and more.

"Sir, yes, sir." C.C. replies unable to do anything else at this point but agree.

"Good, good, dismissed Captain." He bids pleased to have this all arranged.

She exits the C.O.'s office closing the door behind her and walks slowly out of the building not nearly as happy about this turn of events as her C.O. seems to be. It all seemed simple enough when she walked in but now she has to find a bridesmaid and where is Dog going to find a best man. This will not be a normal wedding so she is at liberty to chose an unconventional bridesmaid she decides and she has six while Dog is stuck with Harv and Moss which should work out fine she supposes as she returns to her quarters informing Dog of their wedding ceremony.

"It won't be so bad." Dog responds though he knows she has grave doubts. "Once the ceremony is over no one will be giving us a second thought once the real party starts."

"Well there is that." C.C. agrees only she was counting on quick and over with.

"I'll speak with the Major General. If Falcon were still around he would've stood with me so his brother can stand for him. I'll ask the M.P.s as well. You grab your flight and if they don't feel it's dignified to be bridesmaids tell them I'll shave their legs and stuff them in dresses." Dog suggests with a slight smile.

"And I would be tempted to help you." She responds because they owe her at least this much.

"That's the spirit." Dog remarks knowing she will get the hang of going her own way soon enough.

The two days pass in a surreal haze for C.C. as word has spread through the American and Allied flights stationed through out the base causing her to be congratulated right and left on what she is still not certain is the fifth biggest mistake of her life. Worse Dog has disappeared and she wonders if he had cold feet because she is certain he is no where on base since his M.P.'s are clueless this time. Her flight agrees to stand up with her no threat required and all preparations seem to be going as planned, or so she hopes.

Before the wedding and while wondering if Dog plans to attend his own wedding she is doing some preliminary packing since she will be leaving shortly after the wedding. The whole base is now aware of the standby status to come and she is contemplating her return to the states and civilian life with less jubilation than others.

"Such dark thoughts on our wedding day." Dog accuses while standing in the doorway to her room finding her frowning down into her trunk.

"Just planning ahead." C.C. replies turning to find he looks perfectly fine now after his ordeal and she supposes she will have to get use to him just appearing behind her.

"Incorporate this into your plans." He suggests holding out a file folder to her.

"Orders, sir." She remarks dryly as she takes the folder glancing from it to him as he smiles at her.

"I know better than that." Dog responds leaning against the door frame more tired than he should be and not ready for this mission but he is shipping out first thing in the morning regardless. "The papers I signed are inside and the address you need to find Malinowski. Once he sees my letter along with a copy of our marriage certificate he can take orders from you or you can have him turn everything over to you."

"I'm not cleaning out your bank accounts." She informs him bluntly. "You'll need money once you hit State side."

"Just as long as you have unlimited, and unquestioned, access I don't care what you do with it." Dog reminds her because he might not be alive to spend any of it.

"I'll make sure." She confirms as she puts the file folder in one of her packed bags. "You went for a desert stroll again, didn't you?"

"It was tough getting back on base." He admits as he warns her. "You may want to consider the possibility I'm not coming back."

"You'll be back and state side soon."   C.C. informs him confidently as she pulls the pink rabbit's foot from her pocket. "You still have this mission to accomplish yet."

"If I come back I won't be coming back for that pink scrap of fur." Dog mutters as he reaches for her pulling her in close then turning to pin her up against the wall as most discussions with this woman will have to be held this way for safety sake. "I'll be coming for my wife."

"Not even married yet and we've moved to threats already." She comments but she thinks she knows him well enough by now to know the rabbits foot objective being incomplete will dig at him like a splinter in the back of his mind.

"I have something for you." He responds reaching into his pocket keeping an eye on her as cats are notoriously unpredictable.

C.C. watches as he reveals a gold ring but it is nothing like she has ever seen before and about the size of a man's class ring glittering with jewels sparkling in the over head light. He places it in her hand but she has to move the ring out of direct light to even see it clearly. It is a gold jet circled nose to tail with engraved detail to form the ring but there is a snarling cat's head above the cockpit.

The cat's eyes are green stones possibly emeralds and the cat's face is carved in great detail so even the fangs are clear to see. Reaching out from near the cat's chin is a paw with pointed opals for claws leaving jagged rake marks in the jet as if grasping it. Even the cockpit shield is a gem of some kind so smooth and clear it looks as if it is lit from inside while the after burners just below the cockpit have red stones like rubies.

If all the stones are real then this is one costly ring but it is the detail which holds her spell bound because the craftsmanship is incredible.

"An extraordinary woman deserves no ordinary ring." He informs her as he takes the ring and places it on her finger smiling with satisfaction when it fits her perfectly.

"I didn't get a ring for you. I though we would skip that part of the ceremony." She comments still stunned and a little uncertain how to respond because he did not just pick this up off the shelf at any jewelers.

"Leave the rings out." He responds since he has no need for a reminder he is married. "Buy me something later if you like. I terrorized three artists to have this made for you so when you look at it you'll remember I know what's important to you."

"Not gold and jewels." She mutters if this is what he thinks.

"That's not what you see when you look at this ring." He responds with certainty. "You don't even care what the jewels are or how much it's worth. This is what's in your heart."

"Jets, maybe." She admits because she is not certain now how she survived without flying before she joined the Air Force but she is not too certain about the snarling cat. "I've never snarled at anyone in my life."

"You snarl at everyone and before long I'm hoping you make sure everyone notices." Dog informs her and he is certain she will find her way before long. "You're a very perceptive woman but you ignore what you feel and pretend you don't see. That's about to change because you won't be able to hide anymore and everyone is going to notice the real you."

"I suppose you believe everything you read in fortune cookies as well." C.C. responds feeling uncomfortable under his direct gaze.

"Soldiers of fortune don't need cookies and neither do you." Dog comments pushing her comfort zone and the rest will be up to her.

"We need to get changed." She responds because they are suppose to be getting married in a very short time but he does not move, or let her go, which is when she realizes he is debating whether to kiss her or not. She is not certain how she knows this, she just does. "Are you going to kiss me or not?"

"I'd like too." He admits honestly. "I'm just trying to figure out if I need an escape route before you try to kick the shit out of me for taking liberties."

"You just gave me the most incredible ring I've ever seen. No one has ever given me something so thoughtful in my entire life." C.C. informs him knowing he went to a great deal of trouble to have this made not to mention risked death. "You can steal a kiss for this without worrying about collateral damage."

"Duly noted." Dog replies not needing to be told twice as he leans down kissing her until his head begins to swim so he backs off slightly. "What would I get if I bought you a jet?"

"A swift kick. I'll be buying my own jet." She warns while leaning against the wall for fear of falling to a puddle at his feet but they have things to do. "We have to get into dress uniforms."

"I was thinking more along the line of getting you out of your clothes." He admits wondering if he can change her mind.

"We're getting married today, almost right now." She replies since he seems to have lost track of time.

"Good." He comments staring at her a moment longer as he releases her slipping quickly out the door.

She takes a moment collect herself before stepping away from the wall while glancing down at her hand and the unfamiliar weight there. She has never seen herself as he seems to and she does not understand what he means by ignoring her feelings, she feels things very strongly and sometimes it is all she can do to contain them, but she knows for fact she is not blind as he implied. With a frown she begins changing for her wedding to the very large dogmatic man in the other room.

They arrive together at the packed mess hall which has been converted into a not very similar church bower by throwing white sheets over the serving counters but effort was put into making decorations consisting mostly of whatever could be found on base including blown up rubber medical gloves for balloons. One empty table contains the C.O.'s promised cake though not tiered like a wedding cake usually is but someone did do some fancy flower icing work on it and the C.O. himself frowns upon seeing what she is wearing when he stands by the door waiting to escort her through the crowded tables to the other end.

He surely has to realize the only formal clothing she has here is her dress uniform so if he was expecting to see her in a dress he was doomed to be disappointed. Also given the mistake in her enlistment paper work she was never issued a women officers dress uniform which includes a skirt but the C.O. holds his peace and walks her to the minister standing before Dog with his groomsmen and Check on the other side of the open space with her flight. The ceremony is short just as she had hoped it would be as 'I do's' are exchanged and the kiss at the end releases everyone from their respectful silence as the mess hall erupts with cheers.

"Stand fast." The C.O. orders the wedding party. "Move in closer together. You need a picture."

She does not dare argue this point as they move in closely as a camera is produced and a picture taken then they are motioned toward the cake table but not for the cake cutting as this is being done for them as the sheets are removed from the serving stations revealing the C.O. out did himself in the cake baking area.

Music erupts from some where as the real celebration begins as C.C. and Dog are being loudly regaled by the married members of her flight about married life as they eat their cake and not all the sparkling frosting is sugar because it obviously had to be carried in so some of the sparkle is most likely sand.

The celebration is loud and pounding with so many crowed into the mess hall at once and talking among their little group becomes nearly impossible as members of her flight drift off along with Harv and Moss. The Major General leans in to speak with Dog then he to rises and leaves. Dog rises and holds out his hand to her but she is fairly certain he does not intend they dance as she takes his hand and she is correct when he heads for the door with people parting before him as if he were Moses. Once outside C.C. finds there is a residual humming in her ears from all the previous noise as they cross the deserted parade ground back to their quarters.

"Impressive." C.C. comments later while looking at the deep red marks from his injuries on his chest but they have healed over as she runs a hand over them only he flinches slightly. "Still tender?"

"Not healed." Dog informs her as he takes her hand and kisses her fingers. "Not ready."

"You look ready to me." She replies with a straight face after glancing down his prone body.

"For you always." He grumbles then rolls with her under him enjoying just being near her softness.

"You'll be State side soon." She responds seriously as she looks up at him. "I know it."

"How?" He asks when he is not so certain himself.

"Because I didn't really want another husband but if I'm going to be stuck with one then it's going to have to be you which means you're stuck with me too. Death is not going to let either of us off so easy." She explains simply

"If you're inferring I'm doomed to married life then I can't think of anyone I would rather be doomed with." He responds but if she is thinking their marriage will be boring and routine then she really needs to reevaluate.

C.C. wakes the next morning alone and once again it is as if Dog was never here but lying on the pillow beside her is the pink rabbits foot making her smile. Looking at the ring he gave her a plan begins to form then four days after Dog's deployment she and her flight are shipped back to the states and what awaits her there is totally unexpected.

Their arrival in the states is an unheralded event given the war is not over but her flight is granted two weeks leave only she is not.   Her orders are to report to the barracks officer for reassignment of her living quarters where she discovers the Air Force has corrected their mistake and she is assigned to a female building, to a female flight, but this is not what angers her. It is when the Sergeant in charge informs her she along with her new flight will begin combat flight training and she realizes her record was not just reclassified but purged of her previous combat training. They allowed her to keep her rank yet have erased her combat status and flight experience, not just during the war, but previous to it.

She stands in her assigned barracks having set her pack down on one of the beds and slowly begins to unpack as she considers her options. Fighting the Air Force would be difficult and time consuming not to mention they would deny everything except possibly portions of her past training and blame clerical error but is this really worth. It seems obvious she has gone as far as she can as a pilot in this man's military and as she pulls out the folder Dog gave her she opens the folder finding the photo of their wedding along with their marriage certificate.

Everything she brought back has been looked through for things illegal or not to be brought into the states like souvenirs that never should have left the country they just returned from.   Their wedding photo apparently did not pass muster. it is still a photo or a copy of the original showing her flight, the Major General, and the two M.P.s but the couple standing in the center under the hanging base pendant are nothing more than dark spots. The military has effectively erased both of them.

Rage nearly consumes her but not because they ruined her wedding picture and tangible proof she served her country in a war. No most upsetting is they have erased all trace of Dog for the second time and he is at this very moment fighting for his country while the military is still denying his existence which is more than she can tolerate. Digging through her pack she finds what she is looking for then repacking her things she heads to the base office and standing before an office clerk she signs where instructed before witnesses effectively ending her career in the Air Force.

Chapter 16
Somewhere in the U.S. of A...

Seated on a commercial plane she is plagued by this weird feeling of displacement possibly because she is not flying the plane and surrounded by people she does not have to salute or 'sir'. Everyone seems more colorful while she is still wearing her desert fatigues and combat boots with only a tan tee shirt which is all she owns. She has garnered some curious looks and a few have asked if she is in the military and when she responds not anymore they move on not sure how to respond except to thank her for her service.

Even stranger is the fact she misses her flight and she has not been asked her opinion on some idiotic or irrelevant issue nor heard a graphic description of a good looking woman in days now. This was so much a part of her every day life she almost expects the guy seated on her left at any moment to graphically describe the stewardess he is so obviously trying to charm every time she walks by.

She has this surreal feeling of being totally disconnected from the people around her and the news pertaining to the war is on every form of media known to man in the airport terminals which only heightens this feeling. She was right in the middle of it a short time ago and knew how many SCUD missiles were found because she is one of the pilots who located them but now she is just another civilian out of the real loop.

She walks off the plane into the airport terminal where people are moving purposely about their daily lives either traveling for business or pleasure while carrying her back pack with clothing consisting of exactly what she is currently wearing. She is not the only one dressed this way as soldiers in ABUs from all branches of the military are entering the terminal from other planes and being greeted by enthusiastic family but surprisingly she is hailed by a man in an Air Force uniform. She gives a nod to Jarvis one of the Night Hawk pilots who rotated out before Dog appeared on base and surprisingly he leaves his obviously adoring family to lope across the space to her then throws a salute.

"I mustered out so you don't have to salute me." C.C. informs him seriously.

"You're kidding right." Jarvis responds stunned by this news as his family has followed him looking expectantly between them. "You didn't let that Major win did you?"

"No, we all went on standby and I was in the way." She responds knowing he will understand why.

"I think they made a big mistake letting walk away." Jarvis offers grimly as he glances around. "Are you meeting family here?"

"Business. I married an Army Ranger and I've come to the big apple to over see some of his affairs while I'm waiting for him to return from deployment." C.C. explains.

"You're husband is over there on the ground now?" Jarvis asks shocked by this and surely she has seen the news. "It's hot and heavy in some places over there C.C. We took out what we could from the air but the ground is still full of rocks and hard places."

"I'm not worried." She responds though a normal wife probably would be it occurs to her now but really she is certain he will return. "He can handle the fighting."

"Do you have a place to stay?" Jarvis asks suddenly concerned as his fiance is clutching his arm while his parents are standing with them and it does not seem right she should be here alone.

"I probably won't be staying long." C.C. admits because once she sees this man with Dog's money she has no reason to stay but Jarvis is looking concerned and she smiles. "If I can practically fly a ton of steel through the eye of a needle I think I can find my way around New York, alone."

"True." Jarvis agrees and just that easily seeing her in this setting he forgot her looks are deceiving. "Keep in touch and you know where to find us."

"That I do." C.C. admits but she does not mention the place because she is certain the girl on his arm would not appreciate knowing it is a strip club where most male pilots hang out off duty and she watches them leave feeling better because she was getting a little disorientated for a moment. She has gone head to head with some of the best pilots in the military holding her own, and then some, so why is she letting all this strangeness get to her.

Checking the blue face of her gold watch presented to her

by the Navy when she completed her Top Gun training she finds it is after thirteen hundred hours so she needs to keep moving. Reaching the main doors she flags one of the many cabs waiting at the curb and after hearing all about the sights to be seen in New York she is dropped off before one of the massive skyscrapers.

Entering she finds marble floors, glass and chrome furniture with over sized real leather couches while everyone she passes is either wearing a suit and tie, or a skirt and heels as the security guards gives her the once over. She should probably be feeling out of place crossing the opulent lobby but this is not her concern at the moment nor has it ever really been her concern.

She wonders why she has always given in to how people expect other people to dress in places like this as she scans the glass enclosed directory near the elevators. Malinowski is on the top floor so she enters an elevator going up only to exit into an equally plush outer office maned by a woman who wears a tailored dress like battle armor and is neither young nor old as she gives C.C. a quick glance but does not look impressed.

"May I help you?" She asks in a bored nasal voice.

"I need to speak with Mr. Malinowski." C.C. requests standing before the woman's desk being judged and found wanting.

"Do you have an appointment?" She inquires skeptically.

"No, but I believe he has been expecting me." C.C. informs the woman who looks grim. "Captain Carolyn Callahan."

"One moment please." She replies pointing to the waiting area as she tries to process this name but not finding it familiar.

C.C. crosses to the little waiting area finding a painting with a plaque reading Founder and CEO of Banking International Financial Corp. Benjamin Malinowski hanging above the seats. The painting is of a man she guesses to be in his early fifties or possibly older having a ring of gray hair around his other wise bald dome. He is smiling in a friendly way from the painting down upon her but she pictured the man who cold bloodily asked for Dog's money since he would never be around long enough to spend it to look more sinister.

She may not have a clear picture of what exactly took place years ago but she cannot picture this investor giving his sales pitch any other way.

"Mr. Malinowski will see you now." The secretary informs her voicing her disapproval with the pinched expression.

C.C. enters the inner office finding it as plush as everything else in the building and apparently people feel safer giving their money into the hands of someone who looks like they have plenty of it themselves. The slim man who approaches her halfway to the desk is smiling much the same as he did posing for the painting only it must have been some years before as the half halo of hair is nearly non existent now.

There is nothing about this man approaching her with hand extended which speaks of opportunistic as he wears a modest, though no doubt expensive suit, but she cannot shake the feeling something is not right here.

"Captain Callahan." He greets as he reaches her.

His apparent delight at meeting her seems genuine but for some reason C.C. cannot bring herself to offer her hand in return so instead she off shoulders her backpack and pulls the file folder from it holding it out to his reaching hand.

This action in no way dims his smile as he quickly takes the file back to his desk where he sits motioning her to the chair across from it. She sits on the edge not certain what she is expecting to happen from a benevolent looking man and normally she would ignore this uneasy feeling but this is Dog's future at stake.

"To be frank with you, my dear." Ben begins as he looks through the folder some what curious about this woman before him. "I never expected Dog to do anything so conventional as to marry."

"I'm not any ones 'dear'." C.C. corrects instantly this man who looks like someone's kindly grandfather but she has disliked him since Dog mentioned him so maybe her preconceived opinion is clouding her better judgment. "And marriage is not entirely conventional, just a state of being."

"Interesting concept and forgive my informal address Captain but you remind me of my granddaughter Rose. She's small in stature like yourself." He replies apologetically. "She also defies convention by insisting upon wearing clothing inappropriate for her gender."

This homely is delivered by a man whom is still smiling benevolently at her while delivering a very thinly veiled insult to both her and his granddaughter. He is obviously judgmental basing his assumptions on institutions like marriage and clothing but she lets this slid because this meeting is not about her.

"Everything seems to be in order." Ben comments lookingthrough the documents as he pulls his paperwork to him which requires her signature but before he offers them to her he wants to be certain he is not making a mistake. "It must be a very interesting story how the two of you met. I take it you were stationed over seas while involved with the Air Force and I suppose his money was very tempting if you had to resort to joining a branch of the military to support yourself."

"Is everything in order to transfer Dog's money?" She asks bluntly not rising to his bait if this is his game and he will find he can insult her all he wants just as long as Dog receives what belongs to him.

"Perhaps it would be best if I continue to over see his investments." Ben suggests not that he is concerned with her loosing it all which is most likely to happen but it is a nice nest egg should he ever need it again. "Some how I don't think you have what is required to maintain his accounts given he will not be needing the money and a wise woman would seek help when necessary."

"That was your last free shot." C.C. warns him as she smiles just as benevolently back at him as if they are friends discussing the weather. "Insult me again and I'll be signing the paperwork in your blood."

"Of course." Ben responds and he should have considered. "A female soldier of fortune then. My what the world is coming too."

"Oh it hasn't changed much when a greedy man convinces a fellow soldier to sign over everything he owns." C.C. replies still smiling. "You must have really been sweating bullets when he survived the war."

"I take my responsibilities very seriously." Ben responds.

"Then you gambled all Dog's money on this little empire you've built for yourself." C.C. counters because it was a gamble. "Now show me where to sign, or better yet, just give me the paperwork so we can both go about our day without blood shed."

"All the account numbers and locations are in this file along with the amount each account holds." Ben replies and he cannot agree more as he finds this woman unsavory. "You are now a very wealthy woman, Captain, but you knew that when you married a condemned man."

"Not condemned and soon to be pardoned." She replies as she takes both folders from his desk and puts them safely in her backpack as she rises to leave.

"What?" Ben mutters rising quickly. "You can't be serious."

"I'm very serious." C.C. reminds him but something about his uneasiness makes her wonder. "I'm hoping you didn't do anything stupid like move the accounts so I can't access them."

"That, no, I don't care about the money." Ben admits and really he does not but what kind of pardon is she talking about. "Dog can't be set loose and he can never return to this country."

"Well thankfully that decision isn't up to you." She offers as she shoulders the backpack preparing to leave.

"I did my duty to ensure he would never be allowed to come back to this country." Ben admits wondering what went wrong.

"So it was you." C.C. comments as she turns from the door to stare at the once kindly looking man who is now sitting looking slack jawed and realizes she understood his correctly. This is the man who sent Dog to prison to be put in isolation and starved. "You sentenced him to hell. The man who gave you everything you now have. Even real dogs know better than to bite the hand that feeds them. Why would you do that to him?"

"I had to." Ben replies but maybe this woman does not know what she married. "He's little better than an animal. He's insane, they all were, and they killed innocent people. How could they possibly consider pardoning him?"

"Because he didn't do any of that." C.C. responds easily. "Dog was unjustly sentenced for a crime he had yet to commit, on the grounds the others in his unit did, and you handed him over to them."

"I had no choice." Ben replies and he would do exactly the same again but they could not possibly be thinking of letting him go. "He'll come here to our homes in this country and kill people who have done nothing."

"He did nothing." C.C. repeats but she can see he is not listening to her so she decides he should have something else to worry about. "If you do anything to try to interfere with Dog coming home or attempt to stop me from accessing these accounts you'll loose more than just everything."

"It's my duty." Ben replies and he must stop what is about to happen. "I take my responsibilities very seriously."

"He's not, and never was, your responsibility." C.C. replies as she moves crossing the space to stand before his desk again so he is looking at her. "Let me make myself perfectly clear here. You do anything to interfere with Dog's return I'll do your granddaughter a favor and deprive her of the sanctimonious ass who is unfortunately her grandfather after I drain all the money out of this over inflated office and make you wish you had stayed in the military."

"I'm washing my hands of both of you." Ben announces suddenly staring into the very green eyes of the short woman who entered his office only moments before as she seems to have morphed into something far more substantial and far more dangerous.

"A very wise decision." C.C. replies stabbing his letter opener into his desk where it stands as a testament to the anger she is repressing and she turns heading for the door again before she gives into the urge to strangle him with his own tie.

She crosses the outer lobby and down the hallway to the elevator knowing what she has to do with an unfamiliar certainty. The man she just left cannot be trusted by friend or foe and when she steps onto the elevator she is considering the quickest and easiest way to deal with this problem. Dog was correct in one respect Malinowski dismissed her at first glance as others do but enough is enough and it is time she made a first impression no one will forget.

Three weeks later C.C. is sitting in the outer office of her brother's law firm waiting for him to finish with a client after jetting all across the country and other parts of the world moving Dog's money out of Malinowski's reach which was step one requiring she buy a Cessna Citation X jet. Step two was contacting the Major General and alerting him to Malinowski's part in Dog's imprisonment and now step three is finding out just whom or what her brother is planning to marry.

She made some purchases along the way deciding to stick with cargo pants, boots, tee shirts, and or tank tops given this is what she prefers but these things come in other colors and can be bought closer to her actual size. Presently she is wearing red cargo pants, yellow tank top, and black combat boots carrying a smaller sized and very expensive leather back pack type purse. She is no longer invisible nor garnering frowns from bank officials and business types because now rather than wearing what was assumed men's castoffs she is presenting a fashion statement and finds she likes being considered eccentric. Her only accessories are concealed in special holsters in the lining of her backpack and will not pass metal detectors but with her own plane she is waved through such things due to wealth and she has never been searched.

The inner office door finally opens and a woman leads a little girl by the hand as they step out into the lobby moving slowly as the little girl has a metal brace on one leg and walks with a cuffed stick on her other arm as she ponderously makes her way across the waiting room to the front door.

The girl glances up grinning up at her mother and the woman smiles back with so much pride and love C.C. feels a tickle of emotion in her throat just watching them. Even the secretary is beaming as the pair passes her desk then out the main door leading out to the parking lot but once the door closes behind them the secretary with no smile whatsoever looks toward C.C.

"You may go in now Mrs. Red Eagle." Comes the cold clipped instruction.

C.C. is not certain why she seems to have this effect on secretaries which has not changed with her clothing but they all seem to take an instant dislike to her. She rises from her chair entering and closing the door behind her finding her brother scribbling something on a legal pad looking serious before he puts on a smile then rises from his chair looking toward the door for the first time.

His smile drops as does the hand he intended to offer to greet her as he stands frozen in either shock or horror then he rounds his desk with a happy shout grabs her around the waist and lifts her off her feet spinning her around. Her pack swings from one strap hooked over her shoulder thumping him in the back causing him to humph at the impact when he stops to set her down while keeping hold of her upper arms as if she will run off if he lets go as they study the changes in each other after years of separation.

"What have you got it there, bricks?" He asks unable to believe she is actually standing in his office after nearly fourteen years, someone pinch him he must be dreaming.

"Actually Glocks." C.C. informs him but before he can process this information the door opens and his secretary is looking at them both with a look which can only be described as absolute shock.

"Susan this is Caro." Carter announces probably sounding like an idiot he realizes but he does not care because his twin sister is home to see him married.

"Oh."   Susan replies taking in the short muscular woman with arms bared for all to see by a tank top but her green eyes and short spiky blond hair are some how familiar then the name finally clicks. "Your twin sister?"

"She's the shorter cuter version of me." Carter teases with a grin.

"And he's the taller more egotistical version of me." C.C. responds instantly.

"Well, this is wonderful."   Susan comments though this tanned aggressive woman is not what she expected given her boss is a very laid back but serious man.   "Shall I cancel your other appointments for the rest of the day? I can put them off until tomorrow, you have openings remaining."

"No." C.C. objects to this plan.

"Yes." Carter replies at the same time.

"I don't have all day to play with you." C.C. informs him bluntly. "I have work for you and some more things I have to get done before you run off and get married."

"Okay, no,"   Carter capitulates reluctantly.   "Thank you Susan."

"No problem." Susan replies closing the door.

"So what have you been doing?" Carter asks looking at her sternly but she looks good. "And did you say Glocks in your bag? You mean the guns right?"

"We have some major catching up to do but not right now." C.C. replies knowing explanations will take more than the allotted hour of this appointment. "The short story you need to know is, I'm no longer in the Air Force, I'm married, and I have a ton of contracts I need you to look over."

"What kind of contracts?" Carter asks instantly all business.

"Property contracts, government contracts, and business contracts for over a hand full of companies." C.C. replies as she sets her backpack on one of the two visitor chairs and reaches in pulling out a hard disk. "If you don't have the correct programs to read these then I'll buy them for you."

Carter accepts the hard disk and rounds his desk to sit inserting it into his computer and after a moment he is seeing twenty files under various names and he opens one with a government defense department seal. His jaw drops when he realizes this is a contract for a military action by a private security firm the name of JRE International Security. He was hoping what is on this drive would give him answers but instead he only has more questions.

"Caro, this is a military unit disguised as private security." He informs her wondering if she knows and looking across his desk to where she sits now looking back at him he is certain she knows exactly what this is. "This is dangerous stuff."

"Carter." C.C. begins sitting forward leaning her elbows on the edge of his desk to look at him. "I've been flying jets, engaging in dog fights while carrying live missiles, I was not allowed to spar in a boxing ring because as a sixth degree black belt I might inadvertently kill someone, and I took munitions training from a unit of Navy Seals after I over came five Marines in a training exercise but I was a little impatient. It's time to face facts Carter. I'm not cut out for the whole home, family, and hearth deal but I'm good at flying, fighting, and shooting. It's time I start using my strengths and stop dwelling on my weaknesses."

"But you are married." He replies looking thoughtful because this is what she said. "Unless the only reason you married is to get into this."

"It was the bait he used." C.C. admits freely. "He doesn't need me to do his laundry or match his socks. I'm to fly his planes and handle all those pesky little details I'm more capable of handling than he is but what he really needs is someone he can trust and someone who truly cares for him. In a way I understand him better than I ever did any of my previous husbands, yet I hardly know him at all, and surprisingly he seems to know me better than I know myself. He pointed out I'm a square peg trying to pound myself into a round hole and it's never worked for me. He seems to really like all my sharp edges."

Chapter 18
Somewhere in the U.S. of A...

"Well, he's probably not wrong." Carter agrees since Caro has never fit the mold the parents tried to stuff her into. "I'll be honest and tell you I don't want to like this guy because he's going to be taking you into some seriously dangerous situations. Now, hear me out before you interrupt. If this is what you're good at and it's what you want, then fine. I'm not going to be one of those, namely mother and father, who tried continually to force you into that round hole. You didn't start this, you knew what you wanted to do, only no one listened. Well, I'm listening and I agree. I found my place in life but from what I know you've tried over and over again with nothing but pain to show for it. If this is what you want then I'm happy for you. I'm still going to worry about you but if you're happy, which for once I can actually see you are, I'm going to have to like the guy."

"Once you get past the shock and awe of seeing him, you'll like him." She admits with certainty.

"What shock and awe?" He asks grimly wanting to know what to expect.

"He's huge and a little tore up." She explains.

"As in?" He responds wanting her to spell it out but then he considers. "You mean he's missing limbs? I can set him up there."

"You what?" C.C. asks blinking wondering where he would get the idea Dog is missing body parts and how does Carter think he can do something about if he were.

"Clarissa." He answers smiling then frowns seeing she has no clue whom he is talking about. "My fiancee, you know, the woman I'm marrying who happens to be a physical therapist for amputees. Did you even read my letters?"

"I read them." C.C. replies defensively but nothing he wrote said anything about what his future wife does for a living. "You kept saying something about her kids so I thought she was divorced with kids."

"No, she works with kids who have lost limbs by accident or

through illness." He explains trying to remember exactly what he wrote but thinking back he might have said her kids because this is how he thinks of them just as she does. "I might not have been clear about that."

"Yuh think." She replies as this sheds a whole different light on this woman. "And Dog is not missing anything but he is scarred up from years of combat action. People are going to look at him strangely if not be totally repelled."

"It won't phase me at all any more." He responds unconcerned. "Most of my cases are personal injury with a few business deals thrown in just to remind me it's safe to drive. I've seen some pretty nasty injuries and Clarissa has as well. We won't be offended by his looks which I've always found cruel since the person cannot help how they look and people should just be happy they are still alive."

"So you can handle these?" C.C. asks pointing to the computer and realizing she may have to accept this wedding.

"Yes." He snarls at her for doubting him. "If there's anything I see I think you should know about I'll let you know. Some times they slide time limits and counter payments in to make who ever signs pay their own expenses, or not get paid at all. I'm on this."

"I knew you would be." C.C. responds smiling because she trusts him more than any one else to handle this. "The property concerns me more than the others actually. I need this property but I'm not going to jump through hoops or deal with anyone stepping in at the last minute and saying it can't be sold."

"I'll do the title check and make sure." He assures her and he intends to be doubly thorough as this is his sister's life here. "Look, since you wouldn't let me cancel my next appointment, have dinner with me and Clarissa tonight."

"Hm. What time?" She asks because she still has some things she wants to set in place.

"Eight at the Wagon Wheel." He suggests hopefully because he cannot wait until she meets Clarissa.

"I'll be there." C.C. assures him as she stands because she still needs to know if this woman can be trusted with her brother's future happiness even though she is not apparently the money grubbing divorcee she thought. "Your secretary has the phone number to reach me. I'd give it to you but you'd loose it five seconds after I walked out the door."

"I don't do that any more." Carter replies sitting back in his desk chair smiling smugly.

"Clarissa keeps them for you." She guesses and his smile falls telling her she is correct as she goes out the door so he can call his fiance.

"So how does she look?" Clarissa demands as soon as Carter puts the car in drive heading down town for dinner with his twin sister. She has been so excited since he called earlier and so happy his sister Caro arrived for their wedding because Carter would have been hurt regardless of what he claims.

"Beautiful, of course, she is my twin." He reminds her acting shocked she would need to ask.

"But she's not a handsome woman." Clarissa teases with a smile.

"She's too cute to be handsome." He replies honestly. "Which has always been part of the problem."

"People don't take her seriously?" Clarissa guesses because this seems to be a common problem voiced by many women.

"People don't really see her at all." Carter admits not certain how to explain this phenomenon which seems to surround his sister like the Bermuda triangle so he gives her an example. "There was a trash can fire at school. Caro sees it on her way to her class from the restroom so she steps into the nearest class room to report it to the teacher, which happened to be my history class, and tells the teacher she sees smoke coming out of a garbage can in the hallway. I mean it Clarissa, the teacher never once looked at her but said, 'Okay I'll see to it', then did absolutely nothing. Someone in our class near the door yells, 'I see smoke', and the teacher is up out of her chair pulling the fire alarm. They evacuated the entire school over a small trash can fire the teacher never bothered to investigate then guess who she blamed it on?"

"Caro!" Clarissa replies in horror. "She didn't, did she?"

"Nope," Carter grimaces because he found out later who did but the damage was done. "The more she claimed her innocence the more trouble she was in. She was grounded once again by our parents which was usually all the time over things she never had anything to do with."

"But why would they not believe her?" Clarissa asks because there must be a reason. Attitude, vivid imagination, or something.

"You're sitting there wondering if my sister is a habitual liar or was really guilty when she claimed not to be." Carter comments dryly because this is what everyone begins to assume. "She didn't do it. I found out who did but every time I tried to get Caro out of trouble the higher the pedestal they put me on for trying to protect my sister and the deeper in the hole Caro went. I stopped because she asked me too."

"But why wouldn't the teacher listen to her in the first place?" Clarissa asks wanting to know because there must be some reason.

"Caro doesn't panic or show emotion of any kind. She's calm controlled, and emotionless some would even say, so I assume since she didn't freak out like the other student the teacher put it down as nothing. Just the crazy Callahan twin making trouble again." He replies because he never really understood why everyone jumped to Caro as being guilty either. "I've never seen my sister loose her temper. Every argument with my parents or teachers was done in a modulated calm voice of reason. And apparently since she doesn't raise her voice or scream everyone assumes she is either not serious or incapable of logical thought so why listen to her."

"So you're saying she was a model child yet no one saw it?" Clarissa reiterates finding this incredible but if Carter says it is true than it must be. Carter rarely speaks of his sister and she assumed because it is painful for him since Carolyn basically from what Clarissa understands ran away from home.

"An A+ student, homework done and turned in on time. At home she did her chores without complaint and some times mine so I wouldn't get into trouble. Never set foot out of the house unless wearing a dress, was polite to everyone, miss manners personified. She never did any of the things she was accused of and took her punishment without a word of anger. She would argue but never raise her voice and accepted the outcome of the argument without fuss. So yes, she was a model child, or she was until she turned nine."

"What happened?" Clarissa wants to know because she wants to know everything about this woman who will be her sister and because Carter really loves his sister.

"I taught her how to be bad." He replies simply with a grin. "She wanted to take Karate classes but our parents said absolutely not but they insisted I should. Dad must have seen or heard something about Karate building character or helping with the physical aspect of playing sports so his mind was set I was going. Caro accepted their decision when as usual they refused to listen so I forged the paper work, showed her how to sneak out of the house, and for six years or so she took Karate with no one the wiser. I believe she said she is now a sixth degree black belt."

"It's no wonder she ran away." Clarissa replies sadly if no one listened to her and being accused of all kinds of things she did not do.

"She didn't run away." Carter frowns looking at her while the car is stopped at a red light. "Who told you that?"

"Your parents always say, 'since she left', every time her name comes up." Clarissa informs him wondering what else they could have meant if not she ran away. "You've heard them."

"I guess I just tuned them out which is what I usually do when ever they mention her name." Carter admits because he refuses to allow himself to be drawn back into old family arguments concerning Caro. "Caro wanted to marry a boy in school who was leaving for college. They said no which was probably the right thing to do considering their ages but Mom and Dad went completely off the deep end. They called her a whore because she must be sleeping with him and told her if she was pregnant after he left they would kick her out."

"Oh my God." Clarissa replies horrified yet she has met his parents and they are really nice. "Maybe she misunderstood."

"Yeah, it's always Caro's fault." Carter responds grimly shaking his head. "Clarissa, I was standing right there listening to the whole argument. Every time they addressed her they used slut or whore then added eternal damnation and the threat of tossing her out in the street if they didn't feel they were making themselves clear about what was going to happen too her. I helped her pack because there was no way she could stay with them regardless of whether it was wise to marry the guy or not."

"I just can't picture them doing that." Clarissa replies confused because she likes his parents and they are so nice, now she does not know what to think.

"They're not the same people they once were." Carter admits knowing he probably should not have brought up what his parents were once like but now he needs to explain. Caro's return might make things awkward and Clarissa will be in the middle of it. "Until Dad's stroke my parents were very different people. They had such strict and unshakable views of home, family, and child rearing it bordered on insanity. They preached God but followed only the scriptures they felt were important. When Dad was unable to work, money was tight, and I wanted to drop out of collage since the cost of my schooling was causing part of the problem and with a full time job I could help them out. Mom wouldn't hear of it and went out getting a part time job which Dad objected too because it broke one of their own very strict rules. It caused a rift between my parents then Dad was cleared to work and Mom had found she liked getting out of the house two days a week and she didn't want to give up her job. The battle lines were drawn and eventually Mom filed for divorce."

"I never knew any of this." Clarissa gasps wondering why he did not tell her.

"There really was no reason to tell you. Every couple goes through hardships and hopefully they come out together stronger." He explains as he takes her hand while using the other to drive through heavy traffic at this time of night. "What you see now is what they became after a trial by fire deal. Both of them had a wake up call at the same time and realized they would have to change if they were to stay together, and I can proudly say they did. But Caro is another matter entirely which is why I'm asking you this now. They speak of her occasionally but before her name was not allowed to be spoken in their home. They even went so far as to tell her never to come back after her marriage failed."

"But they've changed." Clarissa points out because he is describing people she has never met.

"I know you Clari Bug, but this is not something you can fix." He informs her point blank. "I know you can't help trying to fix and heal everyone but in this, please, leave it alone. Caro is not the hateful type. She won't cause a scene or give anyone a piece of her mind. But, please, and I'll beg you if I must, don't keep throwing her in with my parents or talking about them continually pushing the issue. I lost my sister once and I don't want it to happen again. She'll just leave and maybe this time never come back."

"Awh." Clarissa replies sadly because poor Carter is the one caught in the middle and he lost his sister whom he loves so much so when he pulls into a parking place turning the car off she instantly unbuckles her seat belt reaching over with both hands grabbing his face and kisses him. "I promise." Then she kisses him again. "I'll do nothing to drive off your sister." She kisses him again. "I won't push or talk about your parents too much." Then she kisses him again.

"You're going to like her." Carter assures her with a smile and kisses her but not one of those little pecks either until knocking comes from his side of the car. He releases Clarissa and looks out the driver side window finding Caro shaking her head at him.

"Are you two going to steam up the windows or are we going to eat?" She asks with her hands on her hips. "And that lip stick is so not your color bro."

Clarissa laughs as she looks into the face of a blond pixie standing slightly bent over looking in the drivers window then to Carter who does have her lipstick on his mouth. He starts to wipe at his mouth but she quickly catches his hands with one of hers before pulling a wet wipe out of her purse.

"You'll just smear it." She warns him as she wipes it away.

"He's worse than a kid, you have to clean him up before he eats and after." C.C. observes waiting patiently outside the car door and she can see Clarissa is trying hard not to laugh as Carter glares at her.

"Move squirt." Carter warns as he opens his car door then rounds it to open Clarissa's then on the sidewalk in front of the restaurant he preforms the introductions. "Clarissa Kincaid this is Carolyn Red Eagle or so my secretary informs me."

"It's so wonderful to meet you." Clarissa replies and not bothering with hand shakes she grabs Carolyn in a big hug before backing off. "Can I call you Caro or is that for brothers only?"

"Caro, C.C or Cat." C.C. informs her. "I answer to all of them."

"Really." Clarissa replies with interest as Carter is putting his hand on her lower back and steering her toward the restaurants entrance. "So where did C.C come from?"

"My call sign in the Air Force." She admits as they move inside and Carter requests a table.

"Does that stand for Carolyn Callahan?" Clarissa wants to know as they are being led to their table and Carter pulls a chair out for her but her attention is still focused on Caro.

"Yes or Captain Callahan or they called me Captain C.C." She explains as she seats herself since Carter's courtesy does not seem to extend to her.

"And who calls you Cat?" Clarissa asks once they give their

drink orders to the waiter.

"My husband." C.C. replies with a smile. "Actually he some times adds Cool to it."

"Which leads you right back to C.C." Clarissa responds laughing. "I love all these pet names. I was never called anything other than Clarissa until I met Carter. He calls me Clari Bug but his friends call him Cart for some reason only so far no one will explain this to me. It seems to me Car would be more logical."

"Sometimes logic doesn't have anything to do with it." C.C. replies grinning at Carter who is looking at her grimly. "Some times it's the lack of logic which makes it so fitting."

"You know why." Clarissa responds looking from sister to brother who are staring at each other in what looks to be a battle of wills. "Tell me."

"Sorry, sworn to secrecy but you'll figure it out all by yourself one day soon." C.C. responds smiling as she looks down at her menu.

"It's not that big of a deal." Carter informs Clarissa. "It's my name, just shorter." This gets a snicker from Caro.

"Oh my." Clarissa gasps then she has C.C.'s hand in hers as she looks at the ring on her finger. "This is incredible."

"Yes, it is." C.C. agrees. "Not only is it worth a fortune the workmanship is unlike anything I've ever seen and Dog risked getting shot crossing a desert to have it made for me."

"Now that's devotion." Clarissa informs her with a smile as she lets go of her hand after making a thorough examination of the ring. "So Dog is your husband?"

"Yes." C.C. replies unable to help liking this woman of her brothers. She does not have to ask why he calls her Clari Bug because she is as cute as a bug which is a favorite saying of one of their grandmothers. Carter was always repeating it because something about it fascinated his young mind and stuck like glue.

Clarissa is a full figured woman just slightly taller than C.C. with a mane of dark curly hair, she is a talker, likes to hug, and touch which C.C. is certain Carter is more than happy with. Not much hugging and touching in their childhood or talking for that matter so Clari Bug is the type of woman her brother needs to balance out his more reserved self.

"Actually his full name and rank is Colonel Johann Red Eagle. He's an Army Ranger currently deployed somewhere in the Persian Gulf." C.C. informs them both.

"Oh dear." Clarissa replies looking at Caro with concern as Carter looks surprised as well. "Are you worried? Of course you're worried, what am I saying."

"I'm not worried." C.C. replies with a smile. "The only ones who should be worried is anyone who gets in the way of his objective. He's rather single minded that way."

"There are all kinds of stories on the news about ground forces coming out now." Clarissa admits finding this whole war interesting in an abstract way. She really does not want to dwell on war too much because she deals with injured children and war brings about the type of injuries she deals with on a daily basis.

"I'm glad you weren't sent over there. So far the deaths have not been too heavy on our side but every three men who dies is worse than none." Carter comments looking at C.C. who smiles back at him.

"I think you meant to say every man who dies is three times worse than none." Clarissa corrects oblivious to the staring match going on between brother and sister as she gives the waiter her order.

"Yes, that's exactly what he meant." C.C. chokes out then manages to keep from laughing by giving her order to the waiter who then moves on around the table.

"If you both will excuse me I have to use the restroom." Clarissa apologizes before leaving them at the table alone.

"She's going to figure it out soon." C.C. comments with a grin at her brother. "You keep putting the cart before the horse she'll have it."

"I'm not worried about that." Carter replies leaning across the table. "You were over there weren't you?"

"If I told you I would have to kill you or if you tell someone else I go to prison." C.C. responds still smiling but keeping her voice down. "Female military personnel are not allowed in combat."

"That's where you met him." Carter concludes because it makes more sense than her meeting an Army Colonel on an Air Force base in the U.S. and this whole time Caro has been out of the country but why this suddenly upsets him he is not certain. "Sorry but I just realized I don't like you having secrets from me or it was an instant panic at the thought of you being so far away. We're not connected like we use to be when we were kids but as long as you tell me things, or I think I know where you are, I don't feel the loss. I know why you cut the connection between us but please don't cut me out completely, okay."

"I cut the connection?" C.C. asks surprised he would think this because she thought they just out grew it.

"You can still read me." He informs her with a smile and he is sure of it. "If I'm happy, sad, or just plain mad, you know it, but if I try, I hit a brick wall unless we're sitting face to face like this. You cut the connection to keep me out and I understand why. You didn't want me to know what you were feeling, and you were so unhappy for so long, but no matter how hard I tried there was nothing I could do for you. No matter what I did it only made matters worse. You let me go about my life not feeling your misery but I still feel guilty for being so useless to change things for you."

"It's over." C.C. replies simply and she never once blamed him for anything.

"But the wall is still there and you're going to keep it there." He responds with certainty. "For me it's like being adrift in a small boat in a big ocean but as long as I know you're around somewhere I can see land. You cut me out without a word or without knowing anything and I'll be lost, alone, and probably rowing in circles."

"But Clarissa." C.C. begins never realizing she is the one who caused the blank spot between them.

"It's not the same." Carter informs her flatly. "You know I'm alive and well. You don't need a letter or a phone call but I have to rely on those things. And for your information I didn't have the cart before the horse mental glitch until after you built the wall. We finished each other sentences, well now I have to use my brain alone, so stop being so amused because you caused it."

"Really." C.C. responds with interest because she knows he is right about the distance and she always knows where he is or near too. They did finish each others sentences or often said the same things at the same time. "Are you sure you're going to be okay with me doing this?"

"Yes." He responds earnestly. "Just kind of keep me in the loop."

Chapter 19
Somewhere in the U.S. of A...

"Okay." C.C. agrees as Clarissa returns to the table just as a waiter appears with a phone in hand.

"You are Mrs. Red Eagle, correct?" He asks and when she nods he sets the phone before her. "A phone call for you."

"Thank you." C.C. responds puzzled by this as she picks up the phone. "Hello."

"The Colonel seems to think he will have to go looking for you but you're not that hard to find Captain." Major General Aimhurst informs her in case she is interested in knowing. "Carter Callahan's secretary was most helpful."

"Major General sir." She responds in greeting but she is not what Dog will be looking for.

"The Colonel is on his way and has been officially discharged from the military." Aimhurst relays these glade tidings. "The war is officially over as of two days ago but the press was not informed as much clean up was required. The Colonel has been heading a good deal of it since they have discovered he can be very useful."

"That's good news, sir." C.C. admits so everything is going as they planned and hoped.

"Have you had time to go over the government contracts?" Aimhurst asks because there is another reason for this call.

"My lawyer is reviewing them now." C.C. replies looking at Carter as she speaks.

"Put a rush on the one marked Central Rearmost, Captain." He requests. "That one isn't going to wait and I need the two of you on it."

"Central Rearmost, yes sir." C.C. responds looking at Carter who pulls out a note book to write it down. "One week sir?"

"Good." He replies finding this satisfactory. "I'll have the rest of what you need ready before then. Good hunting Captain and try not to run the Colonel too ragged, he isn't getting any younger."

"Are you sure?" C.C. counters. "So far nothing else has worked like it was suppose too."

"Thanks for sharing that concept." The Major General grumbles before disconnecting.

"Dog's on his way." C.C. informs the two people seated at her table as she hangs up the phone and the waiter is instantly there to take it away. "But I need you to go over that contract as soon as you can before you run off and get married."

"No problem." Carter assures her. "Is he coming here?"

"Eventually." She smiles. "I left some bread crumbs for him to follow."

"I know we sent you an invitation but we didn't know you were married." Clarissa begins then is suddenly horrified. "He does know he's welcome, right?"

"The only way to stop him is to plant a tank at the door and even then he would find another way in." C.C. assures her as their food arrives. "He's not bashful. Crashing a wedding won't bother him in the least."

"Good." Clarissa sighs as she picks up her fork and freezes. "The wedding!"

"Yes, Clari Bug, we're getting married in three days." Carter replies with a smile.

"Noooo." She moans. "We have to get Caro's a brides maids dress fitted."

"No." C.C. replies holding up her hands as if to ward her off. "Don't change anything and I'm sorry but I'm not wearing a dress for anyone ever again."

"But." Clarissa begins looking at her questioningly because people will think it strange not to have the grooms sister in the wedding party.

"No." C.C. responds again. "I've been married five times and this time I'm going to be smart and sit in the church watching instead of participating."

"Five." Clarissa replies unable to hide her astonishment as she looks to Carter.

"I only knew about two and this husband to my count would be three." Carter admits holding up a hand in innocence when Clari Bug looks at him.

"Spill it." Clarissa orders. "You married your high school sweet heart who was a jerk, then a cop who was probably just as bad." Now she leaves it open for Caro to fill in.

"Actually he was worse than number one." C.C. replies wondering if her soon to be sister-in-law seriously wants to hear about her failed marriages just before her wedding but Clarissa is looking at her expectantly. "Number three was a wonderful man but just after we married he was diagnosed with cancer and died. Number four was basically a business arrangement. He needed a wife who looked good on his arm and wouldn't nag him about his other women and I needed a roof over my head and three solid meals. Unfortunately his business was shady and he was arrested so I lost the roof, and the money to buy food so I enlisted in the Air Force and never regretted it."

"So you've been widowed once and divorce three times." Clarissa reiterates which is not a good track record but she is married again. "And Dog knows this?"

"Dog is still wondering why I didn't kill three of them." C.C. replies dryly.

"I'm going to like Dog." Clarissa responds with a smile. "Do you need a place to stay?"

"I have a suite at the Regency." She informs her soon to be sister-in-law whom she finds she has no objection too thus far. "So spill, how did the two of you meet?"

C.C. sits back enjoying her meal as they take turns regaling her with the events which brought them together. It is not completely a happy tale as it involves a little boy holding his mother's hand while walking through a cross walk when a drunk driver blew through a red light at an intersection. The mother was brushed aside by the speeding car but the boy was run over and Carter became the families lawyer when insurance refused to pay for the boys injuries. Clarissa was assigned as the boy's physical therapist as the boy began learning how to live with the loss of a limb and use an artificial leg, from then on they were being thrown together unintentionally by the boys family and the court system until they both found them selves looking for ways to be together without chaperons.

Their love for each other is obvious as they speak of the boy and his family in glowing terms, the boy who is now playing soccer, and they tell of his antics on and off the field. Carter never misses an opportunity to point out just how wonderful Clarissa is with all of her patients, while Clarissa is just as committed to convincing anyone who will listen Carter is a hero, a modern day Robin Hood. They are actually a cute couple yet they are both grounded by the hard realities in their daily lives but neither show it or dwell on the injustice of it. They are both heroes from what C.C. is hearing and their goals for the future are the unselfish kind and they are working together to achieve those goals.

The evening winds down and they part ways with hugs but now C.C. has even more work to do. She has to finish getting the home base plans set, complete stock piling supplies, and now put together a wedding gift for her brother and his bride all in the space of three days.

Oh well, sleep is highly over rated anyway.

The day of the Callahan/Kincaid wedding dawns bright and clear as C.C. arrives a little early but even this early there are many people entering the church or standing in groups outside talking. There is a hint of gaiety in the air along with a respectful hushed tone inside the church. She is garnering a good deal of looks which she ignores knowing she is dressed in a fashion more commonly found in the middle east.

During one of her few excursions into a foreign market she purchased a harem outfit but she liked the material and loose fit so much she gave into the impulse to buy it. The pale green loose fitting pants gathered at the ankles with a short skirt to the knees front and back is probably the most comfortable pants she has ever worn. Paired with a white tank top under a little short jacket which came with the outfit she feels it encompasses both casual and dressy at the same time very comfortably and this will possibly be the only occasion where she will have the opportunity to wear it.

She is presently on a mission as she traverses a labyrinth of stairs, hallways, and rooms within the church searching for the bride and groom. This would have been much easier if the wedding were being held in the familiar Callahan church and she was surprised when she reached this address to find it is not which is singularly strange but Carter's relationship with their parents is his business and none of hers. Finding a hand written sign on the door reading 'Bride' but the barely contained high pitched laughter, muted slightly by thick walls and door, is a dead give away.

"Delivery for the Bride." C.C. announces after giving the door a firm knock and a woman bearing some resemblance to the bride opens the door a crack.

"Oh, okay." She replies surprised but opens the door.

The small room with a high ceiling is full of pale and bold

pinks, which C.C. assumes is the brides maids who are chattering away to each other while the bride sits before three mirrors on a stool with a frozen smile on her face just short of shear panic. Hovering next to the bride primping the brides veil is none other than Margaret Callahan, C.C.'s own mother, looking relatively pretty in a classic spring dress and wearing her hair rolled up at the sides gathered into chic pony tailing down her back

"I hope you brought nerve medication." The woman whispers concerned with her daughter's unusual quietness. "Clarissa dear, there is a delivery for you."

"Oh." Clarissa responds wondering just who this person is she is looking at in the mirror and glances over her shoulder numbly wondering if there is some detail she forgot to handle and as far as she knows everything was delivered this morning but she was rushing around so much she may have forgotten something but the glance shows her just who is standing next to her mother and sends her spinning the tall stool making her feel like a revolving wedding cake topper to see her soon to be sister -in-law more clearly. "Caro, you look beautiful."

"Did you actually look in that mirror? C.C. asks with a smile but she suspects Clarissa was some place else trying to tune everyone out. "I come bearing bridal gifts."

"Oh, give it here I'll put it with the others." The woman beside her offers instantly.

"No, these are not that kind of gift." C.C. responds reaching into the big deep pockets along the outside of her legs, which is another wonderful feature of this outfit and pulling out two long black velvet boxes holding them up. She holds one in each hand then with a quick twirl of her arms the boxes blur and seem to spin in the air as one black circle before she holds them apart once again which is another magicians slight of hand she learned to impress a crowd. It seems to work on bridesmaids as well then she motions with one box for Clarissa to turn back around on her stool.

Moving up behind Clarissa she places a box aside while opening the other as Clarissa watches her in the mirror with a frown as everyone has gathered around the mirrors so they can either see the bride directly or from a mirror as the bride is doing.

She pulls out a gold chain dripping with colored jewels from the box and there is a collective inhale of air from the women watching then a swooshing exhale which would have snuffed a candle ten feet away. Clarissa's eyes are wide as C.C. takes one end of the golden chain in either hand and moves it over the brides head draping the chain across her forehead.

"This is a bridal head band mostly worn by brides in India, Arabia, and some other middle East countries." C.C. explains as she looks at the veil already on Clarissa's head wondering how she is going to anchor the chain yet hide the ends.

"Carolyn." C.C.'s mother offers with a smile seeing her dilemma. "Let me take off the veil and we can pin it underneath."

C.C. nods to this plan moving back to allow her mother along with the help of the woman she assumes is Clarissa's mother attend to this revealing a complicated braid of hair beneath. Once this is done they step aside so she can drape the chain carefully across Clarissa's forehead again then there is much primping going on as the veil is fussed back into place and the jewels are adjusted so they dangling down as they should.

"There is one more very important piece." C.C. informs them reaching for the second box finding her mother handing it too her with a bright smile but the bride appears to be in shock and once again the inhale as this time the chain is much longer as she draws it from its velvet and lined box The tiered matching necklace to the head band brings the same reaction from the bridesmaids as she drapes the necklace around Clarissa's neck. Clasping the necklace she steps back as the loops in the chain are adjusted then they all stand back looking at the over all picture of the bride now draped in glittering jewels.

"Caro, are these real?" Clarissa asks in a thready voice.

"If I say yes, do either of you think she will pass out?" C.C. asks after placing her hands over Clarissa's ears from behind as she looks to the two mothers standing next to her.

"Just tell me." Clarissa insists pulling Caro's hands away and she is not going to pass out as she looks at her sister-to-be in the mirror.

"Dog can afford it." C.C. replies so this is not an issue she should be concerned with.

"Does he even know he bought them?" Clarissa asks knowing her soon to be brother-in-law is not even here, or is he.

"He ordered them made." She responds so this is not just a gift from her if that is what concerns her.

"So he's here." Clarissa sighs with relief.

"Well not yet." C.C. admits seeing Clarissa is now frowning

again so she goes on to explain. "After we had dinner the other night he called."

"And you told him he is welcome at the wedding and what did he say?" Clarissa insists still staring at Caro but Caro looks away as if debating if she should say. "Or what did you tell him which made him think I needed all of this?"

"He wanted to know if I intend to kill off my brother's fiancee." C.C. relays dryly only Clarissa is smiling while the bridesmaids are looking horrified. "I told him no and you're perfect for Carter so then he wanted to know if you had a bridal dowry, he's been living in countries where they tend to offer sheep, camels, and such to the grooms family as a bridal dowry. I told him I have no idea what Carter paid for you or what your family offered Carter and he told me he would take care of it. I landed my jet in Saudi Arabia not certain if I was picking up donkeys or jackasses as your dowry or if I would need a bigger plane."

"Your jet?" Clarissa questions her eyes wide with surprise. "You flew a plane?"

"Did you think I walked? I have a Cessna Citation X which will go six hundred plus miles an hour but it's not my F-15 Eagle only it got me there fairly quickly." C.C. responds and she will just have to get use to this slower mode of travel but the surprised look of the bride makes her frown. "What do you think I did in the Air Force?"

"I guess I just didn't connect it in my head and not everyone in the Air Force flies planes." Clarissa replies in her own defense and she never really asked Carter what his sister did in the Air Force so she just assumed land based job since Carter is more of the office type.

"Well, no, but what would be the point of joining other wise." C.C. responds and really it was not her first consideration when she joined the Air Force only now she cannot imagine life locked to the ground. "Anyway at least Dog went with one of the customs in the middle east most prevalent and a Bridal dowry is draping the bride for the ceremony in costly gems so the groom can see what he will be gaining from the marriage but in some cultures it is said the jewelry is just decoration upon which the real jewel is the bride."

"Ah." Comes a collective sigh from the bridesmaids.

"Dog is going to be here, right?" Clarissa asks again because she is really is going to like this man.

"Sure. He'll find me." C.C. replies because he will, eventually.

"Did you even tell him where the wedding is?" Clarissa asks because something about Caro's answer seems evasive.

"He's a big, big, boy, so he'll figure it out." C.C. responds not concerned but Clarissa does not look convinced. "Okay fine. Do you have your something borrowed yet for the something old, something new, something borrowed, something blue?"

"I haven't gotten to the borrowed yet." Clarissa admits. "The veil was my grandmother's so it is really old, the shoes are new, and my garter belt is blue."

"Let me see the garter belt." C.C. replies with a smile.

C.C. moves on to seek out the groom leaving a giggling batch of women in her wake and it was really strange to see her mother again but stranger yet is Margaret Callahan seems to have discovered the fountain of youth. C.C. remembers her mother as a thin pinched faced woman with her mouth always pressed firmly in perpetual disapproval and wearing only dark colors smiling only in public. Even the bridal dowry explanation did not set her mother off given the heathen cultural references and all in all her mother looks more at ease and happier than C.C. can ever remember seeing her but she still has the second half of her mission to complete.

The grooms room she finds on the opposite side of the church possibly to keep even an accidental glimpse of the bride by the groom from occurring. Her knock is answered by a round faced balding man with a mustache and goatee but even before he opens his mouth C.C. can see the sparkle of mischievous in this mans eyes despite his smiling open face.

"Hey guys, the dancing girl is here." He calls over his shoulder into the room getting hoots and howls in response.

"Did you order a recall on a brunette?" C.C. asks as she steps up closer smiling.

"No, why?" He responds playing along with a grin.

"Oh, that's good." C.C. replies looking relieved. "You're going bald naturally and you weren't scalped."

The man laughs and throws open the door then turning he puts an arm around C.C.'s shoulders pulling her into the room facing the tuxedo wearing grooms men, four of Carter's closest friends with Carter, and next to him her father.

"If no one claims this one, can I keep her?" He requests to the room in general.

"You're taken."   C.C. responds because this has to be Clarissa's father whom would make a great Santa Claus if he had hair on his head.

"Rats, foiled again." Mr. Kincaid replies laughing as he lets her go.

"Charlie, this is my twin sister Caro." Carter introduces him.

"Well she's better looking than you." Charlie informs his soon to be son-in-law. "Aren't the two of you suppose to be identical?"

"Sex change." She mutters to Charlie who bursts out laughing again.

"Well they took off more than a few inches didn't they." Charlie responds cracking himself up again as the grooms men laugh.

C.C. smiles at him before crossing to Carter pulling two more black boxes from her pockets but much smaller than Clarissa's. She glances toward her father who surprisingly is smiling rather oddly back at her and did not blown up at Charlies rather sexual joke or he simply did not understand thinking perhaps Charlie is referring to inches as in height. But unlike her mother who looks younger her father looks far older and one side of his face seems to sag though other wise he appears hail and hearty and she turns her attention to Carter who is fussing with his tie while fidgeting around unable to stand completely still.

"Is Clarissa even here?" He asks her wondering if she knows.

"No, she jumped into a limo, or is it suppose to be a white horse and rode off into the sun set." She responds seriously as he fidgets while frowning at her. "If you have to go to the bathroom you better go now. Once you're at the alter and faint all body control goes out the window."

"Caro." Carter warns frowning not appreciating her advise as everyone laughs including their father. "I don't have to go to the bathroom, nor am I going to faint."

"When he goes down." C.C. replies turning to Jake Richmond Carter's best friend since forever standing close by. "I want pictures."

"Done." Jake agrees grinning.

"Really Sis." Carter mutters looking put out with her.

"Really Bro." C.C. mocks with a smile holding up the boxes she brought. "I come bearing gifts for the groom."

"You didn't have to do that." Carter responds seriously.

"I didn't, I just flew a few hundred thousand miles because Dog is a sentimental old softy." C.C. mutters with a smirk.

"Right, Dog your husband, the Army Ranger, is a softy." Carter replies in disbelief. "Just tell me he didn't send you after a gun for me."

"No, but, you're close." She admits smiling as she opens one case to show him nestled in red velvet is a small jeweled scimitar to be worn as a tie tack.

"Whoa, that's cool." Jake mutters as the others lean in to look.

"I think the gun would have been better." Charlie comments. "Never know what kind of trouble my daughter will get him into."

"He can borrow mine." C.C. assures him as she opens the other box showing even smaller versions of the sword as cuff links.

"These must have cost a fortune." Carter objects because they are jeweled not to mention gold. "I can't accept these."

"Fine." C.C. replies carelessly with a shrug. "Go to the alter looking like some poor looser marrying a woman for her thousands of dollars worth of jewelry."

"What did he buy her?" Carter gasps in horror.

"I just told you." C.C. informs him looking concerned. "You know, before you faint, they say your hearing is the first thing to go."

"Don't you have any control over your husband?" Carter asks ignoring her comment because he is not going to faint.

"Just about as much as you have over your future wife." She replies honestly.

"Oh she's got you there." Charlie remarks snickering.

"Make sure he doesn't hit his head okay." C.C. warns the grooms men. "Big goose egg on his forehead or a black eye doesn't look good in wedding photos."

"I'm not going to faint." Carter calls after her as his friends are nodding in agreement to Caro's request. "Really, who's side are you on?" They point at Caro who is now standing by the door smiling as she waves on her way out.

Chapter 20
Somewhere in the U.S. of A...

The wedding goes off without the groom fainting, all though he did sway a bit when he came face to face with the jewelry his wife is wearing. The wedding celebration moves to an outdoor tent surrounded by acres of lush rolling grass but C.C. can only see one major obstacle impairing her view, a hedge which stops and starts, for some reason meandering all over one area of open field. She supposes it is part of a garden border still in the beginning stages but the rest of the area is clear so she reconnoiters outside of the tent before moving inside.

Since the wedding was set for two in the afternoon and over by three Clarissa and Carter are cutting the cake changing the usual order so throwing the bouquet and garter toss, followed by gift opening before the meal and dancing begins seems to be the program.

"Excuse me, Caro?" Ethel calls out smiling as she approaches Carter's sister whom she now knows at least by sight. "I'm Ethel Kincaid, Clarissa's mother. I'm sorry we were not properly introduced earlier but Clarissa was a little rattled, and frankly so was I."

"It's nice to meet you, again." C.C. responds sincerely and she had guessed correctly.

"I wanted to show you where we're sitting if you wish to join us when the food is served." Ethel offers happily. "You don't have to sit with us the entire time but if you need a place to put things or just to sit for a while, feel free."

"Thank you," C.C. replies planning to sit later since she is keeping an eye out for Dog but she follows Ethel to a big round table where Charlie Clarissa's father is seated along with both her parents.

The cake is being served and C.C. takes an empty chair next to her mother because with the sides of the ten raised she finds she has a clear view of both the inside and the surrounding area beyond the tent.

"Charlie tells me you have met." Ethel comments while taking a chair next to her husband.

"Yes, and he seems to have a thing for brunettes." C.C. responds with a slight smile before scanning the crowded tent once again as cross the way Clarissa is tossing the bouquet into a bevy of women.

"Well of course I do." Charlie replies putting his arm around his wife whom is a brunette.

"How have you been Carolyn?" Margaret Callahan asks in a bid to form some kind of dialogue with her own daughter.

It has been years since they have spoken to her and what little they know they gleaned from Carter which is not much other than fine and in the Air Force. She just learned today from Clarissa that Carolyn is married again after her previous divorce which is what caused the previous rift between them. She and Stan were so prejudice against divorce they tossed away their only daughter like unwanted trash which shames them now, but how do they make up for all the years they lost.

"Fine." C.C. replies politely and which seems apparent to her so what else is there really to say as she glances over the crowd briefly once again.

"You haven't seen your husband yet?" Margaret asks as this seems the logical explanation for why she chose to sit next to them when she could sit else where if she really does not want to speak to them.

"I'm sure he'll find you." Ethel reasons because this seems logical to her. "He doesn't know anyone here so he would naturally look for you."

"I'm the last person he wants to see just yet." C.C. replies as Carter is putting on a show with Clarissa as they get to the garter belt and Carter disappears all together at one point under his wife's skirts.

"I still don't understand." Margret admits finding this strange even after it was explained earlier but she is not certain she completely understands.

"Looks kill." C.C. reminds her.

"For some reason she's convinced her husband will come looking for a pink rabbit's foot." Ethel explains to her husband and Stan who were not privy to the brides dressing room but the man has a beautiful wife and they have been separated she imagines for a good deal of time so she does not believe a husband would come looking for a rabbit's foot rather than his wife.

"If it were a flag game it would make sense." Charlie responds and it is the only explanation he can understand for this odd behavior. "Looks kill is part of a game played by espionage and infiltration units." He explains to the others as he looks at Caro for confirmation. "Are you playing a flag game, with your husband, in a civilian setting?"

"We don't actually follow all the rules." C.C. admits because that would really turn a few heads.

"Now I have to ask just who is your husband?" Charlie wants to know because this is taking training a little far.

"Colonel Johann Red Eagle, Army Ranger." She answers truthfully as she watches her brother with a piece of elastic and lace though the fact that Clarissa's father knows what a flag game is for she finds interesting so she continues. "I had seven flights hiding the rabbit's foot and managed to keep it away from him for four days."

"Okay." Charlie responds but he believes three of those four days the Colonel was not looking for it. "We're talking a member of the Steel Man unit searching a bunch of, not meaning to be insulting, but there really is no other way to say this, short, barely hand combat trained airheads for a pink rabbit's foot."

"I find that insulting." C.C. responds narrowing her eyes at him taking her attention from Carter.

"My apologies, but still we're talking about a member of a top unit here." Charlie replies not to be put off. "These guys were ghosts, no one saw them if they didn't want to be seen. My unit was involved in one of their training games in Nam. Those guys were scary."

"Dog won't hurt any one." C.C. responds wondering if he is worried about Dog going crazy like Malinowski was and she will not tolerate anyone thinking this way of Dog.

"I mean scary good. I'm saying he's going to find the flag." Charlie informs her flatly and she is dreaming if she thinks she can stop him.

"It's in the one place he'll never look." C.C. assures Charlie with a slight grin as she turns her attention back to Carter who finally pulls back on the garter belt and lets it fly to the waiting men only one big hand reaches out snagging it in mid air and the men part as Dog seems to rise up above them all to his full six something height turning with a grim look as he heads for her. "And Carter just shot it right to him."

"I would say your plan had a slight flaw." Charlie responds laughing and he knew it would not be as easy as she seemed to think.

"Really." C.C. comments fighting a smile as Dog moves toward them as people move away or blatantly stare like they have never seen a long haired large scarred up Indian before, and they probably have not.

He did not dress up for this occasion unless cowboy boots instead of combat boots are a concession to going out. The tee shirt, probably a 5XLT, is stretched tight from shoulder to shoulder and the short sleeves stretch around bulging arms while hanging below his broad chest like a curtain before being tucked into the top of belted jeans. The jeans are also probably several sizes larger as the belt is pleating the waist band around his impossibly narrow waist while his thighs threaten to rip the seams as do his calves, absently she realizes she needs to have his pants custom made.

"Nice little tour of Americana you sent me on Cat." He compliments as he surveys the two couples and surprisingly recognizing one of them.

"Well, you said you've only seen parts of three states so I thought you should see more." She responds to the accusation she hears in his voice.

"Forget the sight seeing. All I want to know now, is how you did it to me again?" Dog demands as he tosses the garter belt onto the table before her.

"Did what?" C.C. inquires frowning as she looks at the garter belt but there is no rabbit's foot and looks up at him again as he is holds both his hands out empty. "It was right here."

"You hid it so well you lost it?" Charlie asks in disbelief.

"It was right here." Margaret defends her daughter as she takes the garter belt and looks through the lacy frills and white fur but it is not there. "We put it right here."

"We did." Ethel agrees as she too reaches out for the garter belt which Margaret hands to her and they made sure it would not fall out but apparently it did. "It was right here."

"Watch your six Dog, you're about to be attacked by a bride." C.C. warns as Clarissa has made her way through the throng of people and does not show any sign of stopping her forward rush.

She does not even pause before running right into Dog with a jump but rather than be knocked backward like anyone else Dog does not so much as budge. When Clarissa wraps her arms around his upper arms and hangs on grinning with delight his legs are swathed in white lace and silk but he looks bemused as he bends his arms at the elbows and with huge hands now around her waist lifts her higher with seeming ease until they are now eye to eye with her hands on his shoulders.

"Caro said you'd find us and I'm so happy you did." Clarissa announces breathlessly because this has to be Dog no process of elimination was really necessary. "I've never had a brother before and you bought me this lovely necklace and head band. I thank you from the bottom of my heart but I've never had a sister before either so you see things are a little complicated."

"I've never had a sister either." He informs this lovely little dark haired woman who just seems to sparkle with light from the inside. "I guess you and I'll have to figure out exactly how this works."

"I know, isn't it strange." She responds smiling at him glad he agrees with her. "But from what I've heard there is a lot of teasing and well some times you have to choose sides. But I want you to know this doesn't mean I love you any less than I do Caro, okay?"

"I understand completely." He responds with a smile as he sets her down and just as he suspects she goes and stands next to Cat who holds out a hand. The bride reaches into the top of her dress and pulls out the pink rabbit's foot handing it to the smugly grinning Cat.

"I'm sorry." Clarissa pouts as she approaches Dog once again.

"You did what you had to do." Dog informs her having no hard feelings over a scrap of pink fur as he finds himself hugged again.

"You're such a wonderful man and Caro is so lucky to have you." Clarissa comments earnestly while taking hold of one of his hands she reaches for Carter who is looking bewildered. "I'll explain it to you later." She promises Carter taking his hand with her other and smiling up at Dog. "This is your brother Carter."

"Hello Carter." Dog responds holding out his free hand to shake but afterwards he keeps hold of Carter's hand looking him in the eyes. "You do realize, you and I are going to have to stick together or they're going to make toast of both of us."

Carter looks at his smiling wife then to his grinning sister who is waving a pink rabbit's foot at him and even with no clue at all about what is going on he knows no truer words have ever been spoken. "We stick together."

"Good." Dog agrees as Carter guides his bride away as Dog looks to Cat moving in closer leaning down into her face and she promptly brushes the rabbit's foot over the tip of his nose while smiling at him. "You and I are not finished by any means."

"Bring it on Dog." C.C. challenges as she waves the rabbit's foot then it is gone as he takes a chair and stares at her a moment.

"Oh laugh it up Chuck." Dog invites the now bald man seated across the table from him with a mustache and goatee which he did not have years before but Chuck seemed to be trying to hold his mirth then he is nearly falling out of his chair laughing. "You never were any help."

"No wait." Charlie gasps putting out a hand in supplication while wiping at tears with the other.

"Really Charlie it's not that funny." Ethel admonishes him not understanding why he going on this badly, or more so than usual.

"Oh, yes it is." Charlie breathes patting her hand on the table in reassurance but there is no way he can explain what he has seen this man can do and make his wife understand without sounding as if he is loosing his mind.

"So the two of you know each other." Margaret guesses finding this interesting while trying not to stare at the scars on the man who is apparently her new son-in-law.

"We were both stationed in Vietnam." Charlie explains belatedly but it was much more complicated than that but he simplifies it. "We met, if you can call it that, when his unit saved mine. I actually owe him my life probably twenty times over."

"Right time, right place, and your unit was in our way." Dog replies dryly.

"Well it was nice of you to walk over top of us and take care of that little problem." Charlie responds with a grin. "I still have the imprint of your size twenty boots on my body back."

"Sixteen." Dog replies because little does not begin to describe the mess Chuck's unit ended up in before his unit arrived.

"Felt like a twenty." Charlie mutters.

"Looks like a twenty to me." Ethel comments backing her husband though he does not have a foot print in his back.

"And she would know." Charlie assures them just as there is a scream causing Dog to turn looking around but he is familiar with that scream and sure enough his daughter is excited by something is moving through people waving papers before her. "She's headed right for you so what did you do this time?"

"Cat?" Dog inquires because he just arrived and has no idea what is going on but they were opening gifts so he probably should have asked what they bought the couple.

"We're both about to be attacked." She warns him wryly. "We gave them an extremely generous wedding gift."

"Good." Dog responds no longer concerned and it sounded like a shout of excitement not anger but none the less his new sister-in-law throws herself into his lap holding papers in his face.

"Look what your wonderful wife did." Clarissa announces laughing and crying at the same time. "I know it was her but she used your money."

"Stop waving it around and let me look at it." Dog grumbles at her as he reaches out catching the papers and as soon as he does she bounds up leaving him with the paper work to hug Cat only he finds he is looking at legal papers then Carter is leaning over his shoulder looking at them as well. "You know what this is?"

"No, she opened it and I've been chasing her ever since." Carter admits as Dog hands the papers to him and he begins reading them over. "Oh my God."

"Warn me if you' re going to start screaming and jumping around like your wife." Dog requests of his new brother-in-law whose eyes have gone wide and his mouth is working but no words come out.

"Its." Carter begins but then the air rushes out of him in a whoosh so it takes a moment before he can continue. "It's permits, grant applications, and the title to property just outside the city. It is, well it will be, a therapy center for children with physical disabilities. We don't have one nearby so Clarissa commutes two hours to work every day. I was planning to open another office and buy a house with a better commute but this, this, will bring Clarissa's work here." Carter manages then looks toward his sister and they only talked to her three days ago. "How the hell did you put this together so fast? Until you came into my office you didn't even know what Clarissa does."

"I had a little help." C.C. admits and it seemed the right thing to give them to start their new life just as she and Dog are about to do.

"Harv and Moss?" Dog asks and he was certain having the two former M.P.s contact her would be worth while. "I though you might find a way to keep them busy."

"You said I should use them however I needed." C.C. responds which was another part of their conversation before she flew off to pick up his gifts for the bride and groom but she makes sure Carter understands. "Nothing is finalized. It's all prospectus so you can look it over when you get back from your honeymoon and decide if you want to take this on."

"This is huge." Carter stutters as Clarissa dances about giggling and crying in turns.

"You don't have to do it all alone either." C.C. informs him. "There are names of surgeons and doctors who are interested in joining on the ground floor so to speak. We have people who can do back ground checks on the doctors before you approach them."

"I just can't believe you put this all together for us." Clarissa cries still over whelmed as she waves a hand before her own face attempting to stop crying. "It's the most wonderful and thoughtful gift in the world."

"Not to mention it sounds expensive." Dog adds looking at some of the paper work Carter is not blindly staring at. "Building costs, salaries, and equipment."

"Grants for this kind of thing are out of this world." C.C. explains. "They can say no but most of them won't."

"If they hit a glitch?" Dog asks looking at her.

"You've got enough to cover it until it's up and running if necessary." She informs him.

"We." He corrects her grimly. "We can cover some of the costs if the grants won't."

"That's what I said." She responds but really it is his money as far as she is concerned because he bled for every dime of it.

"No, you didn't." He grumbles because his hearing is perfectly fine.

"You're so touchy." C.C. remarks.

"And you're not touchy enough." Dog responds as Chuck bursts out laughing and he looks over the table at him. "I knew you would bend that into something else."

"Clarissa people are getting hungry." Ethel reminds her daughter who is now spinning in giddy circles.

"Oh, we have to finish opening presents." Clarissa responds and they were not even half way through.

"Caro, could you maybe keep them on point with that while your mother and I get the food started." Ethel suggests hopefully.

"Roger that." C.C. accepts this mission grabbing the bride with one hand and the groom with the other pulling them back to the open area where they were opening gifts as the wedding celebration has hardly missed them.

"Charlie, I think our daughter might be a little drunk." Ethel informs her husband as she rises from the table.

"You think?" Charlie responds and it is obvious to anyone with eyes. "The champagnes been flowing since we walked in the door."

"Which is exactly why I want to get the food served." Ethel replies as she and Margaret leave the men.

"Slide on over Colonel so we don't have to yell to talk." Charlie suggests motioning to Margaret's empty chair since the noise volume is increasing and his daughter is not the only one drinking freely. "It occurs to me you haven't met Stan here, have you? This is your father-in-law. He don't say much but not because he has nothing to say, he just doesn't say it."

"I let you do all the talking." Stan responds slowly knowing his smile is lop sided since one side of his face is partially paralyzed and he has learned to speak slowly or no one can understand him.

"See he talks all the time, can't get the man to shut up." Charlie comments as Stan laughs. "So what are you doing now?"

"We have an international security company." Dog informs them both.

"Ah, so you're doing what you did before only you're getting paid much better for it." Charlie responds knowingly.

"Something like that." Dog agrees because he is not far off from the truth.

"So where did you meet Stan's Carolyn?" Charlie asks knowing Stan probably wants to know and he is curious himself.

"It's one of those, if I tell you, I have to kill you deals." Dog informs him and the concept is not an unfamiliar one to Chuck.

"Man I hate those." Charlie mutters so they are not going to hear what is probably a very interesting story. "So what is your wife going to be doing while you're out working?"

"She's going with me." Dog responds assuming Chuck missed the 'we' part. "I'm not leaving the best pilot, shot, and fighter I have at base. If I did, anything she baked me after having to play Susie Homemaker would have poison in it if she didn't shoot me full of holes first."

"You're not joking. You're completely serious." Charlie comments seeing no joking smile on Dog's face so he glances at Stan finding he is looking a little concerned and so he should.

"Why does nobody but maybe a hand full of Navy Seals and a bunch of airheads really see her?" Dog asks no one in particular. "Chuck, she threw me across a room, she can fly anything, even things the FAA has not cleared to be flown, and she can shoot a hand gun better than anyone I've ever seen. She's cunningly viscous with ice water in her veins so I feel much safer having her guarding my six rather than having free time to come up with new and creative ways of killing me if I left her behind."

"Well," Charlies replies not sure really what to say but the woman they are speaking of looks and he starts naming the reasons off. "She's short, she's blond, she's cute, and she's a she."

"She's a tiger in a kitten coat." Dog counters to all this. "You piss that woman off, don't bother guarding your balls because that's not what she's going to tear off."

"What happened to ice water in her veins." Charlie remarks.

"That's the scary part." Dog responds honestly. "You won't know she's pissed until it's too late. She won't throw a temper tantrum or scream and yell threats. You'll be on the ground bleeding before you know what hit you."

"Stan?" Charlie asks looking for corroboration because if anyone should know it would be her father.

Chapter 21
Somewhere in the US of A...

"She doesn't yell or scream." Stan corroborates slowly but really nothing else about his own daughter. "We've never known her very well."

"Come on, you raised her." Charlie reminds him figuring time and distance might make Stan feel this way since they have not seen her in a while but she is still the little girl they raised.

"Not really." Stan replies honestly. "We were trying to mold her into the perfect young lady. We never paid much attention to what she thought or felt. If he says she's capable of these things then he would know far better than us."

"Don't be so hard on yourself." Charlie responds assuming this is only the self doubt all parents feel. "Parents make mistakes and kids don't come with instruction manuals but they turn out just fine in the end."

"I'm not being hard enough." Stan corrects his friend but he never really spoke of Carolyn even with his good friend Charlie. "We expected her to be a perfect young lady at all times. Our insistence at being told if she ever behaved other wise was misconstrued to mean she had behavioral problems. She was bullied by students and teachers all through school and blamed for everything when no clear culprit was apparent. Carter tried to tell us but we didn't understand it ourselves until years after she left home. She spent most of her child hood grounded for misbehavior she had nothing to do with because we chose to believe the worst and when she left home at seventeen it was to escape us."

"That was before your stroke wasn't it?" Charlie asks knowing Margaret and Stan had some pretty harsh views at one time.

"Back before I realized I'm not perfect, yes." Stan admits grimly. "I lost my daughter first, nearly lost my life, and then nearly my wife before I woke up to the fact I'm not judge and jury of this world or the here after. Margaret woke up first after getting out and away from me."

"But Carter." Charlie begins only he does not really know how to phrase the question.

"He's a boy." Stan replies simply. "Boys do what boys do which is exactly what Carter wanted to do. Except for Karate lessons which he didn't want but he admitted a few years ago the six years of lessons we paid for were taken by Carolyn. He helped her sneak out of the house so she could take the lessons she wanted." Stan pauses a moment wondering if they will understand the irony of what he is about to say. "I'm probably the only parent who is happy to hear both his children misbehaved because at least Carolyn got to do one things she wanted but it wasn't from us. It was Carter who gave her that one thing, of all the many things we denied her."

"Ah Stan." Charlie replies with sympathy because what a thing to have to live with.

"If he says she can do all he says, than she can." Stan responds nodding. "He knows Carolyn far better than we ever did and probably better than we ever will."

Dog meets Chuck's glance with a grim look because now he knows whose rules Cat keeps trying to live by and failing to the point of looking for a way out. He would like to punch Stan but he is not judge and jury either and what would be the point. Let the man wallow in his own private hell over what he has done and he did loose his daughter so the best thing Dog can do is to let the man suffer but the women are returning to the table so he moves back to his chair looking at Cat as she sits down next to her mother eyeing him.

"This isn't the commissioned officers mess Colonel." She informs him with a grin as the wedding party goes through the buffet. "You'll have to go get your own plate."

"I think I can manage." He replies but suddenly a plate appears before him along with the bride.

"I got this for you." Clarissa offers giving him a kiss on the cheek. "No hard feelings right?"

"Not from me." He responds glancing at Cat who is glaring at him as the Bride giggles her way back to the buffet.

"I'm so going to kick you." C.C warns him.

"I know." He replies in acceptance.

"Would you like some salt?" She asks reaching or the shaker in the middle of the table.

"No thank you." He answers covering his plate with his hands as everyone else at the table is rising to go to the buffet.

"I now see why you won't be eating anything she cooks." Charlie comments after Carolyn follows the others toward the buffet. "If looks could kill, that one would've."

"Told you." Dog replies feeling vindicated.

The mummer of conversation, the clink of glasses, and silverware nearly drowns out the soft music playing as everyone is eating while Ethel and Charlie regal them with some of Clarissa's exploits as a child amusing everyone at the table.

"Remind me to get your brother a flack jacket for Christmas." Dog comments to Cat after one story involves lawn darts and Chuck erupts like a laughing volcano.

Stan eats with a napkin pressed to the paralyzed side of his face to keep food from spilling out and neither Callahan says much of anything as they eat and listen but Ethel encourages them to share some of Carter's exploits in which they draw a great big blank. Carter to them was the model child and rarely got into trouble while Caro on the other hand was blamed for all kinds of things.

"Carter and Jake did most of their damage at Jake's house." C.C. explains to the Kincaids. "Jake's parents covered for them so they wouldn't know what Carter was up too."

"Really." Margaret replies looking at her daughter. "Like what?"

"They nearly set fire to the Kincaids basement before they put it out." C.C. explains simply.

"Now why didn't Alice or Bill tell us." Margaret mutters amazed as they were close with Jake's parents for a number of years until they divorced and refused to acknowledge either Alice or Bill. She sincerely misses Alice who remarried and moved away understandably not leaving a forwarding address for the friend who shunned her.

"They were scolded and I think the Richmond's chalked it up to a lesson learned." C.C. replies with a shrug and the Richmond's no doubt feared the Callahan's would blame it all on Jake and decide their son was a bad influence on Carter.

"That boy is one surprise after another." Margaret comments shaking her head in wonder. "He informed us he never took a single Karate class we paid for six years worth."

"Really." Ethel responds with interest. "What did he do with the money?"

"Nothing," Margaret admits. "He told us Carolyn took the classes instead."

"Sorry." C.C. offers the Kincaids sadly. "Your new son-in-law is an excellent forger."

Ethel laughs but Dog and Charlie share a look which has C.C. looking from one to the other with a frown but Dog nudges her and points at her plate so C.C. reaches for the salt shaker in the middle of the table and Dog raises a hands in surrender. No one else notices this by play except for Charlie who starts snickering into his mash potatoes and the plates have barely been cleared from the tables when the music volume goes up.

The wedding couple has their first dance then the father daughter dance where Charlie is swinging his daughter all over the floor regardless of the slow tune while she laughs helplessly as Carter dances more sedately with Ethel then Margaret. Clarissa is gasping for air by the time the dance is over but she still manages to fly over to Dog and grab him by the arm tugging him toward the floor.

"Seriously." Dog responds in way of complaint because he made them leave his plate and he was looking forward to more food before they put it all away.

"Seriously." Clarissa replies as she leads him out to the middle of the dance floor.

Carter rounds the table and holds his hand out to Caro who accepts but they both stand frozen on the edge of the dance floor staring as Dog and Clarissa are doing a stately waltz to a relatively modern song then when the beat picks up they are tangoing across the floor and Clarissa has the look of a woman in rapture.

"Well it looks like we have some serious competition this year." Carter comments glancing at his sister wondering if she knew her husband could dance.

"I should have guessed." C.C. grumbles as Carter leads her out to the floor and Dog knowing how to dance is just one more surprise from a man with many.

Dance lessons were part of the Callahan repertoire of proper child rearing and both were expected to learn. She and Carter were actually very good, head of the class, but with Carter being male he was only expected to learn the basics then move on to other things like baseball while C.C. continued, not by choice, with deportment lessons and. She can properly set a table using the maximum number of plates and silverware required to host a gala event or work in a high class restaurant which was the most likely case, and did nab her husband number four.

As C.C. and Carter stride across the dance floor using intricate foot work, touching hands and spinning out to the length of their still joined hands and back Dog and Clarissa have circled the edge and now look poised to cut back across only there seems to be a slight problem.

"I don't know how to do that." Clarissa confesses with a laugh seeing what Carter and Caro are doing.

"Then we'll have teach you." Dog replies simply as he calls out. "Cat!"

She spins and looks toward Dog who is motioning for them to come back following more slowly behind as Dog is teaching Clarissa the movements then spinning around the outside edge of the floor Carter spins C.C. to Dog taking back his wife but Ethel and Charlie are waiting at the edge of the dance floor. Dog spins Cat at Charlie and takes Ethel following Carter and Clarissa around the floor once again.

C.C. is set to follow with Charlie as her partner but finds he has his own version of this dance which bares a remarkable likeness the chicken dance and probably is. She cannot help laughing as she starts flapping her bent free arm as he does every time they push off which begins a chain reaction as Clarissa spins with Carter seeing her father and bursts out laughing falling into Carter causing him to stumble killing their momentum.

The D.J. is paying attention and the chicken song comes on which causes a rush onto the dance floor so the dancing begins in earnest. Dog offers his arm to Ethel to escort her back to the table passing Cat who is also headed toward their table so he grabs her around the waist tucking her under his arm carrying her. He even manages to pull out Ethel's chair for her to be seated while still holding Cat then when he sits he shifts her to his lap keeping her anchored there with one arm. He flips aside the short skirt and runs his other hand down her loose pant enclosed her leg.

"What do think you're doing?" C.C. demands pushing at his hand and elbowing him in the gut.

"Trying to find out what was bumping me in the leg." He replies honestly because there is something in one of her pockets.

"Dog, you shouldn't be groping your wife in public." Charlie informs the man motioning to his own wife. "If Ethel won't let me you can't either."

"Ha, shows what you know." Dog growls at him. "She has a Glock strapped to her leg and there is a slit inside the pocket so she can get to it."

"A what?" Margaret asks as Charlie bursts out laughing.

"Your daughter is carrying a hand gun." Ethel informs her gently.

"Very well concealed too." Charlie comments with admiration because he never would have noticed and no one else did either. "How did you figure it out?"

"It was bumping against my leg when I carried her over here." Dog explains other wise he would never have known.

"You're a fine one to talk." C.C. replies leaning down pounding the side of her fist into the bump just above the top of his boot then hisses quietly. "That is a six inch knife in your boot which is illegal to carry."

"Ouch." He mutters as her action caused the sheath the knife to stab into his ankle. "And the gun is not?"

"I have a license in this state to conceal and carry." She replies smiling over her shoulder at him. "Do you?" And he growls at her. "No, I thought not."

"I really do like this outfit though." Dog informs her in case he forgot to mention it and his first thought upon seeing her was now he has his own harem girl but as they danced he can see how easily she can move in it.

"I could conceal rifles in these pockets if I wanted to." She admits grinning at him partly in warning but he is reaching his hand down into her pocket. "Hey."

"She could." Dog comments in amazement then turns her on his lap to look into her disgruntle face. "You need more of these."

"I bought this in the middle east." C.C. informs him and what would she need to dress up for after this.

"Then have them made here." He responds earnestly. "Jungle and desert, the works, but I'm not real keen on the foot wear."

"You don't like them?" She asks looking at her satin slippers as she props one foot on her empty chair.

"Here they're fine but where we go not so good." He replies then he has the over skirt in both hands rubbing it between them.

"Material will have to be a little heavier."

"You're serious."   Cat mutters realizing he is not just meaning for daytime wear but for jungle warfare. "You want me to wear this?"

"A little beefier version, but yeah." He responds looking at her then tugging at the little jacket. "Don't need this you can wear a regular flak jacket."

"I can wear combat boots with this too but why not just wear regular cargo pants?" C.C. inquires since it is good enough for the military so why not for him.

"You can move better in these and don't tell me you can't." Dog responds grimly and it is not just the material but the cut which makes all the difference. "The over skirt might need to be a little shorter, or it will be in your way, and with what you can conceal in these pockets you might save our lives."

"Hand held sawed off shotguns." Charlie responds slapping the table in front of him. "They're not long so they'll hit her knees and she could stop an elephant with one."

"See, good idea." Dog compliments as Cat is now putting her hand in her pocket. "Hey, what are you doing?"

"Don't panic." C.C. responds and she is not reaching for the Glock.   "I'm measuring and for your information a snub nose machine gun will fit just fine in these pockets." And she shoots a glare at Charlie because why would she want single shot guns in her pockets.

"Well excuse me."   Charlie replies and he should have known better. "Of course you want something which will rip things apart rather than blow them up."

"Well yeah." She snipes back because what is the sense of learning to shoot well if all she has to be is close.

"Caro, are you going to war?"   Margaret asks hesitantly because not only is her daughter wearing a gun apparently to a wedding but they are talking about her carrying more.

"We try to prevent them."   Dog explains dryly which is always the objective but some times requires big guns. "And we'll be going to some pretty nasty places and dealing with some rather nasty people."

"And with Caro fully armed looking so sweet and cute she could probably hide a tank under her skirt and no one would notice." Charlie remarks seeing the logic in this.

"That's the idea." Dog agrees. "Ouch."

"You didn't check her other pocket did you." Charlie guesses.

"No." Dog admits. "Now I have something sharp in my side that's going to leave a mark."

"You really need to get past this glitch you seem to have about not fondling women." Charlie informs him trying to keep a straight face. "She's your wife even."

"I know." Dog replies determinedly not needing the reminder nor is he going to tell Chuck just how pleased he is to be married to Cat. "But give me a break, okay. We've only been married something like three weeks and this is only the second time I've seen her since I said I do. Before that she was set on killing me so I might be a little overly cautious about grabbing any part of her she might not want me to grab."

"And now if I kill him, I'll be a rich widow." C.C. adds smiling at Dog.

"Yeah, then there's that." He replies grimly.

"Dude, you're so screwed." Charlie warns him shaking his head.

"Yeah," Dog agrees with a smile as he looks at Cat. "But what a way to go. But we need to get outfitted."

"Mostly done." She informs him seriously. "Carter went through the contract, didn't see any thing we should worry about, and you need to sign then three days from now we go wheels up."

"Must we." He mutter because they will be flying.

"If you wanted to take a slow boat then we should have left yesterday." She informs him rolling her eyes. "I bought a nice roomy jet which also has the benefit of being fast. You won't have time for a panic attack."

"I don't have panic attacks." He mutters.

"Good to know or I was going to strap you down for the ride." She replies half seriously. "Transportation at the other end is being arranged by the powers that be. No idea what, but they won't let me muck around in international negotiations."

"Which brings us back to preventing a war not starting one." Charlie comments garnering a glare from Caro. "I'm just saying."

"You need outfitted more than me." She informs him.

"You need these pants." Dog counters not budging on this subject.

"That will take time to find the material and have them

made." She informs him wondering if he thinks she can nod her head and they will appear like 'I Dream of Genie'.

"I want you wearing these pant." He demands sternly because they are going to need her in them, he is almost certain.

"I can do it." Margaret offers during a glaring match between her daughter and son-in-law as they both look at her. "I just need what she has on now to use as a pattern and the material."

"Oh I can get that." Ethel replies excitedly. "I work at a material store. You want cargo pants material, wet/dry, and what color?"

"Jungle green." Dog answers looking at Cat to see what she thinks.

"She can sew." C.C. replies shrugging and leaving it up to him.

"Then make it sew." He responds grinning though not quite certain this is a good idea as he does not really want her having to deal with her parents at all.

"Margaret did all the adjustments to Clarissa's wedding gown and the bridesmaids dresses." Ethel offers to reassure him his mother-in-law is very talented.

"Good to know." He comments but this is not his immediate concern and he knows Cat will brush off any objection he puts forth for her well being so they will have to deal with her parents on some occasions like the current one.

"Men?" Cat asks getting back to the really important stuff because they are not going on this little adventure alone.

"I have the three I want." He informs her. "They'll be waiting for us and feeling out the locals."

"Oh goody spies." C.C. comments with a grin because having knowledge of the general atmosphere of where they are going always helps.

"You have spies too so you better get them working." He suggests.

"Already do." She informs him as Harv and Moss the former M.P.s are already looking into the job.

"You know it doesn't sound like she really needs you at all." Charles comments as they discuss what needs to be done.

"Shh." Dog shushes him. "Are you trying to get me killed?"

"She's going to figure it out." Charlie warns him with a grin.

"I know but don't tell her now." Dog argues. "By the time

she figures it out she might like me enough to want to keep me around."

"Poor Dog." C.C. sighs as she leans back against him getting comfortable since he is not letting her go back to her chair. "I keep you around because you make me laugh."

"Hey, that's why Ethel keeps me." Charlie responds with a smile.

"The only reason." Ethel replies dryly causing everyone to laugh as Carter walks up to the table looking a little worse for wear from all the dancing and gaiety. His jacket is gone as is his tie, the top buttons of his shirt are undone, and his sleeves are rolled up while he uses his cumber bun to wipe his sweaty face.

"You're looking a little rough around the edges there son." Charlie remarks looking up at Carter.

"Champagne, dancing, champagne and I think we're calling this party over." Carter informs them honestly. "Clarissa is on her way over here then we're slipping out the back door. Our flight leaves in the morning thankfully at ten not five in the morning."

"You're staying at the hotel near the airport right." Margaret asks but Carter puts a finger up to his lips and looks quickly around and she lowers her voice. "Sorry."

"No one heard and we don't care if you all know. It's some of the others who have ideas for pranks we're dodging." Carter explains. "Aren't friends wonderful?"

"Oh yeah." C.C. comments remembering some of the things Carter wrote to her about. "Didn't you and Jake put a honk if you're happy sign out side of Mark's house when he started working nights, then after Paul got married you plastic wrapped his car doors shut the night before he was to fly to Hawaii for his honeymoon."

"Maybe." Carter replies with a grin.

"It's that reaping and sowing thing at work." C.C. comments smiling back thinking of their previous biblical up bringing.

"Not if they can't find me." Carter replies narrowing his eyes at her as Clarissa comes up under Carter's arm wrapping her arms around him and just hanging there.

"I'm sooo tired." She informs them all.

"Then say your goodbyes and let's go." Carter suggests and she goes around the table doing this with hugs before Carter ushers her out.

Chapter 22
Somewhere in the US of A...

"Where are we staying?" Dog asks Cat with interest.

"Regency, penthouse suit." She answers.

"Ah, nice." He replies but not a place he would have chosen. "Gym?"

"There's a little yuppie work out room in the hotel but two blocks down is a boxing gym." C.C. informs him with a grin. "I haven't gone in but since all I see going in and out are men I decided to wait until I had more time before taking off the doors."

"Can I watch?" Dog asks as he smiles and she seems to be taking the no rules apply theory very well.

"Hey I want to watch too." Charlie responds not wanting to left out of seeing this.

"That would be Jaw Breakers I think." Ethel considers as she tries to picture the businesses located in the area around the Regency. "I think it's a membership only kind of place for men geared toward that type of cage fighting which seems to be becoming so popular."

"Sounds like our kind of place." Dog comments with a nod of approval.

"I'm serious." Charlie inserts because he wants to be there although he is certain it will be the Colonel making all the mess. "I'll even bring a bucket and mop to clean up after she's done."

"It won't be so bad unless they do something really stupid like try to throw her out." Dog comments still grinning as he rises up from his chair keeping his arm around Cat's waist so she is going up with him then he drops her to her slipper feet. "How did you get here?"

"Cab." She answers.

"You didn't buy a car did you?" He asks knowing she would not so why is he even asking.

"What for?" She asks him seriously and she can catch a cab anywhere so why worry about dragging a car around with her.

"Yeah, I already knew that." He responds shaking his head.

"Pilot, kick ass plane, so what would you need ground transportation for."

"Exactly." C.C. replies frowning up at him. "Or I can walk."

"Or you can ride with me." He offers.

"You bought a car?" She asks with interest wondering what kind of car a man as big as he is would buy.

"Well I had to have something to drive all over the country tracking my wife." He informs her. "And no, I didn't fly."

"No wonder it took you so long." C.C. responds but she really should have known, not that it would have changed her mind about sending him all over the country. Each bank held a clue to the next bank leading him to her along with cash if he needed it. She could not just tell him where she would be, what fun is that?

"Good night every one." Dog bids the two couples as he heads for the exit.

"I'll be by some time tomorrow." C.C. informs her mother and waves to everyone else as she quickly follows in his wake.

C.C. is not overly surprised by Dog's choice of vehicle and she suspected it would have to be big so they arrive at the Regency in a black gold trimmed Suburban tall enough she has to use the running board to climb into it. Dog seems comfortable in the drivers seat while C.C. could use a booster seat until finding the seat controls sending her seat up wards so she no longer feels like a five year old trying to look over the dash, all though now her feet barely touch the floor.

"Couldn't you find something bigger?" She asks sarcastically.

"No." He responds honestly and he was some what disappointed.

The parking attendant is looking at the Suburban with trepidation and C.C. is not certain this is going to fit into the lower level parking garage. The attendant finally takes the vehicle keys now looking stoic after his first reaction was clearly to run back to the curb when Dog stepped out of the vehicle towering two feet over him. C.C. hides her grin finding the reactions of people to Dog amusing as she leads the way inside the auspicious lobby with Dog carrying his dirty and sadly patched Army issued rucksack past two staring desk attendants to the private elevator off to one side of the main elevator. She slides her key card and the doors open revealing a small elegant couch at the back of the elevator as they step in but C.C. turns finding Dog eyeing the couch.

"You sit on that, it's going to turn into kindling." She warns him as she presses the button for their floor because the slim stylish couch with thin little legs was never made to hold a man as big as he is but as she watches he tosses his rucksack onto it then watches as if expecting it to collapse. "You break it you bought it."

"Might make a good foot stool." He comments after retrieving his rucksack looking about the inside of the elevator finding they put some effort into sprucing up the inside of what is essentially a steel box on a steel string. "Who sits down in an elevator?" He asks because he has never been in an elevator the ride was long enough to require sitting down for.

"Women in mile high heels with bad arches or they simply want to show off more leg." She explains not really giving it much thought before.

"What about the men?" He asks curiously because he can see the benefits of a woman sitting if she is wearing a short skirt and this gives him ideas as well.

"They're not allowed to sit down." She replies with a smile. "If men are able to sit down next to a woman then all kinds of things might happen. This is a classy hotel and they don't want any of those things to happen in here."

"Really." Dog mutters dryly now knowing why he usually stays in cheap motels. "Isn't this just our elevator?"

"No, there are four penthouse suites up here." She explains as the door opens into a hallway with gilded marble tables holding elaborate flower arrangements with gilded framed paintings hanging on the walls over them. "I'm not sure if they are taken but I haven't seen any one yet."

Dog follows her to a door where she swipes her card stepping into an entry leading down into a sunken fancy living area and the furniture is more substantial then the elevator couch but still very classy, only what really grabs his attention is the view out the large floor to ceiling windows taking up the entire far wall. The curtains are open and the city is lit up spread out in a kaleidoscope of lights as he stares stepping down into the living room tossing his rucksack onto a chair then stands just looking out the window.

C.C. removes her jacket tossing it on a chair in the entry before going into the kitchen area to look through the refrigerator pulling out two bottles of ginger ale finding him still standing before the window staring out. She thought he might like this aspect of big vaulted ceilings, lots of big windows, and no reminders here of the last ten years, or tiny rooms. She also knows what else he will like as she carries the bottles to one side of the windows pulling open the balcony door and walks out then around until she is standing in front of him holding up one of the bottles. Dog grins then he is moving toward the door and out on the wide balcony with her and she hands him a bottle.

"Welcome home, Colonel." She offers tapping her bottle to his.

"Thank you, Captain." Dog responds but his eyes are once again drawn to the view beyond the balcony railing and even the air smells different from what he remembers though what he remembers most is the disinfectants the military uses in their buildings.

This is the first opportunity he has taken to just stop and take it all in since he stepped foot off the plane he unfortunately had to take to get back to the States. He has not had much time to relish his new freedom what with worrying about Cat and how well she has integrated back into civilian life while at the same time trying to find her. The fact finding her was not easy reassured him more than anything she is obviously fine.

"You've earned this." C.C. reminds him wondering if he finds everything strange because when he left for foreign soil America was a much different and possibly simpler place then he spent ten years without freedom of any kind to suddenly come back to this.

"We use to talk about what we would do once we came home after the war." Dog admits and it was a dream his unit all shared of coming home to build a life so he knew each of their plans just as they knew his but he ended theirs.

"What were you going to do?" She inquires wanting to know what he thought of at the time because she can see by the look on his face he is thinking about his unit but one thing she has learned, from her own experiences, he cannot dwell on the past. He is the one who has shown her this and going on should not be a punishment but a new adventure so he needs to do the same.

"Oh I had real high expectations." He replies with a grin as he sips his ginger ale then looks at the bottle. "I'm surprised they still make this." So much has changed but ginger ale managed to survive the change of the times but the massively big Cadillac he asked the car salesman for apparently did not.

"It's a classic." She replies knowing there are a lot of things he probably has never tasted or tried that are truly only found in America "Did you plan on getting married, settling down to work somewhere, and having kids?"

"Nope." He responds grinning finding she is totally off base and if he was going to dream then he planned on dreaming much bigger than what any average person might want. "I planned on owning a big fancy car, living in a big swanky house, and maybe run for president."

"Wow." C.C. replies finding she did not expect this. "Well, you've got the big car, although I don't think it qualifies as fancy."

"I like it." He mutters frowning at her.

"Then it's perfect." She responds smiling back. "As for the swanky house, well let's see. Do you like this place?" She asks motioning to the living room and its over the top decor beyond the window. "Because this is swanky."

"It's okay but I really wouldn't want to live here." He admits truthfully and he feels rather uncomfortable wondering if he will break something if he sits on it or touches anything. Of course if he owned the swanky stuff he might not be so concerned except he would have paid the huge price tag and still be worried about breaking it.

"Good, neither would I." C.C. agrees so they at least agree on this. "How about a rustic cabin with huge windows looking out over wilderness and mountains with a really big fire place?"

"Go on." He instructs with interest because she has his full attention now.

"Big rooms with big heavy built furniture but stylish, not chunky." She continues as she moves to the bench by the balcony railing and sits down. "Polished wood floors, Indian throw rugs, and one of us is going to have to kill a deer so we can mount the head on the wall."

"This is doable." He replies as he moves closer to her finding he likes this picture very much. "So where is this house going to be?"

"Well, some place accessible by air, land, and water." She admits because they will need to be able to get out in any weather with equipment and personnel. "Not too close to civilization, no nosy neighbors, and I don't know about you but I really have had enough sand to last me a life time."

"I'm with you there." Dog agrees as he leans down toward her so he can look into her face. "Just where are you building our house Cat?"

"Who says you'll be living there?" C.C. comments frowning at him because she does not remember including him.

"The really big fireplace you forgot to mention." Dog replies because what would a rustic cabin be without a fireplace.

"True." She mutters realizing she gave him too much information. "When Carter gets back and finalizes the contract I'll be building my house, and your really big fire place, in Alaska."

"Alaska." Dog repeats as he considers the ice and snow issues then realizes with her piloting skills it really does not matter. "Snow mobiles?"

"Of course and I'll even add a big heated garage for your not so fancy car." She offers to sweeten the deal.

"Put a place for my 'fancy car' in your big heated hanger where you'll have all your planes so I don't have to walk all over the blasted place." He suggests grimly because some pilots tend to think like birds, if they cannot fly, they walk.

"I suppose." She agrees grudgingly. "But the whole president thing is all yours. I don't have the patience or any inclination to live in the White House."

"I've out grown that one." Dog admits grimly. "I've had my fill of politics for a while."

"Then you might be in the wrong line of work." C.C. warns him as they will be dealing with a lot of bureaucratic red tape doing what they are about to do.

"But now I can always say no." He responds and this makes all the difference in the world to him. "If there's something about a job you don't like, you tell me no, and we don't go. Deal?"

"Deal." She agrees finding this fair enough as she rises to her feet. "Now I really need sleep and you probably do too."

"Cat." He comments reaching out and taking her left hand stopping her then looking at the ring he gave her sparkling on her finger. "Are we really married?"

"Yeah." C.C. answers with concern. "Did you land on your head?"

"No." He replies and smiles but he wants to be certain she has not decided she is better off without him. "I guess I just want to be sure you want to be with me."

"Even though half the time I want to kill you, yes, I want to be with you." She replies honestly and he seems to accept this as a good thing which to her it is.

"There is something I've never told a living person in my entire life." Dog begins as he gently works the ring he gave her from her finger while she glares at him. "You'll get it back. You haven't taken it off since I put it on your finger have you?"

"Not since I reached the States, why would I?" She asks wondering what he is up to now.

"Read the inscription." He instructs handing the ring back to her and she moves closer to the windows where the light is coming from and as she reads she seems to freeze solid. "I've never said those words to anyone. I never thought I would but it's true, probably from the first moment you told me what you would do to me if I touched you." He informs her as he moves to her and taking the ring from her he puts it back on her finger. "I do love you. I just wanted to say it once, even if you don't want to hear it ever again, and I don't expect you to ever say it to me. Because the words aren't important but really big fireplaces and heated garages are."

"Wow, your love doesn't come cheap does it." C.C. replies not certain what to say while knowing the correct response is to say the words back to him but would they really mean anything. "I'm not sure what love means any more."

"Not surprising considering the only person who has shown you unconditional love is Carter and possibly husband number three." He responds understanding and appreciating her candid response rather than just mouthing the words back. "I never gave love much thought myself until I saw Falcon with Songhai. Falcon didn't have to say a word because it was written all over his face every time he looked at Songhai but with Songhai it was difficult to see, then I realized I heard her love for Falcon all the time. Every time she kissed him good bye, fussed about his eating right, and took care of him in all kinds of little ways. If she didn't love him then she cared about him a hell of a lot and I can be happy with that. I know you care."

"I do." C.C. admits rather grudgingly but she never expected him to say 'I love you' and she was fairly certain his reasons for marrying her had more to do with some noble idea of saving her from herself, having a pilot at his beck and call, and the added benefit of sex but his actually loving her never crossed her mind.

"I'm also hoping sleep is not all you have in mind once you lead the way to the bedroom." He confesses hopefully as he reaches out pulling her close.

"I should make you find it." C.C. responds and he grimaces so she takes pity on him. "Come on Dog, follow me."

Despite falling asleep in the early hours of the morning both rise at O'four hundred hours and without discussion both dress for the gym. Dog pulls from his rucksack a pair of sweat pants cut off just below the knees then sticks his bare feet into his combat boots stuffing the untied laces around his ankles before pulling a tank top on over his head while Cat in sweat pants and flip flops wearing a tank top looks at him amazed.

"Wow, they do make clothes your size." She comments for the tank top is actually loose over his shoulders and chest.

"Some times." He grumbles then looking at her he smiles. "I'm some times amazed they make clothes your size. Must be elves." He catches the roll of tape she whips at him before it hits him in the mouth still smiling as she continues digging around in a gym bag on the bed. "What else have you got in there?"

"More tape." She responds then holds up finger-less gloves, two pairs, one small and one x-large which she tosses him the larger pair. "Hope those fit because they're the biggest they had."

"I can go without." Dog replies but he tries them on finding they fit so no more busted knuckles for him but he takes them off handing them back along with a short piece of leather. "I might need that to tie back my hair."

"Or a hair cut." She responds as she puts the leather tie in the bag.

"My hair has a will of it's own, so we have an agreement. If it stays out of my way it gets to stay on my head as long as it likes." He explains completely serious about this. "When it gets in my way then I cut it shorter but as you can see it usually stays out of my way."

"Whatever." C.C. replies thinking this is the strangest excuse for not getting a hair cut she has ever heard. "Doesn't it get hot?"

"No." He responds wondering why she would think so.

"Most people find long hair hot especially black. It's a wonder your brain didn't fry in the desert." She comments as she zips the bag closed.

"No." He repeats looking at her and having a thought. "Do you want me to cut my hair?"

"Not really." C.C. replies looking at him with a frown. "I just thought it might be more comfortable for you."

"Which is why you keep yours short." Dog concludes finding this interesting.

"Yeah, negotiations didn't go so well for me." She explains shaking her head then carrying the bag out into the living room calling back over her shoulder. "Do you want breakfast first?"

"No." He answers from directly behind her and she jumps. "Sorry."

"I should have gotten you a collar with a bell." C.C. breaths finding his stealth mode irritating.

"What did you get me?" He asks her now with a smile.

"What makes you think I got you anything?" She replies grimly knowing she needs to watch her tongue because that is twice now she has given her future plans to torment him away.

"It doesn't have a bell on it." He responds with certainty.

"Fine." C.C. relents moving to the entry closet pulling out two small square jewelry boxes then handing one to him.

He looks down at one of the few presents he has ever received in his life then opens it finds dog tags sitting on red velvet. The fancy box seems over kill for something punched from tin but as he lifts the tags he finds these are not the usual Army issued dog tags. The weight is wrong for nickle or tin so he is thinking solid silver.

There are two tags as usually issued by the military but there all similarities end. The first tag is simply stamped 'DOG' with a birth date below, the second is stamped REWARD, 1,000,000.00 with a phone number causing him to frown as he looks at her.

"Someone had to know your real birthday so I made a stop. When you were enrolled in school the birth date they were given by one of your parents is far more accurate then the one you gave the military when you enlisted." C.C. explains. "You're forty six years old as of this year."

"That old." He replies dryly not certain he really wanted to know but she went to a lot of trouble to get the date for him.

"I knew you were an old Dog when I met you." She responds grinning as she continues. "The second is a phone number to an active phone account Major General Aimhurst opened for only one purpose. If we should get separated on a job or something happens to you, anyone who finds you can call. Dead or alive they get the reward only we won't tell them the first part until we know which." She explains and she had help with this plan. "Wouldn't want anyone killing you for the reward but this is so you won't be buried on foreign soil with some kind of dinky marker. The Major General wants you home buried at Arlington with all the big shebang but mostly alive if at all possible."

C.C. watches his reaction to this as he stares down at the tags now in his hand as he rubs them between his fingers but she can only guess what he must be thinking as he lifts the chain over his head. The tags fall down to the center of his chest then he looks up at her with bright brown/red eyes but before she can judge his mood he grabs her kissing nearly all the air out of her. Just before she fears passing out he wraps her up in a tight hug which is only marginally better but she can now breath if only shallow breaths as her rib cage creaks.

"You better have a set of tags too." He growls in her ear because the thought of him always coming home no matter what is a very special gift to him and he knows she went to some trouble to find his birth date but he is uncertain if the reward to get him back was her idea or the Major Generals only it really does not matter who thought of it.

"Other box." She manages to gasp then he drops her suddenly snatching the box from her unresistant hand as she leans against the back of the couch catching her breath.

"You're twenty nine." He comments after opening the box and examining the tags finding this amusing.

"It's not polite to point out a woman's age." She glowers at him as he lifts the chain over her head and the tags fall down to hang just between her breasts but she instantly lifts the chain dropping the tags under her tank top like she has done for years in the Air Force then reaches out doing the same to his. It is just a habit she got into because the chain can some times get in the way other wise. "Do you want to put your wallet in the gym bag?"

"Yeah." He agrees returning to the bedroom to get it.

Chapter 23
Somewhere in the US of A...

C.C. grabbing her own billfold breaths a sigh, if she did not know better, Dog looked near to tears and now her own throat is tight. Pulling out the key card she puts her billfold in the bag then Dog's wallet when he hands it to her. Zipping the bag and placing the strap over her shoulder she heads for the door with Dog following.

When they exit the elevator into the lobby more people are present than the night before coming and going with whatever business they have here but most stop to stare or quickly move out of their way. Dog's stealth mode is not working here but she imagines if he wanted he could cross this lobby without being seen he could but how is beyond her.

They walk two blocks to the gym entering the front door with no difficulty as pausing to take in the bangs, clanks, and general atmosphere of a fully functional gym which appears small from the outside but goes on seemingly forever holding four boxing rings. Weight stations with enough lifting equipment for serious body builders and no one needs to wait for equipment but there does not seem to be a locker room, or it is so over crowded they were forced to line the walls with lockers and wooden benches.

Dog nods his approval which gains the attention of a young man sitting by the door who was too engrossed in a magazine to notice their entrance but now he is up and out of his chair to stand before them. He is wearing a black tee shirt with what must be the Jaw Breakers logo printed in white consisting of a bare fist connecting with the face of a hulk like neanderthal and teeth flying out.

"She can't be in here." The young man insists pointing at the woman.

"Why not?" Dog asks.

"We don't have changing rooms for women." He explains but he was told never to say this is a men's only gym.

"She's already changed." Dog informs and he is not being

intentionally difficult but this reason is not acceptable. "Besides, she isn't shy."

"But women aren't allowed." He sputters looking uncertain what to say to make his point more clear.

"Didn't see a sign." Dog replies putting a large finger to the young man's bony chest. "If the military lets women in then by God this place should too."

"But." The young man objects only they simply walk by him and this only a part time job for some gas money. He is not about to physically bar a woman while she is standing next to a man as big as a professional wrestler, no job is worth getting pounded.

Dog heads for a bench before the lockers to take off his boots while Cat is opening a locker with no lock on it so it seems members are not assigned lockers. He hands her his boots which she stuffs inside after pulling out her gloves from the gym bag and her her flip flops soon follow his boot. She offers the other pair of gloves which he accepts but when she swings the leather tie in his direction he waves it away.

"Here now." Comes a gravely voice and they turn finding a bulky guy mostly fat with two hulking guys right behind him. "No women allowed in here."

"Why not?" Dog asks and tired of asking the same question because so far no one has given him a good answer.

"No woman's facilities for one, two this is not some froufrou club." He growls seriously. "No yoga classes to be found here."

"Well, good, to the last two and Cat has seen more than her fair share of naked guys so I don't think anything she sees here is going to shock her." Dog responds honestly. "If your regulars are bashful then you can't blame her for that. They'll have to get over it."

"She's going to get hurt." The guy growls flatly as he looks her over. She has some muscle definition but she is good looking woman and these guys do not always play nice. Someone is going to get hurt and even the Goliath with her is not going to stop trouble even with his looks or fists if they think she is a fun target for pranks.

"Are you really fond of these benches?" Dog asks suddenly as the guy just stares at him as if he does not understand. "Do you care what happens to them?"

"Just some boards, hammer and nails takes ten minutes to

put one together." The guy replies puzzled as to what the hell benches have to do with anything.

"Cat." Dog orders hooking a thumb toward an open area between two boxing rings.

When she reaches the area he picks up one of the benches only four foot long with two, two by fours nailed to make legs like the owner said. Without warning he hurls the bench at Cat who leaps up meeting it in the air with her feet flipping the bench in the air so it lands right side up and she leaps up to stand on it.

"Did you want me to break this?" C.C. asks looking at him wondering just what he is hoping to prove by throwing benches at her.

"He says he doesn't care." Dog replies offhandedly motioning to the guy next to him and she shrugs then jumps up coming down busting the bench in two with her bare feet as pieces of splintered boards fly off hitting the edges of the rings and ricocheting off into the weight lifting area.

"Sorry." C.C. calls out to the men nearly hit by flying debris and when she turns back another bench is flying at her. She leaps catching it and spins it legs down then lands standing on it just as another comes at her. She does the same with this one and now she is standing on both benches stacked one on top of the other. "Hey, now I'm taller than you." She smirks at Dog but her smile fades at the look on his face.

"You lied to me." Dog growls grimly as he marches toward her but she back flips off the stack of benches then tosses the top one up giving it a kick sending it hurtling towards him. He leaps catching it as she did with his feet and is now standing on it facing her. "That was more than a six degree black belt."

"Okay, so I kept taking classes but I didn't have time to test." C.C. replies standing on her own bench. "It takes nearly a whole day to test and with Top Gun training then the Seals wanting me to play in their war games, I didn't have time."

"So what degree are you?" He demands and in answer she sends the other bench flying at him which he spins and stacks on the other standing on both while she gives him the hunched shoulders and hands turned up meaning she does not know. "Can you do this?" He jumps coming down breaking both benches in two with his feet and she scowls at him.

"Freaking Ninja." C.C. mutters after him as she surveys the busted benches enviously.

"So are we good here?" Dog asks the man wondering if he is stubbornly going to stick to his no women rule and the assumption Cat will get hurt.

"We're good." The owner replies wondering what the hell just walked into his gym. He is old school boxing but this fancy woo woo stuff keeps turning up in his gym so he has had to make allowances since right now full contact fighting is where the money is as well as the mind set of most of his members. Why not two more? "I'll warn the guys who didn't see that." He motions to the pieces of wood scattered between two rings but they seemed to have gained the attention of many of his regulars already.

"Might not be a bad idea." Dog agrees but he is not concerned as word will spread to leave Cat be and idiots will have to beware. "If you have a ring free I'll wear her out a little. She's been kept out of rings except for one sparing match with me. They were a little concerned about her maiming pilots and it's been a while since she took down some Marines so she's probably ready to cut loose on someone. I would prefer that someone to be me until she gets some of her pent up aggression out of her system."

"I think we would all prefer that." The owner admits honestly as he points to the empty ring next to where they are standing. "Take that one." And as he watches the woman cartwheels into the ring and the man steps over the top rope. "I don't think anyone is going to be getting much of a work out today but I wish I could sell tickets." He informs the guys standing next to him.

They square off in the ring and Dog knows the instant Cat realizes there is no Chief Master Sergeant telling them to take it slow and easy. He is still cautious of putting too much power behind his blows but at full speed Cat is as fast as a striking cobra.

The voices of the men gathered around the ring does not even register as he and Cat spin, kick, and grapple for submission holds all over the ring. An elbow catches him in the nose so he has a trickle of blood running down into his mouth. He catches her with a fore arm in the mouth and she is drooling blood but neither minor injury has stopped them or even slowed them down.

He has no idea how long they have been at it but when they both try flying kicks and end up on the ring floor neither is in a hurry to get back up. Cat is laying face down across from where he is propped up against the bottom ring ropes and he becomes aware of a steady thumping on the ring floor. Looking over he sees

Chuck standing outside the ring smacking his hand down on it with several men still gathered outside the ring watching.

"Come on Caro." Chuck calls loudly over the men talking around the ring. "You can take him. He's down, get up."

C.C. raises up onto her elbows looking to her side seeing Chuck's grinning face among the other men as she realizes blood is about to drip from her chin to the mat so she wipes it off on her own shoulder. Last thing they need is to slip and break a leg on a wet spot. She focuses on Charlie again wondering what he is doing here but as usual he is talking.

"You've got him on the ropes." Chuck informs her. "Don't be a little girl and wuss out now."

Good old Chuck, Dog thinks to himself as he rolls toward Cat because she is now using her fore arms to crawl to the side of the ring where she is probably planing to strangle Chuck. He catches her by an ankle and pulls her back to the middle of the ring before sitting up again looking at Chuck.

"You of all people should know better than to poke sticks at tigers." Dog reminds Chuck grimly.

"It wasn't a tiger, it was a jaguar." Chuck corrects him. "And I wasn't the one stupid enough to jump on it, that was you."

"It was going to eat you." Dog reminds him.

"Well that didn't work out so well did it." Charlie responds. "You killed it and we ate it. Right now the two of you look like something a jaguar drug out of the bush."

"Feel like it too." Dog replies candidly. "We have a government job in two days and she just cracked two of my ribs."

"Wa wa." C.C. replies with her forehead resting on the mat hoping she has enough strength left to crawl with some dignity out of the ring as they seem to have drawn a crowd who seem intent upon staying.

"Well she's going to have a black eye." Chuck predicts pointing at Caro.

"That's from landing on my face." She informs him pushing herself up to a sitting position on her knees. "The split lip was all him."

"You bloodied my nose first." Dog points out.

"Ha, first blood, she wins." Charlie hoots with glee.

"I like the way you think." C.C. replies with a grin but winces as she blocks the fresh flow of blood from her lip with her forearm.

"I can't wait to hear how you're going to explain this to your parent's when you see them later today." Chuck responds with interest.

"Well, there is that." C.C. replies looking at Dog who is brushing at his nose with the back of his hand and then she laughs despite the pain of her lip because she was having a blast.

"I'd laugh to if you hadn't crack my ribs." Dog responds dryly as he rises to his feet then bends down lifting her with one arm around her waist then simply tosses her over the top rope where she spins in the air landing on her feet just as he knew she would. Cats are cats.

"So what are you two planning to do for an encore?" Charlie asks as the Colonel jumps down from the ring.

"Lift weights." Dog replies though with some difficulty now thanks to his wife.

"Jump rope." Cat answers because her blood is pumping and singing in her veins so she intends to keep it that way.

"What a dull couple you are." Chuck complains as he turns and makes his way out of the gym.

Dog thinks Chuck should have stayed because there is nothing dull about Cat jumping rope. He has two guys who offered to spot for him at a weight bench but between sets he looks over to the small open area Cat found where she is now jumping rope with head phones on. She probably has no idea everyone at one time or another stops what they are doing to watch her and he is not sure what she is listening too but he is certain it must be music because she is dancing to it. The rope is a blur as she turns, hops on one foot than the other, and some times jumps up high so the rope does not touch the floor, frankly he has never seen any thing like it.

"Are you two joining us?" The owner walks up during one of Dog's breaks to ask.

"We won't be here very long." Dog assures him.

"Yeah government job." The owner replies with a grin as everyone over heard and this guy has seen more than his fair share of action which is obvious from his looks but the where is a little murky so this leaves one conclusion. "Mercenaries?"

"International Security." Dog responds but some would say they are one in the same.

"Mercs." The owner repeats grinning still. "You're just pickier about who you work for."

"That's one way to look at it." Dog admits. "We might be back for a while. Our new base isn't set up yet and our lawyer is here."

"Then I'll just leave an open invitation to come when you want." The owner replies holding out his hand to show no hard feelings.

"Appreciate it." Dog admits shaking his hand.

Walking back to the hotel a few hours later they encounter more people on the street as they receive stares but C.C.'s body is still humming with energy and Dog does not seem to even notice the attention he is receiving. She imagines they will get looks no matter where they go or what they wear which does not bother her where once she tried so hard to blend in or at least appear normal. The door man nods politely and opens the door for them but as they cross the lobby one of the desk clerks intercepts them.

"Mrs. Red Eagle, I'm sorry to bother you, but there are two men here wishing to speak with you." The desk clerk informs her motioning to a hallway leading off the lobby.

They follow him to a room with chairs and a television where Harv and Moss seem to be engrossed on lap top computers sitting before them on a glass top coffee table. They look up in unison then snap the lap tops closed rising from the couch saluting and civilian life has apparently not set in for them yet. Both are still clean cut and wearing suits much in the way they wore their uniforms but neither is carrying a riffle now.

"Give it up guys," C.C. mutters. "I didn't salute you before and I'm sure not doing it now. Dog is your boss not your commanding officer."

"Sorry." They reply in unison.

"Come on up." She orders while Dog shakes his head in amusement.

In the penthouse they leave the former M.P.s on their own in the living room as they shower in the massive master bath room. When Dog puts on another pair of blue jeans and tightens the belt around his waist pleating the material C.C. shakes her head. They are really going to have to do something about his clothing she reminds herself as she steps into cargo pants and once she has on her tank top she turns to find him shaking his head at her.

"Definitely need those pants." He informs her because dressed as she is she looks ready for battle but he wants that looked toned down a little.

"Well at least I don't look like I'm ready to loose mine." She responds pointing at his cinched tight belt not appreciating being critiqued about her clothing, those days are over.

"Think your mother can fix this?" He asks but really he is still not too sure about her parents.

"We'll take the combat pair you're going to wear and see." She decides because there is no harm asking. "She'll either have time or not."

"You do realize your eye is going black and you do have a split lip." He informs her because one thing he has noticed about Cat is she never looks into a mirror even now with them in abundance, not even in the little square mirror he saw on the back of her pocket book.

"While you look perfectly fine. Thank you for pointing this out." She grumbles not seeing his reason for mentioning it other than to brag.

"I think your parents are going to notice." He continues and he knows everyone else will.

"And your point is?" C.C. asks still not certain what he is getting at.

"They could accuse me of beating you." He responds flat out.

"So?" She asks not seeing the problem. "I don't care what they think or what they say. It's not their place and they lost all right to tell me what I should, or shouldn't do, a long time ago."

"Did you know your father had a stroke?" Dog inquires and they manipulated her once before so they might attempt to regain control.

"Carter told me in one of his letters." C.C. admits but she never considered what kind of damage this left and truthfully she never asked. "Do you think I should've come running home?"

"No." He replies grimly but he understands from what Chuck and he heard her parents may try to interfere for entirely different reasons now.

"So what's your point?" She asks again not understanding why her parents are even an issue suddenly.

"They've changed." He replies wanting her to consider this aspect and to see if this weighs any differently with her.

"So have I." She counters because she is no longer the meek little girl she once was.

"You're right." He concedes. "I don't know what point I'm getting at either. I never stopped to see if my father is dead or alive and I have a mother somewhere but I'm not about to make the effort to find her."

"So we both come from screwed up families." C.C. responds then shrugs because most people do. "That's in the past and can't be changed. You and I are building a future by our own rules. Mother offered to make the pants so I took her up on it because she can sew, and Dog, I'm going to pay her just as I would have paid someone else to do it. That's the way it is."

"Okay." Dog agrees and it is probably the best way to handle the situation all the way around.

"Lets go see what Harv and Moss have to report and get them working on our future." C.C. suggests while tucking her dog tags under her shirt.

"Really big fire place." He reminds her with a smile.

"You could take a nap in it." She informs him rolling her eyes before leading the way out of the bedroom heading for the kitchen finding Moss in the refrigerator.

"Wow." Moss comments as he backs out of the refrigerator closing the door. "Are you stocking up for an invasion here?"

"The hotel provides most of the food then inventories what is left and charges us for what is missing." C.C. explains seeing his plate of crackers on the counter and the round of brie cheese he is holding.

"Whoops." He replies turning back to the refrigerator.

"Oh for crying out loud." She responds shoving past him to reach the refrigerator. "Dog can afford cheese and crackers, eat it."

"Are you sure?" He asks glancing out toward the Colonel standing in the living room.

"Apparently I'm buying land, building a house with heated garages, and Cat bought herself a jet, so yeah I can." Dog assures the man having over heard as he takes a chair since Harv and Moss seem to have taken over the couch and the coffee table.

"Maybe we should ask for a raise." Harv suggests.

"You're being paid quite well." C.C. counters grimly probably more than they are both worth. "If you choose to spend it on suits this is your problem."

"We need to blend in to the working world of politics and government officials." Moss explains taking his plate of crackers, cheese and two bottles of soda to the coffee table.

"All though the real estate agent we dealt with on the Alaska contract wore hiking boots, hunting camouflage and a hunting hat no self respecting moose would be caught dead being shot by." Harv comments.

"Ooh." C.C. exclaims suddenly popping up out the refrigerator from searching for more ginger ale. "A moose head."

"She's collecting dead animals to hang on the wall." Dog explains to the two men who look confused.

"Just one." She corrects while handing him a ginger ale before sitting on the arm of his chair facing Harv and Moss. "So what are we walking into?"

"The local government's military and security force is too small and too weak to keep all the unwanted out of the country so whenever another government wants someone hiding in their borders they throw open the doors and say go get them yourself." Moss explains. "Nice but not much help which is why our government hired you. They consider this a hunting for a needle in haystack job and if they send military in on a dead end mission then tax payers get bent out of shape."

"So they pay big bucks and hire private instead." C.C. replies getting this. "No media following us, no families finding their soldiers are being used for something other than defending our country, and if there is a screw up they can disclaim all knowledge."

"I knew you'd catch on to this quick." Dog comments with a grin before returning his attention to Harv and Moss. "What I need to know is who has the package?"

"This is where it gets sticky." Harv admits. "Roaming bands of guerrillas all over the place and this band no one seems to have ever heard of suddenly has an American business man as hostage wanting millions for his safe return. The only reason our government is even involved is because this guy's company is contracted by the government for some highly secret project and they need him back."

"So where do we start looking?" C.C. asks looking at Dog knowing he probably has an idea.

Chapter 24
Somewhere in the US of A...

"We contact Rayjo Velasquez." Dog replies simply knowing it will be difficult but necessary. "He and I have worked together before to our mutual benefit. He leads a band of what he calls Freedom fighters and knows everything which goes on, some times before it happens."

"So we get the business man back but what is in it for this guy?" C.C. wants to know.

"Money." Dog informs her simply because what else would these people want, though weapons would be appreciated only the US would never go for handing guerrillas weapons unless they were sure which way they will jump if asked.

"Of course, I should have guessed." She replies dryly but this seems strange at the same time. "The local government is throwing open the door for us to get this business man back and we're going to pay this Freedom Fighter whom I assume wants to over throw the government, so he in turn can use the money to defeat a government which cooperates with us. Am I the only one who finds this sort of wrong?"

"Not at all." Dog responds finding once again he likes how she thinks. "Rayjo is an egomaniac. The government is elected but rather than buying votes to win an election he buys guns and soldiers. He's so busy amassing his army of fanatics and feathering his own nest he doesn't even consider the fact no one will recognize him as president let alone let him keep the title. The UN will step in with America to help and take it back. But in the mean time his own men hate him, continually deserting, and what few he has remaining are all show and no substance. He's been plotting to over throw the government for nearly twenty years while living in jungle luxury. The local government knows where he is but they don't see any reason to waste men or ammunition going in to bring him out and they have bigger problems than Rayjo who thinks they're afraid of him."

"A wanna be dictator." C.C. comments understanding now.

"I truly do like the way you think." He admits out loud. "But be impressed when you meet him. He's more useful when he feels important."

"Duly noted." C.C. agrees dryly because one must keep joke wannabe dictators happy. "So how do we get hold of him?"

"We have the Major General call him." Dog replies because it just occurs to him how this can be done simply and realistically. "Rayjo is not very impressed by a mere Colonel asking a favor. I had someone pretend to be a U.S. official last time but this is risky and he might actually catch on one of these days."

"This is like romper room with little bullies and toys that go bang." She mutters amazed at what they are going to go through to get cooperation from a man who obviously likes his ego stroked.

"So what do you want us to do next?" Harv asks smiling because he likes the way the Captain thinks too.

"Good question." C.C. agrees looking to Dog. "Alaska is on hold until Carter gets back in a week."

"So how are you guys set?" Dog asks and gets blank looks from them. "You have places to stay, seen family and friends yet?"

"Well we kinda hit the ground running." Moss replies looking to Harv who shrugs. "We've been traveling pretty much. I called my sister but she's busy with husband, kids, and work. Seemed kinda rushed to me and my folks are on a three week ocean cruise somewhere in the Caribbean, won't be back for another two weeks, so I'm good."

"My parents are dead and I'm an only child." Harv adds with a shrug. "No one I need to go see and no ex girlfriend I ever want to see again."

"In other words their personal family life is as screwed up as ours." She responds looking toward Dog. "Except we have each other."

"True." He agrees making a mental note to kiss her for admitting this later since both Harv and Moss are watching "No place you want to take a weeks vacation?"

"Not really." Moss responds but concerned about taking a vacation when they have barely been on the job. "Is this a paid vacation we're talking about because if it is we can stay here, I mean in this city not right here, and be fine."

"Get them one of those other suites for a couple of weeks." Dog suggests to Cat with a smile. "We'll take them to Jawbreakers with us."

"Sounds good." C.C. replies hiding a smile or they will know they are being set up to take a painful fall as she waves them out the door with her then down to the front desk where she sets them up with the suite across the hallway. They get their own key cards then retrieve their luggage from the desk attendant as C.C. returns. "Well the kids are tucked in for the time being. We need to get to my parents house." She reports.

Dog is snorting with laughter at her reference to Harv and Moss as she grabs her harem pants and his combat pants to take with them. He is still chuckling in the elevator and as they wait for the Suburban to be brought around by the parking attendant he grabs her and kisses her in front of the hotel and the doorman as the car pulls up to the curb. She does not ask what this is all about when he releases her with a smile on his face as she makes the climb into the car.

Dog parks in front of Cat's parent's house in what appears to be a quiet suburban neighborhood remembering as a child he once dreamed of living in a place like this with families and kids his own age but now after years of fighting in crowded areas he wonders who or what is behind all the closed curtains which gives him the creeps.

Climbing out of the vehicle he walks up the front sidewalk behind Cat to the front door of this sprawling ranch type home wondering what Cat must feel returning to the place she escaped. The dark wood door opens revealing her mother Margaret giving them a big smile which quickly fades upon actually seeing her daughter and he waits to see how she will react.

"Charlie said you had a black eye but wow, it's a whopper." Margaret comments making light of her daughters injuries but the split lip actually looks quite painful. Her daughter's eye is puffy at the outer edge just above her cheek bone up to her eye brow and red now but darker shades of purple are beginning to show.

She is painfully aware at one time her first words to her daughter would have been, 'What have you done this time?', because everything was Carolyn's own fault and her daughter became the scapegoat of their religious beliefs. Beliefs so out dated and unforgiving very few churches, if any, follow them any more so in a sense they sacrificed their love, care, and respect for their only daughter on the alter of their misguided beliefs. There is no going back to undo the wrongs they heaped upon her so all they can do is move forward praying their daughter will give them a second chance and allow them into at least a part of her life.

"It's not as bad as it looks." C.C. replies as she steps in the door feeling a cold chill down her spine because she is entering once again the Callahan shrine.

"You seem to have come out without a mark." Margaret addresses her son-in-law whom looks rather savage but she is no longer blind when once upon a time his long hair would have been enough to dislike him but now she sees exactly how he is with Clarissa and Charlie who says he owes this man his life. How this man feels about her and Stan remains to be seen but utter disgust would not be out of line.

"She cracked two of my ribs. It'll be a couple days before anyone can admire my bruises." Dog responds as he steps in after Cat into the small entry with tile floors and peach colored walls. He closes the door behind him but he does not get the willies in this small area because there are two doorways, one leading down a short hallway and another into a large room, and long panels of windows letting in sun light on either side of the door but he wonders if Cat is the one feeling trapped.

"I don't understand it." Margaret admits honestly shaking her head because it seems the only goal in contact fighting is inflicting damage to each other. "Why do people want to beat on each other?"

"It's a work out." C.C. explains simply. "You sweat and build muscle while working on reflexes. You know the saying no pain, no gain."

"Which is much easier for her to say than me at the moment." Dog grumbles and to his surprise Margaret laughs. "Well, I know whose side you're on."

"Well I certainly don't want to be between the two of you." She comments with certainty then on to the business which brought them here. "Ethel brought me the material. Actually she brought three different types so you can choose. Dog?" She begins but pauses undecided but really she must say something. "What is your real name? If you don't mind my asking."

"Johann." He informs her wondering why she is asking.

"Johann." She repeats with a smile. "I like that, it's very

nice. If you don't mind I would like to call you by your name. To say my son-in-law Dog makes it sound as if I don't really like you very much."

"She has a point." C.C. responds with a grin looking up at him. "I can just see her saying to one of her friends, 'The other day my daughter's Dog was hit by a car', imagine the confusion."

"No confusion, you would be the one driving the car." Dog replies.

"More like a bus." C.C. admits to her mother. "Did you see what he bought parked out front?"

"I did and I think it's very nice." Margaret replies because a big man would need a big vehicle and it looks rather sharp.

"See she likes it." Dog gloats as Stan moves into the doorway leading into the living room seeing them in the entry and with slow shuffling steps he moves toward them.

"Why are you all standing here?" He asks gruffly and he wonders if they intend to beat a hasty retreat once they conclude their arrangements with Margaret. He cannot really blame Carolyn if she does not want to spend any more time here than she has too.

"Dog bought a bus." C.C. informs him simply as her father looks at her then moves to the door opening it to look out.

"Yep, he did." Stan agrees looking back at them with a half smile. "Good looking bus too."

"I need to get started." Margaret mutters shaking her head at her husband. "I have two days, am I correct?"

"Yes." C.C. agrees holding out the harem pants to her. "The skirt needs to be four inches shorter, add belt loops, and make sure the pocket openings are like these so they are difficult to see."

"Yes, I see what they did and they are practically invisible aren't they." Margaret replies after examining the pants now in her hands finding the material feels wonderful and the stitching was very well done.

"Are you going to have enough time?" C.C. asks because she knows they use to keep a very busy social schedule with projects such as church bazaars and care groups.

"Oh, of course." Margaret replies with a wave of her hand. "I should have this done by tomorrow morning so you can try them on and we can make adjustments if needed."

"You don't have to stay up all night or anything." C.C. comments because this time frame seems much faster than she remembers her mother making clothing.

"It won't take long to put them together." Margaret assures her daughter easily. "What will take the longest is taking this pair apart. Oh, I hope you knew that."

"I thought so." C.C. replies having seen her mother copy clothing before and picking out all the seams to use the old as a pattern for the new. "Cut the seams if it's faster."

"Oh no." Margaret remarks horrified by the suggestion. "Then I won't be able to put them back together again."

"It's no big deal." C.C. informs her mother since she doubts she will have another occasion to actually wear this outfit again. "Besides you're going to make a pattern from this one so you can make another pair later."

"But this one looked so wonderful on you." Margaret responds ruefully and at one time she would have never allowed Carolyn to wear such an unconventional and rather suggestive outfit but it suited her daughter's small stature and fit the occasion wonderfully. Far from men ogling her daughter as she would have feared they simply smiled in appreciation at a beautiful woman. Carolyn obviously has good taste and her own style which Margaret is fully aware being her mother she should have encouraged and help develop when Carolyn was a child. Thankfully Carolyn managed it on her own. "The jacket will never match because I doubt I can find a color which will match this. I can have this done in no time, don't worry."

"Well the reason I'm asking for speed is because of these." C.C. replies holding up Dog's combat pants then motioning to him. "Look at his waist."

"Oh dear." Margaret comments seeing the gathering at his waist. "I didn't even notice last night but this is not good. Let me grab my tape measure. I can have this done in fifteen minutes, it just requires putting in darts, simple." She heads down the hallway to her sewing room.

"It's a women thing." Stan informs Dog who looks at him in question. "But they have a point. If you need that belt for something else you're going to be feeling some breeze."

"Never thought of that." Dog remarks because he will loose his pants without the belt and he might need the belt for something else. In his line of work a belt is not just to hold up his pants but something to be used even as a weapon or tool if necessary.

"Let me find out what your waist should be." Margaret

suggests returning and not hesitating reaches around Johann to measure his waist then taking the pants from Caro she heads back to her sewing room.

"Might as well sit down." Stan offers as he moves into the living room.

They follow taking seats on a matching couch and love seat as her father takes his recliner while C.C. glances about finding much has changed in her parents home. The room is far more homey than she remembers and no longer feels like sitting in some kind of shrine, which she found rather daunting to have Jesus, his disciples, and crucifixes all about the room as if judging her. There was even a crown of thorns hanging in the dinning room chandelier she never found very appetizing and wonders if it is still there.

New furniture, carpeting and paint along with the absence of other biblical paraphernalia have made the room far less daunting and there is a very beautiful cross on the fire place mantel she does not remember seeing before. Even stranger are the family photos on the mantel some of both her and Carter and she honestly did not know they had pictures of her other than school photos but the one of her and Carter after he passed his driving test at sixteen she remembers. She passed her test the same day but they bought Carter a car given he needed transportation for his sporting events and the parents wanted a picture of him with his car and just before the shot was taken Carter grabbed her pulling her into the frame. It is probably the last picture of them together in existence because not more than a year later she left.

"You're trying to figure out if that's a cow or a dog." Stan speculates watching Dog who is studying the painting across from where he sits on the sofa above his daughters head. Stan is afraid to look at Carolyn who can have no good memories here and fears seeing the hatred he so richly deserves yet cannot bare to see.

"It's a donkey." Dog replies with conviction as Cat turns on the love seat so she can see what they are talking about.

"It is." Stan admits with surprise. "Everyone guesses a dog or a cow.

"Ears are too long." Dog informs him with certainty. "I know, I practically slept with one when I was a kid."

"Seriously?" C.C. asks eyeing him from where she is now turned so she can look from the painting to him and there seem to be several interesting paintings on the walls she notices now. Nothing of valuable she is certain but interesting enough to hang and they add to this new comfortable feeling of the room.

"I wasn't born in a barn but the barn was warmer than the house." Dog explains without shame. "Animals create a lot of body heat and when I was young we had a barn full but as time went on my father sold them all off. I missed the donkey the most but he was a cover hog. So why is there a Donkey on your wall?"

"It was one of my first attempts at painting." Stan responds not judging his son-in-law who obviously grew up poor and at one time he knows he would have made all kinds of false assumptions based on this information but he is no longer as judgmental or as sanctimonious as he once was. "I painted all of these and you can see I did improve over time."

"Wow." C.C. comments because some of the paintings are good as she rises walking around looking at the paintings but she never knew her father could paint and she thought artists require some kind of sensitivity.

"After my stroke the doctors insisted I needed a pet because it's calming and helps relieve stress but I'm allergic to nearly everything with fur so they came up with painting." Stan explains but it was not as simple as it sounds. "Or rather your mother came up with the idea and convinced my doctors to push it on me. I use to paint, a long time ago, so she decided I should do so again then she began working at a hobby store where she is given half off my paint supplies. How is that for convenient?"

"Sounds like a well executed strategy." Dog comments.

"I was out maneuvered from the very start." Stan agrees which he did not appreciate at the time given he was mad at everyone for a good deal of time during his recovery.

"What exactly is this one?" C.C. asks having found a small painting in the entry she did not notice when they first arrived as she moves about admiring her father's art work and looking at it from every angle the nearest thing she can compare it to is a pink peach.

""It's exactly what it looks like." Stan replies without apology and he still feels justified in painting it. "It's a bare butt. "I call it Charlie."

Dog leaps from the couch as Cat bursts out laughing and his mind reels at what could possibly be named for Chuck and the small painting can hardly be mistaken for anything else as he moves back into the living room with Cat pulling her down to sit next to him.

"Why Chuck?" Dog asks and he can see the resemblance to Chuck very well but he is curious as to what Cat's father has seen.

"That was my next painting after the Donkey." Stan explains and sweet revenge it was too. "Charlie sat right where you are and told me my painting was of a rabbit with constipation. So I did the other painting and when he asked what it was, I told him a mirror."

"How long have you known Chuck?" Dog asks as Cat laughs because this was an excellently planned an executed strategy.

"Ten years or so." Stan replies but he has to wonder. "How long have you known him?"

"I met Chuck in Nam. He was the sorriest excuse for a soldier I'd ever seen." Dog explains grimly and it was not the place Chuck ever should have been. "He was drafted and passed the physical, which was all they were concerned about at the time. Handing him a rifle was the stupidest thing anyone could've ever done because he never loaded it and mostly poked people with it minus the bayonet since he used that for a tent stake somewhere and forgot to pull it out before they moved on. My unit spent three weeks with his and I'm fairly certain we saved his life twelve times before we parted ways. I was actually shocked to see him still alive but if morale was low then Chuck was your man. I think it may be why he is still alive because everyone watched out for him, he was their lucky charm, or he wasn't as inept as he appeared,which would make him one of the bravest men I've ever met."

"Do you know what Charlie does now, or did before he retired a couple years ago?" Stan asks and Dog shakes his head. "He was a physical therapist who specialized in stroke and heart attack victims. He had the highest recovery rate of any one in his field and one of the hardest parts of the job is to keeping people fighting to get back what they lost and not give up. This is how I met Charlie and he is one of the hardest task masters there is but you're laughing so hard you don't really even notice. He taught me to walk again then filled my shoes full of water and put them in the freezer. When I complained he turned to me saying, 'What are you belly aching about, you said you'd never walk again so you don't need shoes. I'm taking the wife on a picnic and these will keep the potato salad cold', then he sewed my left sleeve to the side of my hospital gown so I had to use only my right arm or I would moon the nurses. When I was finished with therapy he looked at me and said, 'You can walk, you can talk, and you can feed yourself but I can't do anything about your face. That was your problem before you came to me so you're just going to have to live with it'. We've been friends ever since."

"But Clarissa and Carter met by accident?" C.C. responds imagining her father's frustration trying not to moon the nurses at the hospital. Public nudity for the stern and morally prudent Stan Callahan is just not done.

"They did." Stan replies earnestly. "Carter was off in college when all this happened and so was Clarissa. We knew who she was and Carter knew the Kincaids by name from us talking about them but not by sight. Carter and Clarissa never met through us. None of the four of us pushed for a meeting since we were both paying good money for college hoping neither dropped out because they found someone. We did what most parents do and compared progress reports on our kids but never introduced them. It didn't occur to us to put them together once they graduated going on with their separate lives which included dating other people. Then a little boy was hit by a drunk driver and they were sort of thrown together so imagine our surprise when Carter starts going on about this girl named Clarissa. We didn't think anything of it until Charlie and Ethel told us their Clarissa is seeing some boy named Carter. When we realized it couldn't just be a coincidence we were afraid to say anything in case we jinxed it. So we played dumb right up until the engagement party when they introduced us to each other."

"How did you keep Charlie quiet?" C.C. asks because she cannot see him keeping a secret.

"I thought we would have to tape his mouth shut." Stan replies honestly. "Clarissa was getting such broad hints Ethel was having fits but Clarissa commutes so far to work and lives else where so most of their conversations were over the phone so Ethel could yank the phone from him or smack him if he got too out of line. Charlie said he was black and blue for months until they announced the engagement."

Chapter 25
Somewhere in the US of A...

"Here you are." Margaret announces holding out the pants to Johann. "There is a bath room right through there, go try them on, and if they fit give me the jeans you have on."

"These can wait." Dog objects knowing she has work to do.

"Nonsense." Margaret replies with a wave of her hand. "You should have at least one pair of regular pants which fit."

Dog does as instructed then comes out in his combat pants meekly handing her his jeans and she promptly disappears with them. Cat stands and walks around him then she holds up her hand smacking it so he does a side kick toward her hand but not connecting.

"Good?" She asks because they still seem to be loose where they need to be.

"Great." He replies standing on one foot and extending one leg straight up in standing splits then putting it back down. "This will do fine."

"Wait, one more test." She requests walking behind him and pulling down on the outer seams of his pants but other than a slight lowering they do not come down without his belt only she notices something else which his bagging waist line hid. "Wow."

"What?" He asks trying to look over his shoulder to see what she is looking at.

"Bodacious booty alert as my flight would say." She informs him. "I'm going to have to start walking behind you to fend off women."

"All I have to do is turn around and they'll run off screaming." He assures her rolling his eyes at Stan who is grinning at him from his recliner.

"So far not one woman we've met coming or going from the hotel has run off screaming." She reminds him dryly.

"The one by the elevator nearly fainted when we left today." He comments or maybe she did not notice the woman sway when she saw him.

"She was hyperventilating." C.C. responds and for reasons which have nothing to do with fear but the woman's eyes never left Dog's chest. "Not the same thing at all."

"Close enough." He replies not seeing a difference.

"This is not horseshoes or hand grenades." She informs him. "Did you see the guy she was with? If we had hung around long enough for her to catch her breath she would've jumped you then and there. I'll have to start carrying mace."

"Why in the world would you carry mace?" He mutters.

"Black belt." She reminds him. "I so much as touch someone and they press charges for assault I get nailed with a very heavy fine because of my training, if not jail time. I told you this."

"Right." He responds but self defense should still be allowed.

"Just don't touch any one." She warns him.

"You've not been in the US in a while I take it." Stan guesses as Dog nods. "Things change. Mobile phones are catching on, computers are becoming the big fade, and they're coming up with remote controls for nearly everything now."

"We had some of those in the military before everyone else did." Dog informs him. "This last war was fought from the air with programmed targeting. Cat's jet was nothing but a computer with wings."

"Hey, it couldn't fly its self." She replies feeling slighted. "The Night Hawks can once they get off the ground."

"It's a whole new world." Stan sighs shaking his head in wonder. "Hard for me to keep up. Clarissa was talking about motorized arms and legs working on brain impulses but this is not as frightening to me as planes flying themselves."

"I agree." Dog admits.

"Me three." C.C. offers and they both look at her. "Hey I want to be the one flying the plane not a computer. Where is the fun in that? Besides what would you need me for?"

"I need you for more than flying the plane, helicopter, or what ever else we come across." He informs her honestly. "I trust you six times farther than I can throw you. Twenty times more than any computer."

"You say the most romantic things." She teases with a grin.

"Where exactly are the two of you going?" Stan asks knowing he probably should not. "Or is it a secret?"

"Yes and no." Dog replies thoughtfully. "We can't say exactly but we can tell you South America which covers a lot of territory."

"And most of it jungle." Stan adds but everyone knows drug lords and other unsavory people hide there where authorities cannot reach them.

"A tropical paradise for our honeymoon." C.C. responds which makes her think to ask. "Did Carter and Clarissa make their plane alright?"

"Yes. Carter called from the airport before they left. He said Jake found where they were staying." Stan grins lopsidedly. "And so did Mark and Paul."

"Whoops." C.C. grimaces knowing pay back was bound to happen. "So what did they do?"

"Well, the limo dropped them off at the hotel and they planned to take a taxi to the airport so no car to mess with. They took turns knocking on their door and shining flash lights in the windows." Stan explains. "But other than this there wasn't much they could do and he thinks hotel security called the police on them. He said he heard talking and saw flashing red and blue lights but it could've been something else."

"And he gets away again." C.C. responds amazed as she shakes her head wondering why she did not get the Callahan luck.

"Haven't you heard." Dog remarks. "Lawyers are slippery."

"Then he's an excellent lawyer." She replies. "He's been training for it all his life."

"Okay, now try these." Margaret instructs Johann as she returns holding out his jeans.

"That was fast." Dog comments as he takes the jeans as he rises.

"There are only so many places to put darts in jeans that won't mess with the pockets so I did it with only four." She explains smiling. "If you gain weight we can let one or two out."

"Some how I don't see that happening." C.C. comments as Dog disappears into the bath room and when he returns she twirls a finger and he turns around in a circle. "Yeah, gonna need mace."

"Before you leave, to where ever you're going, if you let me have his other pants I can adjust those too." Margaret offers. "I also matched the colors of the material Ethel brought me and one matches his first pair so I'll use that color for your pants Carolyn."

"Perfect."   C.C. agrees finding this works out just fine. "Here, let me give you our number and you can call when mine are done so I can come try them on." She writes her number on the pad her mother hands her. "Let's go Dog and get something to eat then check on the kids."

"Good idea." He agrees wholeheartedly when it comes to food but as for the other two they are on their own.

"Kids?" Margaret asks wondering if she missed something as she and Stan follow them to the door. Does their daughter have children they know nothing about?

"Mid-twenty something former Army M.P.s." Dog informs her while grinning at Cat. "She's sort of adopted them."

"Me?" C.C replies indignantly. "Who brought them here and dumped them on me?"

"I couldn't just leave them to fend for themselves." Dog responds seriously.   "Their classes don't start until fall, no real place to live, and the only actual job experience they have is as armed guards which we both saw they weren't very good at. Their computer knowledge is useful."

"They do make good ferrets." C.C. admits because they did just dive right in to whatever she gave them to look for. "They're pets, information ferrets. I think I'll put that in their job description."

"Thank you Margaret for fixing my pants which I didn't realize were broken and Stan for the stories." Dog offers turning to look at the painting by the door and laughing. "We need one of these?"

"No, we do not." Cat informs him as she pushes him out the door. "Talk soon."

Once they reach the truck C.C. looks back at the house then to the road as Dog pulls away from the curb and many things have changed in the Callahan house hold. Her father painting pictures of rear ends and her mother allowing him to hang it by the front door is just one of many. They are the same people she once knew, yet they are not.

They elect to eat out which seems a relatively new experience for Dog and entering the buffet they create something of a sensation but it is just as C.C. suspected as the women who were once drawn to staring at his broad shoulders now spend an equal amount of time staring at his back side. He may think it is his scars which makes them stare but C.C. knows better and scars or no scars Dog is one big hunk of man. When Dog pulls out his wallet to pay the rather stunned looking woman at the cash register C.C. reaches over his arm pulling out his military ID handing it to the woman.

"Military discount." She informs him when he frowns at her.

"Really." He replies with interest. "Wish I'd known that earlier. I could've skipped a couple of banks when I was trailing you."

"I'm surprised they didn't ask for it." C.C. admits because who cannot see just by looking at him, unless they think he was thrown through a few dozen windshields or something.

"They tended to stutter a lot." Dog informs her.

"Women?" C.C. asks knowingly.

"Mostly, yes." He admits looking at her wondering how she knew but she just smiles at him being no help at all in interpreting the reason.

Once they find a table and get their plates they go to the buffet tables to fill them and C.C. has her plate relatively covered but Dog comes back with a heaping mound of food on his. As they eat C.C. catches people looking over at them and grins. It boggles the mind Dog can simply disappear when he chooses when everyone cannot seem to miss him right now. Freaking Ninja.

"I'm going to tell you something." Dog admits suddenly after eating part of the food on his plate since Cat does not seem very talkative. "I like your parents, who they are now. When your father told me they virtually kept you in solitary confinement I really wanted to hate him. but they're not the same people any more."

"No, they've changed." C.C. agrees then grins at him. "It wasn't solitary confinement the way you think. I went to school and had free run of the house including the kitchen. I even managed to sneak out and find a boyfriend."

"Your father says you didn't runaway, you escaped." Dog informs her wondering if he should just leave it at this but he cannot help himself. "You found your escape route with number one."

"Yes." C.C. admits honestly though this was not her original intention. "I realized later when everything fell apart I wasn't as broken up as I should've been by his unfaithfulness and it occurred to me the overwhelming feeling I had to be with him might've been more for the new life he represented."

"Still doesn't explain why you married number two." He replies since she had the new life so why marry again. "You could've done anything you wanted."

"I didn't know what I wanted." She informs him simply. "Nothing I've ever wanted seemed possible, or the correct thing to do, and marriage is all I was ever expected to do."

Dog makes no comment and her parents do have much to answer for but it still does not explain why she stayed with an abusive husband, or maybe it does. Something else happened but she is not willing to tell him the real reason so he will have to figure it out himself only it worries him. He trusts her with his life, and probably will over and over again soon, but he is not so certain he can trust her with hers.

Returning to the Regency neither bother to check on Harv and Moss as they are left with the evening ahead of them with nothing slated they must do. Everything they need arrives tomorrow according to Cat's time table so prowling around the large living room Dog begins to feel a little trapped suddenly and the big windows or not he needs action, or something. Cat disappeared into the bedroom and he wonders if she would mind a little bed wrestling so he enters the bedroom finding she is wearing a bathing suit and 'wow' is all that registers.

"Want to take a swim?" She asks wondering why he is just standing there staring at her.

"I was thinking other impure thoughts." He admits because his wife can fill out the top and the bottom of a bathing suit really well and what is in the middle is not bad either.

"Well, I was saving that for later." She admits only she seems to have energy to burn and sex with him would burn some but not enough.

"I don't have a bathing suit." He informs her then after a moments thought adds. "I don't think I've ever owned a bathing suit in my life."

"But you can swim?" She asks wondering if she has discovered something he cannot do.

"Yes, but normally in a dive suit and never just for pleasure." He explains then catches the swimming shorts she tosses at his head.

"First time for every thing." She informs him then she frowns. "Where did they come up with a dive suit big enough to fit you?"

"Rubber does stretch you know." He mutters as he changes into the shorts finding the tie string comes in really handy then he reaches for a tank top which she snatches from him.

"Are you bashful?" She asks waving the shirt at him.

"Don't want to scare the natives." He replies simply wondering why she would even ask, it seems obvious to him.

"Once the shock wears off the awe factor will kick in." She assures him wondering if she should explain in more detail because he is still looking at her as if he does not understand but she decides he will figure it out for himself before much longer. "Besides, you're more native than they are."

"Okay." He agrees as she is pulling out another bag, webbed this time, fishing around in it. "You seem to have thought of every thing."

"Well almost because I didn't get you flip flops." She admits to which he promptly puts his feet into his combat boots as she puts on a swim suit cover.

"Are you bashful Cat?" He repeats what she just said to him.

"No, cold." She replies with a smile as she passes him to go out the bedroom door. "And don't tell me you didn't notice."

"I just thought they were happy to see me." He responds as he follows hearing her snort in response.

Located on the roof top of the other half of the hotel is the pool and for them it is just a short walk down a hallway from their suite through a door at the end. They find most of the guests had the same idea and there is a party going on around the huge hot tub consisting of college aged people leaving the large pool relatively celebration free. Deck lounges are in use by those just wanting to catch some rays but the whole area is filled with laughter and loud talking as the party is being fueled by a small bar near the hot tub maned by a member of the hotel staff while a pool boy is handing out towels and delivering drinks.

Among this crowd of skimpily clad young people are Harv and Moss ensconced in the hot tub holding drinks with little umbrellas. Harv has a woman practically sitting on his lap in the bubbling water as the two men seem to be having a fine time. She catches Dog's smirking glance in her direction choosing to ignore it as she chooses a pair of empty lounges depositing the bag and taking off her swimsuit cover and flip flops while Dog steps out of his boots. Digging into the bag she pulls out two pairs of goggles but Dog shakes his head when she offers him a pair so she tosses them back into the bag as she puts hers around her neck.

She moves to the edge of the pool which looks to be regulation length with lanes and she breaths in the chlorine scent then a large blur goes by her as Dog shallow dives past her entering the water with barely a splash as he slices into the water leaving her standing now frowning after him. She looks up to find nearly everyone is watching as they have been since they came out the door but she sees Harv and Moss clearly grinning at her.

"Great." She comments to them. "He's Flippers ugly cousin."

This sends the two men roaring with laughter so she suspects they have had one, or two, too many cocktails or what ever the fruity concoction is they are severing with little umbrellas. Dog is now standing in the five foot deep water sluing his wet hair back from his face and she swears she can actually hear a collective sigh from the women around the pool. She dives in no doubt leaving a rooster tail of water in her wake to surface next to him wiping water from her face.

"Been a while since I've been this wet." He informs her with a grin. "Great idea."

"Thought you might like it." She replies then goes on to suggest. "Do a few laps then relax?"

"Oh yeah." He replies more than willing.

She puts on her goggles leading off swimming toward the far end of the pool then spinning underwater she pushes off the wall to head back aware of Dog's large form moving along beside her. She watches for people in the pool but most are along the side walls more interested in staying cool then swimming as they spin again then surge back to the other end over and over until C.C. comes up off the wall letting her body float to the surface as her muscles hum nicely then suddenly she is not laying on water any more.

Dog has some how come up under her lifting her up out of the water as he floats under her like a human raft and she is afraid to move or she will sink them both but what they are doing is not possible, or is it? Maybe he can walk on water.

Dog is having a moment of can this be real as he is lying in cool clean water doing nothing more than floating on a beautiful sunny day with the woman he loves. Sometimes he wonders if he is only dreaming and will wake up in his little cell but he knows this is not possible because how can he dream about something he could never have imagined happening.

Dreams are based on reality yet this is not, nor ever has been, part of his reality. He is thinking about this so intently he looses concentration of his body and sinks both himself and Cat so they both come up sputtering.

"What was that?" She asks lifting her goggles to look at him.

"Lost my train of thought." He admits with a grin of apology.

"Well don't do it again." She mutters without heat as she climbs the stairs out of the pool while frowning at him and the pool attendant quickly comes over holding out a towel for her so she can dry off as she goes to their chairs.

He is not ready to get out yet so he dives under and swims around without really having anything in mind and just enjoying the whole doing what he wants when he wants as he walks on his hands across the bottom of the pool then simply explores the bottom wondering if they should have one of these in their new house.

Yeah, indoor heated pool he decides as he surfaces to ask Cat her opinion only everyone seems to be looking at him and clapping so he looks toward Cat where she is stretched out in the sun drying a short distance away for an explanation.

"We humans breath air." She informs him and he never surfaced once but since he was clearly in no danger no one dove in to rescue him.

"How long was I under?" He asks with interest since he has not been tested in aquatics for a very long time but as he climbs the steps up out of the pool a woman near him makes a funny little noise as he accepts an offered towel from the pool attendant who is staring blatantly at his chest.

"About ten minutes." Cat estimates though she did not actually time him.

"Ten minutes, forty nine seconds." Harv calls from the hot tub. "Probably not a record for you Sir."

"Are you drunk?" Dog asks not that he cares if the ex M.P.s are one way or the other as he dries off while ignoring the pool attendant who seems anxious about something.

"Working on it Sir." Harv admits with a smile.

"I'm the sober one tonight, sir." Moss adds.

"Meaning you lost the coin toss." Dog remarks knowing how this usually works but this is not the same "You know we're not on foreign soil any more? You don't have to use the buddy system to go out drinking here."

"It's a good idea no mater where we are, sir." Moss informs him seriously. "Keeps us from doing something stupid and landing in jail."

"Good." C.C. calls out. "Because I'm not bailing either one of you out of jail while you're on vacation."

"So speaks the real boss of the outfit, sir" Harv comments feeling just mellow enough to tweak the Colonel.

"You're right." Dog agrees seriously. "You're not drunk because you're still talking sense."

"I thought you said the two of you are security consultants." The girl on Harv's lap objects. "Are you suppose to be protecting him? Is he one of those famous football players or something? Because some one ran over him with spiked shoes."

"Those are bullet holes."   The pool attendant gasps wondering how they could be mistaken for anything else.

"We work for them." Moss explains pointing to the Captain and the Colonel but she still looks as if she does not get it and Moss rolls his eyes at the Colonel giving his opinion of the woman his partner is practically wearing.

"Not many people know what bullet holes look like." Dog informs the attendant and he has heard almost everything but this guy leaped to the right conclusion. "You've seen marks like this before?"

"My eldest brother is a police officer and he was shot in the line." The attendant explains looking around to be sure he is not shirking his duties but no one seems to need him at the moment.
"He has one, a puckered scar, like those on his shoulder."

"So you've probably been wondering how I managed to collect so many?" Dog guesses because the brother of a cop might be suspicious and by the embarrassed why the young man is looking at him Dog knows he is right.

"That's a soldier." Harv announces proudly pointing at the Colonel before he can respond and why is the hot tub rocking?. "He's a harbinger of war."

Chapter 26
Somewhere in the US of A...

"I think you've had too much sun and alcohol pal." Moss suggests while stepping out of the hot tub accepting a towel from the pool attendant and they need to leave before Harv gets himself hurt since the Captain is now frowning in their direction. "Up an at'em soldier."

"Whoa, were you two were in the military?" One of the guys asks looking from Harv to Moss for an answer and he did not think they were any older than the rest of them. "Like was he your commanding officer or something?"

"Hell yes, he's a Colonel." Harv answers proudly weaving as he stands in the hot tub adding just in case these civilians have no idea. "Army is the best and to hell with all the rest." He announces but his attention is caught by the Captain coming abruptly out of her chair and stalking purposely toward him which is when he realizes what his mouth said before his brain did any editing. "And the Air Force Captain. I meant Army and Air Force."

"Nice save." Moss mutters with relief as the Captain walks on by without kicking Harv into next week.

"I think it's time we went in." Harv agrees knowing he just had a very close call.

"How long have the two of you been out here?" Dog asks as he moves to follow Cat wondering what is doing at the bar.

"Practically from the moment the Captain checked us in. That's when we found out there is a pool." Moss informs him while making sure Harv does not take a header out of the hot tub.

"O'five hundred, meet us in the hallway." Dog informs them or rather orders vacation or not "There's a gym not far from here. We can't have you two getting fat or lazy on us."

"Sir, yes, sir." They agree in unison stopping just short of saluting him.

Dog shakes his head wondering when civilian life will catch up to the two of them as he continues toward the bar just as Cat turns with two drinks in wide mouthed tall frosty glasses which she holds one out offering it to him. Accepting the glass he sniffs the content but cannot smell alcohol so he gives the pinkish red slush a sip finding it to his liking and drains the whole glass then hands her back the empty glass wondering if there is more.

Looking bemused Cat hands him the other glass turning back to the bar and he is halfway through the second glass when she turns again holding a pitcher of the same pink stuff. She hands him the pitcher and takes the glass back then clinks it to his pitcher before she sips from the glass.

"I thought you might like it but I underestimated just how much or I would've gotten you a pitcher to begin with." She admits still amazed by what he did and has he even heard of brain freeze?

"What is it?" He asks now sipping from the pitcher as they move back to the chairs because it tastes like a very fruity strawberry shake to him and he takes the lounge chair next to her.

"Non alcoholic strawberry daiquiri." She informs him. "I didn't think you drink alcohol and I don't because flying and alcohol don't mix."

"But you're not flying now." He points out.

"But I might be." She replies simply.

"Planning a trip?" He asks because why would she be flying today.

"I just don't like being caught off guard." She responds but she avoids alcohol and does not even a social drink.

"Well if this is how most alcoholic drinks taste then I can understand the appeal to my father." He replies having never considered the taste might be the attraction.

"Adding alcohol does change the taste some." She admits from what others have told her. "For most it's not so much the taste as the results of alcohol. Disconnection, everything is either happier, funnier or sadder and some times one person can hit all three in one evening of drinking."

"My father was the last and he didn't go any where with the other two." Dog comments as he thinks back. "He started when my mother left but if he was hoping for happy, it didn't work. What was it with number two?"

"What makes you think number two drank?" She asks certain she did not tell him or even hint at alcohol being involved in her second marriage.

"Seems logical." He replies carefully knowing he is treading on unsteady ground here between what she has told him and what he just knows. "You said he was a cop right? So what else would make a man like that lose his sense of right and wrong. I think it also explains why you refused to go back to make him pay the way I hoped you would."

"You don't beat up a sick person, it's not going to make them well." She responds bluntly but there for a moment she thought he knew the way the Major seemed to have known what happened in her second marriage but she should have told him before they married. "If you wanted children then you married the wrong woman."

"We have the two , that's enough for me." He replies but there is something there in what she said.

"Those are ferrets." C.C. corrects him ignoring the stab of pain in her heart because there was a child once and it was never even given a chance. "They make better pets."

"You want kids." He comments softly and despite her flippant response there is something there.

"No." She responds with a not phonied look of horror. "What would ever give you that idea? I would be the worlds worse mother."

"No, you wouldn't." He replies confidentiality.

"Oh hell yes I would." C.C. replies positively having proof just what kind of uncaring and unfeeling mother she is but she pushes this back, she pushes it away, and it is one sin she will surely pay for. "There's a restaurant here in the hotel where we can eat tonight, or we can order in from there, or somewhere else."

"I'll think about it." He responds accepting the change of subject.

There is a clue in there somewhere but he will have to work it out later as she is headed for the pool again. He follows finding himself doing laps again which is fine and if this is how she works it out then this is what they will do. He knows it is not a matter of trust keeping her from telling him, nor fear, maybe shame, but whatever it is it burns in her and he is going to make damn sure it does not destroy her..

Back in their suite Dog decides they should order pizza in simply because they can and because he still is not certain if he likes thin or thick crust best. Pizza is not something he has had a lot of even as a child or over seas. It is an American food no matter what anyone says.

C.C. places the order for two large pizzas and a call to the front desk which will allow the delivery person to come up the elevator. Of course later Dog is halfway through both pizzas and still cannot make up his mind but C.C. is certain this will always be the case and the excuse he will use to eat pizza as often as possible. Why he thinks an excuse is necessary she is not certain but whatever makes him happy is her new motto. As he finishes the last piece of pizza she knows having cold pizza for breakfast is going to remain on the list of new things for him to try, probably indefinitely.

"So, I look like a football player?" Dog comments leaning back on the couch and propping his bare feet up on the coffee table while staring out at the view over the balcony railing.

He threw on a pair of his cut off sweats after they showered and Cat is wearing what looks like a mans button down shirt which reaches her knees and the cuffs would cover her hands if she had not rolled them back to nearly her elbows. Over all he is feeling relaxed and replete with a full belly along with a great view, both outside the hotel suite and in.

"I guess to half drunk bimbos you do." C.C. remarks as she leans back against the couch arm and props her bare feet up on his thigh.

"I use to watch high school games." He remarks remembering staying after school to watch then walking all the way home or hitching rides when he could. "Seen some American football here and there but mostly Soccer."

"Want to watch a real American football game?" She asks because she knows over seas, and seemingly every where, football is soccer.

"Is there a television in here?" He asks looking around the living room not seeing anything he would recognize as one.

"A television is rather plebeian for places like this." C.C. explains as she reaches over lifting the arm rest of one of the chairs near the couch pulling out the remote control from the hidden compartment. She points It at the wall at one end of the couch and a section of the wall opens up revealing a large screen television as she continues. "So they hide them but they're top of the line, advanced electronics."

"Of course." Dog responds with a grin as she leans forward pulling a hand full of his hair and tugs. He lets his head follow until he is now reclining against her with his head resting on her breasts with his feet over the armrest at the other end of the couch and all the while thinking, yeah, this is much better. "So you know a lot about ritzy places like this?"

"Number four." She admits simply and she spent quite a bit of time in places like this. "First class all the way and then he would complain about everything. The water in the refrigerator wasn't cold enough, the towels weren't fresh enough, and he insisted house keeping change his sheets just before he went to bed."

"Sounds like a real nice guy." Dog grumbles imagining the trouble he caused management and house keeping because he had money and he could.

"Rich, spoiled, and God's gift to every woman, in his mind at least." She replies but she knew what he was and he only married her for her looks so there was not much else to the marriage.

She made his life a little more convenient for him and kept women from trying to trap him into marriage. She was his security blanket if taken to court by any woman claiming he promised marriage and he paid for her just as he paid for the other women who claimed to fall madly in love with him but really it was his bank account they loved.

"So where exactly in a place like this did you sleep?" He wonders out loud because he knows her last marriage was not a regular marriage.

"Right there." She replies pointing to another door across from them. "These suites are all two bedrooms but one is always a little smaller than the other. Right now it's full of our gear."

"We have gear?" He comments with interest which has not been drawn to the football game on the television.

"What I could get through regular channels and not have officials looking at me sideways, that's what is coming tomorrow with the task force from the Major General." She explains. "I understand now why he didn't just ship it ahead of us because from what you say it probably wouldn't be there by the time we arrived."

"True." He agrees seriously. "The local government would have either confiscated it by accident then misplace it if not out right blaming guerrillas for taking it. If any fraction had any idea or guessed where the munitions are stored they would steal it. Nothing is really a secret when arms get moved anywhere."

"So the task force brings it here and they escort us to the airport the next morning, then it goes from our plane to whatever the Major General has waiting for us at the other end." C.C. finishes understanding the delays more then she did originally.

American laws are one thing but the other government was a big fat question mark for her and really she can see the ever so helpful foreign government's reasons for taking the arms if they have the opportunity. U.S. guns and munitions sent in will be sent again so they do not really see it as stealing if it helps them. But this would put her and Dog behind schedule and possibly give the kidnappers time to move the hostage out of the country or deeper into hiding.

"Does the hotel know they're about to be crawling with ATF officers?" Dog wonders out loud.

"Now, that would be cheating." C.C. replies with a slight smile. "Besides they're getting paid over and above with all the rooms taken by the agents who will be staying here. The additional security will be appreciated once the initial head ache is over and we're actually the type of guests they hope to encourage to stay here."

"Troublesome?" He comments surprised and he would think they would be asked to never come back.

"These big high end hotels all hope to attract influential guests needing privacy and security. If they can't adapt to us then they're not going to have much success with the big wheeler and dealers like political candidates, movie stars, and sports celebrities they want to attract." She explains. "Tomorrow when the task force rolls in requesting rooms and access to security they'll wet themselves with glee."

Dog roars with laughter realizing he can happily spend the rest of his life just listening to her talk and she does not think in one dimension but in full spectrum of what will happen and how it will all work. Other than not understanding foreign governments, which she picked up on quickly, she has a firm grasp of everything else including things he does not know or take into account. All in all he is certain they will make excellent partners in the business side of their lives and the personal side is pretty good too especially from his current position. Or even better in another position as he turns over to face his pillow.

"What are you up to now?" C.C. asks with suspicion but she knows just by the look on his face exactly what he has in mind.

"I'm finding American football is just as boring as European football, or maybe it's the distraction of someone more interesting in the room." He informs her rearranging her clothing to get to his pillows.

"Shall I turn it off?" She asks as she moves so he can get to what he is after.

"Just leave it." He mutters. "I've never had thousands of people cheering me on before. Might be interesting."

Four people walk into the Jawbreaker gym the next morning and Harv looks no worse for his day of drinking and fun in the sun while the young man in the chair by the door does not bother to get up as Dog leads the way to where they sat the day before. There is one section missing benches on either side as he sits to remove his boots and Harv and Moss each carry a small gym bag taking out boxing gloves, head gear, and mouth guards so they have been using gyms somewhere in their travels, right down to ring shoes. The owner approaches with a grin on his rough looking face minus the two guys guarding his back this time.

"I kept this ring open for you." He informs the big guy on the bench. "I don't think I got around to introducing myself. I'm called Crush and since it has been so long since anyone has used my real name I'm not too sure if I can remember it."

"Know how it is. I'm Dog and this is Cat." He replies motioning to the ring Cat has already jumped into. "This is Harv and Moss, they work for us and they'll be taking on Cat today."

"What?" Harv responds looking shocked. "I thought you liked us."

"I do but she cracked two of my ribs yesterday and we have a job." He informs them as Moss slumps against the lockers. "You two are officially on vacation."

"We didn't exactly want to spend our vacation nursing broken bones Colonel Sir." Moss objects morosely.

"I'll help you out." He replies looking back to the ring. "Cat, defense only." She gives him a puzzled look which he ignores as he looks back to the other two. "This makes the two of you offense so you better punch and kick like you mean it or she is going to get bored, then she'll start taking shots of her own. Between the two of you, you should be able to keep her busy."

"Flip a coin to see who goes in first." Harv turns to Moss.

"Boys." Crush responds in disbelief as Dog just shakes his head not appearing inclined to explain and Crush believes he might actually let them go in one at a time. "Both of you better enter that ring and both of you better be kicking and punching or she's going to be tossing you out over the top rope like popcorn." And they both look at him as if he is the one who has lost his mind so he sighs looking at Dog. "If you don't mind I'll coach them so you can get a work out and she gets one too."

"I would appreciate that Crush." Dog admits truthfully and he did not think this would be so complicated when he came up with the idea because both men have seen her in the ring only he did not take into account they still may still think of her as a woman. There might also be some chivalrous nonsense rattling around in their heads about not punching a girl or a fair play issue of two against one, not that they will ever connect with her which is what they will soon find out.

"Hey, coaching is what I do now." Crush informs him with a grin. "Come on boy's I'll show you how to do this. You just do as I say."

Cat warms up as she waits then Harv and Moss are climbing into the ring with the owner of the gym standing at the outside apron and she grins as she dances one way then the other. The owner is calling out to Harv and Moss as they take swings at her and she blocks or dodges them and he does not let up on them either as they keep trying to land blows as she spins and kicks blocking them but soon they begin to wear down. Twenty minutes later Harv is sitting on the floor leaning against the ropes looking winded while Moss is getting slower until the owner raises his arms with forearms crossed. Cat dances back from Moss as he drops his arms as if they weigh a ton looking relieved.

"Do you mind if I put two of my boys in with you?" Crush asks because she is not even breathing hard or worked up a sweat yet. These two are out of shape but he has men who are not and will do as they are told.

"Not at all." She replies because these two are way too soft.

"Mike, Reese, where are you?" Crush calls out but they are not far and neither is most of the men in the gym as once again they are crowded around this ring. The two he wants step forward. "Put on your gear and give her a work out. She's defense only so give her something to defend against. Keep her moving."

Mike and Reese climb into the ring and like Harv and Moss they take jabs at her at first but when her block sends them spinning across the ring they quickly realize they either punch like they mean it or she is going to be knocking them all over the ring. Crush urges them on from ring side and then he sees she is smiling, her arms and legs are going to be black and blue tomorrow, and no doubt hurt now but she has a smile on her face like she could not be happier.

A few years ago if he had a woman like this in his place he would take her all the way to the championships but he is too old now to deal with all of that hoopla anymore. He also knows she would never go for it because this is not a woman who wants to be idolized or collect titles to show off. She trains for only one purpose, same as Dog, to kill, and they have to be the deadliest pair he has ever come across.

"She hits like a truck." Mike mutters shaking out a hand gone numb just from one of her blocks.

"If she was actually hitting and not blocking she would break bone." Crush informs him harshly. "She's trained to break bones and way out of our league boys so just give her a work out and for God's sake don't piss her off." Forty minutes later Mike's side kick is blocked but it does not carry as much steam as before and she hooks his leg sending him ass over teakettle to the ring floor. Reese is also down but she is sweating and breathing heavy so Crush wonders what he should do now. "More?" He asks but he has no clue who else to send because most of the men in his gym other than these two have more ego than sense. There might be one or two others he can trust not to loose their heads when they realize they can get their asses kicked by a woman but he would rather not chance it.

"I'm good." Cat answers with a smile as she moves to the edge of the ring and goes through the ropes, too tired to go over. "That was good. These two are good especially that one there, he has a nasty left hook." She comments pointing to Reese as he rolls out of the ring coming around the outside as she shows Crush the red marks on her right upper arm.

"They could both be contenders as far as I can see but they have day jobs." Crush replies scoffing at the whole idea of working instead of boxing as Reese grins at him. "Their both firemen If you can believe it." "They've got the brains and the talent, but they're not interested."

"We don't need fame or fortune Crush." Reese replies as he looks to the woman. "But I know I've seen you before. I'm thinking Miramar on base of the Navy Fighter Weapons School."

"Yeah, I was there." C.C. admits but she does not remember seeing him.

"Pilot right?" Reese replies grinning when she nods. "Fire crew. We don't miss good looking pilots especially ones wearing Air Force flight suits with big ass Captain's bars. You sort of stood out. I didn't re up with the Navy, missed the war."

"Ah." Cat replies nodding her head because this explains why she does not recognize him and there are always people about a base so it is impossible to notice or recognize all of them by sight unless someone introduces them or they introduce themselves.

"He could have been a war hero." Mike adds with a grin motioning to Reese. "Ladies would be all over him if he fought in a war."

"Well Harv and Moss were there and so far they only seem to attract drunk bimbos so I wouldn't stress about it." C.C. informs them as she points to the two as they lift weights. "Dog was there and drunken bimbo's think he's a professional football player."

"I still don't get it." Dog comments as he now stands next to Crush. "Thanks for getting her a good work out Crush, guys."

"How do you know it wasn't Harv and Moss?" She asks with a grin.

"How long did they last?" Dog asks Crush.

"About twenty minutes." Crush informs him.

"Longer than I thought they would." Dog replies looking impressed then his gaze goes back to Cat. "And I have survived two wars, countless missions, and I plan on surviving marriage by knowing where you are and what you're doing every second of every day."

"Sounds like a very wise plan." Crush comments with a grin. "I should've done that with my last two wives."

"Did they try to kill you?" Dog asks with interest.

"No, just took everything I owned." Crush replies ruefully.

"She already has everything I own. Now all she has to do is get rid of me." Dog comments dryly.

"Poor Dog." C.C. mutters as she jumps from the ring apron going to their locker leaving them to get on with her work out.

"She likes me." Dog replies with a shrug as he sees her put her head phones on and pull out her rope.

"Better keep it that way." Crush advises.

Chapter 27
Somewhere in the US of A...

Upon returning to the hotel C.C. is informed she has two phone messages which she reads on the way up to the suite. The first is from her mother saying her pants are done and the second says her parents are on their way over to the hotel. She was not expecting her parents to come to the hotel and how can her mother possible make adjustments if needed here.

A quick shower and change before returning to the living room she finds Dog on the couch channel surfing though he does not seem interested in watching anything available but is simply changing channels on the television because he can. She only has time to grab a bottle of water from the refrigerator before the buzzer on the door goes off and she admits her parents.

"My this place is certainly fancy." Margaret comments as she looks about never having been in these rooms but her eyes light on her daughter whom has big red marks on her arms. "What happened to you?"

"A really good work out." C.C. replies having to look to see what she is even referring too. "Dog decided to bail on me so I had a couple of house boxers. Dog tends to pull his punches and kicks but these guys let me have it. It was great."

"Oh." Margaret remarks while taking in her daughter's smile and wondering how anything which must have hurt can be great.

"They never actually laid a glove on her." Dog adds as he rises from the couch having turned off the television. "Those are just defensive marks."

"Let me try those on." C.C. suggests motioning to the bag her mother carries assuming the pants are inside. "We would have come to your house so you don't have to run back and forth to make adjustments."

"Oh, I brought my little hand held." Margaret responds taking the small sewing machine from her purse. "I can fix anything with this."

"That's a sewing machine?" Dog asks with interest moving closer for a better look and it is no bigger than his hand.

"My yes." Margaret beams proudly. "Stan gave this to me for my birthday some years ago. It runs on batteries and it is great for doing small repairs and adjustments."

C.C. leaves them discussing the pocket sewing machine trying on the pants and all the changes have been made as she asked. She pulls on her combat boots lacing them up quickly and walks out of the bedroom finding everyone waiting.

Dog does the twirl thing with his finger so she does then he holds up his hand indicating as she did with him to kick. She does just missing his hand then spins kicking again but he grabs her ankle holding her leg up in standing splits.

"Looks like they'll hold." Dog comments with satisfaction.

"I double stitched the seams and it's a thick material." Margaret comments breathlessly because she has never seen Caro move like this before, they never saw her preform the Karate she learned when she was younger and from where she stands it looks very impressive.

"Does the skirt telegraph the kick?" C.C. asks seriously because this is one of her concerns when he suggested she wear these pants.

"No, it follows." He informs her. "Doesn't seem to get in the way. If we left it longer it might have."

"Good call." She admits as she jumps up bringing her other foot up as he releases her ankle allowing her to spin in the air and come back down on both feet.

"Oh my." Margaret gasps for she has never seen anyone move as her daughter just did and she is doubly thankful she thought to reinforce the stitching. She was more concerned with rough jungle terrain not what Caro might actually be doing while wearing these pants. "Do they need any adjustments?"

"No." C.C. replies then realizes she has not tried the belt loops yet. "Wait, let me get the belt."

Crossing to the door of the other bedroom C.C. enters looking for her pack taking out the thick ammo belt and walking out again as she is feeding it through the loops. The belt goes through every one easily as Dog suddenly disappears into the other room and is carrying out her flack vest along with her webbed holster belt for some reason. He hands her the vest while he goes down on his knees to put the web belt on her and this is when it hits her.

"I can't wear a side arm." She realizes looking down at herself.

"Or you won't be able to access the pants pockets." He agrees sitting back on his knees looking up at her. "Damn, this will work, but we have to come up with a better way. You don't really need a side arm with the under arm holster and you can hit a duck in the eye at a hundred yards with it but you'll need the ammo pouches for the other weapons no one will notice."

"Loose the skirt?" She asks looking at him.

"No, that helps conceal the additional fire power. How can you be my secret weapon if everyone can see what's in your pockets." He objects then he frowns back down at the holster belt. "I have an idea."

C.C. watches as he removes the ammo pouches from the belt then begins adding them to the belt she presently wearing and laces them through the pant loops as he goes. She agrees in principal this should work except these pants, which he insisted she wear, are more form fitting then regular cargo pants so now the pants are puckering and bulging in all sorts of strange places including the pocket openings.

"This is so much better now." She mutters dryly as he frowns at his handy work.

"Next pair we lower the pockets." He informs her.

"And just how do you plan to make my arms longer so I can reach into my pocket?" She asks and really she does not want to know. "If the skirt were narrower then maybe the pocket won't gape open so badly."

"Or the upper part of the skirt can be over lapped at the top taking the stress off the side seams." Margaret suggests having found enough breath to speak and Stan did warn her what he suspected their daughter might be involved in but this is a little more than she was prepared for. "If I cut and stitch the back skirt just before the pocket and extend the front panel so it over laps the back seam then the pocket should be fine where it is."

"An idea for next time but we don't have time for that now." C.C. responds knowing the pair she is wearing will have to be picked apart.

"Oh it only took me a couple of hours to stitch these together." Margaret replies seeing this not as difficult as Caro believes. "I'll just make the next pair now and fix these later."

"You still have to cut out the material and we leave first thing in the morning." C.C. responds not seeing this as any faster, or easier. "It's our fault for not quite thinking this through."

"Four hours tops." Margaret replies not interested in whose fault it is and apparently she needs these pants. "I have most of the pattern and plenty of material. Your father is an expert pinner and all I need to measure is where to sew the back skirt and how far to overlap the front. I can chalk mark this pair for those measurements."

"You still won't have a side arm." Dog adds but she will have what he intends and this seems really important to Margaret who is probably sees this as doing something for her daughter when she did not before.

"Fine." C.C. agrees and her mother comes at her with a piece of chalk marking what she needs then moving into the bedroom she changes finding this all a lot of bother over a whim of Dog's. She grabs her wallet on the way back with the pants only to be intercepted by Dog who turns at her side taking her hand holding her wallet with him tucking her arm behind her back. She is tempted to kick him but instead hands her mother the pants and they leave promising to have the second pair done soon. "What are you doing?"

"Give them this one free." He requests releasing her as soon as the door closes and moving away to protect his cracked ribs. "After this, offer to pay for more."

"Why?" She wants to know not certain why this matters.

"Atonement. They can never make up for the years they repressed you but their attempt to give you something after all this time should be rewarded with a thank you not cash." He explains and this deserves better than being treated as hired help. "I know you really don't care, or hold a grudge, but they have issues with guilt and they see this as an opportunity to ease some of it."

"Fine." C.C. agrees and he is correct she really could care less about her parents issues. "Now you owe me a swim."

"Deal." He responds knowing Cat does not intentionally mean to be cruel but thanks to her upbringing she is emotionally distant.

A few laps in the pool and they are laying back on lounge chairs relaxing just enjoying a sunny day. Dog has a pitcher of daiquiri while she has stuck to a glass as people around them swim, talk, and frolic but Harv and Moss are absent.

C.C. is amusing herself by counting the number of times the same woman has managed to walk past their lounge chairs checking Dog out without out right staring. Dog seems completely oblivious but she is contemplating getting wet again when a man in dark clothing and an ATF ball cap enters the pool area from the lobby elevator heading directly toward them.

"FedEx delivery is here." C.C. comments and the guy having over heard surprisingly grins. Wow, a federal agent with a sense of humor.

"I hope stuff like this doesn't go that route or we haven't been doing our jobs." He replies while finding Mr. and Mrs. Red Eagle not exactly what he expected.

He knows the basics from military records faxed to his office but the reality is far different. Mrs. Red Eagle is a cute blond but she also has a small compact curvaceous body and apparent dry wit. Mr. Red Eagle was younger in his photo and his face shows more mileage but his very large muscular body shows considerable action in the field.

"Agent Adams." He introduces himself.

"I'm Dog and this is Cat." Dog introduces them.

"I still need to see ID." He informs them smiling wider now because even as their nicknames state these two are as different as night and day.

"Of course you do." C.C. replies because no one is going to hand over automatic rifles, ammunition, and hand grenades to two people on chase lounges with nicknames, if they did, she would be calling her local congressman herself. She pulls their wallets from her beach bag handing both ID's to Agent Adams.

"Mr. and Mrs. Red Eagle would you please accompany me back to your suite?" He asks handing their ID's back.

"Just bring it with you." C.C. instructs as Dog is frowning at his pitcher. "They'll find it in the suite either after we leave or housekeeping will when they clean the room."

"The two of you would not be indulging in alcoholic beverages, would you?" Agent Adams asks eyeing the pitcher and glass with some concern because he cannot, nor will he, hand high powered munitions to people who have been indulging.

"Non alcoholic." Cat responds as she slides her key card to get back into the hallway leading to their suite. "None of us really want to know what happens if Dog gets a little loopy."

"I don't want to know what happens." Dog admits honestly as he holds the door for her and the agent.

From this point on things happen quickly as their suite is

searched to be certain they are not hiding terrorists. More heavily armed agents arrive carrying in several nondescript cases but a casual observer would not notice, or the concealed flack vests they wear. Dog is asked to verify all munitions are present before they officially turn them over and she wonders what would happen if something were missing but thankfully they do not find out.

"We ask that you do not leave the hotel until we escort you to the airport." Agent Adams requests but he is certain they realize they are now responsible for what they now have.

"How do you feel about visitors?" C.C. asks knowing this will be a sticky issue but they have no other choice. "My parents need to be let up as they have something we need to take with us. Should one of us meet them in the lobby?"

"Everyone coming and going from this suite will be searched. We'll also need to verify I.D." He explains because they cannot have people coming and going from this suite full weapons.

"I think your father will get a kick out that." Dog comments with a slight smile. "A cripple being searched like a dangerous criminal. He'll want to tell Chuck all about it."

"While my mother will be completely mortified." C.C. warns because she is certain her mother has not changed that much.

"The searches will be conducted here in the upper hallway after they exit the elevator." Adams offers as most people do not like feeling like criminals which searching seems to induce." It's only a pat down and we have a female agent."

"If your mother needs to make adjustments it would be easier if they came up than you going down." Dog advises and they are not going to be trusted on U.S. soil with what they now have.

"I'll have them come up." C.C. agrees because what other choice do they have but she wonders what these agents will make of the hand sewing machine her mother carries in her purse as she goes to call her parents letting them know things have changed slightly.

After taking a shower C.C. opens the spare bedroom door and begins the task of pulling out everything she has already purchased. Dog helps her sort armament and ammunition into five separate bags since they have three men presently out of the country waiting for them to arrive.

When her parents arrive despite her warning they look

rather shocked by all the security and their situation does not improve seeing weapons spread out all over the living room. C.C. takes the bag from her mother's hand not certain what to say that is not fairly obvious. She changes into the pants finding she is certain these will work and hopes Dog is satisfied though she is still not certain about this plan of his or the need for it.

"I think these will work fine Mother." C.C. offers as she pulls on the belts and vest finding nothing bags out or open then Dog is tossing her a snub nosed machine gun. "This wasn't on the list I gave the Major General."

"It was as of two days ago." He responds as he watches the machine gun fits perfectly with no one able to see it for the skirt and loose folds of these pants.

"She'll be the best dressed woman in the jungle." Stan comments knowing they should say something positive rather than just stand around staring which could be misconstrued as disapproval. Margaret more than he is having difficulty coming to terms with their daughter's apparent new profession and afraid to voice her concern has rendered her mute. Their connection with their daughter is still very fragile so words of caution or unwanted advise could sever future contact which is what they fear will happen.

"Men are going to notice her no matter what she wears so why not use it to our advantage." Dog responds pleased with the result as Cat is practicing pulling the weapon then putting it back and he knows by the time they leave she will have it down. "They're going to believe I'll be protective of her and that she needs my protection."

"Well of course." Margaret agrees because this only seems logical but the way he said it makes her think he means other wise. "You will be looking out for her, right?"

"Cat's not one for waiting to be rescued." Dog responds with a smile as Cat gives him smug smile in return. "She's also over protective."

"What?" C.C. asks wondering what gives him this idea.

"Don't worry your, 'I could careless', attitude and reputation are still intact. I doubt any one but me has noticed how you protect nearly everyone who comes into your orbit." He offers reassuringly as he turns to her parents. "No one will need to rescue her because she's too clever to need rescuing and she'll be pulling me out of the fire more often than not."

"So your saying you tend to leap before you look?"   Stan asks to be certain he understands what the man is saying.

"No." Dog disagrees with a frown.

"Yes." C.C. agrees with her father but she does not consider this as being protective as much as doing what needs to be done.

"I'm not careless or blind." Dog objects indignantly.

"No, you're dogmatic."   C.C. responds not intending insult but he does seem inclined to leap first to complete a mission then look for a place to land.   "You'll do whatever it takes to complete a mission even if it means throwing yourself off a tall building because how or where you land is not germane to completing the mission so just admit I'm basically your back up plan if something should go wrong."

"Okay."   Dog admits and he does tend to leave some of those details to sort themselves out.

"Thank you for these pants." C.C. compliments her parents. "Sorry about the hassle getting in and for the what you're about to go through to get back out."

"Oh really it's not that big a deal."   Margaret responds now better understanding the reason for it and now she can only hope her daughter will be staying some place safe while waiting to rescue her husband.   "We're meeting Ethel and Charlie in the restaurant down stairs and wondered if the two of you would care to join us?"

"This isn't going any where." Dog responds motioning to the mess in the living room and there are armed guards to be sure of it. "We do need to eat."

"And it is in the hotel." C.C. agrees as she turns going into the bedroom to change back into the cargo pants she was wearing.

"So you're all set to leave in the morning then."   Ethel comments once they are seated in the crowded restaurant having been told Margaret had just finished the sewing project before they arrived.

"Everything is ready, or close to."   C.C. admits then she notices Charlie is smiling at her. "What?"

"You still have what remains of a black eye and now you're black and blue down one arm." Chuck remarks. "I guess I should have gone to the gym this morning, and nice to see you've redeemed yourself Colonel."

"Two of the house boxers did that." Dog replies knowing Chuck will have something to say about this.

"Both at the same time no doubt." Chuck remarks but frowning at this mental picture. "You let two men beat up on your wife?"

"Not my fault she kept blocking the guy with her right arm." Dog informs him wondering how he is suppose to do anything about that?

"Are you slipping Ace?" He asks looking to Caro with concern.

"No." C.C. replies calmly. "The guy was slipping in a nasty left hook and all I could do was block per his orders."

"You handicapped her?" Chuck responds astonished but of course he should have guessed.

"It's the only way to keep anyone in the ring with her." Dog replies defensively. "She would've toss them out, or just knock them out."

"Well why weren't you in the ring with her then?" Chuck wants to know.

"You know she cracked two of my ribs." Dog informs him and Chuck was there.

"Since when has a little thing like that ever stopped you." Chuck demands and he has seen him with worse. "Getting soft in your old age?"

"I'm pretty sure he was blown up on his second to last mission for the Army." C.C. remarks in way of explanation.

"Again." Chuck responds incredulously. "Did you leap on something you shouldn't have?"

"Standing too close to something this time." Dog admits wryly.

"Well it seems his leaping into something is going to be only one of your problems." Stan offers to his daughter.

"Don't forget the whole rich widow thing." Chuck advises.

"Charlie." Ethel admonishes.

The whole meal is punctuated with 'Charlie' from his exasperated wife as Chuck entertains them with exploits from his military experience and a few of these involved Dog who makes several corrections to Chuck's stories but it is obvious to C.C., if to no one else, it is a miracle Chuck is still alive. It is an enjoyable evening but it must come to an end as they leave early in the morning as the three couples part ways in the hotel lobby.

"Be careful you two." Ethel instructs as the young couple move toward the private elevator.

"Carolyn." Margaret calls after them before they reach it. "Bring Johann back safe and sound."

"He's not half bad as far as son-in-laws go." Stan adds with his lopsided grin.

"I will." C.C. replies as they enter the elevator and the door closes. "I think my parents like you."

"Well in order for you to bring me back, you have to come back too." He informs her because he got what they said.

"Then why didn't they just say so?" C.C. asks because it seems a round about way to say something.

"Maybe because after telling you what to do for years they're afraid to tell you to do something now." He suggests but he does not know this for certain.

"Or they think I'll do the opposite to spite them." She replies grinning. "Maybe they don't like you as much as they claim."

"Well, at least, it's a nice looking death trap." Dog comments morosely when they arrive at the airport the next morning.

Cat ignores him already in pilot mode with pre-flight checks while he elects to sit in the cabin which looks more like someone's living room instead of the inside of a plane. He decides if he sits in the middle of the plane he can pretend he is still on the ground though it never really works so he meditates instead.

Chapter 28
Somewhere in South America....

"Please tell me this is a joke?" Cat asks dryly looking at the helicopter waiting on the tarmac for them as their official government greeter drives them toward it in a jeep piled with their gear.

"This all available." The uniformed officer replies without sympathy as he stops the jeep next to the helicopter. "We have too few military transports for American's to play soldier in our country."

It has been apparent from the moment this guy met them at the jet after landing he is only following orders and their being in his country, regardless of their objective, is something he does not tolerate well. As she stands looking at the Huey Bell UH-1 Iroquois made some time in the 1960's used mostly as military transport, and almost as old as Dog, she realizes if worse comes to worse they can flap their arms to get back.

She is not certain they even make this class any more so it is probably held together by bailing wire and mismatched parts, which is not good. Some modifications have been made to the body to hold modern missiles but she will have to check to make sure this is not just for looks.

"No one here is going to hire out a decent helicopter to Americans going into the interior." Dog informs her grimly. "They might not get it back. Just see if it will get us there and hopefully back."

"That is the question." Cat mutters as they toss all the packs onto the decking through one of the large open side doors.

"I'm going to call the Major General and let him know we arrived." He informs her. "The men will be arriving shortly. Please don't kill any of them."

"Am I going to want to?" Cat asks but of course she will or he would not have said anything. "This just gets better and better."

"Once they get use to you there won't be any problems." He assures her but he knows his men probably have never worked with a woman before, not as more then an informant or bait, but once they get past her gender and on board with the fact she is one of them they should get along nicely, or so he hopes.

Cat goes over the helicopter from the inside out wishing this were one of the birds she was asked to transfer to a museum rather than taking up possibly into a fire fight. Engine and structural wise it is not as bad as she first feared and someone did do a decent job of repairing cables. Everything works smoothly but there is one thing missing which she intends to mention to Dog but she hears voices approaching and finds three men sauntering toward her in combat fatigues carrying small hand rucksacks.

They are talking and joking as they approach but when they see her standing beside the Huey their expressions are almost comical. The tall black man grins with a friendly curious expression while the shorter dark skinned Mexican turns up the wattage of his smile and allows his dark eyes roam over her.

The third looks American and seems less impressed by her looks. He does not stop at a respectful distance as the other two do and instead walks right up to her stopping only inches from her. His blatant attempt to intimidate with his height and muscular build falls short of its mark as Cat looks up at him.

"Want to dance?" She asks meeting him stare for stare and she is not referring to the type of dancing done at weddings.

"Carmichael!" Dog calls out as he crosses the tarmac moving toward them from the small office next to the helo pad.

"Maybe later." The man smiles. "Between the sheets."

"You couldn't handle it, or me, anywhere." She informs him earnestly.

"Carmichael, back off." Dog growls as he approaches but of course Carmichael does not listen and reaches out for Cat then he is on the ground. He pops back up like a jack in the box as Dog insert himself between them before Cat does something really nasty.

"Not like you to bring your own 'pillow' Han Dog." Carmichael informs Dog moving to look at the woman around his large frame.

"I brought a damn good pilot who also happens to be my wife." Dog replies bluntly. "And if you have a problem with it, I can do this without you."

"No problem." Carmichael responds looking up at Dog. "Even old Dog's need a soft place to lay down, I get that, but she doesn't belong here."

"She does, accept it or leave." Dog replies earnestly and right now he is kind of hoping Carmichael decides to skip this job. He had forgotten just how pig headed the man can be and Cat will not tolerate continuous taunting for long or she will take Carmichael down.

"Sure." Carmichael retorts as if agreeing then tosses his rucksack into the open side door before jumping in after it but he is not fooled. He did not think Dog was stupid enough to be lead around by his dick and he tends to keep an eye on the woman to make sure she does not get them all killed.

"Cat, this is Jake and Rolly." Dog introduces her to the other two men who have yet to say anything. "I have the coordinates where we're to meet with Rayjo's escort."

"We have a problem." Cat informs him simply and she does not mean just with the men he chose. "This bird is not armed."

"What the hell!" Dog replies looking at her then heads for the office again.

"So you fly much?" Rolly asks in his decidedly heavy Mexican accent.

"Very much." Cat replies and Rolly nods as if her answer satisfies him then he tosses his rucksack in and follows it leaving her facing Jake who smiles.

"Mrs. Red Eagle I presume." He greets her.

"Just Cat." She replies as this will be easier than using her old nickname.

"Cat." He agrees with a smile as he tosses his rucksack in and follows after it.

Dog is not happy when he returns but there is nothing he can do about the local officials hording ammunition and defenses. Promises were made then just as easily broken and now he has to inform Cat. Being this is considered a private action Aimhurst cannot just order someone to bring them missiles so they are just going to have to make do.

"We can't out run anything in this." She informs him as he approaches already knowing the report is not good or they would have had missiles in the launchers.

"It's a good thing I have a pilot who is highly trained in aerial maneuvers." He responds trying to look on the bright side but her smile is not what he expected.

"Which makes for a really rough ride." She imparts wondering if this will change his mind as her smile brightens.

"Fine." He responds resigned to the fact he is probably going to hate every aspect of this flight.

Having forewarned him Cat climbs into the pilots seat and begins warming up the helicopter as the blades loop lazily around making swishing sounds until they are chopping the air steadily faster and faster. Dog commences a radio check of their com links while Cat is also wears a head set so she can talk to the tower and will allow her to communicate with other planes or helicopters they may encounter.

Rolly squeezes through the narrow opening between the back half and the front cockpit awkwardly hopping over the center console to land in the co pilots seat with a grin. When the blades are roaring and up to the proper Rpm Cat asks the tower for permission to take off which is granted. Air bound with the coordinates given to them by the Major General provided by Rayjo they have clear air on a bright sunny day.

Cat is attempting to look on the bright side but there are two dark clouds on her personal horizon, the lack of missiles and Carmichael. Rolly is kicked back in the co pilots seat with a big grin like he has never been in a helicopter before, or he just likes to fly while she wonders if the windows rolled down like in a car he would have his head hanging out panting like a dog with his face into the wind.

She cannot see into the back unless she turns completely around but no one is talking which is probably just as well as she pilots scanning the sky because time wise they are right where they are suppose to be then she sees another helicopter in the distance coming toward them.

"Helo, three o'clock." Cat announces through the com link as she watches the helicopter as it gets larger coming closer so she turns her radio to the frequency suggested on the list of coordinates given to her. "Unknown aircraft this is NB three niner four en route to Montague's Bar."

"This is Montague's Bar, follow." Comes the answer back.

"It's our escort." Cat relays over the com link following as below the jungle looks dense and bright below them.

After a short flight Cat is contacted again and told to land but below all she sees are tree tops as the other helicopter hovers in the distance. She hovers still trying to see just where she can land but there is something about this area not quite the same as the rest of the jungle below then the foliage seems to part and she realizes it is only a camouflage net she was seeing covering a landing pad.

Waiting until the pad is clear she begins lowering them down into the hole surrounded by real trees finding a hut community under the natural canopy. She glimpses men with crossed ammo belts over their chests holding a collection of machine guns and hung with an assortment of other weapons through the swirling dirt and vegetation kicked up by her blades. She really hopes these are friendlies because they are seriously out numbered.

"Shut it down Cat." Dog instructs over the com link.

While doing so she sees Dog exit from the side along with Carmichael and Jake but Rolly remains in the copilots seat looking disappointed the ride is over. Dog is being greeted like a long lost friend with much back slapping as she continues shutting the helicopter down then the crowd formed around Dog parts and a man in some kind of fancy military uniform steps forward with a big smile.

She watches as the two men shake hands with Dog receiving more back thumping from the shorter man in uniform. When she steps out she draws some attention but there are woman here dressed for battle but it seems her blond hair might be a novelty from all the brown, black and red heads. Men and women are staring at her like an unidentified insect so she takes her cap from her vest pocket and puts it on.

"Cat." Dog calls out then motions her in sign with one hand when she turns to look at him.

She motions back affirmative then rounds the nose of the helicopter to find Rolly already has one of the long poles needed to cover the helicopter with the camouflage netting previously used to cover the landing pad.

Between her, Rolly, and the help of two other men using poles they lift the tarp over the helicopter blades managing to cover the large Huey very quickly and sufficient enough it cannot be seen from the air. With her plain green field cap covering her hair and wearing or carrying everything else she needs she leads the way toward the heart of the camp with Rolly following shouldering his rifle.

It is Jake who waves them over toward a row of huts on one side of a clearing as tables are being set up in the center and several small fires indicate some of the inhabitants are in the process of preparing the evening meal. Everyone else not occupied with this task seems to be doing absolutely nothing so obviously Rayjo's idea of having an army is to have a bunch of armed men laying around doing nothing. This is not only unproductive but discipline and battle preparation are a must in any army hoping to succeed so Cat can see exactly what Dog was talking about in regard to Rayjo's chances of ever over throwing the local government.

"We'll be sleeping in here tonight." Jake informs them grimly looking at Cat. "I should warn you Rolly snores."

"Si." Rolly replies in agreement looking regretful.

"He can't possibly snore as loud as Dog." She replies straight faced as they laugh and she just passed some kind test cooked up on the spot between the two men since no one will actually be sleeping much this night. Sleeping and snoring in a place like this is more deadly than drinking and driving down the side of a mountain.

"Dog wants us to meet him in Rayjo's command hut." Jake instructs leading the way and motioning to Carmichael as they pass to follow but it seems Carmichael has already picked out his "pillow" for the night from the look of it.

The command hut is a rather prestigious name for nothing more than a hut slightly larger than the others with maps on the walls and a large table covered in more maps. Dog is leaning over the table and a map as Rayjo is talking in his language while pointing to something on the map with three more of Rayjo's men present.

"Cat, come look at this." Dog instructs glancing up at her when she enters then pointing to the map on the table. "The rest of you listen up. Rayjo knows where our package is being held."

"It is a small group of mish mosh." Rayjo begins in accented English.

Cat listens as she studies the topographical map on the table as Rayjo seems to make up English words as he goes along but he gets his point across. A small group of mixed radicals are hoping to make a big pay day with their hostage but never having done anything like this before they are not very good at it, or at least not by Rayjo's standards apparently.

The only thing these radicals have done right according to Rayjo is the location they chose to hold the hostage which is inaccessible by land and any attempt by air will be seen, then Rayjo who has been making light of this group announces they have some how obtained ground to air missiles which Cat finds rather bizarre and makes them much more formidable then he lets on.

The gist of Rayjo's information is the only way into the encampment unseen is by air but only by flying down out of view through a very narrow canyon. Rayjo rattles off the dimensions of the canyon and speaks of the difficulties involved navigating this narrow space then wraps his arm around the shoulders of one of his men standing beside him.

"Alijond is my very best pilot." Rayjo claims shaking the man who is now grinning but does not understand a word his commander and chief is saying as he does not speak English. "He will fly you there."

"Cat?" Dog asks looking at her questioningly.

"Done." Cat replies confidently.

"Sorry Rayjo, but I'll be using my pilot." Dog informs Rayjo as if regretful for not using the man who is being so highly recommended.

"This woman?" Rayjo asks looking at her finding he would like to have her, but trust her with his life, never.

"If camels could fly my wife could fly it through the eye of a needle." Dog replies earnestly.

"Wife?" Rayjo responds as his eyes light up finding it encouraging his friend is as weak as any man and has fallen under the spell of a woman. "First wife, si?"

"First for me." Dog agrees with a smile. "I'm her fifth husband."

"Five?" Rayjo replies looking at the woman with astonishment then looking back to his friend. "What happened to other four?"

"They didn't let her fly." Dog responds with a serious expression. "No one has seen them since."

Rayjo bursts out laughing and after more back slapping he rounds the table as if to give Cat the same treatment but she flips out a butterfly knife spinning it open and begins using it to clean beneath her nails. This causes Rayjo to pause and pass her by to slap Rolie's back instead, then Jake, and then Carmichael until he is once again pounding on Dog.

"Your wife, she no friendly." Rayjo comments softly as he grins at his friend.

"No, she's not friendly at all." Dog replies knowing Rayjo will not believe a word he says regarding Cat as he continues. "She cracked two of my ribs before we even got here."

"And he has been whining about it ever since." Cat mutters grimly to Rolly standing next to her.

Rayjo laughs again finding Dog's joke is very funny and better than Abbott and Costello but he only has to look at the woman to know none of this is true. His friend has a good sense of humor but he must at least put up a token resistance so his friend will believe he wants him to succeed in his attempt to rescue the hostage but either way Rayjo will win but maybe he can keep the woman.

"Alijond is one of only five pilots who can do this." Rayjo informs the Colonel being truthful this one time.

"Soon there will be six." Dog responds confidently. "We'll leave in the morning but as always you have been a big help Rayjo."

"No, no, first we must eat and celebrate." Rayjo announces for a final feast for his friend is the least he can do.

"Food would be good but I'm sure you'll understand if we skip the festivities." Dog replies with false regret.

"Of course." Rayjo replies sagely as he claps his hands and makes shooing motions for everyone to leave the hut. "Eat, we shall eat."

"Something's off." Cat comments to Dog as she hangs back with him as Rayjo is waving the others before him like an old lady trying to shoo a dog off her lawn.

"Yeah, I got that too." Dog replies leaning close to her. "But until we find out what and how..."

"We play the game." She finishes for him.

"Have I told you recently I love you?" He asks knowing he probably should not say it again but at a moment like this he cannot seem to help himself.

"Three days, four hours, and less than sixty seconds ago." She informs him which has him looking at her surprised. "I noticed and I'm not deaf."

"I want a real honeymoon." He announces.

"Where?" She asks wondering if he is serious.

"I have no clue." He replies honestly.

"Well, think it over." She advises him as she exits the hut looking for food.

"Han Dog." Carmichael calls out just as Dog exits the hut behind his wife. "Maybe we should let Rayjo's pilot fly us in. Look, I know how it is with women but our asses are hanging here."

"I realize we're no longer in the military so I shouldn't expect blind obedience but I am your employer. I'm paying you to come with me but if you question my judgment one more time I'll fire your ass and you can walk back to civilization." Dog informs Carmichael flatly. "We've worked together before so you should know me. I'm telling you now if our asses are hanging, she's the one who will pull them back from the edge. You mark my words Carmichael before this is over she'll save all our lives, if not once, then several times."

"You can't know that." Carmichael responds but then looking at who he is talking too as the fire light flashes red in Dog's eyes he realizes maybe he can.

"She's already saved my life once." Dog informs him candidly. "And another thing, if you think you're bringing a "pillow" into the hut tonight you better think again."

Carmichael watches as Dog moves off into the people moving about the now fire lit camp and his large size dwarfs most of Rayjo's men then he remembers Dog's incredible strength and speed, so it is all coming back to Carmichael now. Dog can do things most cannot and it has been a while so maybe part of him thought he imagined these things but it is all coming back to him now as he moves through the people finding the woman and he sits watching her.

"Great." Cat grumbles into her bowl as she eats something she cannot readily identify but this has become the usual for her, even nostalgic.

"What?" Jake asks looking to see if a bug flew into her stew.

"Carmichael is staring at me." Cat replies as he and Rolly seem to have latched them selves to her like book ends and maybe they are afraid she will take a drink or two of what passes for alcohol here and kill them all tomorrow, maybe this is why Carmichael is staring at her now.

"He's okay." Jake assures her. "He just doesn't trust

anyone."

"Not even Dog from the sound of it." Cat remarks.

"Dog is probably the only person he does trust but then Dog took off and we never heard from him again until now." Jake replies with a shrug. "Probably found some other guys to work with."

"Let me guess." Cat responds grimly playing a hunch. "He was gone a little over ten years."

"Yeah, somet'ing like that." Rolly replies looking at her. "Then he jus' call us like he never gone."

"Did you ask him where he was?" Cat asks but by the way they look at each other first then back at her she realizes it never even occurred to them to question Dog.

Cat sets her empty bowl on a table giving the disgruntle looking people standing behind it a 'thank you' before turning back toward the fire. Rounding the outer edge of the clearing to get to their hut she is grabbed from behind and pulled into the semi darkness between huts. She can smell alcohol as she is spun about and with a few well placed hits her would be attacker is on the ground. She steps back into the fire light finding Dog along with the other three apparently waiting for her.

"What?" She asks.

"Did you kill him?" Dog asks grimly motioning to the guy on the ground behind her.

"No." She answers. "Unfortunately."

"Good." Dog replies darkly. "I can't have my secret weapon going off before the grand finale."

"Which is when?" Cat asks because she is about to fly a helicopter through a canyon and prove she is a great pilot so when does she really get to show off.

"How the hell should I know." He replies putting an arm around her shoulders. "It's nightie night time before anyone else gets drunk and stupid enough to make another grab for you."

"You're such a kill joy." Cat responds as she lets him steer her toward their hut. "I never get to have any fun anymore."

"You get to fly into a gorge which loosely translated is the Devil's Crotch because of all the pilots who tried what you're going to do didn't live to tell about it." He informs her.

"Okay, there is that." She replies as they enter the hut and she kind of likes the name.

Chapter 29
Somewhere in South America....

"Did you memorize just the gorge, or the whole map?" Dog asks as he surveys the cots each with its own mosquito netting and begins taking off his web belt as everyone else is doing but each will have their belt laying in the cot with them close at hand.

"Did you?" She counters as she opens her vest but leaves it on as she lays down on the cot next to his.

"Humor me." He requests as he places his rifle down next to his leg with his finger on the trigger.

"The whole map." She replies as she shifts to get comfortable then puts her hand in her pocket on the gun there.

"Gotta love a woman with a photographic memory." Dog responds as he grins up at the hut ceiling.

"So if you get lost, all you have to do is ask me." She offers knowing he never will but this brings her to what she wanted to ask him, without asking him. "You know like when you were lost for ten years."

"I wasn't lost." He mutters, he and the military knew exactly where he was.

"But you did just disappear for ten years with no explanation." Cat reminds him knowing the three men in the same hut are listening as she wonders how long it will take Dog to realize he needs to fill in the blanks, or maybe not. "Inquiring minds may need to know."

"It's kind of embarrassing." Dog comments realizing he has not given these men any explanation for his disappearance and they were between jobs at the time going their separate ways as he was working with Anderson, his go between, setting up their next job. "I was setup and imprisoned by my accountant which is rather pathetic, so now I have to wonder what happened to Anderson."

"Did he suspect you might blame him?" Cat asks because if so she has a very good idea Dog will never find him.

"Until you rattled Malinowski I did think it was Anderson." Dog reminds her so he might have to find Anderson. "I didn't try calling him."

"Some how I don't think he would have answered." Cat replies and the poor guy has probably been looking over his shoulder for the last ten years. "Who takes first watch?"

"I do." Dog answers. "Rolly, Jake, then Carmichael."

"I can take a watch." Cat comments frowning at being left out.

"We took a unanimous vote without having to vote we would prefer you get a full six of shut eye before taking us through anything remotely called the Devil's Crotch." Dog informs her knowing no vote was needed.

"Si." Rolly responds from his cot.

"I second that motion." Jake chimes in.

"I third." Carmichael adds.

"You're out voted four to one, go to sleep." Dog instructs her knowing she will only take short naps in a strange place, strange uncomfortable cot, and strange animal noises, some of which are not animals, but Cat will get more shut eye then they will by not taking a watch which is the goal.

"I'm not sure you translated that correctly." Cat grumbles realizing she is left no room to argue about the schedule. "It looked more the Devil's butt crack to me."

Devil's Crotch, the correct translation, opens below them starting as a gentle water runoff then gradually widening as Cat pilots the Huey helicopter toward their destination. Further along it appears to be just a gorge cut in the jungle floor by hundreds of years of water flow and no where near Grand Canyon scale but give it a few hundred years more and people will be vacationing here she suspects.

So far they have encountered no difficulties in leaving Rayjo's camp or in the air. Rayjo's rag tag army gave them a rather desultory send off when commanded by their fearless leader to cheer them to success.

Cat prepares to drop down into the gorge and through the com link she can practically hear the men in the back take a deep breath and hold it, while Rolly in the copilots seat is grinning like a kid on an amusement park ride. Thrilled anticipation and no fear, which makes Cat fairly certain Rolly does not do this kind of work strictly for the money.

They descend into twilight leaving the sun at the top of the gorge as Cat maneuvers the helicopter slowly but steadily through the rock crevasse were trees have taken root clinging to the rocky cliffs and jutting out into the gorge. Luckily most of these are in wider spots where they get sunlight from above allowing them to grow here, and way down below is a flat glassy ribbon of water.

Cat keeps the helicopter steadily moving forward below the lip of the gorge navigating the twists and turns while keeping the chopping blades from touching the rocky edges. Just one brush, no matter how slight, could break a blade or send the helicopter careening into the other side of the gorge without warning and disaster would quickly follow.

She now hears heavy breathing over the com as trees sweep by the open doors on the sides as she rises just enough for the blades to clear a section of trees. One section is so narrow she has to tip the helicopter side ways which requires more speed and the blades send up a spray of water.

"Jesus." Jake breaths over the com link as he clings to the safety harness to keep from sliding on the decking and dropping through the open side door into the water below. They all buckled in for this ride but seeing the ground rush by the side of this bird is a sight he was not prepared for.

Dog cannot meditate this trip away as he clings to the safety netting grimly but the urge to jump out is not as strong as it usually is which he knows has nothing to do with the gorge they are in and everything to do with the pilot. They should be getting close to what Rayjo referred to as the beach.

At some time a rock face gave way sliding off into the river causing sand and sediment to build up against this rocky obstruction. Not only is the spot wide enough to land but safe enough to walk on so they can climb from there up what remains of the cliff without being seen. Not ideal for bringing out a hostage, or for a quick get away, but if they move carefully no one will ever know they are here let alone gone by the time the hostage is discovered missing. This is the plan anyway but things do go wrong.

Cat can see the beach and sets down but still one runner is in the river and she has the helicopter turned facing back facing the way they came simply because she would rather head back through familiar territory then face the unknown part of the gorge reported to be impassible if they do need to make a quick get away. Rolly climbs out bending low below the blades and splashing through water to get to the beach.

"See you soon." Dog promises Cat over the com link looking at her through the bubbled window as he stands a safe distance away.

"Or I'll come get you." She warns him as she watches the others pull rope from their packs and prepare to climb the cliff face while she lets the blades slow. She will keep the helicopter warm and ready for a quick get away if needed but all she can do now is watch as they scale the wall of rock and disappear.

Twenty minutes later Cat hears the chit-chit-chute of automatic gun fire in the distance over the low hum of the rotors and she powers up the helicopter which takes no time at all to get to the rpms needed for lift off. Even over the now loud thumping of the blades overhead she can hear the faint sound of gun fire drawing closer so the men are provably going to be coming to her hard and fast. A rope spools out over the edge of the cliff followed by a man fast rappelling down, his feet never hit the side of the cliff until he is half way down before pushing off, and sliding down the rope air born again telling her whoever it is was at a dead run when he started down.

She cannot see who because of looking up into the blurring blades but once on the ground she sees Jake headed her way as two more ropes hit the ground soon followed by men. Rolly is running toward her and Dog has what must be Carmichael over his shoulder as he runs full out for the helicopter reaching it before Rolly or Jake who had a head start while not hampered by carrying a two hundred pound man. Rolly throws himself into the copilots seat with his boots leaking river water.

"Go." Dog orders from the back over the com link.

"Hang on." She warns as small plumes of sand are being kicked up from the guns just out of range.

"Shit,shit." Carmichael groans from the back.

Cat ignores this as she lifts the helicopter upward heading back down the gorge at a fast clip leaving what is obviously a failed hostage extraction in her wake of blowing sand and water. She stays down in the gorge since the hostage takers might have missiles though they have no idea if this is fact or not. Reaching the point were they inserted into the gorge while ignoring the steady stream of cussing coming from Carmichael she lifts the helicopter up only to find a helicopter in their path as the dash of her bird gives an electronic ping sound.

"They try lock missiles on us." Rolly remarks.

Like she does not know what this sound means Cat thinks grimly as she spins the helicopter diving back down into the gorge. The other helicopter does not follow meaning this may not be one of the five who can fly the gorge and they cannot lock missiles from above but they can follow along the top waiting for her to rise again then tag her with missiles.

She is piloting the gorge at a much faster clip as turning around is not an option until they reach the wider beach area as she mentally pulls out every trick she knows then discards most of them. What she would not give for her fighter jet right about now or just missiles on this helicopter but these things are not going to magically appear.

"Cat?" Dog calls out wanting to know what she is going to do and he wants to be ready.

"Give me a sec." She responds as a plan comes to her as they reach the beach where armed men are now standing at the waters edge with rifles and she spins the helicopter going back down the gorge yet again while sending their attackers diving for the ground but soon metal pings come from gun fire. She feels a burning sensation along the out side of her right leg just as one of the dials on her console does a not so nice dip but neither of these things concern her now. "I'm taking us up, give that bird a steel raking. I'll keep him between us and the ground missiles."

"They'll get a lock on us." Jake replies wondering if she has thought of this and if he can so can the enemy.

"Not if you keep him busy." Cat responds not waiting for a debate on the subject. "Get ready."

Dog and Jake belt themselves as best they can while crouched in the back of the helicopter near the same opening. Each is armed with a semi automatic assault riffle held by a strap securely across their bodies using one arm to keep the rifles from flying around as they are pitched this way and that as Cat navigates the gorge.

"Set." Dog informs her after receiving a nod from Jake.

"On my three o'clock." Cat responds as she lifts the helicopter out of the gorge so the side opening is facing the on coming helicopter as the loud chit-chit-chat of two rifles comes in a steady staccato from the back amplified by the open com link.

Rolly without being told is bent over hugging his knees as she looks over top of him judging the location and distance of the other helicopter by the blades which is about all she can see but she can picture well enough the problem the other pilot is having. He cannot turn away or have the sides of his helicopter raked with gun fire and since the helicopter has not gone down the glass is bullet proof but no one likes to be shot in the face regardless and what she is counting on is he either looses his nerve making a mistake or the missiles from the base lock onto him.

The other pilot tries rising up but she counters keeping him in line with the door opening and the guns but she knows the instant he realizes he has a bigger problem coming his way. As the helicopter turns she can just make out the pilots panicked look before she speeds off in the opposite direction pouring everything she has into getting them as far away as fast as she can. The boom of the other helicopter exploding does not even rock them as Rolly sits up right once again smiling at her then his face falls.

"Cat is hit." He reports over the com link as he scrambles to unhook his harness holding him in his seat then he has a bandanna in hand while brushing her skirt aside and tying the bandanna over the gash just above her knee.

"Cat!" Dog roars from the back.

"Stop yelling." She calls back as she grimaces at the pain in her leg but this is not a consideration at this time. "We're hit and going down." Then looks at her fuel gauge which lights up and adds. "Now."

She reaches over with one hand shoving Rolly back towards his seat and he scrambles to re hook his harness while she scans the leafy terrain below as the engine sputters. She sees what she hopes will be a soft landing spot as she hovers a moment over the area as her console beeps in alarm then she hits the kill switch.

The blades instantly begin to slow but the helicopter begins to rotate as she struggles to hold them over the area then they drop down into the tree tops. She grabs her harness holding on because from here on out she has no control over what happens but the blades are breaking and not kicking them around as they would have at full speed which was all she could do. Now she hopes something catches them sturdy enough to keep them from smashing full force into the jungle floor and in the end the tail catching in a tree does the trick.

Dog unhooks his harness then begins untangling himself

from the contents of the interior which now includes tree branches and the cargo netting that once held their gear securely is tangled up with everything. Not helping is the fact the helicopter finally came to rest at a ninety degree angle after several sudden starts and stops before resting more securely but only a glance out the door shows him they have reached the ground.

Once he is clear he pauses to check on Jake who is moving slowly but alive so he checks on Carmichael who is still safely harnessed into his seat and waves him off. Jumping out of the helicopter he turns finding the tail hooked in the Y of a tree and the runners are driven into the ground but not enough for the cockpit to be smashed as he first feared. Prying open the pilots door he can see Rolly stirring while hanging in his harness so he turns his attention to Cat. She is also hanging in her harness slumped forward and he begins using his hands to go over her checking for broken bones.

"You picked a fine time to cop a feel." She warns him grimly as she reaches for the harness release.

"I have to pick my opportunities very carefully when dealing with you." He responds as he wraps an arm around her so when the harness clicks open he catches her body weight then helps her with the shoulder straps. When she is free he has her in his arms resting his fore head on top her head for a moment just breathing in relief then turns off his com link then hers he whispers in her ear. "Limp a lot when I put you down."

"Why?" She wants to know.

"Plan B." He informs her as he lets her feet slide to the ground carefully. "The wound is just a nick, right?"

"Yeah, might have clipped my cannon." She warns patting her pocket and the gun hidden there.

"Ankle same side will work." He suggests just as quietly.

"Got it." She replies asking no further questions as she uses the side of the helicopter as a crutch to limp away then louder asks when she looks into the back seeing Rolly standing on the other side. "Any one else hurt?"

"Still just Carmichael." Dog answers reaching past her to pull a pack out of the rubble to look through it. "He has a hole in his shoulder."

"Package wasn't there, was it?" She asks grimly looking at Carmichael who seems put out by this whole mess.

"Hell no." Carmichael swears. "We were set up."

"Let's keep that to ourselves when we get to Rayjo's camp." Dog orders him. "I'm sure he'll have a good explanation why the package was not there and we're going to pretend we believe it."

"Good old Rayjo." Rolly comments shaking his head sadly as he begins pulling things out of the back on his side. "No trust any one no more."

"He's not expecting us back." Jake adds thoughtfully. "He's not going to have time to set up another ambush. We push hard enough we might catch him with his pants down."

"Which is exactly what I plan to do." Dog informs them finding what he is looking for which is the medical kit. "He might have to give us the real location this time especially if he is certain we won't be coming back a second time."

"How do we convince him of that?" Jake wants to know because they have a fifty fifty shot of making it out again.

"We'll be short a pilot so we use his. We're one man short so now he only has to worry about three men getting away." Dog informs them with a grim smile.

"Hey, I'm good to go." Carmichael objects and he is not being left behind sitting out Rayjo's much deserved payback. "He's going to pay for this and I want to see it."

"Which is why you and Cat are going to milk your injuries and stay behind." Dog responds looking pointedly at him and deadly serious. "This gives Rayjo a boost of confidence and leaves the two of you available to bail us out."

"And why would we want to do that?" Cat asks looking just as serious.

"Because it's what you do." Dog replies and all anyone has to do is look at this helicopter to see the proof. "It's why the Air Force cried when you left, why the Navy is still trying to find you to reenlist, and the Army is still trying to come up with the right incentive to lure you in."

"I didn't see any tears." Cat comments because there were none to see.

"You weren't looking in the right places." He responds grinning at her but the Major General certainly did. "You were up for three promotions just as soon as you reenlisted which is what they thought you were going to do. But you took the other option they forgot about. They didn't see that coming nor catch what happened, or how, until you were long gone."

"Now you tell me." Cat mutters wondering why he did not

tell her this sooner.

"You weren't going to reenlisted." Dog replies confidently. "That's not where the action is so why bother telling you what the Major General found?"

"Full disclosure." She replies but he is right, she would not have reenlisted if she had stayed but still he should have told her now she does not feel as if they tossed her out on her ear.

"Fine." Dog mutters handing her a pack. "Be a girl about it."

"You're so going to pay for that." She warns him.

"Then you'll have to come get me won't you." Dog replies as he looks toward the others. "Rolly, Jake, make a litter for Carmichael. I'll carry Cat. Make it look good which is really bad."

Dog takes Cat aside to see to her wound which is only a crease thankfully but he cleans and wraps it under her pants but there is nothing he can do about the blood or the burnt bullet hole in her skirt. He then wraps her ankle on the same leg making it look like it is very swollen so the bandage is large then feels her frown when he goes over the rifle she was carrying in her pocket to make sure it was not damaged.

"I can see where I rate." Cat comments as he is giving the rifle a much more thorough going over than he did her.

"I need you and your claws fully operational." Dog remarks and satisfied the bullet which hit her did not hit the hardware she is carrying. "You're going to need this."

"Right." Cat responds but it is the when and where she is beginning to wonder about.

They do make a rather pathetic picture as she limps into Rayjo's camp while Carmichael is carried on a litter. They are dirty, covered in bloody scratches, and after walking miles to reach the camp tired does not need to be an act. Unfortunately more pathetic is the fact they have to wake the guard so he can alert the camp they are coming in and entering the camp they are greeted like long lost friends once again.

Rayjo apologizes profusely over and over while promising someones head will roll for selling him false information. They are put in the same hut as Dog accompanies Rayjo to make plans and find the missing package. Carmichael is disgruntle about playing invalid which makes the whole thing more realistic so there is no need for him to act. Rolly and Jake are playing nurse maids by bringing them meals and making sure they are comfortable. Carmichael is in the process of telling Rolly just what he will do to him if he asks one more time if he needs help going out to take a piss when Dog returns.

"Well he has other information he says he discarded it as being unlikely." Dog informs them but he had to put up with the apologizing and vehement promises of retribution on their behalf from Rayjo for sending them on a wild ducks chase. Dog did not bother to correct him as he watched his old friend scramble to figure out where to send them next and apparently for Rayjo biting the hand which has paid him quite well in the past is not something he wants everyone to know he is doing. "I think this is the real deal. He's a little negligible on the details and exact location but his pilot will get us there he assured me."

"Not going to make this easy for me, are you?" Cat grumbles because a simple north, south, east or west would be helpful if she needs to rescue him.

"If this were easy you'd throw down your toys and go home." He responds knowingly and he is not worried about her finding him.

"He's going to have everything he has waiting for you." Carmichael warns grimly. "He's either helping these people, or they are his."

"Old Rayjo has graduated from pocket dictator to extortionist in the last ten years or so." Cat predicts to no one in particular.

"Shame too, he has been useful in the past." Dog mutters shaking his head while grinning at her. "Hate to see something happen to him."

"Yeah, I can tell." Cat replies as she makes herself more comfortable on her cot which is not much since her leg throbs, her ankle will not bend, and there is a long piece of steel running down one leg out of sight from everyone. Welcome to her world.

"We leave first light." Dog informs them. "Let's dig that bullet out of Carmichael."

"Now?" Carmichael asks but the look Dog gives him is not a pleasant one and he lays back on the cot remembering what Dog warned and right now he is in no condition to walk anywhere.

"Can't think of a single thing I'd rather do." Dog responds but he does produce a bottle of what the natives are drinking. This does not stop the cussing and name calling as Rolly and Jake hold him down while Dog grimly digs out the bullet.

Chapter 30
Somewhere in South America....

Cat using her make shift crutch made from some kind of tree root, or branch, stands next to Carmichael who has his arm in a sling as the helicopter carrying Dog and the others lifts off with Rayjo's pilot. Rayjo is aiming a smarmy smile her direction as if he knows a secret she does not and she is relieved when he walks off with some of his men because she is not in the mood to be polite to him.

She is not liking being left behind and she really is not pleased to be left with Carmichael. Dog in the night leaned over toward her cot telling her to watch over Carmichael and use him however she needs to. She knows what she would like to do with him, toss him off the nearest cliff, because his sulking about being left behind is irritating which she is certain it is not an act.

Carmichael watches as Dog's woman limps away wondering what the man can possibly be thinking to have brought her here, and okay, she is a halfway decent pilot he will give her that but this is no place for a woman. Especially a short cute one who looks like she sweats sugar instead of salt. What is even stranger is Dog whispering in his ear to do what this woman tells him or she will kill him.

Rrrright, she will pull the Glock she carries under her arm and plug him, ha, it would be like taking candy from a baby, and the whole prison for the last ten years thing is bogus. What military installation could hold Dog if he wanted to be free? None. He has been running other guys for his jobs and this time seeing as how things are expected to go balls up he needed men who are expendable so, hey Carmichael, I need your help on a job. Maybe the wife is expendable too which is why he brought her, cheaper than divorce.

It is a long morning as Cat sits before their hut in a camp chair swatting bugs and thinking of all kinds of nasty things she will do to Dog when she gets her hands on him again. Carmichael has been moving around camp then for some inexplicable reason sits in a chair next to her. He does not say anything at first which is just as well but this does not last long.

"You do realize you and I are expendable to a man like Dog?" Carmichael asks just to be sure she knows what is what.

"You are, but I'm not." She informs him flatly as she stares out at the unwashed army which has yet to do anything military like and have so far laid around in the shade.

"Great," Carmichael grumbles because now he is certain she is not real bright. "You really think he's coming back?"

"No, he's not coming back." Cat responds grimly wondering where this man was when Dog told her to come get him. "We're going after him."

"Right." Carmichael replies with a laugh for the woman is clueless, a babe in the jungle. "He has bugged out before and he just did it again."

"He didn't bug out." She mutters shaking her head wondering how this guy even functions without a brain.

"The whole prison thing is bull shit." Carmichael replies laughing but not with humor. "No prison cell can hold the man."

"Solitary confinement, bread and water. Starved and without human contact, they can keep him and they did." She replies grimly and this is fact. "They were too chicken to just shoot him, or no one would man up and give the order. They wanted him dead but no one wanted their hands dirty doing it."

"And how do you know this?" He asks figuring this is the bullshit story Dog fed her.

"I saw what was left of him." Cat replies grimly and it still angers her. "Muscle and bone, clothes hanging like they belonged to someone else, and talking like he didn't know silence is golden. Couldn't get him to shut up."

"How?" Carmichael asks while he considers what he is hearing and starving Dog would take a long time. "How did they get him? He was ready for another job, we were on standby then nothing."

"His accountant set him up." Cat responds angrily and she is still keeping tabs on the man through Harv and Moss but she thought she had made this clear the night before but Carmichael must have fallen fast asleep. "Malinowski was stock piling Dog's money but the minute Dog started talking about heading back to the U.S. and to hell with the consequences he freaked out."

"He was skimming money?" Carmichael reasons or why else would he freak.

"He knew one of the Steel Man unit other than Dog. Saw him go nuts and was more than willing to give Dog as much money as he wanted, as long as he never set foot in the U.S." Cat explains grimly.

"Mother fucker." Carmichael exclaims because this does make sense. He knows of Steel Man but was too young to meet them as a unit and he has heard the stories from men who did know them in the day who still hide from a war long over when they threw down their guns and ran. Carmichael knew who and possibly what he was dealing with when he said yes to Dog the first time out. "What changed? Something changed."

"Another war." Cat replies. "A way out, friends in high places pulling for him, and an honorable discharge from the military because they need him out here working."

"So where did you meet him?" He asks but his mind is reeling because if what she says is true this is not just another job and if Dog is square with the military then this is a sanctioned operation.

"If I told you, then I'd have to kill you." She replies. "For some reason Dog wants you alive but so far the only thing I can find you're good for is being used as target practice."

Before Carmichael can respond they hear the sound of a helicopter approaching and she is up probably faster then someone with a bad ankle should be but she remembers to hobble to the landing pad as the helicopter begins to descend through the tree canopy. It is difficult to see who is inside until the blades slow and the vegetation settles then the pilot exits but he is alone. Rayjo comes out of a group of his men as the pilot begins talking quickly then Rayjo turns to face her and Carmichael looking grim. She knows the trap has been sprung as Rayjo approaches.

"Be ready." Cat warns Carmichael as she tries to look like a worried wife.

"I'm sorry but the Colonel and his men, they are gone." Rayjo announces hiding his relief they are finally done with this but he is not too happy with the pilot who should have stayed and brought back the bodies. He must buy better men, ones who can follow orders.

"So you say." Cat replies pulling her Glock which is an

obvious move they expect and two men hold guns on her while Carmichael is disarmed from behind. They seem satisfied she is thoroughly cowed when she tosses her Glock to the ground and they lower their weapons standing to either side of her while two men hold Carmichael by the elbows to keep him from charging Rayjo or running off. They do not seem to think she is a flight risk as with a glance she finds they are smiling confidently at their leader.

"I am so sorry little wife." Rayjo responds while tamping down the glee he feels for he is certain he will be able to keep the woman with little effort.

"Not as sorry as you're about to be." Cat informs him smiling back then jumps straight up split kicking the two idiots to either side of her all while pulling the machine gun from her pants pocket. It comes out just as smoothly as she practiced as she twists in the air taking out the men holding Carmichael then she is standing before Rayjo with the hot end of the gun pointed at his chest. "Now you tell me where my husband is."

"You cannot do this." Rayjo sputters in disbelief looking at his men who have backed away making no attempt to dispatch the woman as the other is now armed and behind him.

"She just did." Carmichael replies poking one of the fallen rifles into Rayjo's back while tucking her Glock into his waist band while his mind is still reeling, his life did not even have time to flash before his eyes, she was that fast.

Together they maneuver a still disbelieving Rayjo toward the helicopter at gun point without making themselves clear targets but no one makes any attempt to help their leader. Cat was counting on the fact no one in camp would risk death or even know how to handle a situation like this. She is certain the real fighting will begin once they are in the air over who will take over command if they do not just grab what they can to sell off as Rayjo with his hands tied is strapped into the copilots seat with Carmichael keeping a rifle on him at all times. The added bonus is the helicopter is already warmed up so she kicks it up to speed only taking seconds as they lift into the air.

"Hand me my Glock." Cat orders Carmichael as she moves the helicopter off a safe distance from the camp then sets her machine gun between her and the door not wanting it any where near Rayjo. Carmichael reaches through from the back handing the gun to her instantly since he is wedged in the opening behind the center console between the storage lockers keeping Rayjo covered with his rifle. "Now you're going to tell me where your pilot left Dog."

"I realize this is a shock but he is gone." Rayjo replies sincerely trying to reason with this stupid woman who does not seem to understand the meaning of gone then bang and his foot feels as if someone just poured acid on it. He begins cussing as he realizes the woman has shot him in the foot, just like that, no warning. "I can tell you nothing if I am dead."

"You're only going to wish you were dead." Cat informs him calmly with a smile. "Next will be your ankle then your calf and then your knee. Oh look, you have a whole other leg for me to work on after that."

"He is dead." Rayjo roars then bang and he did not think anything could hurt anymore badly as he screams looking at his shattered ankle and all the blood on the floor of the helicopter. This is when he realizes she is going to do what she says and she has never so much as looked in his direction as he rattles off the coordinates.

"Carmichael take him in back and tourniquet his leg just below the knee." Cat orders over the com link even though he is right behind her then she yells over the noise so Rayjo can hear. "Keep him alive and if he has lied to us start cutting off his fingers. I hope your knife is duller than mine because I really want him to feel it."

"Yes Ma'am." Carmichael replies finding he never expected this but, hell yes, he can and will take orders from a woman as he pulls Rayjo into the back screaming and crying all the way.

Cat pours on the power sending the helicopter shooting over the trees below checking gauges and familiarizing herself with this helicopter then she grins when she finds what she was hoping for as they near the drop point but the com links are only good up to a few hundred feet so hailing Dog will not work unless she is hoovering practically on top of him. Of course, it is another cliff with a steep drop off and the only clear landing place is on the top of the cliff but there is no sign of anyone down there as she circles looking.

"Damn it Dog. Where are you?" She mutters out loud.

"Right here." Comes the reply. "Land."

"Are you landing?" Carmichael exclaims from the back noticing they are going down. "I don't see anyone."

"Dog said land." She informs him wondering why he did not hear but then he must have been occupied with Rayjo.

"I didn't hear anything." Carmichael comments as he looks out the side door as they drop down on the cliffs edge then he sees three people coming out of the tree line. One is being half carried and he recognizes Rolie's grinning face then Jake but the third trying to hobble along with an arm over Jake must be the package. "Here they come."

"Dog?" Cat calls out scanning what she can see of the tree line but she is not seeing him.

"Get up and away, I'm coming in hot." Dog warns her.

"Or cliffs." Cat mutters and she is somehow suppose to catch him as Rolly climbs into the copilots seat. "Clear?"

"Clear." Carmichael calls back. "What about Han Dog?"

"He'll meet us." She informs him wondering if his come link is working correctly as she lifts the bird up and swings it around in a big loop. "Buckle up tight."

"Meet us where?" Carmichael mutters wondering what the hell she is talking about.

"In the air." Cat responds as she swoops in toward the cliff again as Dog runs from tree cover with what looks like a very angry army behind him as she lines the side door up tilting the helicopter slightly so he does not run headlong into the beating blades then Dog is leaping toward them. "Do we have him?"

"He's on the runner. He's been hit." Carmichael calls back.

"Get him in, we have company." Cat warns seeing two helicopters headed their way and right now she is not counting on them being friendly. "Put some hustle into it."

"Clear." Jake shouts.

"Buckle in." She warns shooting the helicopter straight up.

"Cat?" Dog grumbles because the helicopter is tipped forward going at high speed.

"Company." She informs him closing her eyes in relief at the sound of his voice before pouring on more power.

"Out run them." He suggests but it is not his preferred option especially how he feels at the moment.

"She is headed right at them." Rolly informs him with his eyes big and a grin on his face.

"Cat?" Dog calls out tiredly and all he really wants right now is a nice smooth ride.

"Guess what I got?" Cat replies in sing song voice.

"Well, don't play with them too long. I'm probably bleeding to death, the package needs some care, and who the hell made a mess of Rayjo?" Dog asks suddenly realizing all the blood on the decking is not his.

"Your wife." Carmichael informs him with grin.

"Jesus Cat." Dog mutters grimly. "He's a friend of mine."

"Was." She corrects as her console beeps then whistles. "Tag, you're it." She mutters as she flicks the toggle switch and both missiles fly off as she turns the helicopter gaining altitude as the other two helicopters realizing their danger dive for the tree tops but neither make it and she is already heading for the city leaving them far behind. "I really didn't expect them to send anyone out looking for Rayjo."

"Probably wanted to make sure he's dead and not coming back." Jake suggests but no one else offers an explanation.

They are intercepted by two more helicopters before reaching the outer markers of the airport and it takes her a while to convince them they are the same people who left in the Huey two days before so they are escorted down.

The local guard, U.S. embassy diplomats, and assorted personnel greet them once they are on the ground. The hostage is taken for medical attention over seen by a diplomat while the local guard is not happy they lost the Huey but Dog suggests they keep the Black Hawk they arrived in and the reward for Rayjo when he is turned over to them. They seem satisfied with this and as far as Cat is concerned even without the money involved they are getting the better end of this deal.

A jeep takes them to the Cessna and she watches Dog whom has been bandaged around his middle but he seems to be alright and not the bloody nightmare of before. The air field attendants have the stairs down in readiness for them as she hauls both their gear up the stairs as Dog stands facing the three men at the bottom of the steps. Dumping the packs just inside the door she comes half way back down the stairs waiting to see what comes next.

"I owe you one Carmichael." Dog offers with a slight smile. "You can dig this one out of me on the way to the States."

"The offer is tempting but you know I can't go back." Carmichael reminds him and he has the really dull knife he did not get to use on Rayjo.

"This was a U.S. government funded operation. I can't have men working for me the government doesn't know about anymore." Dog replies easily. "So I had to get you an honorable discharge. You can go back with us now and a job or you can stay with whatever comes along. But if you stay with me you're going to have to take orders from a woman and she'll kill you if you mess up."

"I sorta got that impression." Carmichael responds looking up at the woman who keeps a machine gun in her pocket while wearing a skirt. "Your secret weapon?"

"Pocket sized dynamite." Dog agrees.

"You're so going to pay for that too." Cat responds grimly.

"Yep Carmichael, one of these days she'll probably kill me." Dog informs the man seriously. "So do you want to watch?"

"It should be interesting." Carmichael responds picking up his pack and going up the stairs as the woman comes down to let him by but he cannot resist. "I'm on to you. You won't kill him."

"I hope you can grow wings really fast." Cat warns him but he looks undaunted as he goes up the stairs as she frowns after him while thinking she has found someone she really wants in the ring with her.

"Rolly how about a trip to the U.S.?" Dog offers as Rolly grins back but shakes his head. "I have the paper work. Green card working visa to enter the U.S. for employment so as long as you work for me, you're legal. You quit working for me, they kick your ass out again. I know you've no ties in Mexico anymore."

"Which I still don't believe." Jake interjects looking at Rolly. "You have to be the only Mexican I've ever met who doesn't have brothers, sisters, uncles, and cousins, all living in one town or under one roof."

"I believe that's stereo typing." Cat comments frowning at Jake.

"No, that's fact." Jake replies not at all detoured by this. "I can't believe there isn't one living soul in Mexico he is not related too."

"They all in America." Rolly responds as he explains. "Illegally."

"Sorry Rolly, but you'll be legal and paying taxes." Dog warns him.

"They no speak to me." Rolly mutters shaking his head sadly then he grins. "Is okay, they no speak to me now."

"Freaking greaser." Jake mutters as Rolly cheerfully goes up the stairs onto the plane.

"Are you in Jake?" Dog asks.

"Now I know how a cheap date feels." Jake grumbles as he picks up his pack and heads for the jet. "I'm the only one you didn't have to pay to get into the States."

"They're so not living with us." Cat informs Dog as she follows him up the stairs. "I'm not building a compound or a dog pound, I'm building us a home."

"I think the kids are old enough to fend for themselves." Dog responds grinning as he reaches the top of the stairs turning back toward her. "Besides you're the one who brought up their abandonment issues."

"I can't wait until you heal again." She warns while standing in the narrow hallway between the cockpit and the cabin. "Because next time I am breaking your ribs."

"Can we wrestle first." Dog offers as he leans down to her. "This jet is really fast right?"

"Not fast enough." She mutters hearing kissing noises from them as Dog leans in and the sooner she is rid of them the better she will like it.

After take off Cat kicks back in the pilot's seat with the jet on auto pilot and alone with her thoughts until Rolly enters the cockpit with a smile taking the copilot's seat but he says nothing seemingly content to just look out the front window as they slice through the sky. She continues doing her own mental evaluation of the mission and the only area needing improvement from her point of view is the transportation waiting at the other end. Maybe they should have tried hiring private but short of buying a helicopter from some individual she doubts anyone would rent to them having the same fear as the government did when it comes to having it returned. Arguing the point they would not have lost the Huey if they had been given missiles would have been futile but it all worked out in the end though Dog being shot was not part of the plan.

Her mind keeps going back to what happened on the cliff and she is positive she heard Dog tell her to land but for some reason Carmichael did not and she knows she did not imagine hearing him. The Major General told her part of the project Dog was involved with intended to develop mental abilities which she presumes would include mental telepathy of some form only Dog showed no change in the testing and the Major General based his whole premise on the fact he could prove Dog was not like the others in his unit and the military cleared him.

She also finds it strange how certain Dog was she would need the pants she wears and the hardware they would conceal before they even left the states but maybe this was just some sort of premonition or an innate sense of preparation for every eventuality. Given the number of missions he has been given over the years being overly prepared is probably second nature to him.

She is so deep in thought it takes her a moment to notice a light flashing on the console and Rolly is giving her a questioning look as she puts her headphones back on finding the nearest tower is trying to contact her to relay what seems to be a phone call from the states. With a frown she asks them to put the call through wondering if the Major General has a need for them again so soon.

"Hello?" Cat asks not certain whom she is speaking to.

"Oh thank God." Margaret gasps with relief. "I didn't know how to contact you but Charlie seemed certain one of the air towers could. I hate to bother you while you're on your...trip but we really didn't know what else to do. Your Father and Charlie have been calling the consulate while Ethel has been on the phone with Clarissa who is nearly hysterical and trying to keep her calm."

"Mother?" Cat asks sitting up in her chair because none of this sounds good. "Just tell me what has happened."

"Carter's been kidnapped." Margaret responds and even saying it out loud makes it sound unbelievable. "I don't understand how this can happen and in broad daylight no less."

"Mother, take a few breaths and give me a minute. I want Dog to hear what you have to say. Okay?" Cat suggests as she begins flipping switches. "Just stay on the line and give me a moment."

"All right, yes." Margaret replies breathlessly. "That's a good idea."

Chapter 31
Somewhere in South America....

"Dog, we have a situation." Cat announces over the intercom. "I'm going to put a call on speaker through out the plane. Everyone else shut up." Cat links the call in. "Mother, Dog can hear you now. Tell him what you just told me and breath."

"Yes." Margaret agrees trying to remain calm. "I'm just so scattered I forgot I needed to breath for a minute."

"Hi Margaret." Dog greets the woman curiously while seated on the sofa in the cabin where he is feeling like Cat beat him up after Carmichael dug the bullet out of him.

Jake and Carmichael are now sitting across from him in chairs with a table between them playing some kind of two handed card game but they are presently looking at him and no doubt wondering what is going on just as he is.

"Oh Johann." Margaret sighs uncertain where to even begin. "I'm so sorry to bother the two of you."

"It's okay Margaret we're on our way back." Dog replies sitting on the edge of the couch now as fear comes through the trembling voice. "Just tell us what's wrong?"

"Well, Charlie and Ethel received a phone call from Clarissa this morning." Margaret explains trying to give them what happened in the proper order. "Clarissa told them she and Carter went out in the ocean on a chartered boat which included a guide who was showing them the sights from the water when another boat came up beside them."

"Remember to breath Mother." Cat suggests as her mother is talking in a rush.

"Yes." Margaret responds realizing she needs to get a grip on herself if this is going to make any sense but this is the strangest thing she has ever heard of happening. "Three men boarded their boat holding guns and they simply took Carter."

"It's going to be okay Margaret. Did they say why?" Dog asks looking toward the hallway to the cockpit as his hands clench into fists on his knees as he pictures several different scenarios occurring and none of them good.

"They've taken my son hostage for money." Margaret announces with disbelief clear in her voice. "They told Clarissa they will kill Carter if she doesn't pay them. My God Johann, they want a million dollars. We don't have that kind of money and neither does Charlie and Ethel."

"They know they won't get the whole amount Mother." Cat informs her mother but it is a very steep starting point. "They'll negotiate but if they won't money isn't a problem for us, okay."

"We suspected Johann is financially sound but that's not why I called." Margaret replies because she would never ask them for money, unless absolutely necessary, and only to save Carter. "It's just that Charlie and your father insisted I keep calling and trying to get through."

"They were exactly right. This is what we do." Dog informs her and he is worried Chuck will go charging into this situation which could get Carter or himself killed. "Where's Chuck now?"

"He's on the phone with the American consulate. I mean who else do you call when an American has been kidnapped in a foreign country. It was all we could think of. Clarissa has been with the local police and they don't really seem helpful." Margaret explains in a rush still unable to process what has happened or how it even could.

"Where is Clarissa now?" Dog asks as he rises from his chair to pace the confined space and he needs to know where she is or she could end up dead.

"Well, they wanted her to stay in the hospital but after the police took her statement they never came back. When she didn't hear anything from them she left the hospital to go to the police station. They told her they are looking but they never even asked her for his photograph. How can they look for a man when they don't even know what he looks like?" Margaret asks now nearly hysterical herself because if the police are not willing to help then what hope do they have.

"Margaret we'll find him." Dog promises but he is missing a piece here. "I need to know what happened to Clarissa and why was she in the hospital?"

"They hit her." Margaret sniffs and they can hear through the phone connection she is probably moving a tissue to her nose. "They hit her and knocked her down in the boat then kicked her and told her if she doesn't pay them they'll do worse to Carter."

Jake and Carmichael draw back in their chairs as Dog's muscles bulge in his arms and shoulders as he raises his closed fists in the air and his mouth opens in a silent roar directed at the jet ceiling. The man is practically shaking with maddened fury as the veins pop out in his neck and they are more than aware they are seated in an enclosed plane with a man capable of crushing bone. They have never seen Dog this enraged and it is not a sight they really ever want to see again as the woman on the speakers is crying with the deep sobs of pure terror.

"Mother." Cat calls softly her fingers dug into the arm rests of the pilots seat. "Where is Clarissa now?"

"I'm not certain." Margaret admits for she has lost track of the conversations going on around her. "I thinks she's talking to Ethel on another phone right now."

"Margaret." Dog decides quickly as he takes a deep breath striving for control. "We need Clarissa's phone number to reach her."

"Okay." Margaret breaths turning to Ethel and interrupting her conversation then relays the number.

"I've got it." Cat confirms. "We'll be contacting her so she needs to be off the phone so we can call."

"Okay, but what do you think we should do. We want to fly there but we may need the money to get Carter back." Margaret responds helplessly but even with their savings and pensions along with the Kincaids they might reach half the money these people are demanding.

"I need all of you stay where you are." Dog orders bluntly biting back his anger so it does not come out as an order. "Just tell Chuck to stand down. He'll know what that means."

"Okay, tell Charlie to stand down." Margaret repeats breathing in relief because she can finally be doing something even if it is passing along a message. "Ethel is off the phone with Clarissa."

"We're on our way to her now Mother." Cat replies but she needs to radio in her changed course then relay a call so they have to end this conversation quickly. "This is what we do Mother and we'll get Carter back."

"Okay." Margaret replies sighing even though she does not know how this is possible but it does make her feel better for the moment. "Right. Thank you."

"I'm radioing the change of course." Cat informs Dog over

the intercom after the connection is broken. "They're so fucking dead."

"You got that right." Dog snarls as he reaches for calm again. "How close are we?"

"An hour." She informs him grimly. "I'm cutting that in half."

"After we get through to Clarissa I need to call Harv and Moss." Dog replies as the plane begins to rumble louder then to shake slightly as he looks toward Jake and Carmichael. "Hang on we're about to set an air speed record for this class of jet if at all possible."

"Mind filling us in." Carmichael requests as he buckles into his seat belt as Jake does the same.

"I have Clarissa." Cat announces over the intercom then a moment of static. "Clarissa, Dog is on."

"Dog." Clarissa cries hopefully.

"Clarissa, I need you to do something for me." He informs her and his guts clench at the sound of her shaking voice as he motions Jake and Carmichael to wait for their explanation.

"Dog, they took Carter. They had guns and they just took him." Clarissa babels into the phone surrounded by strangers in a strange place where no one seems to want to help her. "I couldn't do anything to stop them. I couldn't protect Carter the way Caro protects you."

"Honey you've got this backwards." Dog replies softly but his face is a mask of rage. "Cat beats me up."

"Okay, maybe some times, but if anyone else tried to hurt you she would beat them up. The only one allowed to beat you up is her." Clarissa responds laughing and sniffing at the same time. "I want to learn how to beat people up the way Caro does."

"Honey, you have better things to do with your time." Dog informs her truthfully. "And you have a big brother now to beat people up for you."

"Yeah, I do." Clarissa sniffs with a little laugh. "Are you going to beat them up Dog?"

"Oh yes, I am." He agrees unable to stop the growl in his voice. "Then I'm tossing what is left to Cat to finish off."

"I think you might have that backwards." Cat informs him grimly.

"Oh the you two are so great and this makes me feel so much better." Clarissa interjects wistfully. "I wish you were here."

"We'll be there shortly." Dog assures her. "But I need you to go to the U.S. embassy and stay there."

"But the police need to look for Carter." Clarissa replies sounding confused. "They're not even trying to find him. One even told me to pay them and forget about it."

"Clarissa, please, you have to do this for me." Dog instructs her actually wishing this death trap could go faster. "I need you there."

"But Dog." Clarissa replies in a drawn out voice.

"Clarissa, get your ass to the U.S. embassy now." Cat orders in a modulated voice to imply she is very serious.

"Or what, you'll beat me up." Clarissa snaps back. "Well someone beat you to it. He was big and ugly."

"Like Dog?" Cat asks half serious trying to keep Clarissa from remembering for the time being or she might end up a puddle on the floor of where ever she presently is.

"Noooo." Clarissa replies drawing it out . "Dog is not ugly, he's beautiful. Stop saying mean things about my big brother Caro."

"Fine, fine." Cat relents closing her eyes because she happens to agree but she has to get Clarissa to cooperate and do as Dog wants. "But Dog wants you at the U.S. embassy. You wouldn't want to disappoint Dog would you?"

"No, I wouldn't." She replies sounding uncertain. "I like Dog."

"I know you do." Cat admits wishing with all her might this plane could break the sound barrier but she has it at top speed way beyond the manufacturers recommended limits. "Then do as he says, okay?"

"Okay." Clarissa responds finally.

"Take a cab." Cat suggests because the last thing they need is for her to burst in to tears at the wrong time and get her self into an accident.

"Don't have a car. I'll take a cab." She agrees then there is a dial tone.

"Drugged?" Cat asks over the intercom because Clarissa can be a little spacey but there is a sharp mind there only not just now.

"Or concussed." Dog replies from his knees on the plane floor where he has been since Cat started using him to get Clarissa to cooperate. Why he is on his knees he is not certain, maybe praying for the first time in his life.

"Shit." Cat replies because she had not thought of this but at the consulate they will get her medical help if they feel she needs it, if she even gets there. "Shit."

"Just get us there. Preferably in one piece." He suggests knowing his Cat wants blood too. "Rolly get your ass back here." Once Rolly makes his staggering way back through the shaking plane to take a seat Dog finds he cannot stop pacing. "Here's the situation. Cat's brother Carter just married Clarissa, they're on their honeymoon. I think you can gather the rest."

"Why was he targeted?" Jake asks.

"He's a lawyer." Dog replies grimly.

"All American lawyers are big money." Rolly remarks as if this is just a fact of life.

"That's what seems to be going around." Carmichael agrees grimly even though it is far from the truth for most. "Someone probably asked him what he did for a living and he said lawyer. Wouldn't have seen any reason to say something else or know any better."

"Most places like these are tourist traps but not many kidnappers." Jake considers because obviously they went to a popular honeymoon spot on foreign soil. "They scalp the tourists over the tables, face to face, and with a friendly smile so no need to get nasty when they willingly hand over more money than they should."

"Probably why the police are not acting." Carmichael responds. "Either they have no clue what to do or they don't want to acknowledge it even happened which is not good for drawing more tourists if word gets around."

"Dog, Chuck would like to speak to you." Cat relays before transferring the call to the com just to give him a heads up because Chuck does not sound happy.

"He's going to want to help." Dog predicts and the last thing he needs is Chuck in the middle of this.

"Send him to Harv and Moss." She suggests having alerted the two M.P.s their vacation is over. "He'll at least be in the loop if not boots on the ground."

"Patch him through." Dog instructs because he does not need a while card in the mix but Cat is correct and they are talking about the man's daughter. "Chuck."

"Don't tell me to stand down you son of a bitch." Chuck roars angrily. "I know I was a sorry excuse for a soldier but this is my daughter over there and I'm not sitting here with my thumb up my ass waiting for you to do something."

"The hotel where Cat and I stayed. Harv and Moss our IT guys are staying right across the hall." Dog informs him quickly. "I need information Chuck anything Clarissa may have told you, any little thing she may have mentioned which might have helped the kidnappers select Carter. They were watched, followed and he was snatched. They may have noticed or seen someone and never even knew it."

"Okay." Charlie breaths. "That's my little girl Colonel."

"That's my little sister." Dog reminds him. "She can take me to my knees faster than Cat and in a much nicer way."

"How is Caro taking this?" Charlie asks grimly not realizing she can hear him as well.

"If the plane doesn't shake apart and the wings don't shake off she's okay." Dog informs him seriously. "You might have to come pick us up."

"We'll do it." Chuck promises just as seriously. "I need a Steel Man."

"Yeah." Dog replies after Chuck disconnects but the man was more settled by the time the call ended. "Good call sending him to Moss and Harv."

"You don't have many friends." Cat replies. "You can't afford to loose any."

"Yet you don't seem to have any." Dog reminds her finding this a curious thing for her to say and he would think she would say he has too many.

"I don't need them, you do." Cat replies truthfully because he does. Dog needs people to interact with and solitary confinement must have been the worst form of torturer for him. "Besides, I have you and you're the only headache I need."

"Of course." Dog replies with a grin as the intercom clicks off and he turns back to the guys. "I think my wife may love me."

"May?" Carmichael asks in disbelief and if the man needs proof he has it. "It's obvious to me if you're in danger anyone who stands in her way is nothing more than raw meat for her to turn into hamburger."

"That's just what she does and she doesn't really even have to like the person she's saving." Dog responds so this is not proof of anything but Cat doing what Cat does.

"It seems clear to me she would throw herself on a live hand grenade to save you but not so much for us." Jake adds his view of the situation just from the impression he has of the woman already.

"Which is exactly what I don't want happening." Dog replies pointing to Jake who just voiced one of his biggest fears. "If any of you notices her pushing the edge too far then pull her back."

"And just how are we suppose to do that?" Carmichael asks finding what amounts to an order is asking the impossible. "She split kicked two guys out cold, drew a semi automatic rifle while still in the air, and popped the two guys holding me before her feet even touched the ground." And to prove what he says is true he unbuckles his safety belt then stands turning around holding out his arms. "Do you see any blood splatter on me? No, you don't because those guys were dead before they even hit the ground. What you see here." He motions to Jake, Rolly and himself as he goes on. "Are just slabs of raw meat she'll turn into hamburger if we do anything that puts you in danger or try to stop her from reaching you. The safest place for us is behind you because you're the only person here she won't tear through. So my plan is to not do anything stupid which might jeopardize you and live to see another day."

"Not a bad plan." Dog agrees and maybe the key to keeping Cat alive is for him to be more careful about what he is standing next to if explosives become an issue. She would, probably cheerfully, sacrifice herself for him so he needs to make sure she never has the opportunity.

Somewhere in the Caribbean.....

Cat is cleared to land at a moderately sized airport with colorful signs along a chain link perimeter fence advertising all the local businesses and what they have to offer the thousands of tourist which flood into this vacation hot spot every year. She requested a private area to leave the jet away from the busy terminal filled with incoming tourists and other regularly scheduled aircraft.

During the flight she radio relayed a call to have the Cessna structurally inspected by a qualified mechanic from where she bought the jet. They did not ask why mainly because she paid them in advance to go through all the hassle of sending someone and money talks when dealing with very large expensive purchases.

With packs in hand they exit the jet seeing a long dark car heading across the tarmac toward them and she knows it is too soon for the mechanic to have arrived so wonders what kind of welcoming committee they should be expecting. When Major General Aimhurst steps out of what appears to be a limo she is somewhat surprised but Dog does not seem surprised as the two men shake hands. She knows Dog asked Harv and Moss to contact him but thought only as a courtesy since they would be out of the country longer than expected if he should need them.

"Clarissa Callahan, I've been informed, is presently established at the U.S. embassy. She has a mild concussion and cracked ribs which she was told at the hospital where she was taken previously but walked out disregarding the local doctors orders but she is being monitored now and will be staying at the embassy under observation." Aimhurst relays first and foremost as this is no doubt a concern to them. "The police have no information on the hostage takers what so ever but I do have some information you may find useful. I'll tell you all about it during the drive as it may effect how you wish to proceed. It's a long drive given this is the height of the tourist season so the streets are packed."

"How did you get here before us?" Cat asks as they pile into the limo and they were much closer than he would have been if in the states.

"I'm reluctant to tell you given what I was told you were expected to fly last mission." Aimhurst admits because things did not quite go as arranged there so she may not be too happy with him. "A fighter jet then a Sea Hawk helicopter to the U.S. base here and it's at your disposal if you should need it."

"Consider yourself redeemed." Cat replies and it will be a far cry above even the Black Hawk which was probably twenty years out of date.

"Do any of you require a doctor?" He asks since one man seated across from him has an arm in a sling and he ignores Dog's obvious injury knowing medical treatment will not be required there but even the Captain has a bullet hole in her skirt which he cannot see below to know the extent of. "Were you shot Captain?"

"Grazed." Cat replies but she is impatient with all the niceties. "Tell us what you know about Carter."

"The police as I said will be no help at all. This falls outside their jurisdiction of muggings and minor thefts." Aimhurst reiterates to be certain they understand local help is not forth coming. "There is however a Navy carrier further down the cost which has been engaged in tracking pirates plaguing the coastal waters in a rather large area. They've had two sightings of the pirates boat and a SEAL team has done recon to no avail but one of those sightings was very near where and when Carter Callahan was taken. The Navy is convinced it was the pirate or the pirates may have seen who did take Carter but it is the only lead we have at this point."

"It's a start." Jake comments but not much of one.

"What did the SEAL team learn during their recon?" Carmichael asks with a frown because they should know more.

"SEALs are trained to associate and blend into any surroundings but in this case it's far more difficult. There's an element unique to this area. A combination of guerrilla fighters, water mercenaries, and the locals who are wary of anyone who can speak with the proper dialect." Aimhurst explains so the problem is not translating and being understood but being understood too well it seems making the locals suspicious of them. "None of the locals are talking."

"Ocean slang, jungle slang, and large heaping cups full of salty slang." Dog remarks nodding his understanding.

"We'll fit right the fuck in." Carmichael replies confidently.

"Yes, I believe so, even dressed as you are." Aimhurst agrees and he knows Dog has the ability to mimic any social surrounding. "You fit the example of the clientele in several establishments these pirates or kidnappers, if not one in the same, may frequent."

"No shower and no clean clothes." Rolly mutters then grins.

"I'm not going to fit in." Cat realizes immediately which grates to be relegated to the sidelines when it is her brother they are looking for.

Chapter 32
Somewhere in the Caribbean....

"Unfortunately not." Aimhurst agrees because being a woman does not disqualify her but the fact she does not look aged nor tough will. "We've been offered full cooperation by the Navy of the carrier off shore. They really want these pirates and they fully believe they have your brother. Captain, you have full access to anything you may need or deemed necessary and they're willing to assist in a ground search."

"Is the Navy attempting to sweet talk my wife away from me?" Dog asks because they seem very cooperative.

"Of course they are." Aimhurst responds wondering why he would even ask. "You knew they were interested in her before you somehow talked her out of the Air Force, who by the way, has finally figured out they made a colossal mistake when they fixed their so called 'error' in her military record. When the Navy found out they ex-sponged her combat record completely they became certain she would re-up with them no problem."

"They deleted your combat training?" Dog asks surprised by this as he looks at Cat as she never told him this.

"Is this important now?" Cat asks finding it totally unrelated to the here an now but then maybe he is worried she will jump on ship with the Navy. "Nothing would change. The Navy would make me top dog when I'm in a cockpit but once my feet are on the ground I'm nothing more to them then just another flea on the same dog. I chose which Dog I'm going to be on top of so let that be the end of it."

"There is a hotel three blocks over catering to rougher clientele." Aimhurst inserts into the silence while the Colonel is smiling at his wife and she is glaring back at him. "We'll drop you off here so we don't draw unwanted attention or gain suspicion. I'll see the Captain to the embassy."

"Once we're in we'll make the rounds." Dog agrees knowing he should tread carefully around Cat at the moment because her anger with the present situation is very close to the surface so he just advises her. "Stay locked and loaded."

Nodding an affirmative she watches the men climb out of the car while it sits idle at a busy intersection and she has seen nothing of this city but traffic clogged streets, brightly dressed people walking by and crossing where they will between cars through the dark tinted windows. Their driver up front behind a dark wall of glass must have the patience of a saint and nothing about this crowded place appeals to her.

"I can arrange for you to stay in an adjoining room to your sister-in-law." Aimhurst offers now paying more attention to the rather odd outfit she is wearing but despite the dirt on her clothing and the surface scratches on her face and arms she still looks harmless and cute. "I could also arrange for a change of clothing as well."

"Thank you but no. I can sleep on the floor in Clarissa's room and Dog's reference to 'locked and loaded' is what I'm concealing with what I'm wearing." She informs him then slides the machine gun partly out of her pocket then back.

"Very clever." Aimhurst comments and nothing about her clothing suggests she is carrying weapons of that caliber. "Very well concealed I might add."

"Dog's creation from something I wore to my brother's wedding. He was very insistent about it actually and claimed it might be useful which it was." Cat explains wondering what he will say to this. "I really shocked the natives."

"I imagine you did." He responds with a slight smile though there is an underlying question. "As I told you before the Colonel's intuitive abilities kept him in the Steel Man project but the telepathic abilities they had hoped to generate were never evident as with the others. The test proved this along with past records if this is your concern."

"I'm not concerned." Cat responds but she is almost certain something is evident just not what anyone in the project was looking for but she changes the subject. "This is all a little above and beyond a military adjacent duties to a private security company."

"Well, you could say I have a vested interest in the two of you Captain." Aimhurst replies but this sounds too clinical for his liking. "The Colonel was my brother's best friend which to me makes him family, if this makes sense to you, so what affects him in a way affects me as well."

"As I see it you've repaid any debt you may feel you owed

your brother when you had Dog discharged." Cat informs him. "It's not a debt you have to keep paying."

"And what if I told you I've never had family in the true sense." He replies so maybe she will understand there is no debt to pay. "I first began looking for Falcon when I was a teenager but children whom are considered difficult in those days were institutionalized passed from system to system until adults then the law can deal with any problems they may cause. I went looking because the people who adopted me did so out of pity, not love. I stuttered, was born with on leg shorter than the other, and was generally not liked by other children for those very reasons.

"It's a wonder the Army took you." Cat comments but he has not stuttered so he probably grew out of it only the leg issue would be difficult to overcome and she never noticed a limp.

"An insert in my shoe corrected the problem so they had no grounds to deny me entry" Aimhurst responds with a smile. "My adopted parents used me as a crutch to bolster their sense of saintliness given my issues and had no interest in helping me over come them."

"I'm the least intuitive person in the world and even I can see where this is going." Cat informs him after having assumed he had the normal childhood Falcon was denied. "Bullied much."

"Every time the adults turned their heads but unfortunately they looked back in time to see Falcon beating up another child who was making fun of me." Aimhurst admits grimly but no amount of explanation kept Falcon from being in trouble. "Excessive aggression they called it and decided it would be best to separate us as if he were inflicted with an illness I might catch."

"Well, I tried to give you an out." Cat admits but it seems he is just as messed up as the rest of them. "This dysfunctional functional family already has two information ferrets and you saw the three kids with abandonment issues but it's not too late to change your mind."

"I'm not going to change my mind." Aimhurst responds confidently no matter what issues they may have. "I believe we have arrived."

Glancing out the side window she sees a tall white stone wall and as the car negotiates a turn then stops momentarily before proceeding passing through tall black wrought iron gates she finds attended by Marine guards. Old curved trunk palm trees line the long U shaped driveway leaving a clear view to a large white stone building resembling a tropical plantation or palace and when the car stops before it five marines are standing in the shade along the front or at least she only sees five.

"Who did this use to belong too?" Cat asks because she knows the U.S. would not have built it.

"Very astute Captain." Aimhurst comments as the door is opened by a Marine. "One of the first joint efforts to rid this area of drug lords and part of the deal to establish a U.S. presence."

"Good deal." Cat responds now standing beside the car looking up at the blending of tropical looks yet modern design while shouldering her pack as the Major General leads the way past men who salute him along the way.

The inside does not disappoint and there is nothing sterile or clerk like about the massive entry with stairs winding up from both sides to the second floor and a railing running across the second story connecting the two. It looks to her like the owner just stepped out and the diplomats just stepped in as the largest ceiling fan she has ever seen hangs from the central ceiling looping slowly and moving the thick warm tropic air within mixing it with the cooler air being pumped in from somewhere. She sees more people moving about dressed colorfully with some uniforms thrown in as the place is heavily guarded as if they expect the former owner to try to reclaim his home by force.

"This is Captain Callahan." Aimhurst introduces to the woman who approaches them dressed in a white linen pant suit. "This is Lisa Holman one of the assistant directors who has arranged everything for Clarissa's stay."

"Our condolences." The Mrs. Holman offers sincerely understanding by the last name this is some relation to the unfortunate man. "We have Clarissa upstairs but she is understandably very upset. We check on her every hour as instructed by the doctor and so far she doesn't show any lingering effects from the concussion. Abductions aren't normal this close to the coast which is why we discourage American tourists from traveling to the interior where there are roaming bands of guerrillas."

"From my understanding the open water isn't much safer." Cat responds resenting her condolence implying Carter is dead and her reference to unsafe areas when Carter and Clarissa where clearly not in one of them. "I would like to speak with Clarissa now then maybe you could direct me to the police station, or officer who took the charter boat captain's statement."

"We discourage citizens from involving themselves in such matters." Mrs. Holman responds. "It's best to leave this matter to the local police."

"My brother didn't intend to be involved." Cat counters grimly. "But I intend to find the people who involved him."

"Mrs. Holman, I suggest you do as she asks." Aimhurst requests before this escalates any further and he even introduced the Captain by rank while it should be obvious from how the Captain is dressed she did not come here to vacation. "The Captain has the full cooperation of the U.S. Navy in this matter and is not known for patience."

"And she is armed." One of the two Marines adds who drew closer at what seemed an altercation. "I can attest to what she can do without a weapon."

"Lee." Cat greets but never takes her eyes off the woman before her. "I would like to speak with Clarissa now."

"Certainly." Mrs. Holman responds leading the way to one of the staircases while wondering if this is some sort of joke.

"You don't make friends do you Captain." Aimhurst comments softly as they follow behind the woman.

"That's Dog's department, not mine." Cat informs him just so he knows.

"You know that Marine?" Aimhurst asks curiously.

"We met once." Cat admits as they walk side by side down a wide hallway at the top of the stairs.

"With your feet or your fists?" Aimhurst asks out of curiosity.

"A little of both." Cat admits as the woman stops before an arched door.

"She hasn't left her room by choice and we can't in good conscious allow her to leave the compound until we are certain she is out of danger." Mrs. Holman informs them. "I will see who spoke to the charter captain."

"Thank you." Cat replies as the woman walks away. "See I can be nice."

"I suspect only when it suits you Captain." Aimhurst responds with a slight smile. "If you need to contact the Colonel just let me know and I can get word to him."

"If we're family then it is Cat and Dog." She corrects him then adds. "I'll be speaking to Dog shortly. He'll want to see and speak to Clarissa himself so if you have anything to pass along be here about sundown."

"I'll alert the Marines on the gate to allow him entrance." Aimhurst responds then wonders why she is looking at him with her head tilted as if she does not understand what he just said then a thought occurs. "He's not coming in through the front gate."

"How quickly they forget." Cat comments. "But then I haven't seen him walk on water yet so I'm sure that'll come as a surprise."

"Would you mind if I speak to the police and the charter boat captain directly." Aimhurst offers given she will want to spend time with her sister in law.

"Be my guest but if you find anything useful." She begins.

"I'll be here at sun down." He promises then leaves her.

Cat knocks softly on the door then a little harder and when there is no answer again she is now concerned as she tries the door finding it is unlocked so enters. The room is darker then the hallway but she can still see clearly since the curtains drawn over the windows cannot completely block the sun blazing beyond.

Setting her pack by the door she tries to locate Clarissa among the shadows amid chairs and a couch in a very nice setting more like one would find on a patio than inside a house but there is an archway suggesting another room which she walks towards just as Clarissa appears in the opening holding the hand set of a portable phone to her ear.

"Oh my God." Clarissa gasps with a start finding Caro suddenly standing before her as she clasps her side as pain shoots through her. "It's just Caro. I have to go. Yes, I'll call you as soon as I know anything."

"You didn't answer the door." Cat comments noting Clarissa looks pale and one side of her face is bruised but other than this and the puffy eyes she looks fine only her short quick breaths tell a different story.

"I was in the bathroom off the bedroom getting more tissues because I've run through the living room supply." Clarissa explains having disconnected with her mother and unclasping her side to show Caro the wad up tissues in her hand. "I'm a wuss remember so all I do is cry."

"You're not a wuss." Cat mutters as she grasps one of Clarissa's arms guiding her slowly to the wicker couch because neither self blame nor tears are going to help Carter then she opens the curtains to let the sunlight in. "You may be part vampire." She turns back to find Clarissa squinting now and a thought occurs to her and people with concussions might have issues with light. "Does the light hurt your eyes?"

"No, for the hundredth time." Clarissa replies frustrated while taking short shallow breaths. "Why can't anyone understand I don't want to see the sun and the ocean. I came here to see those things with Carter and he's not here."

"Good, anger works better for me." Cat comments as she gingerly sits next to Clarissa finding the short coffee table before them covered in used tissues and she is glad she missed that crying jag but she is tearing up again. "Can we just pretend we're discussing one of your patients. You don't cry all over them do you?"

"Of course not." Clarissa replies horrified at the thought. "I know how to departmentalize my emotions and present a confident appearance because a child's physical and mental welfare are more important then how I feel." Then having explained she realizes she probably should have considered doing this sooner. "And Carter's welfare is more important than my own misery."

"I didn't say that." Cat denies and for all they know Clarissa might be in worse shape than Carter.

"They said they wold kill him Caro if I don't give them a million dollars." Clarissa gasps out wincing with pain having forgotten to take small breaths.

"They only said that to scare you so you'll do what they want." Cat assures her but Clarissa is tearing up again so she goes on. "They can't collect if he's dead so they'll keep him alive. Right now they have to."

"Right now?" Clarissa repeats looking to her sister-in-law wondering what she means. "When do they not need to keep him alive?"

"When they have the money." Cat replies truthfully and few kidnappings actually end happily on both sides. "We have to find him first."

"But where do we look?" Clarissa asks and she never considered even once looking for Carter herself but maybe she should have. "Shouldn't the police be looking for him?"

"Actually the fact they aren't is good." Cat informs her. "They stand out and if they even get close the kidnappers could kill Carter and hide his body."

"What!" Clarissa gasps grabbing her side and she never

even thought of this.

"Look, let's just not talk about this." Cat suggests because now she has alarmed Clarissa when all she intended was to reassure her Carter is in no danger for the moment.

"Oh, well, let's just talk about the weather." Clarissa responds staring at her sister-in-law in disbelief then realizes she is probably over reacting again or just reacting when she should be thinking so taking a calming short half breath she asks. "So where should we be looking for Carter?"

"We can't." Cat responds irritated and rises from the couch to pace. She just came to check on Clarissa, reassure her, and find out what she knows about the situation they may not know but in only a matter of seconds she has sent her sister-in-law from one extreme to the other. "Look, have they contacted you again about the money?"

"No." Clarissa responds softly as she watches Caro pace wondering what she is missing because apparently she said something wrong.

"Did they at any time tell you not to go to the police?" Cat asks just to be certain but no one mentioned this during their calls.

"No." Clarissa replies or she would not have gone to them pushing them to find Carter, which was apparently a mistake. "Carter said you and Dog have a security company."

"Several actually." Cat replies as she looks out the window finding the sun is heading down and hopefully Dog will have some word of Carter. She has always considered herself a patient person but the Major General did not seem to think so, and apparently others, which they may be correct as this waiting is not suiting her at all. "It's not important."

"Oh, I think it is." Clarissa replies as she watches Caro and is really seeing her maybe for the first time. Her sister-in-law has a dark mark on her face near her eye which might be what remains of a bruise while there is definitely bruises up and down one of her arms, and when Caro turns toward her she notices a burnt hole in the skirt on pants similar to the ones she wore to their wedding. "Caro, what exactly do you and Dog do?"

"Whatever it takes to get the job done?" Cat responds watching Clarissa who is staring at the hole in her skirt so she amends. "With whatever is necessary."

"You deal with people like this, don't you?" Clarissa asks as she looks away and now she is beginning to understand why

Carter was so hesitant about talking about what Caro does but she was thinking their work ran more along the lines of protection and Carter has a certain amount of client confidentiality to maintain only now she thinks it might have more to do with causing her to worry. "Tell me what happens? Tell me what I'm suppose to be doing?"

"You're doing what you're suppose to be doing." Cat informs her or at least she is now.

"No, tell me all of it." Clarissa insists because there must be more and if Caro knows what will happen then she wants to know. "What should I have done?"

"Clarissa, there isn't a check list when someone is kidnapped." Cat responds and it seems Clarissa is back to self recrimination again. "Each situation is different. If the assistant director here were as quick to handout assistance as she is handing out blame and condolences you would've been here safe much sooner."

"Why wasn't I safe?" Clarissa asks because she is not the one they threatened to kill.

"If they don't think you're trying to get the money they could have revisited you to get their point across or worse." Cat admits though she is not about to go into detail.

"Or they might hurt Carter to make sure I know they're serious." Clarissa responds and this never occurred to her until now.

"Look, I need to know if you've ever seen these men before?" Cat asks which is a key point here. "While out eating or shopping, any place other than where you last saw them."

"No." Clarissa responds but the police asked her the same question only rather than get upset at being asked the same thing again she considers why everyone is asking. "You think they were watching us and, oh my God, they still are."

"They can't see you in this compound." Cat assures her when Clarissa stares at the open windows with trepidation. "But they know where you are, now, so they can contact you."

"I've been on the phone." Clarissa responds looking at the handset on the table. "I didn't even consider they would try to contact me."

"If they tried calling here they would've been told you're on an international call which is fine." Cat replies but missed messages at the hotel where they were staying would not have been. "They'll assume you're making arrangements for the money.

Realistically they know you can't get that kind of money in one day and it would've reassured them you're working on it."

"I've been doing everything wrong." Clarissa mutters and why is there no information for what people should do in this situation. "You know all of this because this is what you do, isn't it?"

"One of our companies specializes in what is called regaining physical assets." Cat admits which is the job description on the open market without actually advertising they find kidnapped victims. "No two situations are alike and there really is no right or wrong unless the kidnappers told you specifically not to do something."

"They just said to get the money." Clarissa replies which is all they seemed to care about but they were clear they would hurt Carter if they did not get their money when a thought occurs to her. "You could pay them. You and Dog have the money but I told Mother to sell the bridal dowry Dog gave us so that might be enough."

"Clarissa." Cat begins not certain if she should tell her the truth or lie at this point because paying these people will most likely not get Carter back the way any of them wants him to be. "Just let Dog and I handle this."

"Handle what?" Clarissa asks because it seems to her the money is the only problem. "You give me the money and I can get Carter back. But you didn't come here to do that, did you?"

Chapter 33
Somewhere in the Caribbean.....

Cat looks toward a darkened corner of the room as the sun is setting behind her meeting the dark eyes with a touch of red reflected in them as she tries to formulate an answer to Clarissa's accusation. The fact Clarissa is correct makes no matter because no amount of money will get Carter back alive or well. So rather than answer she turns back toward the window hoping Dog has the answers because nothing she can say at this point will make things better and from past experience she knows she will only make matters worse.

"What's wrong with you?" Clarissa demands as she rises slowly from the couch intending to make Caro look her in the eye and tell her she will not help her brother.

"Hello Little Sister." Dog greets alerting Clarissa to his presence as gently as possible so as not to startle her but she jumps and gasps clasping her side anyway. "Sit back down Sweetheart."

"Dog." Clarissa manages to gasp so relieved to see him and now she knows everything will be alright as she complies sitting back down not that sitting is any more comfortable. "You have the money so we can get Carter back."

"No." Dog responds as he moves to her and kneels taking her hands in his while she looks at him horrified by his answer. "If we pay them then Carter is as good as dead."

"You don't know that." Clarissa objects but looking into his eyes she realizes he may know and Caro did say they must look for Carter. "We have to find him first but where do we look?"

"I have a good idea." Dog admits very aware Cat is standing by the window and he interrupted what was beginning to look like a very nasty confrontation between the two.

"Where do we look?" Clarissa asks repeats grasping at this ray of hope wanting Carter back.

"Cat and I will find Carter." Dog corrects her and counters her instant objection before she can form it. "You have to buy us time.   They'll call wanting to know where their money is or how soon you'll have it.   You have to stall them with nothing but the truth."

"The truth." Clarissa repeats not seeing this as helpful at all. "The truth is we don't have that kind of money."

"Yes, you do." Dog responds and maybe at some point she will have the head dress and necklace appraised for insurance purposes but for now it is of no matter.   "When they call you need to tell them your money is tied up in gems and it will take time to have them converted into cash.   Even if they decide they want the gems instead of money it will still take time to get them here.   You don't actually know their current worth and would have to have them appraised to find their current worth on today's market."

"You think they'll be willing to wait for an appraisal?" Clarissa asks not seeing this as logical given these people seemed to be in a hurry and want cash.

"Probably not, but they might be willing to take a chance it's less then what they are asking." Dog admits though this is not the point.   "We're not buying Carter back regardless but buying time to find him.   By sticking to the truth and giving them an option they must debate you're giving us what we need."

"Time." Clarissa mutter realizing she does not have to lie because she has no idea what the jewelry is actually worth.   "I'm glad you don't need me to lie because I'm a terrible liar."

"I guessed as much." Dog admits giving her hands a squeeze of reassurance.   "I know you can do this but you won't be alone.   Major General Aimhurst is a friend of mine."

"Aimee.   Spelled the French way for a man." Cat comments without turning from the window.   "He's your brother.   The brother of my brother is my brother."

"Aimee." Clarissa repeats nodding for this makes perfect sense to her.   "What will Aimee do?"

"Whatever you want short of looking for Carter yourself.   He can hold your hand if you want him too but he's going to be staying close by until this is over." Dog responds and she will not be alone waiting and worrying.   "I need you to rest and be able to think clearly for tomorrow which is going to be another long day for you. Why don't you put a cool cloth on your face and prepare for bed."

"I'm not going to be able to sleep a wink." Clarissa predicts as he rises holding out his hand to help her up and giving him a brief hug she moves off slowly into the the bedroom.

"Here are the coordinates of where we need to start looking first light." Dog comments as he moves to stand next to Cat then holds out a list to her. "This is what we need from the Navy and bring that team of SEALs with you. Drop them off with me. There's a clearing just in from the inlet which will work."

"So it's a pirates holiday then." Cat responds guessing the inlet is where they took their ship into the interior. "The Navy is making them nervous so they lay low with a little kidnapping to off set what they're unable to take."

"Which makes them amateurs at this game." Dog warns her grimly. "They think they know how to play but no one is watching this building and they may not have been watching Clarissa after they took Carter."

"Which means they also don't know they need to keep the victim alive for at least a certain length of time for proof of life." Cat mutters not seeing this as a good thing.

"Their chosen profession requires they board ships hold weapons on people and take what they want then walk away." Dog reminds her. "The weapon this time is Carter so they expect Clarissa to hand over the money and they might think like piracy they can just simply walk away."

"You're basing a lot on a guess they just steal and don't kill their victims." Cat remarks wondering what he knows that he has not told her.

"The Navy isn't after them because of murder but because the ship they have was stolen from the Cuban military." Dog replies and she has such a quick mind. "It runs silent."

"So they work at night." Cat responds thoughtfully and they could approach any ship unheard, board the other ship, and wave guns getting what they want only there is still a problem here. "They just took a man in broad daylight. There are three witnesses this time."

"And they have one of them but aren't even watching the other two." Dog replies which suggests they have not figured out their mistake yet. "New game, new rules, and they don't even know the basics of a snatch and grab which is leave no witnesses who can identify them later."

"At some point in time they may realize their mistake." Cat warns him not seeing this information as reassuring.

"That would require the police actively looking for them." Dog responds and if no one is asking after them by description they have no idea they made a mistake. "You're right you know. Your bother is one very lucky man."

"Right now that doesn't bother me as much as it usually does." Cat admits as she glances at the list again. "Is the second item really necessary or are you testing the Navy's full cooperation?"

"I believe an example should be made. Kidnapping is not popular here and I would like to keep it that way." Dog responds but yes he is curious as to how far they will go to lure his wife away.

"This will do it in a big way." Cat predicts as she folds the paper putting it in one of her pockets and truthfully she is curious as too just how much pull she will have with the Navy.

"Dog left?" Clarissa asks as she enters the room again only seeing Caro as she looks around the room. She changed clothing which took time and is holding a cool face cloth to the side of her face and it does feel better.

"He needs to rest too." Cat replies not even bothering to look for him knowing Dog just melted into the darkness from where he came as she turns to Clarissa. "Nice PJ's."

"My honeymoon." Clarissa reminds her sister-in-law though it is one of the more modest outfits she brought to wear and even the robe she threw over it is meant to show off her legs but this is not what she wants to talk about. "You knew what Dog said about what will happen if they get their money so why didn't you tell me."

"Because you wouldn't have believed me." Car responds simply. "You believed him without question and I really didn't want to go into detail about how I know what I know."

"Is this kind of thing what you and Dog do?" Clarissa asks curiously as it seems they would not have much to do if so. "I mean this kind of thing can't happen very often."

"We own several companies and each specializes in a different area of security." Cat admits which is all Clarissa really needs to know.

"I thought security would be preventing something like this from happening." Clarissa responds as this would seem more logical to her.

"We do, but we're also hired when things are beyond securing in the normal way." Cat replies and she read each companies files while jetting all over and things can go really wrong before they are hired to fix them. "We need to get some shut eye. I have to be in the air by O'three hundred."

"You could have told me." Clarissa repeats with a frown.

"You don't even want to believe what I'm telling you now." Cat responds as proof of fact. "We'll get Carter back and that's all you need to know, or should be worrying about."

"Carter told me no one ever believed you when you were younger." Clarissa comments as she watches as Caro tosses the pillows on the couch to one end and it seems she intends to sleep on the couch. "Normally people who lie add detail, or too much detail, trying to convince everyone what they're saying is truth but that's not what you do. You're telling me flat out all I need to worry about is getting Carter back but I have the feeling you're leaving out an entire book of details so I'm having trouble believing you."

"Maybe I'm trying to spare your feelings." Cat responds sarcastically not certain just what Clarissa is getting at as she lays down on the couch and not certain she wants to know.

"That's it." Clarissa responds as it dawns on her. "You exude this aloof personality but that's the lie."

"I haven't slept in something like thirty six hours so could we do this analysis of my personal issues at another time." Cat suggests and she cannot help how she looks.

"But it's not you but how people perceive you which is why no one believes you." Clarissa responds honestly as she considers what she just discovered from her own response. "You're not doing it intentionally and really there is nothing you can do about it. You're not cold and unfeeling, or cute and dumb, but one of these is what everyone perceives of you upon first glance. Okay, second and third glance as well."

"And your point is?" Cat asks not sure why Clarissa looks like she just discovered some shocking reality.

"My point is, I believe you." Clarissa responds confidently. "You're sparing my feelings by not telling me some horrible circumstances you know from situations like this because you're not either of those things people see you as. I see you Caro, and I'm sorry for putting you in a position where saying nothing was your only option while I was thinking all kinds of horrendous things about you. I should've listened to what Carter was trying to tell me but I really didn't understand until now what he meant."

"Clarissa." Cat mutters as she closes her eyes not really

wanting to talk about this. "Go to bed."

"Sure." Clarissa agrees but her mind is still reeling from what she has finally figured out about her sister-in-law. "Good night."

Cat leaves the compound under darkness having spent a good deal of the night waking periodically to check on Clarissa whom true to her word was never sleeping and only pretending to be. Now relieved and reassured her sister-in-law's concussion is not as bad as she first feared Cat is driven to a military base where she is passed through security with only a glance over so having friends in high places has its perks.

Lifting off in a flashy new high powered Sea Hawk helicopter she heads directly for the floating fortress several miles out in the ocean requesting and receiving permission to land without which she would end up a greasy spot on the ocean waves. She touches down on an upper helicopter pad and two men approach her as she steps out returning their salutes finding she knows one of these men.

"They finally let the little girl get dirty." Lieutenant Killdare comments with a smile taking in her strange pants and there is no mistaking the bullet hole along with the bruises and scratches. She has been in some action but he does not even have to ask to know who won the fight.

"When I own part of the company there's no one to stop me now." Cat replies finding her old friend is looking good but that was never the problem with Dare.

She spent a month with Dare and his SEAL team participating in training exercises knowing all the while the only reason she was asked was because of his interest in her personally and the Navy's hope to lure her to change branches after she qualified as a top gun pilot. Neither option worked for her and they parted as friends but Dare does not know the meaning of surrender in any situation which is what makes him good at his job if not so good in personal relationships.

"Private security I heard." Dare admits but he cannot see how this would keep a woman like C.C. busy or satisfied only he was not able to come up with anything that would entice her to stay, both in the Navy and with him. "I can't see you negotiating a hostage release."

"When the hostage is my brother there is no negotiation."

Cat informs him seeing his look of surprise as she looks toward the ships second in command. "I need to see your superior."

"He has been appraised of the situation and is waiting for you." The seaman admits having stayed out of what was a some what tense greeting and knowing there is some history here. "If you'll follow me."

"You'll want in on this." Cat suggests to Dare as she follows the seaman into the ship. "I need your team."

"My team doesn't freelance." Dare warns her as he follows curious about what this woman is up to. She has been like a splinter in his mind for a long time now and when he heard she was coming aboard he wanted to see her but now he is more interested then ever.

"But you do follow orders." Cat mutters knowing this well enough and she knew he was ordered to be part of her life at one time and Dare takes his duties very seriously.

"It wasn't an order." Dare responds in a low voice knowing she is taking a jab at him. "Two totally separate deals."

"I believe you but I'm an all or nothing type of gal." Cat informs him as the seaman holds open a door for them and she enters finding a dapper gentleman with flaming red hair and a glint in his eyes green eyes of both intelligence and speculation as they stand before his desk.

"Captain Callahan I presume." The ships commander comments and he is glad he was well briefed before her arrival or he would have thought this is some kind of joke. This short slightly battered woman has the face of sunshine but she is dressed for combat if one ignores the skirt and even that has a bullet hole in it. "It's a pleasure to meet the woman who has over set the Air Force and put the Navy on notice there are bigger fish in the sea. It seems the Army may have won your hand without even asking for it."

"I didn't marry the Army." Cat corrects his assumption. "I married a man who use to be in the Army."

"You're married." Dare blurts out totally shocked by this as he looks at her not having heard this.

"Hell froze over." Cat replies not sure how else to explain it when at one time she told Dare this would have to happen before she ever considered marriage again as she addresses the matter at hand and not having time for anything else. "I was told my company would have your full cooperation."

"Not your company, you specifically." The Commander corrects her. "A last ditch effort I believe to promote good will in case you should change your mind about the private sector."

"Right now I don't give a rats ass about the Army, Navy, Air Force, or Marines. I need to find my brother who has been kidnapped in these waters before a band of pirates realize just how a kidnapping is really suppose to work, so are you willing to help or not?" Cat asks not willing to listen to any recruiting babel or promises other than this one thing.

"Whatever you need is yours." The Commander replies and he is beginning to see behind the bright face to the shrewd woman beneath. "I agree the timing is not right for this type of horse shit when a man's life is at stake."

"I need Dare's team for a ground search. We'll meet my team at an inlet we believe the pirates used to escape your net." Cat responds as she takes out the list and hands it over the desk. "Ground tracking equipment put into the Sea Hawk and a tech to run it."

"Yule has a busted wing but he can run a board." Dare offers and he knows the signs well enough to know C.C. is not playing any ones game right now so he needs to focus on now, not what could have been.

"A little heavy artillery goes a long way." The Commander comments seeing one of the things on the list which seems extreme.

"If my husband thinks it's necessary then it is." Cat assures him..

"Your husband, Colonel Red Eagle, is a bit of an enigma even to the Army where he served over thirty years from what I've been told." The Commander responds looking at this woman as he considers but he said whatever she needs only this seems to be what her husband needs. It seems to him they can help each other. "I'm going to ask for a favor in return. We need that ship these pirates have obtained and we need it in one piece."

"Our company motto seems to be, 'Whatever gets the job done', so I'm not making any promises." Cat replies unwilling to bargain when Carter is her first priority.

"She doesn't negotiate." Dare comments just so the Commander knows he is not going to get anywhere this way.

"Then get your team ready." The commander responds handing the list to his second. "Have it all put on the Sea Hawk.

Good hunting Captain."

"Thank you." Cat replies as she follows the second in command out intending to wait at the helicopter as men appear placing systems on the bird which are not standard equipment but portable enough to be added to any aircraft or boat.

She takes the time to radio into the main land tower as the sky turns an inky color just between night and day as her call is relayed to the aircraft people checking over her Cessna. She is listening to the list of stress fractures and assorted other problems caused by her hast as the SEAL team emerges onto the helicopter deck.

Dare walks up to where she stands near the open front door with headset on listening to all the safety violations she committed pushing the Cessna beyond manufacturer recommended limits and she rolls her eyes at Dare who has the audacity to smile back.

"Just get me another jet." Cat interrupts the lecture she is being given. "I need it brought here and if your pilot can wait he can fly back the other once repairs are complete. You have my money and your additional experiences so either do it or I'll take my business else where but if you think something like this will never happen again then you're wrong. So decide now if it's worth the effort, and just how badly you want my companies business. You have an hour to decide and if a new jet isn't here by this time tonight we're done."

"Money talks." Dare comments because she seems to be tossing it around as he tosses his gear into the back of the helicopter.

"Not loudly enough when they think their reputation will suffer if I tear apart one of their jets." Cat comments grimly as she returns the headset to the seat and understanding in some respects but what she does is not their problem as she moves away from the doorway to allow the technicians installing the radar equipment access. "I may have to go with surplus military grade aircraft at this rate."

"Join the Navy and they'll let you fly anything you want." Dare suggests because she could change her mind.

"Now you sound like an enlistment poster." Cat mutters knowing that is not all she wants which she thought he understand only to find out he really did not know her very well at all. "SEAL's accepting women now."

"Not really." Dare admits which he knows is what she said

she wanted but the reality is far from what she may believe.

"I'm not just a pilot you know." Cat informs him which he never seemed to see beyond the one skill set she used most often.

"I know, but in a team every member has his or her place." Dare explains which he did before to no avail and she is a great pilot but that was never enough for her he supposes.

"Be honest Dare. You never saw a place for me on your team except under you." Cat responds confidently and his ego was an obstacle which has no boundaries.

"Not true. You can fly circles around me and I know it." Dare admits freely. "But why couldn't that be enough with me. You're obviously piloting for your husband so what's the difference?"

"He doesn't just need a pilot." Cat responds easily and she is beginning to understand just how much Dog does need her. "He needs someone to catch him when he falls regardless if we're on the ground or in the air. He trusts me explicitly. You only trusted me within the boundaries of what you think are my limitations and only within a controlled situation where you dictated what I was allowed to do and what I was not. I don't have any limitations now."

"Apparently." Dare responds glancing down at the whole in her skirt. "You're safety was my first concern."

"Exactly why we would never have suited." Cat responds because his need to protect her tipped the scales in his direction. "He doesn't try to cage me with his concern, and he has yet to order me not to do anything."

"Have you considered he might just be using you to his own ends?" Dare asks.

"Which makes he and I equals in just about every aspect of our marriage." Cat remarks with a slight smile.

"Captain, we're good to go." Yule calls over from the passengers side of the helicopter hating to break up what appears to be a private discussion only he and the guys realized this pilot is really not Dare's type right from the start.

"Load up." Cat calls out to the men as she glances up at the sky as the sun begins peaking over the horizon.

She is allowed clearance to lift off heading directly for the inlet then once again she is looking down into thick jungle as she hovers allowing the five SEALs time to rappel down into a relatively open area before moving along the ribbon of water often hidden by trees as Yule is scanning for life signs below.

Chapter 34
Somewhere in the Caribbean.....

Dare and his men wind up the ropes they used to repel down from the helicopter as the still weak sun light creates darker patches of shadow around them but there is no sign of the men they are suppose to meet. It seems this former Army colonel is not much on punctuality and he knows in a matter of minutes the sun will be bright enough to light this area up like Christmas making them easy to see if anyone is even in this part of the jungle.

"Suppose they got lost?" Crew asks teasingly though they usually do not work with private companies so maybe this is normal.

"Just how many people are we suppose to be rescuing." Eman mutters thinking they would have been better off on their own.

"If we yell Marco loud enough maybe they'll find us." Gordy suggests as a joke.

"Polo." Dog responds stepping out of the shadows next to the man who last spoke and he will give the man credit for being well trained enough not to jump out of his skin. The others do just as well when Rolly, Jake, and Carmichael appear out of the shadows among them. "Sorry we're a little late but we had to walk in. You have our pilot."

"The Hell Cat give you pretty boys a nice ride." Carmichael comments with a sneer.

"Stow it, or walk home." Dog warns and he really has not missed Carmichael he now realizes. "Did you bring what we asked for?"

"Yes sir." Dare responds instantly to this large man who is not the old doddering fool he half way hoped and some what expected.

"Jake, I'll let you do the honors." Dog orders and Jake picks up the large rectangular box the Seals brought with them slinging it by the strap over his shoulder as he turns on his com link. "Cat, track north west along the water way."

"Roger that." Cat responds as she turns the helicopter in a loop passing over the clearing once again.

"We fan out staying in communication working along this side of the water way. Our Intel says these regulars have a place out here but they stay in this general area of the inlet." Dog outlines his plan. "Keep an eye out for anything irregular as we move. Our kidnapped victim could be any where out here by now."

"Why not just check out the structures?" Dare asks thinking these men will not be holding a hostage out in the open. "We could save some time going from house or shack directly."

"Because this man is my wife's identical twin." Dog responds looking at the young officer and this man if any should know what this means. "He's a Callahan and staying put regardless of who is guarding them just doesn't seem to set well with either of them."

"You think he'll try to escape." Dare mutters as he considers this and his previous experience with this man's wife. "Is he military?"

"No." Dog admits which is what will make this tricky. "He's going to have absolutely no idea how to survive out here or how to figure out which direction he should go, but he is the lucky Callahan so escaping and staying alive until we find him is within the realm of probability. His ace in the hole is Cat in the air."

"The heat imaging should help before it gets too warm." Dare agrees.

"She probably won't need it." Dog mutters as he motions with his hand they should move out.

Clarissa sits at a wrought iron table situated in a pretty little courtyard garden within the embassy security walls and seated across from her is a distinguished gray haired man with gray eyes if stern features who introduced himself as Major General Aimhurst. The sun rose on what promises to be yet another gorgeous day, just as the vacation pamphlet promised, only there is a dark cloud hovering over her this day. The previous day also started with such promise and turned into a living nightmare so she is cautious of expecting too much from today.

She accepted this breakfast invitation more from curiosity than any real need for food, and quite possibly looking for a distraction. Her nightmare beginning the day before has not yet ended even though she has yet to sleep, or possibly she is asleep and will wake up any moment to see Carter's smiling face.

"Thank you for accepting my invitation, Mrs. Callahan."

Aimhurst remarks fearing she would not and she probably should have slept in this morning because from the look of her eyes any sleep she may have gotten was not peaceful. Still a very pretty woman despite her wane smile and slightly battered features but there is an almost haunting sadness in her blue eyes.

"Please, call me Clarissa." She offers realizing the uniform he wears instantly gives one the impression of stiff and formal but there is a kindness in his eyes she notices being seated this close at a rather small table.

"Clarissa." Aimhurst amends and he spent the previous afternoon walking in this woman's foot steps looking for some clue as to who has her husband but what he found in her wake was only a string of very sympathetic people with no memory of anything useful. He had hoped to give her some factual insight into the people holding her husband but all he can give her is supposition as to the type of people these maybe and pull from past experience of kidnappings which have ended happily to reassure her. "Given the situation and the lack of constant demands..."

"Could we talk about something else." Clarissa suggests as her mind feels bogged down with worry and there is nothing he can say which will change this so she wants to talk about anything else.

"Of course." Aimhurst responds not certain what they have in common to discuss but he can understand how her husband's absence is a very difficult subject for her.

"Caro says we're related in a way since you're Dog's brother." Clarissa comments seeing she has clearly put this very confident man at a loss for words.

"I'm afraid I don't follow your meaning." Aimhurst responds because he knows of no way they are related. "I'm not actually his brother and he is your brother by marriage."

"I think you've been adopted and Cat told me your name was Aimee. Not the girl form but the French form for a man." Clarissa informs him since he does not seem to realize this and it is nice to know something for a change that no one else does. "I think Dog collects family which is one of the things I love most about him. I feel as if I have known him all my life."

"Yes, it is some characteristic of his nature I suppose." Aimhurst responds not mentioning the clinical term the military gave it. "From his wife's perspective he has two ferrets and three men with abandonment issues to date."

"Dog in some ways looks very fearsome but he's just a very big man with a very big heart." Clarissa comments and she saw this when she first laid eyes on him but her sister-in-law is an entirely different matter. "Caro is much the same I just discovered though she hides it very well."

"I'll give you tolerant and faithful." Aimhurst responds from his own perspective but does not see the Captain as being overly loving.

"Then she has fooled you as well." Clarissa replies confidently because she finally saw what is behind the veneer. "I think she has fooled many people."

"If you say so." Aimhurst remarks but he has seen and heard exactly what Cat is capable of which takes a certain mind set not considered loving and caring. "I would say her disposition is more protective."

"Then we'll have to agree to disagree." Clarissa responds thinking he is wrong as what appears to be a waiter moves up beside her.

"Mrs. Callahan, you have a phone call." The man informs her.

"Oh." Clarissa gasps and it must be the kidnappers as her mother knows she intended to have breakfast with Aimee. "Oh my God."

"You need to take this call." Aimhurst instructs as the woman across from him seems frozen. "Have the call transferred to her room."

"I don't know if I can do this." Clarissa hisses as her breakfast companion rises from his chair and attempts to assist her from her chair only her legs have gone numb with fear. "Dog told me what to tell them and it sounded so simple but what if I say the wrong thing."

"There is no wrong thing to say at this point but if you don't take this call it would be the worst possible thing you could do." Aimhurst informs her as he helps her rise and keeps an arm around her as he guides her toward the stairs. "You must appear to be cooperating and give them time to find him."

"Yes, that's what Dog said." Clarissa replies and feels reassured when he seems to agree but this does nothing to calm her fears. "But no one has told me what will happen if they refuse to wait."

"Or you're fixating on what will happen because you already

know." Aimhurst counters as this is a very bright and introspective woman who has probably come up with all kinds of scenarios which no one had to mention. "They want money, it's as simple as that, and you want your husband back. As long as they are convinced they have a chance of getting it they will not harm your husband for now."

"Just as long as they don't get it is my understanding of the situation." Clarissa comments as she leans heavily on Aimee's arm as they go up the stairs.

"Yes, that would be bad." Aimhurst agrees knowing the chances of her husband surviving would be slim to none once they have what they want and they are taking a gamble now that he is even still alive. "Just buy them today to find him."

"And if they don't?" Clarissa asks but she suspects she knows.

"You'll do fine." Aimhurst assures her as he opens the door and enters with her just as the phone rings but he makes certain she is seated before handing her the phone as she has gone pale. "Your husband needs you to do this for him so forget about everything else."

"Shouldn't I be asking them to prove he's alive." Clarissa whispers as if they can hear her which she knows is ridiculous since she has not even answered the phone yet.

"Not at this time." Aimhurst suggests for multiple reasons he does not voice. "Just talk to them."

"Right." Clarissa replies as she picks up the handset with a shaking hand. "Hello."

Aimhurst remains by her side nodding to her as she explains about the jewels and the delay offering them to the kidnappers if they do not want to wait for an appraisal. It seems clear by her side of the conversation he is hearing Dog is correct about this not being something these pirates do but then Dog's ability to assess a situation has never been in question.

"They'll call back after they decide if they'll take the jewelry as it is not knowing the cost." Clarissa informs Aimee after disconnecting feeling like she has just run a marathon and having difficulty catching her breath.

"Just relax." Aimhurst advises and retrieves a bottle of water for her from the mini fridge he saw when they entered. "The hard part is over. They'll be calling only to tell you yes or no."

"Why doesn't Caro or Dog want proof Carter is still alive?"

She asks now finding this odd as well as frightening.

"Proof of life can come in several nasty forms." Aimhurst warns not willing to go into detail at this stage. "Also Dog believes they have your husband in the jungle beyond the city where there is no phone reception. We don't want them to believe keeping your husband alive is more trouble than they're willing to go to by running back and forth. Also any proof they give us could be falsified in advance. Did he say when he would call back?"

"Some time this afternoon but I'm to have the dowry sent waiting their decision." Clarissa replies while thinking a lock of Carter's hair would really not be sufficient proof then her mind conjures up all sorts of things like fingers. "I think I need to lay down."

"Excellent idea." Aimhurst agrees as she is sheet white and shaking as he helps her up from the couch and to the bedroom then into bed. "You did great."

"My husbands imminent death is great incentive." Clarissa responds weakly and all this time she was thinking all she had to do was pay them and everything would be fine but she had begun to realize even before the advice of others that she was not looking at the situation correctly. "I should call my parents and Carter's parents are probably worried sick."

"How about I do that for you." Aimhurst offers and he should probably call the doctor to see her but he is not certain what they can do short of sedating her which would not be good when they call back.

"Would you please? Clarissa responds as she gives him her parents number. "I think they're together."

"If not I'll be sure they get the message." Aimhurst assures her as he closes the curtains in the room and moves to the couch while wondering just what to say and what not to say. This is beyond his experience and training but he is certain being firm and confident their son-in-law will be found when he really does not know for certain will help in the short term.

"JRE International."

"This is Major General Aimhurst." He replies puzzled because he just dialed the number Clarissa gave her. "Mr. and Mrs. Kincaid would not happen to be there."

"Yes, sir. Along with the Callahans sir." Harv replies looking about his and Moss's suit where both older couples have been staying with them since the day before. It seems Mrs. Callahan cooks when she is upset but she has nearly set the place on fire once already and Mr. Kincaid curses their boss with every other word as he paces the suit. It is Mr. Callahan and Mrs. Kincaid whom concern him the most as they are quiet seated in chairs saying very little and staring off as if they could drop over dead at any moment. "Whom do you want to speak with first, sir?"

"How about speaker phone if you have that capability?" Aimhurst suggests and this will save time having to repeat himself over and over again though it will add some confusion he is certain.

"I'll get them all together, sir. Hold on one moment, sir." Harv suggests and he also intends to make sure nothing is left cooking on the stove.

"Who is this?" Chuck demands to know now that they are all seated about a small table with the phone on speaker.

"Major General Aimhurst sir." He replies not expecting the hostility but given the situation he expected fear only some people express anger instead.   "I'm the Army's liaison to private contractors and I am working with JRE International."

"So what is the military doing to find our son?" Margaret asks and some what relieved they are involved.

"I'm afraid this is not considered a military situation. Our advice would be to hire private security such as JRE and even the FBI is some what restricted in this area which is still a foreign country with only a U.S. presence not an occupation. Given the official view of the locals they're not interested in calling in the FBI as they want to pretend this never happened but the embassy director here has been calling the local government demanding more only with no success so far. I actually think this is a good thing and keeps the playing field open for JRE to move about without restriction." Aimhurst responds knowing this sounds more dire than it is.

"So what are Dog and Caro doing?" Chuck asks though he knows the men they are staying with have been relaying information to them.

"Captain Callahan has the full support of a Navy carrier off shore here. She has a Sea Hawk helicopter and ground surveillance equipment. The Colonel is on the ground with a team of Navy SEALs and given the information they have gathered they have an idea where Carter Callahan may be held but they're covering every inch of ground to be certain." Aimhurst explains so the military is doing something but their priority is not the man in question. "Clarissa just spoke to the kidnappers moments ago and bought the Colonel and Captain more time to look."

"How did she do that?" Ethel asks because her daughter is not very astute when it comes to things like this she is certain.

"By insinuating it would take time to get the gem stones in her possession to her current location and having them appraised for current value." Aimhurst responds and leave it to Dog to come up with such a plan. "If they want an appraisal done they'll have to wait so we have bought an additional twelve hours but if they are willing to accept the gems value unknown we have bought at least six hours. It all depends on how greedy or how smart these people are but we'll know shortly when they call again in a few hours."

"What gem stones?" Chuck asks looking about the table.

"The bridal dowry." Ethel responds while staring at Margaret who also knew instantly what he was talking about. "Was that why Carter was taken?"

"Oh no." Aimhurst replies though this dowry thing seems strange. "He's a young handsome American and a lawyer is the word going around which to some instantly equates dollar signs to those who think they know more than everyone else. He could have just as easily been taken for a movie star as all Americans are deemed rich but in this instance he seemed an easy mark for money of a band of pirates who are taking a vacation while the Navy carrier is in the area."

"Wrong place, wrong time." Stan mutters and maybe Carter is not as lucky as Caro claims.

"I'm afraid so." Aimhurst admits and it really is as simple as that. "But you have the best private security company in the business right in the family and the Navy has a vested interest in keeping the Captain happy."

"By Captain you mean my daughter Carolyn I'm assuming?" Margaret asks because now she is not so certain and she just learned this from Harv and Moss when they more or less moved in on the two men. "She was a captain in the Air Force is what I believe."

"Yes she was, but she was invited to participate in the Navy fighter training program." Aimhurst explains wondering why her parents whom he assumes he is speaking to do not know this. "When she aced the program the Navy was certain she would wish to join them only she was presented another opportunity but now that she is no longer in the Air Force the Navy is actively attempting to recruit her. Captain Callahan is a top gun pilot but as a woman she has had to prove her qualifications repeatedly and I can't say I blame her for not wanting to have anything to do with either branch given the way they have treated her in the past."

"And the Steel Man she married doesn't like to fly." Chuck comments and he would find this hilarious if he were not so worried about his daughter and Carter.

"I beg your pardon." Aimhurst replies not certain he heard correctly.

"Dog hates to fly." Chuck repeats not certain what he said that was not understandable. "None of our unit dared make fun of him or Falcon would have had our asses, pardon my French."

"You knew the Steel Man unit?" Aimhurst asks unable to believe what he is hearing.

"The unit I was with in Vietnam worked in tandem with the Steel Man Unit. We spent three hellacious months together swatting mosquitoes and being thrown at immovable objects. We didn't last long after they were sent elsewhere and I'm one of only two left." Chuck admits sadly because most of them died too young.

"I would very much like to hear about that at a later date if that is agreeable to you." Aimhurst suggests then realizes he may not wish to speak of it. "Falcon was my biological brother and I never saw him again after I was adopted but he was considered un-adoptable."

"Sure." Charlie agrees having no problem with this. "Feather Head had a wicked sense of humor so I have lots to tell about him. But right now look after my daughter."

"I'm doing exactly that." Aimhurst promises. "She's resting now and I'll let you know as soon as I have word from the Colonel, the Captain, or the kidnappers."

"Thank you so much." Ethel responds and people looking after Clarissa, even perfect strangers, is better then thinking of her daughter being all alone at a time like this then there is a dial tone.

"I wonder if we'll ever really know our daughter." Margaret comments as she reaches across the table taking her husbands hand.

"Just don't ever step into a boxing ring with her." Moss advises getting a frown from Harv. "I'm just saying."

Four hours and a few deserted shacks later Cat is still flying slowly along the inlet river course and swinging wide occasionally to cover more area on either side while the men below trudge through, over, and around on the jungle floor. It is slow and painstaking work when the heat of the sun is now messing with Yule's equipment sending heat signatures for every pile of vegetation with moisture generating heat.

She is skimming the tree tops to give Yule the best range for accuracy but this equipment is more accurate in cooler climates, or night as it was intended only this would alert the kidnappers they are being actively sought and might send them into hiding as they did with the Navy carrier. The last thing they want is the pirates panicking about being located and this time rather than just hide their boat they could very easily hide Carter's body and none would be the wiser.

"Structure I think one click further west." Yule informs the Captain. "Good size structure. Might want to swing over closer so I can get a better reading."

"Roger that." Cat replies as she moves the joystick to comply but then stops as she suddenly has the strange feeling she is going in the wrong direction. She swings the helicopter around and moves to the north as Yule looks at her probably wondering what is wrong but says nothing. She cannot explain even if she tried as she moves slowly along then hovers over the trees.

"I've got a heat signature down there." Yule confirms wondering why she went this direction. "Could be an animal."

"No." Cat comments as she keys her com link knowing she is going to sound crazy but she cannot shake this feeling. "I think I found him."

"Of course you did." Dog responds and he knew all it would take is getting her in the general area of her brother. "The two of you are hardwired."

She gives him the coordinates rather than ask what he means by this but once again Dog has proven he knows far more than any person really should. It is almost like he can see the future but if this were the case then he would know everything before it happened and much of that could have been changed, so maybe he has premonitions of some kind. Either way it would have been something the Steel Man project would have been interested in but they nearly cut him from the project which makes no sense at all, unless he intentionally failed the tests.

Chapter 35
Somewhere in the Caribbean.....

Carter has heard near death experiences make people reflect on their past mistakes and regrets though at the moment his only serious regret is not honeymooning at Niagara Falls. He is also not anywhere near dead yet, but the threat has been hanging over his head for a while now and presently an immediate concern. The fact he might have been safer staying with his kidnappers has crossed his mind a couple of times but they were pretty adamant about killing him if the money did not come through and since neither his nor Clarissa's family have that kind of money it seemed prudent to take his chances.

Escaping was relatively easy given the locked door of the room they put him in was the only sturdy wall of the building and he timed his escape to coincide with the coming daylight but what he did not completely comprehend is the jungle that now surrounds him. He was a boy scout and received basic of survival training but navigating a wooded area is a far cry from this dark, damp, and rather fetid terrain he has found himself smack in the middle of, or so he can only guess.

The sun is no help with direction when it does not penetrate the foliage around him so he can only hope he is going in the right direction but given he does not know where he is or which direction to go he could be walking in circles. Climbing a tree he hoped to see from this vantage point a village or the city but all he can see is more trees taller than the one he climbed.

The sound of an approaching helicopter makes his heart beat faster but looking up he realizes no one is going to spot him for all the foliage still above him and as the helicopter recedes he thinks of Caro. He regrets being unable to help his sister more when they were kids and maybe it was a mistake to quit trying but it was what she wanted only did he do the right thing. He hears the helicopter again growing louder and wonders if he dare climb any higher to try to signal it when he glances down seeing his brother-in-law standing on the ground looking up at him.

"We have him Cat." Dog informs her through the com link as he studies Carter from the ground. "He's a little scrapped up but other wise looks fine. Keep looking for the boat or a dwelling near here."

"Roger." Cat responds closing her eyes in relief and when she opens them she finds Yule grinning at her. "Let's find Dare's boat."

"That was Caro." Carter announces pointing upward from his perch in the trees as more men gather below him.

"Of course." Dog calls back. "Can you get down from there on your own or do we need to come up and get you. Maybe you want to stick around and hatch something while you're up there."

"The view was better from the boat." Carter admits as he reaches up to grab the branch above him. "I'm sure getting down will be much easier than climbing up was."

"Just don't come down the hard way." Dog suggests as he watches Carter carefully pick his hand and foot holds which is made more difficult by the fact Carter is barefoot. "Did they think taking your shoes would stop you from running off?"

"I think so." Carter replies though he is not certain what they were thinking when they took his shoes. "They even double locked the door but the walls were so rotten all I had to do was pull the boards from the nails."

"Do you know which direction you came and how far?" Dog asks once Carter is on the ground and they have him seated on a log as one of the SEALs with a medic kit looks over his feet which are tore up from the tree most likely.

"Not hardly." Carter responds and if they had not found him he knows he would have died wondering about in here. "For all I know I was going in circles. This isn't the woods by the lake where I went to boy scout camp but I thought I would be better off out here then sticking around until they found out I'm poor."

"You might be but your wife isn't." Dog informs him but they need to find these pirates before they take off again. "What can you tell me about the place they held you?"

"It was a two room shack from what I could see of it. Rusted out old truck in front I saw on the way out. I never saw what they brought me there in but there was only the truck when I left and I don't think it has an engine." Carter replies trying to be helpful but really there was not much more than that. "What do you mean Clarissa is rich?"

"I'm beginning to hope you put her dowry in a safe before you left." Dog responds as he keys his come link. "Cat, it's a two room shack, rusty junked truck in front."

"North, south, east, or west?" Cat asks because this is still a needle in a really big haystack.

"Not my fault this time, blame your brother." Dog suggests.

"I think we found the boat so I'll track out from there." Cat responds, and now she knows to get Carter a compass for his birthday, but this lack of being given a direction is getting old.

"Expect a compass for your birthday." Dog informs Carter as he rises on his wrapped feet.

"I'm more concerned about what you gave my wife." Carter replies honestly as one of the men hands him a bottle of water.

"Ammunition if she should ever need it." Dog responds and it seems simple enough to him. "Delicate looking women need big guns."

"Or in his wife's case snub nosed semi automatic rifles in her pockets." Carmichael mutters and finds Han Dog frowning at him. "I'm not complaining, mind you, but it does make me wonder what you gave his wife."

"One point four million dollars worth of jewels and gold." Dog responds easily and grabs Carter to slow his decent as he sits back on his log abruptly.

"No wonder they kidnapped him." Dare remarks and that would be good incentive.

"No one but Cat and I know how much they're worth and Clarissa only wore them once at a private gathering. Even she doesn't know how much they're worth." Dog responds.

"He's a lawyer." Jake adds.

"Lawyers filthy rich." Rolly comments looking around him not understanding why no one seems to know this.

"Slum lore." Jake explains. "They all hear how lawyers in America make the most money and they believe it so you must have told someone you're a lawyer which made you a prime target."

"Of pirates needing money because the Navy here was sniffing too close to their front door and they needed an income until the Navy moves on to something else." Dog comments looking at Lieutenant Commander expectantly.

"You think we drove them to ground?" Dare asks but it does seem a little abnormal for pirates to take up kidnapping. "This must be their home port."

"No wonder no one was talking." Crew mutters and if these men are in their home port others would cover for them.

"Carmichael got lucky." Dog admits because these people would have closed ranks to protect their own no matter what they did.

"Literally." Carmichael responds with a satisfied grin.

"Now we have to wonder what he told her in return." Jake remarks and it had to be Carmichael who found the hostile ex girlfriend of one of the pirates.

"I have a possible on the shack." Cat informs the men below unaware of the conversation taking place. "We can't get a positive on the shack or the boat."

"I'll take a look." Dog replies motioning to Jake to hand over the large box he has been carrying as Cat gives him the coordinates.

"We'll go with you and your men can see to your brother-in-law." Dare responds.

"Negative, I move faster alone." Dog counters as he shoulders the strap of the rectangular case while watching the Navy commander knowing the man's main concern. "Don't worry, you'll get your boat. Head back to the clearing as the city is across the water inlet and will take longer to reach on foot."

"Or we could take the boat back down the inlet." Dare disagrees and it seems their working relationship with a private contractor is at an impasse because he has his orders.

"It's basically a cigarette boat and only holds six but the inlet is shallow so one would be the limit." Dog replies so either the SEAL has not been paying attention to the water depth or he just does not care enough about anything other than having the boat in his possession and he knows it is the latter. "You would make better time if you came out later from the city to retrieve your boat."

"Sir, with all due respect, I'll be coming with you." Dare responds as he looks to his men. "Accompany these men back to the clearing"

"Cat, I'm inbound." Dog informs her as he heads for the coordinates she gave him but it is not long before the Lieutenant Commander is trailing far behind and since he is using their com and not the SEAL's equipment to speak to her he adds. "Your boyfriend is determined, I'll give him that."

"I don't have a boyfriend." Cat mutters aware Yule is seated next to her.

"Former then." Dog corrects though only on her part. "But not from a lack of initiative on his part."

"His orders were to show me around so to speak." Cat counters so Dare had a reason for being with her which had nothing to do with anything personal. "As it turned out he showed me everything I couldn't be in the Navy and never understood why I wouldn't settle for less."

"Your no SEAL groupie." Dog comments and the man obviously never knew what he had in his sights or he never would have expected less from her.

"Is this really important right now?" Cat asks not wanting to rehash the past. "Or is this jealousy?"

"No, just wondering if you care enough about him to track him in case he runs into trouble." Dog remarks as he kicks it up a notch leaving the man even further behind. "He insisted upon coming with me."

"Yule might care." Cat admits as she looks over to the man with the goatee and arm in a sling as she shuts off her com and in a louder voice calls over. "Do you have Dare?"

"Ya, he says your husband might be lost." Yule replies having just been on the com with Dare. "He wanted me to locate him but I'm not sure if I found him or a cheetah. Whatever it is is closing in on the location we gave them fast."

"If Dare had done what Dog asked he would have brought the boat to him." Cat responds not feeling at all sorry for Dare's predicament. "Tell him to wait by the inlet."

"It's not a cheetah." Yule relays to Dare and since there are no other large heat signatures in the area he has to believe her. "The Captain suggests you wait by the inlet. Not spoken is you might get your ass left behind."

"What?" Cat asks when Yule motions her to change frequencies.

"Just how old is your husband again?" Dare asks as he stands looking around him but he cannot even hear the man any more.

"You of all people should know better than to judge anyone by height and now age as well." Cat suggests but she could add gender only she is certain that would go over Dare's head as she switches back to Dog's frequency. "Give him the boat."

"I intend to." Dog replies and that was the plan all along. "I think this is it but I'm going in for a closer look around."

Cat keeps the helicopter high and off to the side of their target not wanting to alert them as she scans the treetops and horizon waiting. This time there is no way she can fly in to Dog's rescue as this jungle is thick so if he falls or jumps from anything down there she can only radio for help which is a situation she does not like.

"Clear the area." Dog warns over both com links.

Cat swings wide but she is already high enough to miss the explosion which billows up through the trees in the form of smoke and debris then through a small gap in the trees she sees a long boat moving along the inlet water way with a very big man with long dark hair piloting it. She heads for the clearing to pick up the teams following the inlet back toward the beginning but other than an irregular seam in the trees barely discernible no one would ever know there is a water way down there from the air.

Dare sees but does not hear the boat approaching as he stands at the gray-green waters edge and this stealth capability is why this boat is being much sought after. The large dark skinned man eases the boat close to the bank cutting the engine and tossing him a rope. Holding the boat steady on the nearly none existent current he remains silent as the man jumps down into the water and wades to shore then he decides to say what needs to be said.

"Does C.C. know you just killed possibly five unsuspecting men?" Dare asks making sure his com link is off because he does not think she would stand for this kind of thing.

"What Cat doesn't know yet is I didn't just kill six men." Dog corrects Killdare's assumption. "She will be disappointed at first but will settle for her brother's kidnappers being stranded out here with no shoes, transportation, or shelter. They'll have to head for the city where the local authorities are already waiting for them or die so they have a fifty fifty chance which are better odds than she would have given them."

"Disappointed." Killdare comments not believing this.

"You've never seen her angry, have you?" Dog asks certain of the answer.

"C.C. doesn't get angry." Killdare counters seeing her as one of the calmest people he has ever met.

"Cat is always angry but she has learned to hide it very well."

Dog informs him with a smile and it is obvious Killdare never stood a chance. "Without an outlet for her anger she would eventually self destruct given time."

"So you give her this outlet." Killdare comments but he had intended to give her much more.

"No, I give her opportunities." Dog replies but he is not certain a man so steeped in what he feels is the natural order will ever understand. "And ammunition."

"Live rounds or wealth?" Dare wonders out loud.

"Both in her case." Dog admits as he motions to the rope which Killdare hands him so he can hold the boat steady for him to climb aboard.

"I'll let the men know your on your way when I reach the clearing." Dare offers knowing on the water he will be faster while thinking this man has a strange view concerning women.

"Thanks." Dog responds as the boat moves off and a man like Killdare would never consider putting himself in a vulnerable position even for a woman he claims to love since he does not see himself as anything other than an alpha above others. Killdare should not, but will be, very surprised shortly just as Killdare probably will be surprised by people for most of his life given his mind set.

Cat hovers near the clearing waiting for the men to arrive which they do followed by Dog then Dare with the boat whom even she can see has a stunned expression on his face. Yule awkwardly with one arm in a sling climbs into the back dropping rope to the ground when she is positioned over the clearing. She cannot see the men below her as she waits for them to climb or be hauled up the ropes then Carter is moving cautiously between the seats to take the copilots seat.

"Do you remember the church picnics you weren't allowed to play hide and seek because it was un-lady like?" Carter shouts over the noise of the helicopter to his sister who looks quite confident amid all the switches and dials before her while he is worried about touching something he should not. She hands him headphones and motions for him to buckle in then her voice comes loud and clear in his ears without yelling.

"I remember." Cat replies not certain why he is asking as she notices the surface scrapes and torn clothing but he looks to be fine. "Why?"

"It's one of the few times our parents did me a favor by not letting you do something." Carter responds with a smile. "I would've always been it."

"Or I would have been." Cat counters because they would have probably always found each other.

"We're secure Cat." Dog informs her.

Cat changes frequencies and asks. "Where do you want me to drop off your men Dare?"

"The land military base is fine." Dare responds as he navigates the water inlet knowing she has Navy equipment to return. "Crew can pilot the helicopter back to the carrier if you can get a ride into the city."

"Roger and thanks" Cat agrees so they can deal with returning the equipment and helicopter because she wants Carter and Clarissa out of here today.

"He didn't kill them." Killdare informs her because he wants to know what her reaction really will be.

"You know for a guy who looks tough as nails he has some serious weak spots." Cat comments with a frown. "I find it somewhat disappointing."

"And he said you would be disappointed." Killdare responds and now he is left to wonder. "He also just out distanced a cigarette boat going twenty knots on water running through jungle."

"I've actually seen him do worse." Cat responds leaving it at this because jungle or desert Dog can really move.

Somewhere in Alaska....
Eight months later.

"Yes, we'll be there." Cat assures her mother over the phone as she wrinkles her nose at the mess she is presently viewing on her kitchen counters.

"We look forward to seeing you both again." Margaret responds truthfully because it seems like ages not weeks since her daughter and Johann moved into their new home so far away after returning Carter and Clarissa home. Her daughter and son-in-law stayed at the Regency for nearly six months while their house was being built so she and Stan grew use to seeing them when they were not out working in some God forsaken place doing something extremely dangerous.

It has occurred to her this distance may work out to be beneficial in the long run. It was becoming increasingly difficult for her not to voice her concerns given she now has some inkling of just what the couple does for a living. She lives in fear of alienating her daughter once again by saying the wrong thing or pushing her daughter to be something she is not nor never was.

"Same goes." Cat comments and strangely enough she has come to know her parents better than she ever did and they have become different people yet the same in some respects. "I heard Aimee is staying with the Kincaids."

"He was but he had to leave yesterday I believe" Margaret responds having met the Major General herself. "It's heartbreaking to think about. He never saw his brother again after he was adopted."

"Falcon's whole life was more or less a tragedy." Cat comments which her mother will never know the half of but fact is poor Falcon was doomed the moment he volunteered to serve his country.

"Charlie plans to go with him when he brings Falcon's body back to be buried with honors." Margaret informs Carolyn but she probably knows this as it was Dog who told them where he buried the man.

"I'm glad to hear it. Dog offered but Aimee turned him down." Cat replies pleased to hear he will not be going alone after all.

"I imagine going back would be hard for Johann." Margaret agrees thinking this is for the best though she is not certain what exactly happened to Falcon but she knows the two men were close friends.

"Is everything ready to move forward after the ground breaking ceremony for the Therapy center?" Cat asks changing the subject because what only Dog and Aimee know is two bodies will be brought back since Dog buried his brother with the woman he loved as Falcon would have wanted despite how her death came about. They should remain together forever and what the military does not know will not hurt them.

"As far as I know." Margaret responds but Carolyn did much of the ground work for the event about to take place. "I never realized just how much is involved when a medical center like this is built and I assumed they just put up a building then installed the equipment they need. Even the EPA is involved and environmental studies were made like they are building a nuclear plant or something."

"Bio hazardous waste." Cat comments because even a therapy center falls under the same considerations a hospital does. "They managed to cut through all the red tape fairly quickly."

"I'm not sure why they're in such a hurry to have the center completed. I thought they would take their time." Margaret admits because they were just married not long before and have yet to have time to settle into that transition but they went on another honeymoon with less drama than the first and just dug right into this new therapy center.

"It's a labor of love." Cat replies but both Carter and Clarissa discovered just how uncertain and short life can be so they are apparently not wasting a moment of theirs.

"How did you manage to get the grant for the pool?" Margaret asks having heard the difficulties they were having with this aspect of their plans but she was told Caro fixed it. "Carter said the grant people were rather set on certain stipulations he was not willing to grant."

"I just pointed out a few things they didn't consider." Cat responds but in actuality the grant did not go through so Dog had Carter draw up his own grant which Dog approved. "Sorry, I have to cut you short but I have to get some cleaning done around here before we get another job and have to leave again."

"A housewives work is never done." Margaret quips without thinking then realizes being a housewife seems to be the last thing Carolyn ever wanted to be, or so she assumes. "I'm sorry, I mean..."

"Mother, I'm a wife and I have a house, but part of the problem is we're not home very often, or often enough as the case maybe." Cat responds honestly and it is not the same as what her parents wanted for her by a long shot. "We share KP duty and as we speak Dog is cleaning the master bathroom, because he lost the coin toss. We need a cleaning service but he is resisting muttering something about privacy."

"One day a week should be enough." Margaret agrees but she is smiling as she tries to picture her large son-in-law cleaning a toilet and for some reason it makes her want to laugh.

"That's what I think." Cat replies hearing another muffled oath coming from the master bedroom. "I have to go make sure he is not ripping out the plumbing."

Chapter 36
Somewhere in Alaska....

They built their home with everything they both wanted right down to a moose head on the wall over a massive stone fireplace and included things like heated stone floors, large heavily insulated windows which gives them an incredible view of a pine tree studded mountain valley presently covered in several feet of snow, and added whatever modern advancement they wanted to try like the little robot disk running around the floors vacuuming but there is one problem they did not foresee.

The two people living in this secluded scenic paradise are either pigs, which she does not believe is the problem given their military training, or they are gone most of the time often leaving on only an hours notice. She is seriously tempted to toss the mess of left over food, plates, and pans from the counters to the floor and let the little vacuum handle it only the poor thing might choke and die given the extent of the mess.

They hired several people from a nearby village and cities to come once a week checking such things as jet fuel for the three jets she now has in the heated hanger further along the mountain, the vehicles including snow mobiles and ATV s housed in the same hanger, and one man plows the landing strip with a snow plow also in the hanger but no one comes in the house to maintain anything except coming near enough to haul loads of fire wood stacked out the back door.

Even the kids, Harv, Moss, Rolly, Jake and Carmichael, living in a near by city have a house she and Dog had built with five bedrooms, five private baths, two communal living rooms, and a massive kitchen with sit down dinning have employed a full time cleaning woman

She wonders again if she should be worried about Dog because this insistence for privacy is not like him when giving orders to people is practically second nature to him and he generally likes people around but he has yet to arbitrarily order her around. The man is naturally drawn to people and people to him like a magnet. He actually enjoys speaking to them so this self seclusion makes no sense to her and if he enjoyed cleaning she would understand only so far this does not seem to be the case at all.

Picking up after themselves is one thing but leaving then coming back to dishes they could not wash due to the abruptness of their departure and have now been sitting for a week is ridiculous. They will be having pets next of the small furry skinny tailed variety along with insects better seen out of doors and it is a wonder there are not bears, mountain lions and wolves with their tongues stuck to the windows now.

"Bath room is done." Dog announces as he approaches crossing the wide open living room seeing Cat just standing at the kitchen counter with dirty dishes from their meal a week ago still on the counter. "Problem?"

"I forgot to bring home C-4 from our last mission to do the dishes." Cat replies and that is probably what it will take.

"Just throw them out and we'll buy new." He suggests not seeing a problem and some of food never should have been left but it could not be helped, they had to go.

"I like these dishes." Cat informs him folding her arms and staring at him because she did not intend for them to be disposable.

"Okay." Dog comments uncertain just which way he should jump because his Cat is not looking friendly which is not a good sign. "I was going to go clean the pool."

"I might drown you in it." Cat warns him because if he cannot see the problem they have growing steadily worse each day, each mission, and one free day between is not going to correct then maybe she needs to get nasty.

"What did I do?" Dog asks because he has been cleaning so how can he have done anything wrong.

"We are hiring weekly cleaning people and a pool person so when we come home, after however long we're gone, we can do what we want to do." Cat dictates flatly waiting for an argument.

"But then we would have people here." He replies knowing she does not want people around or why would they live in the middle of nowhere. He kind of likes the isolation too as long as Cat is here and he knows how impatient she gets when they are surrounded by people so it is nice to come home to their own piece of deserted wilderness.

"Just once a week so when we come home I can take a swim and relax in what does not look like green jello." Cat responds because this has gone on long enough and she is tired of it. "I want to curl up in front of that fireplace right now and make love to you then take an nap but I can smell what we ate a week ago and it smelled much better then."

"Fireplace." Dog comments glancing over his shoulder at the mammoth creation behind him and he really likes that pile of stone, with or without a fire, because they can just lay there on the nice thick soft, imitation, bear skin rug where she some times runs her finger nails through his hair scratching his scalp, or she rubs his stomach, and the sex is pretty incredible too. If he is really lucky he can have all three if Cat is in a mellow mood and it is his trifecta of heaven on earth but when was the last time they did any of that. The fact he cannot remember when the last time was is some what alarming. "You wouldn't mind people coming in?"

"You're the one who suddenly doesn't want people around." Cat informs him and it was not her idea.

"Five minutes with the kids and you're trying to decide which one and exactly where you want to put your foot to do the most damage." He informs her and having other people around does bother his Cat so this is the only place she can be without bother.

"Morons don't count and this would be different." She responds grimly because they would be hiring qualified help not the incompetent helpless they work with.

"Then we hire." Dog agrees and if Cat has no problem with this then neither does he but now that she mentioned it. "About the nap idea?"

Then build a fire, Cat thinks to herself, and he instantly turns heading for the fireplace but stops abruptly as if frozen in his tracks. Cat rounds the island counter moving to stand before him seeing his eyes are closed and when he opens them he stares at the polished wood floor rather than look at her.

"Did you honestly think you could hide this from me?" Cat accuses wondering why he even tried and he has read her mind several times now or his instructions have come to her as if he is speaking directly to her only he is miles away. "The project worked on you and not the others but that's not your fault."

"The project didn't work at all." He counters gruffly and he knew she would catch on because she is smart and quick but he had really hoped she would over look it. "It was a train wreck that killed five men and countless others before them because the DNA patch couldn't give them what they didn't all ready have. All the brain activity they were so excited about was just their minds being torn apart. I could project and receive thoughts before I even entered the military which is what drove my mother away."

"Why didn't you tell me?" Cat asks and she thought he trusted her since she has saved his bacon often enough and it surprises her just how much his admission hurts but then she considers what else he said. "How does this have anything to do with your mother leaving your father?"

"She was cooking dinner one night and the frying pan on the stove caught fire. She didn't notice with her back turned working on something else so I shouted fire but I didn't actually say anything. She turned around and put the lid on snuffing out the fire then looked at me as if to praise me for warning her then she realized I hadn't actually said anything. It wasn't me she was furious with but my father and the look she gave him I'll never forget. It was a look of pure hatred like venom dripping from her eyes." Dog explains remembering it all like it happened yesterday. "She started screaming at him, things I didn't understand at the time about witches, voodoo, and things like that. He tried to calm her and to reason with her but she wouldn't listen to anything he said. She called him a demon and me his spawn so I think my father had the same ability and at some point in their marriage he promised never to use whatever ever this is. She apparently didn't know it was hereditary and I'm certain if she had I never would've been born or she would've left long before then. She walked out the door that night not taking anything with her except my father's heart which I guess he tried to fill the hole with alcohol and I never saw her again."

"You think I would leave you, because of this?" She asks now insulted but then his own mother walked out on him so what is he suppose to think. She does not understand how the woman could leave her own child like that but then she has no room to condemn anyone when she killed her unborn child. "You should've told me."

"I did. I told you I killed my unit and you should be able to figure out the rest with what you now know." He replies as he looks at her and it was the only draw back to marrying a smart capable woman like Cat but she is glaring at him now so he spells it out for her. "I kept them in the project by making it seem they had the ability they were looking for. If not for me they would've washed out, gone home, and lived normal lives."

"No, none of the men who washed out did any of those things." Cat corrects him wondering were he came by his information because it is not true. "Everyone who participated in the Steel Man project died. You're the only one left, or weren't you listening. Once the project ripped up their minds there was no going home and the others before may not have gone out like your unit but dead is dead. If you some how manipulated the tests then you may have kept them from dying much sooner because they would have kept trying to perfect their super soldiers making matters worse, and you were the one they were thinking of tossing from the project. Aimee says your intuition of what the others would do kept you from being washed out."

"He said before the project." Dog realizes as he considers what the Major General said when he was listing off his complaints, before, during, and after the project he had said and men were given the DNA patch but rejected for the project. "Twenty men signed up for the project."

"And only six showed any sign the DNA patch worked so they tested the six in the project but they continued to attempt to get the DNA patch to work with the others until they started dying so they gave up and washed them out. Some died as their bodies started shutting down after three patches while other went quietly insane but the end result was the same, they all died." Cat explains and obviously he does not know the full extent of the project. "If you manipulated the tests so they could stay in the project where all they did is monitor them for advancements then you lengthened their lives by years."

"They did it to some of the men more than once?" Dog asks and first time was bad enough.

"I should have considered you wouldn't know." Cat replies nodding and though he was part of the project he would not have been told anything other than what they felt was necessary. "I called Aimee back after he called to tell me you were on your way home, I was having dinner with Carter and Clarissa. I wanted to be sure they couldn't change their minds if they saw or heard something about you they felt was too similar to the others in your unit. I was going to make sure they didn't know but Aimee already knew exactly what the differences were which is why he brought in a genetic scientist. The difference was the brain activity the people running the project saw as an improvement was just their minds being shredded by the patch. Your brain activity never changed, then, or now and after all this time there is no chance of it happening. It was proof positive. Nothing you do or say from here on out can reflect back on the project, you can't be used as proof of their genetic tampering, and that was their main concern, keeping the secret."

"They don't need to kill me to hide the evidence." Dog responds finding this not what he expected all the way around and part of him has wondered if they might change their mind but Cat was already finding the answers looking for ways to protect him, again.

"You already had what they were trying to induce in the others and the DNA patch may have made it stronger, like the rest of you." She adds and he has been laboring under a mountain of guilt that was unnecessary. "I suspected the first mission and you have talked to me in my mind several times since, or read my mind, so I began to think either you thought I would tell some one and have you kicked out the country back into a little cell, or now it seems you thought I would just walk out on you like your mother which proves when it comes to increased intelligence the patch did absolutely nothing because you're still an idiot."

"You love me." Dog reasons because she was worried about him. "Carmichael thought so."

"I wouldn't believe anything he said either." Cat admits honestly and when they returned from their first mission they took all five to Jaw Breakers. Carmichael claimed to be a bare knuckles champ but Crush did not believe him any more than she did and added one of his membership guys. Neither Rolly nor Jake felt the need to prove their manhood by stepping into the ring with her while Harv and Moss refused to go near any ring with her in it. She took great pleasure in tossing Carmichael over the top rope after only ten minutes unable to tolerate his showboating any longer and the fact he landed badly on his shoulder and he is wearing a sling for two weeks was an added bonus. "What happened to my not having to say it?"

"You don't even think the words." Dog informs her then realizes she might take this the wrong way now that she knows what he can do. "I don't read your mind all the time but every once in a while I take a peek and you're still planning new and painful ways to kill me."

"But are you dead yet?" Cat counters since she has obviously not implemented any of those plans and the reality is all she has to do is not, 'do what she does' as he calls it which would have killed him three times at least by now with no effort on her part at all.

"No." Dog responds and here is a very obvious sign he missed as he grins at her while she frowns back at him. "Enough said."

He wraps his arms around her lifting her up and the fact she lets him even though she is clearly not happy with him is yet another sign she loves him which this time he does not miss. He carries her to the rug before the fireplace kissing her for the first time without worrying about risking life and limb but a sharp stab of her finger below his ribs a few moments later has him backing off. Looking down into her beautiful frowning face he cannot help smiling back because her parents may have wanted her to be the perfect lady but she is the perfect warrior woman for him.

"I love you." Dog informs her.

"Seriously, you talk entirely too much." Cat informs him when they could be doing something else.

THE BEGINING